CN01594138

ENCORE

20p

ENCORE

Julie Harris

CENTURY
LONDON SYDNEY AUCKLAND JOHANNESBURG

First published in Great Britain in 1993 by
Random House UK Limited
20 Vauxhall Bridge Road, London SW1V 2SA

Random House South Africa (Pty) Ltd
PO Box 337, Bergvlei 2012, South Africa

Random House Australia Pty Ltd
20 Alfred Street, Milsons Point, Sydney, NSW 2061
Australia

Random House New Zealand Ltd
18 Poland Road, Glenfield, Auckland,
New Zealand

The catalogue data record for this book is available from the British Library

Printed and bound in Australia by Australian Print Group

Happy the eyes that see what you see, for I tell you that many prophets and kings wanted to see what you see and never saw it; to hear what you hear and never heard it.

Luke 10.23

For my daughters and David.
Special thanks to Terry.

CHAPTER 1

WHEN THEY came to her father's door, the crowd was screaming her name. She appeared in a nightgown and cap, confused, squinting into the rising sun. She barely had time to question aloud before the strong hands seized her.

'There it is!' came the cry as her ginger cat darted out of the door and away with a frightened yowl. 'There's her familiar!'

'She bears the fruits of blasphemy!' another woman cried.

'Consorting with the devil!'

'An abomination to the Lord!'

Hannah, blinded by the early morning sun, tried to see the faces. Was one Nell of Craigmore? Nell who had brought her fevered baby to the Dougall house and cried for help?

'See how she's cursed us!'

'Tis she killed my son!'

'Tis she made me barren!'

'Tis she causing the sheep to die!'

'Tis she conjuring the storms! Consorting with the devil!'

'No! I'd consort with no one! I'd curse no one! Nell of Craigmore, I tried to help you. Why are you doing this?'

But Nell's eyes were mad. 'This be what Michael Maginley found in the McTaggart bothy!' Nell held high a small clay doll and showed it off to the hungry gathering. 'See the elf-arrows to the heart! Is Mairie McTaggart not this whore's teacher? Did Mairie McTaggart not confess? This one has the witch's mark! We'll not suffer another witch to live!'

And as they chanted 'Kill the witch! Kill the witch!' Ian the Fisherman and Michael Maginley from the kirk tore apart her father's house.

The chanting grew louder as Michael Maginley came out with his arms full of small clay dolls, all pierced with shards of wood.

Hannah had never seen them before and Nell of Craigmore spat in Hannah's face. 'Kill the witch!'

'Seat belt.'

Rebecca woke with a start at the flight attendant's quick touch. She snapped her seat belt into place. But the image lingered. She closed her eyes. The terrified pregnant girl was still there, reaching out to someone, tormented, confused.

No, Rebecca thought and rubbed her face. Not again. Leave me alone.

The image refused to dissolve, still reached out, pleading for help.

I can't help you now. Not here.

It slowly faded. The pregnant girl was gone, but Rebecca knew she'd be back. She would return and return, a persistent ghost determined to haunt until someone knew, understood, and released her.

Rebecca glanced at the man beside her. They had talked intermittently for the entire flight from Sydney and now he was dozing. He'd said his name was Joel and that he worked in security but offered little else. In a way she was glad he was not a talker although a little more conversation would have alleviated the growing boredom.

He was snoring again until one huge intake of breath woke him with a start and he fell off his hand. It took a few seconds for him to orient himself and Rebecca envied his ability to sleep on a plane.

'Going to London for a holiday?' he eventually asked.

'If a week-long conference can be considered a holiday.'

'What sort of conference?' he asked, appearing suddenly interested.

'Oh . . . mainly healing,' she said quickly, not wanting to go into too much detail because people often barraged her with their ills and Rebecca would rather talk about the weather than the recurring kidney complaint cousin Joe inherited from Uncle Fred. 'I'm demonstrating.'

Joel waited for her to go on. Nothing came. 'Demonstrating what?'

'Different kinds of healing. I'm talking about alternative medicine, mostly.' She gazed out of the window and sighed as he had done when she had asked his vocation. If she told him she used herbal remedies and massage just like the pregnant girl who haunted her constantly and was probably burnt as a witch

300 years ago, Joel would demand a parachute. Most people would.

'What's so funny?' he asked.

'Nothing, nothing.'

'You don't look like a healer.'

'You don't look like a security person.' She glanced at his honey blond hair, the diamond stud in his right ear and his baby face.

'I was once bodyguard to the President of Malta.'

'What, only once? Does that mean he died?'

'Scout's honour, it's true.'

She laughed quietly and turned away. At first, sleep was pretence. When next she was aware of anything it was fifteen minutes ETA, Heathrow.

She lost Joel amid the swirl of agitated people. Rebecca waited patiently and scanned the crowd of hurrying faces, most intent on two things—catching a plane or getting out of the aiport as quickly as possible. All Rebecca wanted was a decent bed and time to recuperate. After this nightmare of the airport, she was going to Thurlestone, South Devon, and after the conference she was off to Scotland to check out her ancestral heritage and collect as many epitaphs from as many kirkyards as she could locate in ten days. She also knew that when she got there, she would never want to go home again.

Glasgow, she thought. I'll find the real me when I get to Glasgow. And perhaps when I get to Glasgow, that pregnant Scottish witch will stop haunting me.

She yawned, fumbled in her pocket for a Mintie and looked around for signs indicating baggage collection. There was no rush—her bag would not appear first. High above on a walkway she suddenly saw a man she felt she should have known. Something about him was terribly familiar. She gazed at him from a mist of semi-exhaustion until he smiled. Rebecca automatically looked around to see who he was smiling at. Then she was pushed impatiently from behind and when she glanced up again he wasn't there. Then at the carousel, she was two seconds away from reaching for her blue suitcase when a leather-jacketed arm grasped it. 'Hey, that's—' she said. It was the smiling man. 'That's mine.'

'Yes, I know,' he said, in a soft, American lilt. 'Would you come with us, please, Miss Miller?'

'How do you know my name?'

Then Joel, her flight companion, appeared and as the American gave him the suitcase he said, 'We can't talk here, Rebecca. Please come with us.' There was insistence, almost urgency in his eyes and Rebecca looked from him into the other man's face. He may have been wearing civilian clothing yet she knew instinctively that he normally wore a uniform—jungle greens. She suddenly had an impression of him dressed completely in black, with a submachine gun slung across his back. She retreated from the image but he reached out and held tightly onto her arm.

'We'd like to get this over with as quickly as possible,' Joel said quietly. He walked off, her suitcase in his hand. The other released his hold and stepped back to allow her to walk first.

'But . . . but . . .'

'Customs will wait.'

'What's going on?' she asked.

Again, the American smiled. 'After you, Miss.' And as she walked across the grey carpet and was shown into a small waiting room, he was one step behind her, so close she could smell him.

He closed the door and two others stood up as if it were a reflex action because she had walked in. Something else she was not used to. One, a small man with silvering, receding hair stepped towards her, hand outstretched. 'Charles Rudd. How was the flight?' Before she could reply, he said, 'Take a seat, Rebecca.'

'What have I done?' she asked, instantly paranoid. The man had a sponge-rubber handshake.

'No, no, you've done nothing. Please sit. Tea? Coffee?' It was a polite offer.

'No . . . Thanks,' she added as an afterthought.

'Please sit. I know how you must be feeling.'

She glanced at Joel but he was not meeting her gaze. He'd sat beside her for the past eighteen hours, on and off. He'd even grabbed her hand tight and held on reassuringly for each massive air pocket. He'd sensed she wasn't a good flyer. Now he looked guilty. As if he had known this was waiting at the end of the line. Security? No wonder he hadn't elaborated. 'Will someone tell me what's happening?' she asked, impatience rising. What in hell had she done to warrant this?

'We will talk to you when you sit.'

Rebecca took the only available chair.

'First and foremost, you are not being detained.'

Rebecca glanced around the small room and at the four faces

watching her intently. 'If that's the case, why is there wall to wall . . .' she decided it was not wise to call these people gorillas. She glanced at the two by the door—perhaps *guerillas* was the better word.

Rudd tried to smile. Yes, she thought. A politician's smile. 'I'd like to introduce Leon Carter. He's with the United States Central Intelligence Agency.' She received a nod and a large hand stretched to meet hers. It seemed a friendly, firm handshake, even if she immediately sensed men hiding behind newspapers. Such covert images did not suit Leon Carter's face yet the truth lay in his touch. She smiled at him and he smiled back. Any ice which may have been present quickly melted.

'Commander Nolan, United States Navy.'

'Miss,' the tall American said. He was by the door and offered no hand—his were safely hidden behind his back. Familiarity hit again, its origins indefinable.

'And you already know Sergeant Joel Barrett.'

'Sergeant?' Rebecca repeated, while Joel pretended the paintwork on the wall was a surrealistic masterpiece—another safety manoeuvre.

'And you're from what? The Australian Embassy?' Rebecca asked.

'In a way you may understand, I'm from every embassy you could imagine.'

'You didn't answer my question.'

'Have you heard of the World Council of Nations?' he asked, his tone condescending.

'In futuristic fantasy books.'

Charles Rudd smiled with the sincerity of a Bengal tiger. 'Each man here, Rebecca, is associated with that very organisation. We'd like your assistance.'

The sudden silence seemed extremely loud. Rebecca waited, reminded of the long wait on the plane for Joel to explain what sort of security work he was involved in. 'My assistance? With what?'

'Let me put it to you this way, Rebecca. May I call you Rebecca?' Rudd ploughed on, without waiting for an answer. 'In July of 1991, six years ago, the London office of the Society for Psychical Research received this.' He took two yellowed sheets of typed A4 paper and put them into her hand. 'Tell me if it's yours.'

Rebecca looked down at the prediction of a black American President's death, a well-worded account of how, why, when and where, made when she was eighteen years old. She scanned it quickly. Few gruesome details had been omitted. Touching the paper brought the past back vividly. A teenager pacing the balcony at four in the morning, fighting the recurring images of an assassination. Her father appearing, so very sick, so very annoyed. She could read his mind: Not again. What's she seen this time? Another earthquake?

I was there. I saw it happen, but I was there.

Where?

England.

Her father sighed, recovered from a fit of coughing and told her again, that it wasn't possible. How could she be in England watching some black man shot as he stepped from a plane when she lived on the other side of the world?

I was there! I saw that black man die! It won't leave me alone! It won't go away!

Who was he, love?

She'd told him—her father the sceptic, who then told her there would never be a black president. Never. Never.

Forget it, Becky. Leave it be.

But she hadn't. She couldn't. It kept returning, repeating. Haunting.

Leave it be.

Wise words in hindsight. If he were alive now he'd be jumping the queue to repeat his favourite expression: *I told you so*. Now she knew why. Here, she had the President's prophesied demise, the CIA, a world council . . . I've been watching too many movies, she thought, once more unsure of the boundaries between fantasy and other people's reality. All her life it had been her problem. Sorting out the crowding images, learning to conceal that she saw what others did not. Learning to hide her perceptions, her talents. Learning to respond only to the grey 'reality' around her. Then, as she got older, letting some of her gifts emerge, enough not to frighten others into calling her mad. Enough to be regarded as acceptably 'psychic', even to be asked to help the police.

'Is it yours, Rebecca?'

'Yes, it's mine and you know it's mine,' she said, looking at the four faces in turn, settling on the navy officer. Some kind of suicide soldier. 'How am I supposed to help you people?'

'You would do this voluntarily?'

'Do bloody *what*?' she snapped.

'Assist us.'

'How? Look, I've come here for a healing convention, all right?'

'We know what you're here for, Rebecca. I am asking if you will cooperate?'

'How?' she asked, anger rising. The American by the door shifted his weight.

'You'd be assisting us by acting in an advisory capacity with the Nighthawks anti-terrorist squad—'

'With what?' she interrupted.

'Commander Nolan will give you those details later.'

'Try giving me the details now.'

'The squad was formed by and is answerable to the United States Secretary of Defence. The Secretary of Defence is also the chairman of the World Council of Nations. Nighthawks anti-terrorist squad is based in England, although we have priority security clearance world-wide.' The commander was softly spoken and seemed fairly patient but his words sounded very rehearsed. 'We're responsible for diplomat safety.'

Diplomat safety and many other things too, which were not made public. She caught impressions of smoke, of grenades, of men in black abseiling down walls, of sub-machine guns . . . of a nightmare.

'Look, I am hearing words and nothing makes sense. I think you people have made a mistake. Forget it. You don't need me.' Rebecca rose quickly and made for the door. The commander did not move out of her way. Rebecca looked up into his dark eyes and knew she'd need more than a forklift to move him aside. The next statement stopped her abruptly.

'Do you want the first black President of the United States to die just as you saw him die six years ago?'

The calmness of the voice was colder than the question. She turned to Leon Carter. 'Of course not. What do you think I am?'

'Will you agree to assist us?' he asked.

'What in God's name do you think I can do? You're CIA and they're the lethal bodyguards,' she said, indicating the commander and the sergeant. 'What the hell do you expect *me* to do?'

'Rebecca, we know you are a gifted psychic who more often

than not has willingly cooperated with—'

'Spare me the compliments, okay?'

Charles Rudd took over. 'Rebecca, we have a file here from the Australian Federal Police which you are quite welcome to read if you wish.'

She looked at the file in Rudd's hands. It contained all the cases she had helped the Queensland Police with—she'd lost count after eighteen—and federal operations as well.

'It details, in sumarised form, twenty-three separate cases ranging from kidnappings and rape to serial murders and disappearances which were solved with your voluntary assistance by the Queensland Police Department.'

'So?' she asked, shakily.

'Do you want to see this?' Rudd asked, impatience rising imperceptibly.

Rebecca rubbed her face. 'No, my memory is not that poor.'

'We would like the same measure of voluntary cooperation and assistance to avert this prophesied assassination of Robert Glover,' Leon Carter said quietly.

'You've got to be kidding me.'

'I wish I could be kidding you, Miss Miller. In November last year, the fourteenth to be exact, you gave what you call a reading for an American woman. Do you recall?'

Rebecca signed. 'I give readings to fifteen people a week. How am I supposed to remember one American woman?'

'You visited her hotel room in Brisbane. Room 101, the Sheraton. We have it on videotape, Rebecca, as well as a statement from the agent—'

'The agent? She was CIA?'

'And you were one hundred per cent accurate about her past, her present and what, we realise now, remained of her future.'

Rebecca closed her eyes. 'The red Celica.'

'Exactly. She died in a motor vehicle accident three weeks ago in Los Angeles. She was—'

'I don't want to know!'

'She was a passenger in a red Toyota Celica. I realise you're tired. I realise this is difficult and possibly imcomprehensible.'

Possibly? Another understatement. She sat down again, put her heavy shoulder bag on the carpet and ran her hands through her hair.

'Now, it's obvious that you knew she was going to die and it's also obvious you concealed this from her. It disturbed you. You hid it well. Very well.'

'And maybe if you'd seen what I'd seen, Mister Carter, you'd have been disturbed, too. But what if I'm wrong about the President? Has anyone stopped to consider that I might be wrong? That I made that prediction when I was just out of high school for God's sake?'

'Given your track record . . .'

'What if I'm wrong?' Anger emphasised each syllable.

'I certainly hope you are wrong, Rebecca,' Charles Rudd said. 'But you can see our position if in fact, you are correct, as in the past you have apparently proved to be, many, many times. Your failure rate is minimal. Will you help us?'

Rebecca read Charles Rudd easily. He was impatient to be gone, to get this little duty over with. She wondered if he was late for a game of golf. Either that or he was spellbound by a new watch—he couldn't keep his eyes off it.

She studied Carter. Lead-lined. Joel Barrett. He tried to smile. The navy officer watched her constantly. She had the impression of an eaglehawk hovering near him. The symbol of the hawk she understood fully. 'Are you people really expecting this assassination?'

'What do you think, Rebecca? In 1991, this man was an air force pilot, virtually unknown. You gave us his name six years before he nominated.'

'And won,' the navy officer added.

'I have told you, I'm in England for a conference.'

Four faces studied her, each expression basically identical.

'A replacement can be found for that,' Leon Carter said quietly.

'Can or already has?'

No answer.

'It seems as if all this has been preparranged and I'm the last to know.'

The navy commander scratched his chin and inspected the carpet.

'Do I have a choice or not?'

'Yes, you have a choice,' Leon said quietly. 'You can help us avert the death of the new President which you saw happen six years ago or you can walk out now. Personally, I don't think you're the type of person to turn your back on anyone needing help. And personally, I believe that if Glover was to be assassinated, the aftermath of Martin Luther King's death would be trifling by comparison.'

Rebecca studied her thumbnail. Martin Luther King. Dead years before she was born but his message lingered on and was born again with this ex-air force pilot who had defied incredible odds to become President. Loved by everyone. *Almost* everyone. 'You want me as an advisor to the anti-terrorists?'

'Yes. As explained, the squad is responsible for diplomat safety and will be assisting security when the new President arrives in England.'

'If I agreed, how long is this likely to take?'

'We can't be sure. The President's stopover in England would depend on the next World Council and summit meeting in Zurich.'

'I've never heard of any World Council, let alone this supposed summit meeting. Is it some kind of secret society that rules the planet?'

No one answered. 'Rebecca, please realise that Robert Glover has not yet been sworn into office and what we are doing now is taking necessary precautions to ensure his safety when he arrives here.'

'But by the time we finish this conversation, he'll be President, won't he? You think there's a conspiracy to kill him after he takes office, don't you? Maybe he's a target because he's black? He's charismatic. He's a man of his word? Or is it because his own people are his first priority?' Four sighs answered her questions.

'Be assured you will be made comfortable at the Nighthawks headquarters in Wiltshire.'

She glanced at the navy commander and he smiled at her again. She looked away, quickly, and felt her face heating.

'Could we have a decision?'

'You want a decision. Great. I step off a bloody plane to this. You want me to help you keep Robert Glover alive. Me.' She laughed, almost hysterically and then all mirth faded. She studied the faces again. If she were not needed she would not be here.

She thought of what she had seen in an altered reality so long ago. She saw again the man's bright, sincere smile. The moment he lifted his hand to wave . . . 'I'll do what I can,' she said quietly.

She felt four small waves of relief swamp the occupants of the small room while a tidal wave of exhaustion nearly drowned her. An official form on a clipboard was placed on the small table. 'What's this for?' she asked.

'You'll be paid for your services as a consultant parapsychologist.'

Consultant parapsychologist? Rebecca took the offered pen, and stifling another yawn, she signed. Rudd witnessed and the head of the CIA, Northern Operations, pounced on the clipboard.

'I'll leave you in the commander's capable hands, then.' Rudd shook her hand without warmth or gratitude and mumbling something that sounded like '*good girl*', he departed for his game of golf, taking his leather case of police file photocopies with him.

'We'll be in touch,' Leon Carter said, a satisfied grin overtaking his face.

'I was afraid you'd say that.'

'This means a lot to us,' he tried, a half-hearted attempt at reassurance which Rebecca received with a blank stare. 'Catch you later, Commander,' he said to the navy officer and departed with the clipboard under his arm.

The commander nodded to Joel, who also departed. Rebecca didn't understand the smile passing between them.

She was left alone with the navy officer and this, too, she felt had been prearranged. Perhaps the intangible familiarity was mutual. Neither could look into the other's eyes for any length of time without immediate discomfort. But when she thought he wasn't looking, Rebecca studied him. Six-two. Long-fingered artistic hands. His skin was naturally tanned, his eyes and his hair were dark. He was possibly the most handsome man she had ever laid eyes on. If his hair were longer and straighter, he could get a job as an Indian extra in a cowboy movie. He caught her tiny smile but did not react to it. Perhaps he caught her thoughts, too.

'What are we waiting for?' she asked.

'Our transport.'

'Which is?'

'Chopper,' he said.

For a while the silence was thick. 'I've forgotten your name.'

'Kelly Nolan.' Again, he shifted his weight from one foot to the other.

'Is Joel really a Nighthawk?'

Kelly nodded.

'He was on the plane with me.'

He nodded, but this time amusement crossed his face. Joel had been a lot more than just on the plane with her, he'd had her under constant surveillance for three months. While the rest of the squad froze their butts off in England, Barrett was sending scenic postcards from the Gold Coast. Kelly hoped someone had remembered to take the topless sunbathers off the notice board.

'Something amusing?' she asked.

'No, Miss,' Kelly said and turned his attention to the carpet once more. It seemed safer than looking into her eyes. They were a slightly different colour to what he had anticipated: very, very blue indeed. She was also shorter than he'd expected—she was barely five-three and her shoes had a good one-inch heel. She would be easy to lose in a crowd.

'Kelly, can you tell me what's really going on?'

'I thought we just did.'

'No, all I heard were words that didn't make sense. Maybe I'm dreaming.'

'Welcome to fantasy land,' Kelly said with a little grin and she watched the way he walked across the room—one foot heavier than the other. He seemed shy. Shy and brimming with questions he dared not ask except one. 'What do you really know about the assassination attempt, Rebecca?'

'It was a long time ago. You would have read all those files because I know all this has been well-organised. But one thing's certain. My father was right. He told me to back off because it would only lead to trouble.'

'Hindsight, right?' Kelly asked with an impolite grin. 'One thing bothers me about this.'

'Only one?' Rebecca asked.

'If you're so psychic, why did you let yourself get into this mess?' Before she could form a reply to the question—one he might believe at least—he picked up her suitcase and said, 'Transport's arriving.'

'How do you know—' She was interrupted by a polite if persistent beeping noise coming from the depths of his coat. He took out a very small radio, hit a button, and replaced it. Rebecca glimpsed the butt of a handgun tucked under his arm.

He opened the door and beckoned her out. She walked close by and he caught her perfume. Light, lingering.

'There's something you're not telling me,' she said.

Holding her bag and her hand, Kelly said, 'I like mysteries. Pretend we're long-lost lovers. Can you do that?' And he walked off with her, taking long, confident strides into the depths of the airport, weaving his way through the crowd, his grip tightening when she hesitated.

The sign on the door said Authorised Personnel Only. She glimpsed the armed security guards and noticed that two of them nodded to the commander in friendly recognition. The door opened and closed behind them.

It seemed so final. She was leaving Heathrow behind, exiting quite differently from the way she had intended. She was leaving with a man she didn't know but thought she recognised and, for some foolish reason suddenly she couldn't remember why or even how she'd come to be here. Nothing made sense inside this fog. She felt alienated, distant, dizzy.

Rebecca pulled out of the strong grip and came to a sudden standstill. Around them noise grew in intensity. Men driving small tractors. Tarmac shuttle buses, refuelling trucks. Kelly was speaking, impatient, but she couldn't hear his voice. And the air was cold. Inside, she was cold. She wasn't sure which felt worse.

'Come on!' Urgency in Kelly's eyes. He grabbed for her hand.

'No!' She pulled away. 'I refuse to get into that thing.'

She pointed to an army Kiowa a hundred yards across the tarmac. The chopper's back door was already open and Joel stood by, waiting.

'Move!'

'No! I can't, Kelly!' she yelled over the noise. 'I'll die if I go out there!'

'It's not going to crash! If it does, I will hold your hand and we can die together, will that help?'

'I'll die if I go out there! I'm not joking!'

'Oh, for Christ's sake, come on!'

There was no escaping the grip this time. Kelly had her upper arm, tight. He was hurting. Still, she hesitated. Baulked at full sight of the Kiowa. 'Come on, there's nothing to worry about. It's not going to crash.'

'But it isn't that, it's—'

'Move!'

'No! No! You don't understand!'

Kelly dragged her unwilling body across the tarmac. She was

stronger than she appeared and it was raining now, lightly.

Kelly, still holding her arm, threw her bag in at Joel and turned. It only took a moment—the small orange glow appearing on the white blouse, travelling quickly to her head. As he pushed her away, hard, he heard the thud as the projectile embedded in the chopper, close to his head. The girl went down, crumpling on wet tarmac. She'd been hit.

Rebecca felt the hands. Warm hands, pressing on her neck. It was hard to breathe. She was cold. Very cold. So noisy. Flying again. Flying?

Rebecca opened her eyes. 'Kelly?'

'Easy, sweetheart. Won't be long now.'

He was lifting something bloodied from her neck, replacing it with something clean. She couldn't move. Lead-weighted. She tried to touch his hand but her body refused to cooperate. She couldn't swallow. Tasted blood. 'Burns. It burns.'

'I know. I know.' And he pushed hair from her eyes. 'We're nearly there. You're not going to die. Unlike you, I am never wrong. Okay?' Reassurances? Trying to joke? She tried to reply but nothing would come. She saw another face through the haze. Joel? Then there was nothing except a peaceful warmth.

Kelly held his hand out for another dressing. Joel wasn't bold enough to speak—few were when the commander's eyes turned black from bottled rage. Everyone who had been into the commander's quarters and had seen his drawings, paintings and sketches knew who this girl was. Someone would die for this.

'Harlem!'

The pilot turned with the answer to Kelly's intended question: 'Twenty minutes.'

'Make it ten.'

Headquarters and barracks for the Nighthawks anti-terrorist unit were situated near Salisbury, in Wiltshire. Broadmeadows was a run-down mental institution well over 200 years old when leased and modified by the United States government in 1982. It now covered twenty-five hectares and was mostly heavily wooded—hidden amid the woods were an SAS training ground, three kill houses and nine obstacle and training courses. The base itself, set on three hectares, comprised four buildings of old, white-painted sandstone—administration, personnel quarters, infirmary and gymnasium. A tree-lined drive ran from the main gates to the car park. The helipad which doubled as a baseball diamond was attended by a welcoming party of three—the Medical Officer, Captain Michael McLaren; a medic, Mitch Stafford, and the Commanding Officer, Colonel Pete Hamill. But as the Kiowa landed, Kelly knew forty pairs of eyes were on red alert.

The duck was finally landing on their pond.

You will make this female civilian welcome. You will not invade her privacy. You will comply with any request providing the primary objective of her presence here is kept as a priority at all times. You will not offend, you will defend—more will-nots than wills. A will-not to a Nighthawk caused a certain amount of curiosity.

Kelly alighted and stood back while the medics stepped in and Rebecca was taken away on a gurney.

Pete Hamill didn't speak at first on the short, slow walk inside. 'Washington's been informed,' he finally said while Kelly waited for the inevitable. 'What the hell happened?'

The second in command related the details of the attempted hit as seen from his perspective. He could offer no more.

'She willingly cooperated?' Pete asked.

'Then. She may not now.'

Kelly took the stairs to his quarters on level three. He walked into his room—a small haven he called home—closed the door and rested his head against it tiredly for a little while. Home. Photographs amid the Eastern junk. A few books he never had time to read. The red Persian rug he'd bought in Karachi. The cushions from Turkey. A remote-control stereo and a hundred old sixties tapes. His great grandfather's lance and head-dress. A collection of sabres and one 300-year-old scimitar. Yes, Kelly thought. This is home and home's a junkyard.

He stripped, showered, and changed into his greens, back into normality. He lit a cigarette, coughed and knew that soon he'd have to give up. But soon never came. He studied his reflection in the bathroom mirror, shook his head and reached for what remained of the Southern Comfort on top of the cupboard. He found a glass and poured a good amount before walking barefoot to his bed.

He lay and studied the ceiling for a while, his glass resting on his chest. Every time he closed his eyes, he saw her face. He'd been seeing her face for eight years. And worse, she knew him, too. He'd seen that in her eyes. Felt it when he took the excuse to touch her hand to lead her out of the airport. Any excuse at all.

Kelly sat up, downed his bourbon in one gulp and felt it burn a trail to his toenails.

And there she was. On the wall, among the other works of art—something else he rarely had time for these days. In almost living colour, a painting of a girl with long blonde hair and huge eyes. Eyes that followed his every movement, that knew every thought. He'd seen her a thousand times and for eight long, lonely years, he had waited for this meeting because he'd known, he had *known* that she was real. She existed somewhere, not just in his mind. She'd first appeared to him on the *New Jersey*—in that 1989 Australian summer—standing there in his mind's eye, begging to be drawn, begging to be found. Kelly had hopefully scanned every blonde girl who walked on board on every port the *New Jersey* had called into. There'd been hundreds of blondes, but none quite like her. For eight years he'd searched and the past four months had felt like forty years after he'd watched that CIA videotape, seen the face, the smile, heard the voice. And he knew that dreams were not lies because sometimes they came true. And turned into immediate nightmares.

They're the lethal bodyguards, not me.

We're off to a good start, girl, he thought and pulled his boots on. He did not look at the painting on his way out.

CHAPTER 2

For two days she huddled with Mairie in a dark corner of the cell, waiting for these people to see their mistake but watching instead others being taken away to the tower.

Some didn't come back.

Hannah was worried for her baby and for Mairie who couldn't see but knew so much. Be my eyes, lass. Be my eyes, she had often said but Hannah had not seen this coming. Nor had she dreamt it possible. Who would do such things to Blind Mairie? She'd always helped people. Why were they hurting her so?

'Hannah?'

She looked up. Redmond. At last he'd come to take her away from this madhouse. She grabbed at his knees but he pushed her away. 'No nonsense now. Come.'

He heaved her to her feet and left Mairie McTaggart grasping at the air and howling, 'Not Hannah. Not my girl. She's innocent! You'll not take her—'

'I'll be right now, Mairie. I will.' But nothing Hannah could say would stop the old woman's howls and curses. 'Don't you see he's come to take me home? I'll be right now.'

'No, Hannah. You're wanted,' he said quietly as he walked her up uneven, slippery, flagstone steps. 'Catherine told Nell of the mark on your breast. I couldn't stop 'em.'

'But why? Was it you told Catherine?'

'Will you not trust me?'

'But what is this they say? What be the dolls? What be these elf-arrows?'

'Quiet, now. Quiet.' He pulled her along and she couldn't resist. But before he opened the final door he looked down into her eyes. 'If you confess, if you say what they want to hear, the baby'll save you. Do you understand me, Hannah? They canna hurt you for you be with child.'

'Confess to what?'

'Devil's work.'

'I'd not do the devil's work. You know that.'

'Aye, but you canna convince them, so confess.' He pulled her into the huge, dark room, a room lined with living shadows. Faces of people she once knew, people who had come to be cured of their ills but who were now barely recognised. The arms holding her upright before the judge and inquisitor were strong.

'She's young,' someone said and the voice was foreign to Hannah. 'Heavy with child.'

'Name?' another asked.

'Hannah Dougall.'

'Let the charges be read.'

But Hannah understood none of the words, nor did she understand their questions. 'No, it is not true. I'd not be cursing anyone. I'd be helping with the medicines, not hurting people.'

'Aye, is true enough. She tends the ill.'

'With the concotions of the devil given her by Mairie McTaggart!'

The judge looked down into the girl's eyes. 'Be this true?' James Daley asked.

'The good Michael Maginley, he knows I'd not harm a soul. I've helped his boy through the fever and my own da's been ill two years now. You know that, James Daley. Was I not the one who helped your good Lady? Tis God who helps me, not the devil. This you know.'

'And who's the father of the bairn? Was Mairie not the one to witness you copulating with the evil one?'

'I'd not know of this you say!' Hannah tried to turn to Redmond but she could see him nowhere. 'Tis Redmond Innes' baby. All the village knows.'

'Tis the devil's spawn! She's been seen dancing by the waters in the moonlight! She has the mark!' Nell of Craigmore screamed.

'I've no mark! Will ye not let me go back to my da? He needs me! He's ill! He's dying!'

'She has the witch's mark!' Nell said happily.

Rebecca woke, disoriented. Hazy. The pleading Scots voice gently echoing—*'I've no mark, my da needs me'*—and softly sliding back into the recesses of another time. Another place.

She could hardly breathe. There was an incredible burning

pressure on the side of her neck. She couldn't touch it. Her arms were weighted and in her left hand, an intravenous tube.

Stone walls again, but they were a stark white, not dungeon-like. Her eyes readjusted to a hospital room. Hospital? What had happened? The cogs of her memory slowly started to turn forward, into the appropriate year, 1997. The flight. The airport. Something vaguely reminiscent of Robert Glover and world councils, questionable pleas for help.

The commander and a chopper.

Nothing though could be associated with this room or the dull aches throughout her body. Where the hell am I now? she wondered.

She tried to turn her head towards the door. Her body still felt weighted. There was a corridor leading to a larger room, much like a nurses' station. And the smells hit her then—cold, clinical, antiseptic. But the nurse who plodded by and looked in was dressed in marine greens and his face was bearded.

Nighthawks? They must have taken me to Wiltshire, she thought. She heard echoing voices. Male voices. Footsteps approaching.

She turned the other way, slowly. One small window was set high on the wall. Vertical bars. A prison? Rebecca closed her eyes and the image of dark slimy stone flooded back. *Straw on an earth floor. Straw that stank. It was wet, putrid.*

Rebecca tried to move and, after a tiring effort, managed to push the bedcovers back a few inches. She wore her nightgown. Her skin was very pale, almost translucent. An unquenchable thirst plagued her. The smell returned, twice as strong. The smell of death and decay swarmed and all light disappeared. The walls were dark again. Stained. She heard the voices clearly, male voices, howling, crying, screaming. A madhouse. This place had been a madhouse.

No! Take it away!

Immediate response. The walls were white, clean, bright again. She stared at an empty water jug and a sparkling glass, upside down on a paper doily.

'I'll get some ice, okay?'

She turned to the voice. An Australian voice. It wasn't Joel. Small, amused green eyes smiled at her.

'Where am I?'

'You're quite safe. You'll be fine, Rebecca.'

'Who are you?'

Mitch flashed the ID and clearance pinned to his jungle green shirt. 'Sergeant Mitchell H. Stafford at your service and if I can ask a dumb question, how do you feel?'

'Cold. I'm cold. Thirsty. I can't move.'

Mitch studied her eyes for a little while, unsure. 'Captain!' he called and a few seconds later, Rebecca heard the sounds of heavy boots on polished tile. The medic retreated and the biggest man Rebecca had ever seen loomed into the room.

'Come back to us, have you?' he asked in a thick Glasgow accent. Her blood curdled at the sound of his voice. He came closer, adjusted the drip, checked her eyes and stuck a thermometer strip across her forehead.

'I want to see Kelly Nolan.'

'Aye, lass, in time.'

'I am not a lass. My name is Rebecca and I want to see Kelly right now.'

The Scot sighed. 'Aye, aye. Soon.'

'What's happened to me?'

'You were shot, Rebecca-lass. No major damage but we're mindful of infection and you'll be mighty sore a while yet. So we'll conserve your energies and getting upset's no answer.'

'Upset? *Upset?* Why should I be upset? I want Kelly Nolan and I want him now!'

Someone by the door cleared his throat and two heads turned instantly. Kelly. 'Careful. You'll blow a gasket,' he said to Rebecca.

'I'll blow more than a gasket.'

'I take it you'd like some time with the wee lassie, Commander?'

'Thank you, Captain. Close the door on your way out.'

Rebecca remained quiet until the door had closed. 'Who's he think he is?'

'He's the Medical Officer.'

'And what are you supposed to be? Chief safety-for-civilians officer?'

Kelly put his hands behind his back, the safest place. 'No, I'm second in command. And I'm also sorry for what happened to you.'

'You're sorry?'

'Yes. I know exactly how it feels.'

'I don't want to know about your battle scars. I want to know why someone tried to kill me and nearly did. What's going on?

Is this the extent of your protective custody?'

'The fact is, if I hadn't pushed you out of the way, you would be dead. I intercepted a head shot.'

'What do you want? A medal? How are you supposed to keep the President alive if you can barely keep me alive?'

'The bullets basically missed you.'

'It doesn't feel like it.'

Kelly waited for more. He knew he deserved it. She wasn't as angry as he'd expected. Simply upset. Confused. Weak and possibly in shock. 'Why?' she asked. 'Who would do this?'

'We don't have that information right now.'

'But you expected it.'

Kelly neither confirmed nor denied it.

'Oh, great. What the hell have I got myself into?'

He avoided that one, too. 'Look, I know you're tired, so why don't you—'

'Go away!'

Kelly studied her as objectively as he could. One moment a threatening demand for his immediate presence and next, instant dismissal. 'Is that what you want? You don't have any questions?'

'I want to go home.'

Kelly looked away from the tears welling in confused and frightened eyes. 'Right now, that isn't possible.' But briefly he wished it were. She didn't belong here. Someone else, maybe, but not her.

'Get me out of this room.'

'Rebecca, you can't be moved yet.'

'Get me out!'

'Is it this room?' he asked, all too aware of what the problem was. Kelly himself hated being down here for any length of time, and if anyone else could feel, hear and see what he did, it'd be her.

'Was this place some kind of prison?'

'No, just an institution for the criminally insane. Welcome to Broadmeadows, Miss Miller.' His sudden smile was radiant and the deeply tanned skin browner if possible against the jungle greens. He wore the uniform so well.

'I hear cries from these walls. You hear them too, don't you?' she said quietly, her voice beginning to rasp.

'Cries?'

'I know you do.'

'Look, how about you concentrate on what you know, and let me concentrate on what I know.'

'Where are my things? Where's my jewellery? I came here with—'

'A small gold crucifix, a watch, opal ear studs and a sapphire ring. You'll have them back very soon.'

'Thank you.'

'I'll let you rest awhile.'

'Kelly?'

He turned back at the door.

'Thanks for what you did.'

'Anytime. It'd be easier if I knew when to fly the white flag.' With a small smile, he was gone.

His smile lingered. Lingered like the memories firmly embedded in the stone walls surrounding.

Emmanuel, help me block this.

Push it away.

It's too strong to push away.

Push it away.

It's all so simple to you, isn't it?

Close your eyes and take good advice.

Rebecca slept because in sleep there was no pain, no confusion.

It was late afternoon when Kelly came back and sat for a time, arms folded, watching her sleep. She was restless. Talked a lot. Mumbled. Now and then, he'd hear a word in an accent thicker than McLaren's. It seemed to be a voice he knew, returning in a waking nightmare.

'I know nothing of this y'say. I've no name but Hannah. I've no mark of a witch.'

'Show this mark to the court,' James Daley said with a sigh.

Hannah felt the hands of a stranger pull her nightgown apart and every man in the room watched eagerly as Nell of Craigmore lifted Hannah's arm so that under her swollen left breast the mark of the witch appeared—a large dark mole.

James Daley rubbed at his face tiredly and nodded to the one sent from Inverness—the Pricker, who rarely failed to find the mark of true guilt.

He approached Hannah and she stared at what he wore—the ruffles at his throat, the fine linen of his coat. She'd never seen finery like it. A rich man yes, and his eyes were grey, as grey as the loch in winter. His two helpers took the nightcap from her head and one held her while the other took shears to Hannah's long dark hair.

The man from Inverness sank to his knees on the flagstone, touched the hair and ordered it be buried in the kirkyard. For then it seemed, Satan would be able to find nowhere to hide.

He said a prayer, his voice calming, soothing. A soothing whisper none could hear but Hannah. His eyes seemed to reflect the sea, his voice seemed to be the gentle waves, stirred by a breeze. She drifted off to his voice: 'There be no pain. There be no pain. There be no pain.'

Hannah was laid naked on the hard stone floor but it felt as if she floated on water and her eyes closed as expert hands kneaded, stroked, searched for the devil's mark, that elusive, invisible place which heralded no pain.

And all watched as the one from Inverness took a long brass pin with an ornate grip and he plunged it deep into the girl's shoulder. She screamed and the eyes of the Pricker smiled. He stabbed again, into her side. Again, into her thigh. Her hand.

'Enough!' Redmond Innes cried. 'Can you not see the lassie's innocent! Can you not see she feels the pain!'

The Pricker looked at Redmond Innes, at Hannah Dougall. He watched her eyes carefully as he leaned over her face, his body swaying ever so slightly, side to side, as he whispered to her again. Again she was back at the sea, at the sea. Yes, there be no pain.

And when he thought it was time, he took the largest of his pins from the cushion around his waist and this he plunged to the hilt in the young girl's left breast.

And she felt nothing.

'Here lies the devil's mark and here be the witch.'

'You'll not suffer a witch to live!' Nell screamed, ecstatic. 'Burn her in a barrel of tar! Burn her alive!'

The Pricker pulled out his pin and a thin trickle of blood followed. Hannah saw it but didn't understand it.

'What say you, Hannah Dougall?'

Hannah, blinking, dazed, looked up into James Daley's eyes. What had he said? But he shook his head and banged his fist on his table to quiet the noise, releasing her from the Pricker's hypnotic spell. 'She'll be kept in the dungeons till the child comes. Bring in the next.'

Nell of Craigmore's mad eyes were wide with joy.

Kelly started awake from his own recurring nightmare: a scene played over and over in which he seemed bound and gagged and unable to help that poor, pregnant little girl. 'Rebecca?' She didn't wake. 'Rebecca?' Louder. Still she didn't wake. She seemed to be fighting unseen hands until she grabbed his by mistake and blue eyes opened, startled. 'You okay?'

She focussed on Kelly's face. There were no dungeons, no hooded men taking shears to her hair, or men with mesmerising grey eyes stabbing her body with thick, long pins. She was not Hannah. This was not 1662. It was 1997 and a concerned navy officer was leaning over her.

'You were dreaming.'

'No, I was there.'

'You were dreaming. Trust me.'

Trust me, Hannah, Can ye not trust me?

Rebecca's face drained of colour. It's him, she thought, pressing her head back into the pillows. This is *him*. No. Impossible. But I felt familiarity. And I know *he* did, too. Rebecca had a death grip on his wrist and she tried to let go but her fingers had locked.

'Just a dream, Rebecca. You were right. It happens to me all the time when I'm down here.'

When she had calmed a little and finally relinquished possession of his arm, Kelly poured her some water and watched as she tried to drink and touch her hair at the same time. He wanted to tell her that yes, she still had hair and yes, the IV was now gone. 'Want to talk about it?' he offered.

'No. No. I just want to get out of here.'

'I'm not the doctor, Rebecca.'

Mitch arrived with two dinners balanced on a tray and was instantly dismissed with, 'That'll be all, Sergeant.' Kelly settled to eat and was aware of Rebecca's unceasing, thoughtful stare. 'Aren't you hungry?' he asked.

'Starving.'

Kelly took the cover off her dinner. A quarter of a crumbed chicken lay beside a salad.

'I can't swallow.'

'Have you told Mike?'

'Who's Mike?'

'The MO. The doctor.'

'No. I know what the cause is. It'll be better tomorrow.'

'So you're not going to eat that?' he asked, hopeful.

'Oh, take it. Take it and leave me alone.'

Before he retired for the night, Kelly ransacked his room in the futile search for a two-year-old sketchbook. He couldn't seem to find it, but it had to be here. It had to be. He sat in the middle of his room, defeated, tired and surrounded by a shambles of books, pads and stray artwork. 'Shit,' he mumbled. 'I'm going crazy.'

He left the mess for the morning. It could wait. He stripped to his underwear, pulled the bedcovers back and remembered the box under his bed.

The sketchbook was discovered and pages turned until the target was found. The image from a recurrent dream of four months' duration, two years old and titled simply, 'Hannah'. Young, pregnant Hannah, her hair roughly shorn, huddled in rags into a corner of a prison-like cell. Her despairing eyes raked him. Looking at it again, he relived the desolation he'd felt when committing the image to paper. Her desolation. Her despair. Her hopelessness. He felt as if he'd been there.

Hannah.

Kelly glanced up at the girl on the wall. She was blonde. Hannah was dark. But what lived behind the eyes of each felt the same.

You're finally going crazy, he told himself and killed the light. But he knew from past experience that if Hannah was recalled there would be no such thing as sleep.

'Come with me, Hannah. Your father sleeps. No one's to know.'

She looked away, unsure.

'Come', he said again, as impatient as always.

How she loved him—so handsome, eyes of a summer sky, hair of the sun. How she hesitated. 'I canna leave him. He's ill. He's dyin'—'

'And will you not think of me? Will you not think of the livin' for a change?'

'Tis not right, this we do.'

'Stop the nonsense and come,' he said, taking her by the hand, leading her out of her father's house and into the darkness. 'We'll watch the moon rise over the water.'

Hannah watched the moon rise, seeing the beauty, feeling no fear of the night because he was with her. 'The moon's almost the colour of y'hair. Oh, such a wonder it is.'

He turned to her, an odd look in his eyes now. Then he kissed her and laughed at the way she tried to object.

'This feels wrong. You be wed to my cousin.'

'Ah, Catherine. Catherine, who nags and complains and cries. Tis you I want.' He pulled her close, then straddled her in the long grass and looked down at her, smiling. 'I swear, there'll come a day when you're mine alone.'

'I'm but fourteen—'

'And I canna wait any longer. I'm bein' sent to Aberdeen. You'll not see me for months. I need you now, Hannah. Now. If you don't let me soon, I'll go mad. Will you let me, Hannah? Will you let me, tonight?'

Rebecca woke quickly, disorientated again. For a while she still felt as if she were Hannah, being seduced in the moonlight . . . It made a pleasant change from stinking, damp, dark castles and men with their faces covered by hoods.

Someone was in the room. She hadn't seen this one before—he was at the most twenty-two, baby-faced and blue-eyed.

'Morning,' he chirped. 'Didn't mean to wake you. I'm like an old Cadillac, the older I get, the noisier I am.'

Another American in marine greens, who, when he changed her water, hummed the 'Teddy Bear's Picnic'. 'Pardon me for humming, Miss, but the lyrics are obscene and not meant for a pretty lady's ears and we are under order to de-fend not o-ffend.'

He put a thermometer strip across her forehead and took up her wrist. She let him take her pulse, and he scrawled his verdict on the clipboard dangling from the end of the bed. He was whistling now.

'Do you have a name?'

'Faraday.'

'Faraday what?'

'Faraday Faraday, Miss, but Jamie'll do if you want to get technical.' He read the temperature, gave her a Groucho Marx smile and recorded his findings.

'Am I normal?' she asked.

Jamie inclined his head, peered over the top of an imaginary pair of glasses and asked, 'Vot iz diz normal ov vich you speak?' Rebecca laughed as he pushed his imaginary glasses back in place, fumbled his way to her blindly and stuck a stethoscope into his ears. Eventually. 'Think arctic,' he warned, pulling the covers back. Rebecca winced at the sudden cold as it hit her chest. She watched his face as he listened to her heart. Jamie's serious moments were unmistakeable. 'How long have you had this murmur?'

'Since I was seven. How long have you had five girlfriends at the one time?'

'Since I was seven.' He picked up the skin tape from the side of her neck and ripped the dressing off. But there was very little to be seen. 'Can I ask a dumb question? When did you get wounded?'

'Yesterday.'

'That's what I thought.'

'Has it healed already?'

Jamie nodded.

'Good,' she said, touching her neck, feeling only a slight smoothness of scar tissue and an incredible itch.

'Your résumé informs me you're a healer. A hands-on healer.'

She nodded.

'Did you do that?'

Rebecca smiled at him.

'How's it work?' he asked, warily.

'I might show you, one day.'

'One day?'

'You'll find out.'

'Would the mystery girl care for some breakfast?' Jamie asked.

'You can call me Rebecca, you know.'

'And get my pretty little ass kicked? Give me a break, Rebecca, give me a break!' And off he went, this ray of bright sunshine, returning ten minutes that felt like half an hour later, balancing what appeared to be a very heavy dinner tray.

He should have been a clown, she thought. When she glimpsed his face, she automatically brightened. His natural joy was contagious. And she needed it more than her medication for arrhythmia. 'Compliments of the ration assassin. Nighthawks motto—if the food don't kill you, the medics will.'

'Yes, I believe that.' Rebecca lifted the lid and saw bacon, eggs, tomato, two slices of toast and a dollop of something brownish-grey. Mushrooms? she wondered. 'Are you going to have a coffee with me?'

'Ah, the lady not only heals with her hands but she reads minds, too.' Jamie departed and returned a while later with his coffee mug. He sat near the bed, quite comfortable with his feet on her locker.

'What time is it?' she asked.

'Early. Morning, I think. Hang on, no, it's, by God, it's daytime.' Jamie sipped his coffee and watched her eat, noticed she didn't touch the meat. That made sense, too. Psychic. Healer. All sorts of things could this little lady do, apparently. 'I'll let Frank know he has a vegetarian to experiment on. That's if you're willing to risk it, of course.'

'Would you do that?'

'For you, mystery girl, I'd do anything.'

Rebecca had an inkling of why Jamie Faraday had a minimum of five girlfriends at any given time. 'You can smoke if you want. I don't mind.'

'Well, you should. Don't you know you can get lung cancer sniffin' other people's smoke?'

'I'm not going to die of lung cancer. Possibly a bullet, the way things are turning out.'

'Don't say that.'

'Why not?'

'If you're like me, saying it's enough to make it happen. Man, I think flat tyre and sure as . . . ah, I'll get one.' Jamie lit his breakfast, watched her sugar her coffee.

'Jamie, you can be yourself.. There's no need to mind your language.' You haven't heard me yet, she thought.

'Can I ask you a dumb question? When did you first discover you could heal?'

'Oh,' she said quietly. 'I suppose I've always been able to see and feel people's pain. Relieve it. There are many people who can, you know. I've been told my touch is a real buzz.'

'Yeah?'

'Yeah. Come closer.'

Jamie obliged and sat on her bed. Rebecca reached out and put her hand flat on his forehead. After a moment she whispered, 'You've got kidney stones.'

'No, I have a headache,' he whispered in return. 'How can you see the pain?'

'It shows in what you might call the aura. So does disease. Whatever it is, it's a diagnostic tool for me. What are we whispering for?'

'Good question,' Jamie said and went back to his seat and his previous position. He picked up his coffee and caught her expression. 'Yeah, yeah, I know. It should be water, not coffee and booze.' But she was right—her touch was a buzz and she had, somehow, relieved him of his constant headache. His blood pressure was probably down, too, but he was too lazy to check. 'They tell us you can see futures, too. Stuff like that.'

'I try not to wherever possible. The more you know, the less you want to say. The less you can interfere with someone else's life the better. We're all here for a reason, you know. We're only here to learn.'

'But I'm asking what's it like having that sort of gift? Being able to see the future and that kind of thing.'

Rebecca almost choked on her coffee. 'Gift? It's more of a curse.'

Jamie recoiled, pulled a horrified face and squeaked, 'Unclean, unclean! Away, begone!'

'Yes, some people tend to act that way when I'm around.'

'Why?' he asked, wanting to know. 'You seem okay to me.'

'Some people want answers that are often best found by themselves. Give them an answer that they can't find themselves and they expect a trail of constant miracles which I refuse to provide. There's no learning that way, Jamie. We all have to fall over a thousand times before we can walk properly. But the healing is so different. I studied alternative medicine after my—'

'Jesus, don't tell the captain.'

'He's bound to find out sooner or later.'

'Do me a favour and make it later. Please. Around here we fill them with pethidine, patch them up, fill them with pethidine again and when they're right, they're back on duty. Ninety percent of our cases are injuries, not disease and there is a difference, so for Christ's sake don't sprout alternatives at the captain.'

'Pethidine?'

'That's how it is.'

'Then I feel that the captain and I may clash.'

'Rebecca, you don't know the guy.'

'And you don't know what I can do. Besides, I've clashed with worse than that big Scot before. I can hold my own where necessary.'

Jamie didn't doubt her for a moment. His backache was slowly dissipating and for the first time in two days he was free of his headache. Attributed to a few kidney stones.

'As far as I'm concerned there's one sin in life and that's not using, to the best of your ability, whatever gift or talent you may have. Give me your hand.'

Jamie didn't hesitate. Her fingers closed around it and her face creased into a smile. 'Well?' he asked. 'Am I a healer or a comedian?'

'You have the touch of both.'

'Ah, but only one am I paid to use.' Jamie finished his coffee and leapt to his feet. 'Back to the salt mine. God, I love this job, I love it.'

Rebecca watched him depart and what little sunshine there was disappeared the moment he closed the door. It appeared again when she called his name and his face peeked around the partly open door. 'I need a shower.'

'Need a good-looking guy to wash your back, too?'

CHAPTER 3

SHE WAS standing by the window and she felt brand new. Happy. Until Kelly walked into the room. 'The lethal bodyguard has returned,' she said before she faced him.

'Referring to me?' he asked, not expecting a reply.

Faraday was right—he could hardly see where that bullet had grazed. There was barely a scar left. Her hair was loose, damp and a very light scent wafted across the room to meet him. She wore a very thin nightgown. He looked away.

Someone—he suspected Faraday—had lent her a ghetto-blaster which took up most of the available space on her locker. Rebecca turned the radio down. She moved like a dancer in bare feet. Give her a month, Kelly thought, there'll be fifty guys falling over themselves for an opportunity to talk to her. Alone. 'You shouldn't be out of bed.'

'There's a lot of things I shouldn't be. The first that springs to mind is in this place. The second is alive. You shouldn't leave me alone down here. It gives me too much time to think.'

'About what?'

'How the hell I'll get back to London. To the conference.'

'You agreed, Rebecca.'

'And you were supposed to guard this body.'

'You're alive, aren't you?'

'That's not the point.'

'Tell me what is.'

'Five minutes in England and someone tries to kill me. You don't know who—'

'I never said I didn't know. Have you ever considered the possibility that you're with us for your own protection? If it was so easy to attempt a hit at Heathrow, how easy would it be if you were standing in front of three hundred people doing . . . whatever it is you do? What *do* you do?'

'I'm a healer, a naturopath, if you like, and stop changing the subject.' She went back to the window and he tried to discern her overall shape.

'What more do you want me to say?' he asked. 'I'm sorry. We'll do our best to make you comfortable.'

'Good. Get me out of this room.'

'That's up to the captain.'

'The captain isn't here. I feel okay and you outrank him. Don't you?' She turned to him.

'I'm not a doctor and I'm out of my depth down here.'

'I'm not. Sign me out, Commander. Quick. All is forgiven if I leave this room right now.'

Kelly tried hard not to smile. She had persistence, an admirable quality providing it didn't become nagging. No doubt she'd try it on Pete, too. Pete. He'd nearly forgotten why he was here. 'Two things, okay? Are you listening?'

She regarded him coolly. She knew instinctively that she would rarely win with Kelly.

'You'll be having some visitors later today. If you feel you can't manage at any stage, they're gone.'

'You mean there'll be people asking me questions about what I saw. The assassination.'

'Later. Right now they want you assessed by some parapsychologists. That's this afternoon. And tonight some CIA goons are coming to talk to you.'

'I thought Nighthawks were working with the CIA on this? Leon Carter was with you at the airport.'

'Yeah.' He looked away. 'The CIA's part of it—they have to be. But that doesn't mean we have to like it.' In fact Pete Hamill was furiously trying to get Pentagon authorisation to ban the CIA from further involvement, but Kelly didn't tell her this. He didn't want to confuse her any further.

She sighed. 'Funnily enough, I don't mind talking to the CIA nearly as much as the prospect of the parapsychologists. Show me a white-coated professor and I have immediate shutdown. What I do can't necessarily be repeated in laboratory conditions. It's spontaneous.' In fact, the idea terrified her. She had always managed to avoid being tested this way, afraid that her particular powers *would* be demonstrated, once and for all, rather than the reverse.

'You think they'll be disappointed?'

'I think they won't be able to prove anything one way or another, scientifically. Science can't explain what happens. No one can. But it's not magic or mysticism or witchcraft. Whatever it is, it's been in use for as long as mankind's been mankind.'

'Yeah.' He was thoughtful. 'But once they *did* call it witchcraft, and they burnt people for it.' He watched her carefully and saw the shudder that went over her. *Hannah.*

'People fear what they don't understand,' she said. 'What they call the unknown. That's why someone's trying to kill me—out of fear of what I know or have some supernatural access to. That's true, isn't it?'

'Perhaps. If there's a conspiracy to kill the President, they'd want to put a spoke in any wheel that might interfere, whether they believed it or not.' Saying it reminded him that he'd meant to go through all the access files again, to try and find where the massive security breach might have occurred. How had they known who to shoot at at Heathrow? How had they found out times and places so efficiently? Who were they? 'I have to go,' he said to her. 'I've got work to do.'

'And so have I, apparently.'

'Unfortunately, yes. That is the reason you're here.'

Rebecca sighed and sat on her bed.

She had nice legs. He turned back at the door. 'Oh, the second thing. The CO will be down to speak to you shortly.'

'CO?'

'The commanding officer. And it would be better if you called him Colonel unless he tells you otherwise.'

'Why?'

'It's polite. It's also standard procedure here.'

'You don't care what I call you,' she said, a smile passing across her eyes.

'Perhaps you assume too much.'

'I've heard Jamie calling you by your first name.'

'You mean Sergeant Faraday?'

'And are you going to demand formality when you're the CO?'

'Sorry?'

'You'll be Nighthawks' commanding officer by March next year.'

Kelly studied her for a little while. 'Can I be frank with you?' He paused.

'Go ahead,' she said tiredly.

Kelly ignored her appraising look as much as he was able to.

'Now, personally, I think it's unnecessary that you're here and if I can be totally honest about this, I don't want to know who, what or where I'll be in March next year. You don't have to prove you can read fortunes to me. Clear?'

True, she thought. He knows exactly what's going to happen. 'I'm not trying to prove myself to anyone, Kelly. I'm just allergic to formality. This place has as much inner warmth as Tasmania in June and if it weren't for Jamie, I'd have gone stark raving crazy by now. I don't care if you think Jamie's the resident clown. If it weren't for him, I'd be on the road, hitching back to London.'

Kelly sighed and came back into the room. He fished in his pocket. Eventually he withdrew a small plastic packet. He gave it to her. 'The jewellery you requested. I don't want you thinking we're thieves as well.'

Rebecca looked at the small cross on the gold chain. She smiled at Kelly, opened the packet and put her earrings in—medium-sized opal studs. But she couldn't clasp the cross successfully, so Kelly helped. He needed to touch her, yet all he did was fasten the chain and step back. Always, step back. 'The cross was my mother's. She gave it to me a week before she died. I was seven at the time.'

'Yes, I . . . No wonder you wanted it back.'

'You know I was seven when my mother died?'

Cornered, Kelly nodded.

'Do you know what she died of, too?'

'No,' he lied and she accepted it, much to his relief. 'Like I said, if you feel you're not ready, or able, to talk to these people today, you let me know.'

'You'll be with me?

'Yes, as an objective observer. I'll stand in the corner and listen.'

'Kelly, how much *do* you people know about me?'

'As much as is necessary. Look, I realise that this isn't the kind of atmosphere you're used to, and it's not what a person like you would approve of, but there's precious little I can do about that. Okay?'

'No. It's not okay. You say I assume too much? What sort of person do *you* think I am?'

Give me a while and I'll let you know, Kelly thought, but remained silent.

'You don't know me. You can't know what someone's reactions

will be by observing them from a distance. I can't know what you're thinking or feeling because even if I wanted to, I couldn't invade your privacy like that. So don't you dare assume things about me. I could be a closet axe murderer for all you know.'

'Look, we'll learn to get used to you, so for God's sake try a little reciprocation,' Kelly said quietly and departed.

'Hail,' she whispered, pulling a face at him as he walked out.

Pete Hamill heard the whisper very clearly, smiled to himself and took the headset off. He gave it to Barney Quinn.

'Clear enough, sir?' Barney asked.

Oh yes, he thought. *You'll be Nighthawks' commanding officer by March next year.* If she was right about Glover, then he'd be taking his promotion and new posting to the Pentagon within twelve months. Pete's inner joy was immediate but concealed.

'That'll be fine, Quinn, but the heartbeat's annoying now she's wearing the crucifix. Are you sure the device is waterproof?'

'Put it this way, sir. It's indestructible providing she doesn't get shot right in the middle of the cross and if she does, who'll give a shit what she can't talk about?'

Pete, deep in thought for a moment, said. 'Back-up with the ear studs in order?'

Barney re-selected the monitor and offered the headset again. Pete listened for a while—he heard the radio in her room. 'I want it all on tape—however, use discretion when you're editing. And when Carter and Samperi come, I want a separate master, uncut, on my desk when I return from London. Clear?'

'Sir.'

And the boss departed.

Barney listened in. Nothing but the radio, so he tried to complete his crossword. Only a few gaps remained. A word for short, feminine. Starts with P. Ends with E. Six letters. He stared at the wall, waiting for inspiration and the answer came through his headset, immediately. 'Petite?' It was a surprised, female whisper.

'Petite!' Barney cried. 'That's it.'

'Emmanuel?' she whispered quietly. 'Is that you?' There was no answer, so she shook her head slightly and closed her eyes.

Barney called the infirmary. Jamie answered the phone. 'Is the female alone?' Barney asked.

'Yep,' Jamie replied.

'Are you sure?'

'Is the Pope a Jew, man? Give us five, I'll check.'

It took five seconds for Jamie to turn on the camera, monitor what was happening in Isolation and deliver the verdict to Barney. 'She's alone.'

'She's talking to some guy called Emmanuel. Are you sure there ain't no one under the bed?'

'Call you back, Barney.'

'Jamie turned the electronics off, went into Isolation, smiled at Rebecca, dropped to his knees and peered under the bed. Not a thing. He looked up, sheepishly. She was peering down. 'Lost your little black book?' she asked.

'No, no, checking for insurgents.'

Rebecca leaned over and peered under the bed, too. 'Damn,' she said softly. 'I always wanted to know what an insurgent looked like, too.' Jamie gave her a dumb grin, pulled a face. Rebecca watched him leave and the door closed. 'And I thought *I* was mad,' she whispered.

Jamie picked up the phone, hit '1' and waited. The CO walked in, his timing as impeccable as ever. 'Colonel,' he said, then into the phone, 'Quinn? She's alone. Do you suggest I run a few schizophrenia tests? If so, we'll start on you,' and Jamie hung up. 'Quinn thinks she's crazy.'

'Why?' Pete asked.

'She's talking to someone who isn't there.'

'Her voices may not be imaginary, Faraday. How is she?'

'All systems fully operable, sir, apart from arrhythmia.'

'What's that in my language?'

'Dicky heart.'

'She has a heart condition?'

'It's under control.'

'Christ, I hope so,' Pete mumbled. 'Carry on.' Jamie put his feet back on the desk and returned to his magazine. Pete saw the cover photograph of an amply endowed red-head. 'Whose is that?' he asked.

'Mitch's, sir.'

'Keep it out of sight when the woman's around.'

'Yes, sir.' For a while, Jamie thought Hamill would confiscate it.

'If she's a feminist, she'll take offence. And we don't need her believing that we're a bunch of animals.'

'Course not, sir.'

Pete walked away, down the corridor towards Isolation and Jamie was hit by mirth.

Rebecca heard the polite knock and wondered who it could be. Nobody else knocked. The door opened and a blond appeared. He was in greens, wore a red beret with the Nighthawks emblem, had summer blue eyes and looked no more than forty-three. He was tall and, for a man, lithe. Almost magnetic.

'Rebecca,' he said, walking to where she stood by the window. He offered his hand. 'Pete Hamill. Nighthawks' Commanding Officer.' Rebecca accepted the offer. His hand was cool and strong, and something else she couldn't focus on. 'You can call me Pete when no one's around, however, if others are present, you'll address me as—'

'Colonel?'

Her word derailed his train for a second. He squeezed her hand and let go before her impression could crystallise. 'We'll do our best to see you're comfortable while you remain with us.'

'Good, let me out of here.'

'I'm sorry but that decision remains with Captain McLaren.'

'I thought you'd say that. What's that?' she asked, pointing towards the distant horizon, at the Wiltshire landscape struggling for a balance between winter and spring, the rolling hills of the palest green. Pete followed the pointing hand but was more interested in her face than the view he'd become too accustomed to.

'What's what?'

'There. It looks like a church spire.'

'That's Salisbury Cathedral, but you'll have a better view from your quarters.'

'When I get there.'

'When you get there, yes. Thank you for your voluntary cooperation.'

'It was more like emotional blackmail.'

'In what way?'

'Leon Carter says to me, Do you want the President to die? To me. Me, who'll save a moth from drowning in the bathtub. I don't know whether my cooperation was voluntary or stupid but I suppose if you grab someone who's suffering terminal jet lag and put her in a room with four large men, who tell her she's essential to helping keep the new American President alive, she's bound to say whatever they want her to say. Right?'

'Are you telling me your decision was forced, that you did not have the right to choose? If so, a few heads will most certainly roll.'

Rebecca regarded him with a mixture of scepticism and curiosity. She didn't know if he was for real or not. 'What's done is done. I'm here, I'm alive and everyone's happy. Everyone except the person who tried to kill me, right?'

Pete didn't comment except to say, 'It will not happen again.'

'Tell me about this place,' she said. 'It feels like . . . an asylum.'

'Until 1912, Broadmeadows *was* an asylum for the criminally insane. I'm sure any ghosts were scared away fifteen years ago when the Nighthawks moved in.' Pete watched her face closely as she peered out of the barred window and her breath fogged the thick glass.

'And what do you know about ghosts, Colonel?'

'Not a lot.'

'Good. You play wars, I'll play peace. You stay on your side of the fence and I'll stay on mine. How does that sound?'

'Sounds fine to me.'

'Are you going to talk to me or do we politely discuss everything except what needs to be discussed?'

'Would you like a coffee? I could use one.'

'That'd be nice. White with two.'

The colonel went to the door and told Jamie to get 'Two NATO standards.'

'Two NATO standards coming up,' came Jamie's echoing voice.

'Feeling okay?' the CO asked, trying to sound sympathetic, she thought, but something was missing. Maybe he was trying too hard.

'I'll be happy as long as Jamie doesn't decide to leave.'

Amusement flickered across his magnetic eyes and faded just as quickly as it appeared. 'I do apologise for the mishap at Heathrow.'

Someone tried to kill me, she thought, and he calls it a mishap. 'It's always comforting to know someone wants you dead. Just makes it more interesting when it's someone you don't know.'

'As I said, I am sorry that had to happen.'

'Why *did* it have to happen?'

Silence.

'You're not going to tell me, either. Is this sparing my feelings or keeping me in the dark? You know, "what she doesn't know can't hurt us".'

Jamie arrived with two coffees in hand, then retreated quickly and closed the door. Rebecca sat on her bed and sipped at her cup.

'For now, all you need to know is . . . Do you mind if I smoke?'

'They're your lungs, Colonel.'

She watched as he took a cigarette out of a gold case, tapped its end lightly and reached in his breast pocket for a gold lighter. The flame was low, blue and instant. He looked into her eyes as he inhaled and she was frozen solid by the ice-blue eyes staring at her. Judging. Weighing. Deciding. This man wouldn't need a gun to kill. Or any well-used lines to seduce.

'Yes, there has been one attempt on your life. I won't go into detail. Suffice to say, you're alive.'

'Thanks are due to the commander.'

'We think we know who is responsible. Unfortunately it can't be proved and even if it could, nothing could be done about it.'

'Great.'

'In some areas we're restricted by higher authorities.'

Rebecca wondered who was higher than the Secretary of Defence.

'We need your cooperation. We've studied your talents very closely. If you weren't useful to us, you wouldn't be here. We need to know all that you know so steps can be taken if needed to avoid this . . . shall we say prophesied assassination. I realise this is not going to be easy for any of us.'

'Because I'm a female civilian.'

A very pretty one, he thought. 'There's another organisation which we have reason to believe employs people who also want to know what we want to know. We are trying to have their access to you denied.'

'Why? Are these the people who tried to kill me?'

'Nothing as yet is certain.'

'The CIA? But Leon Carter was at the first interview . . .'

'That was necessary. But perhaps their motives are not, shall we say, in accord with ours. Or very wholesome.'

'So President Glover does intend upsetting a few private apple carts?'

'We do not know how widespread the conspiracy is.'

'Now it's a widespread conspiracy? When you find out, let me know the outcome.'

'Rebecca, I know as much as you.'

'But you don't *know* what I know. I might know that Robert Glover wears green socks and uses Mickey Mouse hankies. *You* might know who his enemies are and that's the difference between us. That's why I keep saying I don't know how I can help you people, but no one listens to me.'

'I've read the police files so thoroughly they're committed to memory. I've seen the videotape of you with the CIA operative. The prediction you had filed with the Society for Psychical Research was leaked to the American government by a parapsychologist reviewing files.'

'When?'

'Four months ago. You have been under surveillance and twenty-four-hour protection since then, although you were not aware of it.'

'Joel followed me around for four months?' she asked, horrified because she hadn't known, hadn't even had an inkling.

But the colonel let her question ride. 'Now, Glover was, as you predicted, sworn into office two days ago.'

'I feel sorry for the poor bastard.'

'Why?'

'Because he's black. A wise man once told me that everyone's blood is red. A shame so many people can't see the wisdom in that. I still don't see how I can help you people.'

'Rebeca, I repeat, if you weren't useful you wouldn't be here.'

She rubbed her face. An overwhelming sea of emotion was swelling like a tidal wave. 'I don't know what I can do,' she said, tears emerging in her eyes.

'Nor do we, precisely. But your . . . foreknowledge, if you like, seemed too detailed and too accurate, so far, for us to ignore it. We may have to ask you to try and relive the assassination vision for us. Many times, perhaps. If we could pinpoint who holds the gun—even who's in the crowd . . . if you can identify them in time, we can prevent it. And that's all-important. You'd have a general idea of the consequences if Robert Glover was murdered?'

'It was long before my time but I know what the consequences of Martin Luther King's assassination were. It will be a thousand times worse with Robert Glover because both black and white voted him in against all odds. The people love him.'

'That's right.'

'Because he's a good man, whatever colour he is. Or don't you think like that? Is it just a job for you?'

Pete looked away from the expression in her eyes. He was used to studying people, not being a subject himself. 'There are times when, if I stopped to consider where a man's goodness might lie, I'd get a bullet between the eyes. Perhaps you should think on that. In time you'll have a different perspective.'

She lay on her bed, pulled one of her pillows out and held it tightly. For a moment, all Pete saw was a frightened kid.

And worse, he felt sympathetic.

'How many people do you think might be involved in this assassination conspiracy? Providing there is one?'

'You're here to help us find out. Any ideas now might prove valuable.'

And he was so eager to know but he was clinging to thin air. 'Miracles,' she said. 'You're expecting miracles from me.'

'Not necessarily.'

'Already there are people who don't want me alive because they think I know things which would be damaging about them. The commander was expecting what happened at Heathrow. Everyone seems to be expecting another try at me, too. That's why I'm staying here, surrounded twenty-four hours a day by anti-terrorist soliders. Right?'

'You're here for your protection, yes.'

'This advisory thing. What's expected?'

'This . . . clairvoyance of yours. Do you know what it is? Where it comes from?'

She thought for a moment, trying to find language he'd understand. 'It's as if . . .' she began hesitantly, 'as if each of my senses has a double. As if I have five sixth senses. It can't be proved, except by hindsight. If what I predict turns out to be true, it's believed *then*—not at the time I experience it. All I know is that I'm usually right.'

'And that's what we're trying to avoid here. The President dead, and you being right in hindsight yet again.' He was thoughtful, frowning. 'If you could describe the whole thing to us in detail—who else is there . . .'

'I don't think I can force it. I can only give you what I see, what I'm allowed to know.'

'Allowed?'

'Colonel, you have to answer to someone, don't you?'

'Yes.'

'So do I.'

'Who?' he asked, perplexed.

'You wouldn't understand. It's a different chain of command and a different higher authority, and it's all inside me.' She knew by the look in his eyes that he *didn't* understand.

'Please tell your higher authority that I think all this is futile.'

He was frustrated at finding there might be no answers to his questions. 'Nothing is futile.'

But trying to convince you surely might be, she thought. 'Does Robert Glover know about me?'

'What do you think?' He clearly wasn't going to answer.

'How many men are in your Nighthawks? Or is that classified information, too?'

'Fifty-four.'

'How many women?'

'No women. We're an anti-terrorist squad. Elite, if you like. We're a family. A large, close family.'

Of professional killers who wear black uniforms and abseil down buildings and throw stun grenades before they shoot at anything not lying down. I suppose a close family is better than none at all, she thought.

'This evening, you'll be interviewed by two CIA field operatives. Carter, you've met. Samperi, you haven't yet.'

'Are they suspected conspirators?'

'You met Leon. Did he feel like a conspirator?'

'I could have been on Mars for all I knew.'

'Rebecca, if it wasn't safe for you to speak with these two people, I would not allow it. Trust me. Commander Nolan will be present throughout and any time you wish the interview terminated, all you have to do is say so. Now, unless you have any more questions?'

'None you'll answer.'

Pete smiled at her and finished his coffee.

'Well, I'll let you rest now,' he said. 'But if you remember anything—anything—more about your vision of Glover's assassination than is already in the file, please hold onto it.'

She hesitated, then she said, 'That file's six years old. I've had that experience again, at other times since then.'

'What? Jesus, is it always the same?'

'No. Sometimes it's quite different—oh, he always gets shot, but the background scene changes.' She faltered, unwilling to let herself dwell on those images. Fatigue washed over her.

The colonel stared at her, impatient to find out more. But he could see how close she was to exhaustion.

'Okay,' he said reluctantly. 'We'll leave it for now. Get some rest.'

'I'm not what you expected, am I,' she said, not a question.

'Is anyone?' he replied and with a nod, he departed.

Rebecca cuddled the pillow again. Tears stung at her eyes and fought for outlet. Tears. No way on earth would she let any of these people see her cry. Who here would understand? Oh, God, she thought, sniffing. What if there was no conference at all? What if this had all been an orchestrated excuse to bring her to England?

If you're so psychic, why did you let yourself get into this mess?

She glanced around the isolation room and the walls closed in, quickly. I can't help them, she thought. I can't. And President Glover will die.

Jamie came in quietly, as if he knew she needed someone. He put a large, warm hand on her shoulder and she grabbed that hand and held it tightly. He whispered his reassurances—he seemed to be the only one who truly cared.

And in the small communications room, Kelly gave the headset back to Barney.

CHAPTER 4

THERE WERE four men waiting in Interrogation A when she walked in after lunch. She'd had a short sleep, and then Frank had sent some fruit and milk to the infirmary, but she still felt exhausted, and she wondered if she'd be able to perform on cue for these men. How she ached for another female face, how she'd hoped to find one among these researchers.

'Come in Rebecca,' Pete Hamill said. He was friendly, pleased that something concrete was about to happen.

She studied each of the men as she was introduced. She touched their hands in greeting and found no threats or hostility among them, just an impersonal curiosity. They began by asking her basic questions, and at first she only needed to answer yes or no. Matters of fact, of file.

'Yes, it's true I work mainly through psychometry. I have found missing people. Yes, I've helped with the odd murder investigation. Before I came here I was much in demand, yes. I still am, but for different reasons.' She shot a wry look towards the colonel.

'For what were you in demand?' Professor Gottsbaum asked.

'Spiritual healing and naturopathic medicine.'

'You are how old?'

'Nearly twenty-five.'

'And you claim to have had this gift all your life?'

'I claim nothing.'

'Psychometry is one of your abilities, yes? To you it is what? How would you describe it to us?'

'It's . . .' she hesitated. She had thought about this a lot, but wasn't sure how much she wanted to reveal to these people. 'It's as if I tune into the residual memory. A memory that's somehow been imprinted into an inanimate object by the force of a person's emotions. The impressions can be spiritual, emotional, mental and physical—sometimes all four together, depending on how intensely the person has lived, or how intimate the object is.'

Her statement surprised them somewhat. Not many natural pyschics were that articulate about their abilities. The youngest of the men took off an old fob watch and gave it to her without saying anything. She closed her hand over it.

'It was your father's watch,' she said. 'He stole it in a card game. It was a joke, I think, there's a lot of amusement here.' She studied the Oxford University student. 'There's remorse, too. Your father wanted your forgiveness for something, Michael.'

The young man's face drained of colour.

'Let him go, Michael. There's a lot of possessiveness and jealousy here, which led to rejection and hatred. Your father was tormented by it, so are you. Let it go.'

'He's been dead for five years.'

'But you haven't let him die. You've fed on your hatred of him. It's time to stop.'

The young man took the watch back in silence. Rebecca knew he would not approach her later. His interest in the paranormal was intellectual, not for its healing powers.

After another half an hour or so of questions she was handed a teaspoon. 'Can you bend this?' Professor Gottsbaum asked.

'Yes,' she said, furious at being asked to do tricks. Her anger fused the spoon in her mind as she closed her eyes and pictured it lying on the desk, welded into a circle. She opened her eyes. The ends of the spoon had touched and melted together. Her yawn looked like indifference to the men, when it was genuine tiredness.

They put her through several routines with more spoons, placing her at distances further and further away. Each time she managed to meld it into a circle, or some other pleasing shape. They seemed genuinely excited at her ability to perform on cue, but she knew it was a combination of anger and exhaustion that kept her so intensely focussed. She doubted she would be able to repeat the performance on another day and vaguely pitied these people who had so little understanding of what she was doing.

They had barely begun. They took her to the library, where equipment the professor had requested was set up. There she was hooked to a bewildering array of machinery—bio-feedback monitors, others to record alpha, beta, delta and theta brainwaves. Something else that measured electrostatic and electromagnetic fields. A polygraph that read physiological changes associated with stress—heart-rate, respiration and body temperature. She had sensor pads glued to her head, arms, shoulders and ribs. She felt like the centre of an electrician's nightmare.

Then four video cameras were set up to make records of her every reaction, these in their turn to be registered, computer-enhanced, on the sophisticated equipment the squad already possessed. When everything was in position the men went out, leaving her alone in the library. Under total surveillance and alone.

From a microphone the questions began again. When? Where? How? How often? She watched the scrawling graphs on the screen, the regular patterns of her heartbeat, the blipping lines of her various brain waves. No change in the regular ups and downs when they asked her to bend yet another spoon on the desk, and she did. No change when they asked her to describe her vision of the President's assassination. The merest hiccup in several graphs at once when her father was mentioned, a bigger one when she was asked the unexpected question: 'Who is Emmanuel?'

'How do you know about Emmanuel?' He was her secret, she would not share him.

'Is he a so-called spirit guide?'

'He exists in my world, my private world. You have no words to describe him.'

They persisted for some time, but she was stubborn. She would cooperate as much as she had to, to help avert the President's murder, but she would not let them violate her innermost visions and beliefs.

Finally, when she was kept upright in the chair almost entirely by the various straps and wires attached to her, they called it a day. Professor Gottsbaum, a trained doctor, had finally noticed her white face and the purple hollows under her eyes like bruises. 'The little one is exhausted,' he said. 'We have much of interest here to discuss. We can come back again. Let her go, now. She is extraordinary,' he said in an aside to Pete Hamill.

'She has her moments,' Pete agreed sardonically.

'What effect has she on the men here?'

'It's too early to tell, but so far everyone who's met her seems to be under her spell.'

'Yes,' the professor mused a while. 'I would like to test her healing skills. Perhaps next time.'

She was sitting by the window and deep in thought when Jamie made another entrance, in the late afternoon. He had a huge bunch of roses in a vase, a bud clenched between his teeth as he Spanish-danced his way in, plonked the vase down and offered her the bud, Romeo style. Rebecca, feeling unwell, looked away. 'Don't tell me you're declaring everlasting love already?' she asked, wearily.

'They're from Colonel Hamill,' Jamie said, brightness fading.

'Well, it's not every day I get roses from a gorgeous blond who has a wife and four kids.'

Jamie wondered how she knew Hamill had four kids. 'Why are you out of bed?' he asked. He'd seen how pale and shaken she was when they brought her back from the library.

She shrugged. 'Don't bug me or I'll call you Sergeant. Aren't you too young to be a sergeant?' she asked.

'It's the lowest rank here.' He was worried about her trivial, subject-changing questions. She looked terrible. A pulse was visibly thumping in her throat. Erratic. Her breathing was strained, too. The eyes were dull, the skin almost grey. Concern welled.

Rebecca sensed it. 'What's out there?' she asked, pointing vaguely to the south, towards the assault courses and the training grounds.

'That's where the teddy bears have their picnics. Looks like they're having another right now.'

'I saw smoke there before, thought it might be a bushfire. And a chopper hovered over it but didn't drop any water. Just two people.'

'It's a simulation. An exercise.'

'Oh. They're being honed on the finer points of wholesale slaughter and mass destruction. I see. And is the commander out there?'

'Commander Nolan is Chief Instructor.'

'Chief Instructor for what?'

'Everything. Mainly the finer points of wholesale slaughter and mass destruction. Please get back into bed.'

'No. I'm enjoying the view.'

'Rebecca, you need rest.' He was being serious. No jokes. No comedy routine.

'Don't nag me, Jamie. I'll be fine. Look. There's that smoke again. Do you think I could watch them do their simulations one day?'

'You wouldn't like what you'd see. Please get into bed.'

She smiled at his gentle persistence. 'What time are these CIA people coming?'

'Tonight. Maybe.'

Rebecca rose slowly, but even so the movement was too much. The exhaustion was obvious because Jamie grabbed her arm. She felt like a rag doll. 'It's only jet lag,' she explained and wiped beading sweat from her face.

'Yeah, right.' He put her into bed, reached for the oxygen mask above her head and brought it down.

And she knew what to do with it. She also grumpily submitted to an ECG being attached after Jamie had calmly panicked when he put the stethoscope on her chest.

McLaren had left on exercise in Buckinghamshire with ten members of the squad, Stafford had taken twenty-four-hour leave. The CO was in London and Jamie had his first ill, as opposed to injured, patient. He made doubly certain she took her medication and he sat with her for a little while until the ECG showed some sign of regularity, albeit vague.

'If it's true you can heal others, why can't you help yourself?'

'It should make you feel worthwhile, because nothing except orthodox medicine can help me with this.' Much to her inner disgust. 'Give me an hour, I'll be back to normal.'

'Is it some kind of congenital disorder?'

'I don't think so.'

'It's brought on by emotional stress?'

'Jamie, isn't there a solider with a fractured toe who needs you desperately?'

'Nope.'

'How about half a dozen girls with broken hearts then?'

'Nope. Well, maybe one or two—' His lighter moment passed. 'What did you really see when you were eighteen?' he asked, wanting to know. He was so curious.

She sighed and studied the ceiling, then spoke in a flat voice. 'I saw a black man walk out of a Learjet and he lifted his hand to a crowd of people. He was smiling. A moment later, he was dead from a bullet between his eyes.'

'You *saw*?'

'Just as I'm looking at you now, only it's like being in a movie theatre with two features playing at the one time. You're aware of both simultaneously. It's something you get used to. In one feature you have reality, or what we perceive as being the present. In the other, you somehow skip time into another reality, either past or future.'

'How'd you know it was Robert Glover?'

'I *saw* a newspaper stand on a crowded sidewalk. I could see all these people who seemed stunned. Dazed. Shocked. Then I saw a paper—the *New York Times*—and a paper-seller with tears in his eyes. I can even remember what he looked like. It was snowing and he had a bright red woolly cap on his head. The headlines said, "President Robert Glover dead". The date was December 10, 1997 and I don't know what was worse, feeling the hopeless desolation of all those people or having watched him get a bullet in the head. It wasn't symbolic. Even then I knew the difference. It was very real and it was going to happen.'

'What did you do?'

'I tried to ignore it, hoping it would go away. But it didn't. It repeated, over and over and over.' Like all these questions they keep asking me about it, she thought. Even Jamie.

Jamie watched carefully. What to anyone else would have been some kind of waking nightmare, soon forgotten, could not be so easily laid aside by this little lady. He gazed at her as she lay there and much more than a pretty face and a lovely body was visible. Something from within seemed to be glowing at him. Something about her made him feel useful. Special even. Again he longed to touch, if only to hold her hand for a while.

'I had no one else to tell except my father but we'd never communicated very well. He'd often look at me as if I were totally crazy. I think I unnerved him too much.'

'How'd you do that?'

'Knowing things. Seeing things. When I was seven years old I knew what had killed my mother.' She was quiet, pensive for a little while and Jamie didn't volunteer what he already knew. 'When I was thirteen the doctors decided I had some kind of brain embolism because I'd pass out and start babbling in foreign languages or telling complete strangers their life stories. It had to be a major brain dysfunction. I know it was terribly embarrassing for my father.'

'Was it a dysfunction?'

'No. Most of my teenage years were a succession of doctor's surgeries, CAT-scans, psychiatrists. You name it, Jamie, I've had it. Something, anything to find a cause for this encroaching insanity of Hugh Miller's only daughter. You asked when I first knew I could heal? During one of my attacks. I grabbed one of the specialists and within forty-eight hours his glaucoma was cured.'

Jamie didn't disbelieve her—she relieved pain with a touch, he'd experienced it himself. Whether she was aware of it or not seemed to make no difference.

'He went on helping people years after he should have been totally blind, and he was the one who looked beyond science and found my answer. He knew a psychic who took one look at me and knew what the trouble was. So now I can control my so-called brain dysfunction because I know what it is, and I heal people as well. That's what I'm here to do. Not tell fortunes or look into futures which aren't mine to know about.' She didn't describe the years of emotional pain, the disbelief, the fear in people's eyes before she learned to harness her power, to present herself as 'normally' psychic, something they could understand, if not totally have faith in.

'That's it?'

'What did you want? A bolt of lightning? A burning bush or two?'

He grinned at her. His amusement was opaque.

'Jamie Faraday, what are you thinking of doing?' she asked, but Jamie didn't answer. 'I'll be fine. I'll be firing on all eight cylinders tomorrow. I won't be like your black '57 Cadillac convertible.'

'No visitors tonight, though,' he said, watching her closely. 'No way. No visitors. You're not strong enough to talk to these guys.'

'It'd be best to get this over with as quickly as possible. Get them out of the way.'

'No. Stop arguing, woman, you won't win.' He headed for the phone, but the CO wasn't answering his pager. Jamie was patched through to the second in command.

'Commander?'

Kelly turned and barked, 'What?'

Mannett was holding a mobile phone. 'It's Faraday.'

Kelly took the call and watched two men undertake a simulated clearance in the kill house. Straw dummies had been moved about in the room, and today's elected volunteer, Harlem, was tied to a chair.

'What's the problem, Faraday!' Kelly yelled as Pugno hovered the Kiowa over the building and birthed its twins—black-robed and roped.

'Commander, I'd advise you to cancel tonight.'

'What! Speak up, I can't hear a damned thing!'

'Cancel tonight!' came the yell.

Kelly stopped talking until the two had finished playing with their Skorpions and Harlem emerged, pleased to be alive.

'What?' Kelly asked again.

'Sir, you have to cancel tonight.'

'What's wrong? Is she sick?'

'I don't want to risk any unnecessary stress. You know what I mean. She's worn out from this afternoon.'

'I'll be there in five,' Kelly said. 'Griinke!' he barked. Ammo appeared with one demolished straw terrorist over his shoulder. 'Take over.'

'This dancing by the sea, it feels wrong. What if we're seen?'

'Feel, feel . . . Hannah, you understand nothing. Come with me. I can open the door to a new, wonderful world.'

'I like the world as it is.'

'Do you? Why is it then I only see your smile when I'm near?'

'I'm only happy when you're near,' she said shyly.

'You must come with me tonight. You belong with us, Hannah, not locked in a stinkin' wee house with an old man who canna even recognise his own daughter.'

'He's my da! He's ill!'

'When he dies, what'll you have?' His hands were so strong, his eyes bright. 'Don't you want to learn new things?'

'I can read and write,' she said quietly as she felt his hands touching her body. It felt so nice, so good. But his beard was always tickling. Scratching.

'And who might'a taught you?'

'You did and I love you for it but this dancin', still, it feels wrong. I'd rather be here with you. Just you and me.'

'But you're chosen, Hannah. Have I not seen the mark? Have I not touched it?'

'But I've many marks. Is not to mean I'd be chosen by anything. Oh, y'should'na do that. Not my nose—' She objected to the playful touch, closed her eyes when he kissed her. He was kissing her neck, his hands tickling her breasts and sliding lower, and lower. 'You should'na do that,' she giggled. Hannah knew what would happen, soon. She knew. And she didn't mind because it made him so happy, even if it hurt. He said she let him do things that Catherine wouldn't. And if she loved him, she'd not say no. Never.

'Hannah, I've promised t'bring you.'

'No. I would do anything for you but not this. I don't want'a be dancin' when it be not allowed. You know what Michael Macginley would say if we was seen.'

'But Michael Macginley's coming.'

Hannah touched the huge hand between her legs. 'No. No. My heart says it be wrong.'

'You don't love me at all, then.'

'But I do.'

'No. No, if you loved me you would do as I say!' He rolled away and rose to his feet. Redmond walked off to find his horse. Hannah tried to get dressed but he'd already gone.

'Redmond, you canna leave me here! I don't know where I am!'

He had disappeared into the thick darkness, the fog.

'Where are you!' she screamed. There was no reply. 'If I promise to go, will you not come back! I canna bear the darkness!'

Kelly, dressed in black flameproofs and wearing his beret, stood by her bed. He listened to her crying whispers, 'Will you not come back?' while she lightly tossed about. Her sleeping face was almost grey in colour, beaded with sweat. She was hooked to an ECG, the sensors glued to freckled shoulders, breasts, ribs. And it seemed that Faraday's instincts matched Kelly's.

He turned to Jamie and nodded his approval. Jamie, relieved, departed quickly.

'Rebecca?' Kelly said quietly and put his hand on the cool, bare arm.

She woke quickly, drew the sheet higher to cover what he had already seen. 'I thought you were having a picnic in the woods with the other teddy bears?' she asked, weakly.

A chair was by the window. She'd been watching the action out on assault five. 'I'm cancelling your interview with Samperi and Carter.'

'Why?'

'I'm also bringing in a doctor, a Major Hauser from Enfield. Call it a second opinion.'

'What the hell's Enfield?'

'It's an airbase hospital.'

'Kelly, you're wasting your time. You could bring in every specialist in the world and all they'd find is a murmur and the odd irregularity. You're making a fuss over nothing.'

Kelly was not convinced by her pleading face, either. He thought she looked like shit. 'There will be no visitors. Your interview will be cancelled altogether.'

'Don't do that. Let them come. I can manage.'

'No. It's a risk I'm not prepared to take. I'm looking at one sick lady, here.'

'Kelly—'

'No. Final. Don't argue with me.'

'It could be a grave mistake you're about to make.'

'I am well aware of what it could and could not be. And you're lying there looking like that telling me about grave mistakes?'

'Kelly, please. I'll be a new person tomorrow.'

He looked down at her, not convinced. She knew she would never win with him, never.

'Stubborn, aren't you?' she mumbled.

'I'm probably worse than you.'

Apparently, he had no idea of what he had just said. 'I will hate to have to say I told you so. But when you see me walk onto your baseball diamond tomorrow afternoon at three p.m., you will know that I mean what I say.'

Kelly wondered who had told her about tomorrow's game, scheduled for 1500 hours. 'No visitors.' He was unrelenting, even as he left and he answered her heated call again with a negative while his boots clacked along the tiles, then up a flight of stairs.

'You're just making it worse!'

No reply. He was gone.

'Stubborn bloody man,' she mumbled.

You are critical?

Rebecca watched the familiar gold mist manifest into a glittering sphere and hover six feet from the floor.

He sees.

Yes, I know.

Could it be that he sees that which you cannot? Trust is needed.

Trust?

The door opened and Jamie came back in. He walked straight through Emmanuel, his only reaction to scratch the back of his head and look about, vaguely.

Soon there is one more for healing.

Rebecca was given a visual impression, swift and immediate..

'Jamie, is Casualty ready?'

'Huh?'

'We have a compound fracture and one severed artery arriving at any moment.'

'We got what?' Jamie asked.

'Let me help you. I *can* help, Jamie. You can't do this alone.'

Jamie studied her. Part of him wanted to cooperate—the part he'd been taught belonged to illogical, irrational thought. Her eyes were sparkling, her skin not as transparent. She looked good. The commander comes in, Jamie thought, talks for a few minutes and, it seemed ludicrous, but could he actually recharge this girl's batteries?

'You can't set a fracture like this on your own. Take this off me?' she asked, throwing back the sheet, picking the glued sensors from her skin and wincing. 'Quick. There's not much time.'

Jamie hesitated, but after a quick scan, all, if there had been any, danger seemed negligible. He took her off the monitor, then heard the call, 'Faraday! Where the hell are you!' Jamie's face paled instantly. This girl was spooky.

Ammo Griinke appeared, and balancing against him, Billy Macpherson. Jamie indicated the treatment room and Ammo deposited his heavy burden onto the table.

Rebecca appeared from under the sheet with a hopeful look in her eyes. 'Okay, okay,' Jamie threw her nightie at her on his way to the treatment room.

'What happened?'

'Fucking fool got tangled on descent. Christ, his arm's a—'

'Ladies present, sarge,' Jamie said and Ammo turned to the door quickly. There she was, washing her hands with Hibitane, long hair tumbling over one shoulder. Pretty. Just like the girl plastered all over the commander's walls. Shit, Ammo thought. This is weird.

But weird had yet to be formally introduced.

'Excuse me, Miss,' he said. 'I didn't realise you were there.'

'No problem, sarge, I've heard worse.' Rebecca walked barefooted past the mountain of a sergeant who watched every movement she made.

She looked down at the black-clothed soldier. His face was lacerated and agonized hazel eyes fought to focus on her face. His pain was apparently unbearable. One leg was raised and the splinted, crudely bandaged forearm lay across his chest. Jamie took up scissors, ready to cut through the flameproofs. 'No, Jamie. Wait a moment.'

Billy stopped breathing at the sound of the voice. Soft. Wonderful. He saw the blue eyes, the hypnotic smile. She put her hand on his forehead and he felt immediate warmth penetrate his head, his neck, his chest. Everywhere. It was a tingling warmth that dulled the agony. He was numb. Numb and floating.

'Okay, now you can cut the sleeve.'

Billy moaned from the release of pain. He didn't feel the scissors or the pull at the sleeve. He lifted his head and looked at his arm. Shattered bone protruded below his elbow, blood still spurted.

He didn't feel a thing.

Rebecca, without gloves, put her right hand over the jagged wound and closed her eyes. To Billy, the entire room seemed to glow.

He looked up at her with dazed, hazy eyes. To him, she was an angel. All she lacked were the wings. He touched her face with his good hand to make sure this wasn't a fantasy. Her skin was as soft as it appeared. As he had hoped it would be.

She looked down into his eyes and smiled at him. 'Feels good, doesn't it?'

'Magic,' Billy whispered

'What's your name?'

'Billy—' He let his hand fall and moaned with pleasure. Anaesthetised in ecstasy. I'm in love again, Billy thought while the room constantly dimmed and glowed. He could hear her voice but it was only sound now. Soft, flowing sound. Faraday was cutting through the uniform and her left hand, flattened on his bared chest, filled him again with a buzzing warmth. Then he could breathe without pain and soon, there was nothing.

'Let me—'

'No, Jamie. Just a little while longer. Put the sutures away, we won't need them.'

'But you can't—' Jamie's words faded when she lifted her hand to show him the wound, '. . . do that.' Blood no longer spurted.

Rebecca looked into Jamie's astounded eyes. 'He'll probably sleep for twenty-four hours, but after that he'll be back at work, as good as new.'

'I'm not seeing this. It can't be possible.'

'Then it must be an illusion, Jamie Faraday.'

It took almost an hour, an hour that passed in the space of five minutes. Billy's arm was bloody, splinters of bone no longer protruded four inches below the elbow, the blood vessels had repaired and all tissues had healed completely. His arm was as pink as a newborn baby.

'Let him sleep.'

Rebecca was not aware of the observers until she turned, holding bloodied hands high, then she saw them all crowding in the doorway and spilling out into the corridor.

Kelly was leaning against the wall near the Hibitane dispenser and basin, watching her curiously. 'He's all right now,' was all she could think of to say. 'He'll be fine.'

Kelly flicked the tap on. 'Disperse,' he said and the men dispersed, quietly. Not a good sign. 'You,' he said to Rebecca, 'can get back to your room, get back into bed and I will be in shortly to speak to you.'

Rebecca put her hands under the water and smiled at his threat. 'Don't order me around, Commander. Don't even try.' But his eyes were frozen and ice emanated from him in waves. Rebecca washed the solider's blood from her hands and forearms, dried them on a paper towel and departed.

Standing at the end of the corridor were half a dozen men in black. She disappeared into her room and prepared for the blast of more arctic air when the commander had finished with Jamie.

Jamie was in trouble, could not—probably would not—explain himself. One raised voice echoed around the ten-bed hospital section. Jamie's replies were a succession of 'Yes sir, no sir. I'll remember that, yes sir . . .'

Rebecca heard the footsteps on the tiles. The squeak and clunk of heavy boots. One seemed lighter than the other—she knew who it was before the door opened and the commander came in. He was quiet but there was no associated calm. Rebecca studied him closely and decided to speak before he did. 'I knew that man would be injured. I helped. What did you expect me to do? Sit here and vegetate?'

'You are not being paid to perform miracles.'

'I do not perform miracles. I don't want to be paid. Billy was in pain and losing a lot of blood.'

'You're referring to Sergeant Macpherson.'

'I'm referring to a man with a broken arm, one severed artery and three broken ribs. He could have been out of action for months with injuries like that. He was one breath away from a punctured lung. If the fracture hadn't been set properly, he might have lost total use of his arm. I'm sure you'd want that as much as he would and I'm doubly sure Jamie wouldn't have wanted that responsibility. Why are you so angry?'

Kelly was silent for a little while. 'It was hard enough briefing the men on the reason for your presence here. Most of them are sceptics and it would have been better for all concerned if they had remained so. Now I find I'll have to brief them over again on the relative unimportance of what seems a miraculous healing which eight men have just witnessed. Would you like to help me do that, Rebecca?'

'If you want me to. But they wouldn't understand a word I'd say.'

'Jesus,' Kelly whispered. 'It's hard enough understanding what we saw.'

'You shouldn't have been watching.'

'Put it this way, it was impossible not to see.'

'A true sceptic will be able to reason it away.'

'Rebecca, listen to me.' Kelly pulled his beret off, threw it on top of the stereo and ran his fingers through his hair. 'Okay, you're some kind of miracle healer. How come we didn't know that? How come the *world* doesn't know? Have you always been able to do it? How come the pilgrims aren't beating a path to your door?'

She stared at him, then turned away.

'Kelly, I keep it confidential—so do my patients. I don't want a path beaten to my door. I don't want laboratory conditions and endless tests to see if I'm genuine or a fraud—the sort of thing they're doing to me here. The experiments to see how I do what I do!' I've felt like a freak for enough of my life, she thought. I don't need any more. But it was true that since she'd been here she'd felt her powers intensifying, as if something—or someone—in this place was acting as a catalyst. And it was not like her to be so careless—not checking that no one could watch her with the injured man.

'I usually make sure there's no audience,' she said weakly. 'And the results aren't usually so—dramatic.'

'Well if I hadn't seen it, I wouldn't have believed it. But you must remain anonymous while you remain with us.'

'All I did was help him!'

'Not like that. Not again.'

'You want my help but you won't allow me to help where I truly can? That doesn't make sense.'

'We have a major security breach. This security breach was the cause of the attempt on your life at Heathrow. I don't want anything like this leaked, too. Our unit is officially non-existent. Drawing attention to your abilities draws attention to us.' He must have been upset. He was raising his voice.

'I'm a healer, Kelly. I can't help it. When someone is injured or in pain—'

'No! You are one very sick lady who thinks she's Joan of Arc, Jesus Christ and God knows who else rolled into one.' Anger lit her eyes and she forced it down quickly. 'From now on, you will assist in the infirmary only with permission from the MO. You hear me? The Medical Officer. You are not here to heal. Is this understood?' He tried, but deep-seated agitation kept him from looking her in the eye. He picked up his beret. 'It's bad enough that you're female. The last thing I need is for fifty men suddenly becoming injured and in need of miraculous help. They'll be queueing for miles after this little display.'

'I don't believe I am hearing this.'

'I have a unit to run!'

'What do you want? A medal or a chest to pin it on?' she yelled. Jamie came in, opened his mouth to speak, saw Kelly's eyes and retreated, quickly. 'It's fine, Jamie. The commander was just leaving.'

Kelly fixed her with his best stare, which she mirrored, easily. As he was leaving he heard her say, 'If you put me back on that machine, Jamie Faraday, I'll turn you into a boil as big as Vesuvius before it erupted.'

CHAPTER 5

'ROSES?' ASKED the female voice, interrupting her grateful drowsing. Rebecca saw a tall brunette standing by the door. She was in army uniform and carried the inevitable bag.

Rebecca sat up in bed. 'I think it's the colonel's way of apologising.'

'Major Hauser,' the woman introduced herself, unsmiling.

'Rebecca Miller,' she said, just as officially.

'You're the Australian psychic?' Major Hauser asked.

'Unfortunately, yes.' Rebecca wondered if the doctor had expected dark wavy hair, black eyes, a strange accent, large earrings and a turban.

'I'll tell you this at the outset, Rebecca. I don't like civilians and I don't believe in ESP. It's all crap to me. I think this is a total waste of time, yours, mine and theirs. So you'll tell me exactly what it is you've been diagnosed with and we'll start from there.'

'There's nothing wrong with me apart from the occasional heart irregularity and I have medication for that, so you can go now.'

The major studied the morning's ECG printouts. 'It would help if you'd cooperate.'

'I'm not sick. Do I look sick?'

The woman was deaf. The torture bag was opened, the futile rigmarole began. She has the bedside manner of an out-of-control tank, Rebecca thought and answered the succession of barked questions as best she could without retaliating in the same manner. She refused to feed the woman's glowing embers. Was it Rebecca's fault that Jamie had panicked, incited Kelly to panic, and made this woman come forty miles to check on one civilian patient when she was about to get ready for her first date in three months? Of course it was. At least, the major thought so.

'Why don't you like civilians?' Rebecca asked, gently testing the waters.

'What?' the woman barked and took the steth out of her ears.

'Why don't you like civilians?'

'I don't understand them.'

'Weren't you ever a civilian, Major?'

'No. My entire family is, has been and always will be, army.'

'Oh.' Rebecca had always believed that the world would be a far better place without the need of the military. And tender touches like this woman's. Not one inch of Rebecca's body was overlooked in her thorough examination. She took blood. Rebecca wondered if she'd ever be able to use her arm again. The wound was padded and taped and blood still flowed. 'Tell me when you realise there's nothing wrong. Then they might let me out of here so I can do whatever it is they want me to do.'

The major said nothing. She packed her weapons and re-read what seemed to be a file. The patient's existence seemed forgotten until the head raised and murky green-blue eyes stared at Rebecca. 'It says here that your mother died of breast cancer. Is this true?' she asked.

'How the hell do these people know that?' Rebecca asked, question for question, but the major repeated hers, more forcefully this time.

'Yes, it's true. I'd like to know how you people found out.'

'You're supposed to cooperate with us, Rebecca.'

'And what else does it say? Can I see that?'

Lou-Ann Hauser handed the file to her. Copies of her parents' respective death certificates were paperclipped among the file's many questionnaires. Rebecca was surprised to be reminded that she'd had chicken-pox when she was eleven. On and on and on. 'This is a gross invasion of privacy,' she said quietly.

'It would help us understand you better if you cooperated by answering my questions.'

'Who's us? The World Council of Nations or the entire U.S. Defence Forces? What more do you want to know, Major? It seems as if it's all here. I hadn't heard from my brother in twelve years. It's nice to know I have to go to England for the American Army to tell me he's in the Australian Navy.'

'Is something bothering you?' the major asked, quite sincerely.

'What else do you people know about me?'

'Only what's necessary.'

What is the limit of necessary? Rebecca wondered.

'How about we have a cup of tea?' the major asked.

'And then?' Rebecca queried.

'Then you can tell me how you managed to heal Sergeant Macpherson's arm.'

'Did Jamie tell you?'

'No. Commander Nolan did.'

When she said Kelly's name the blue-green eyes came alight.

'But you said you didn't believe in the paranormal.'

Lou Ann smiled. 'Kelly told me what you'd done.' She barked at Jamie to make tea, and when he mumbled she barked at him again. Her voice was chalk screaming on blackboard.

After the longest half hour of Rebecca's life, the major left none the wiser and Rebecca was glad, for soon, she knew, she'd be out of the isolation room. She'd managed to convince the major she was feeling well enough to be discharged. Now all she had to do was wait.

And if the colonel thought the Nighthawks had scared all the ghosts away, then he was mistaken.

The walls were ancient brick, painted white. Old walls with too many memories. For two days now, she had been ignoring what she felt, saw, heard, and mostly, smelled. The old asylum for the criminally insane . . . She wondered if Kelly ever felt what she felt.

Yes.

Emmanuel, are you sure he sees?

Yes.

It's no wonder he's always on edge.

You will help.

But he's a sceptic.

You will help.

Rebecca repacked her suitcase and changed into a pair of jeans and a shirt. She brushed her hair, added a trace of makeup to her eyes and waited. And waited. 'Come on, Kelly,' she mumbled. Get me out before I go as crazy as those poor people they used to lock up in here.

When he arrived, he had just showered. He was wearing a pair of jeans which seemed old favourites, white Reebok sneakers, and a dark blue shirt. His hair was damp, swept back. 'Would you like to have dinner in the mess?' he asked. 'Are you up to it? You've had a pretty crowded day.'

'Anything to get out of here.'

His eyes sparkled with what she thought was amusement. 'I see you're ready. You must be psychic.' She gave a sarcastic smile. 'I'll show you to your room after we eat. Follow me.' He picked up her suitcase and walked off up the corridor with Rebecca almost running beside him. He took a left at the first T-junction. Rebecca took a left as well and ploughed headlong into a large uniformed body. He had three stripes on his sleeve. She finally found a face. 'Watch where you're going, Pip.' He stepped aside and strolled on. Rebecca watched him walk away—the one who had brought Billy in. He'd apologised for swearing and now he was calling her Pip.

'I'm waiting.'

'I'm coming, I'm coming, keep your shirt on.'

Kelly was stationary at the opened doors of an elevator.

Rebecca baulked.

Here we go again, he thought. 'Something wrong?'

'I'll take the stairs. I need the exercise.'

'Scared of flying. Scared of elevators. Anything else I should know about?'

'Yes, but you won't believe me.'

'Try me,' Kelly said.

'If I go in there, it'll short circuit.'

'Why?' he asked.

'I don't know. I have a drastic effect on some electronic equipment and elevators come second to pacemakers.'

His eyebrows raised in a silent question. She nodded.

'Major Hauser left strict instructions that any physical activity was to be kept to a minimum. No stairs. You are to take the elevator.'

'Don't say I didn't warn you.'

Kelly hid his thoughts and she came into the lift with him. The door closed, the lift shuddered to life.

'That man I just ran into—'

'Sergeant Griinke. We call him Ammo.'

'He called me Pip.'

'Short for pipsqueak.' Kelly folded his arms and waited. Rebecca folded her arms and waited. Nothing else was said. She smiled at him and he tried to ignore it. Her smiles were contagious. Inviting. Kelly shifted his weight.

'You look good in jeans,' she said.

It was probably the last thing he expected to hear. He said nothing. A quiet one unless aggravated.

'Most men lose it when they hit thirty. You must be . . . thirty-eight?'

'Five,' Kelly said. 'I'm thirty-five.'

'I'm—'

'Yes, I know how old you are.' There was silence for a little while. Then the elevator shuddered to a halt between floors two and three.

Kelly cursed silently. Lou-Ann's advice had been to watch her carefully and keep her environment stress-free. She'd wished him luck and departed. Smiling. Lou-Ann rarely smiled. That alone had given him cause for concern.

'I am not going to say I told you so.' The silence echoed until she continued. 'At least the light's still on. It could be worse. It could be—'

The light flickered twice and died, too.

'What'd you go and say that for?' he said. She didn't reply. She grabbed for his hand and held tight. He knew the touch. Instant fear. She's also claustrophobic, he thought. 'It's okay. Auxiliary power's bound to come on at any moment.' His arm went around her, holding automatically, Lou-Ann's words of warning foremost in his mind. 'Don't like the dark much, I see.'

Rebecca didn't answer. A fear of sudden darkness had been her lingering cloud for twenty years. She'd known this man a very short time—if in fact she knew him at all—yet when her anxiety rose, however imperceptibly, his touch was reassuring.

'Maybe next time you'll believe me and save us both some embarrassment,' she said. 'If there is a next time. We may never get out of here alive. We might be found in six months—'

'Here,' he said and put something in her hand. 'Give you something else to chew on apart from my ear.'

Rebecca put the wad of gum into her mouth.

Silence. For a little while Kelly basked in it. 'How do you do it, Rebecca?'

'What?'

'This ESP stuff.'

'You should know. You're psychic too.'

Silence.

'Mostly I tune in, like a radio or a TV, but sometimes I'm taken by surprise.'

'It's as easy as that for you?'

'Thoughts and emotions are powerful things. Understanding the inexpressible is the hardest part. Choosing, discriminating, getting specifics is at times impossible. Isn't it?'

Silence.

'You see, too, don't you?' she said.

No reply.

'Do you believe in coincidence, Kelly?'

'Why?'

'I was wondering what I'd do if the lift suddenly stopped and it stopped. Do you think it was coincidence?'

'Absolutely.' He knew it wasn't.

'I'm beginning to wonder what I'd do if it started again.'

The lift shuddered into life. The light flickered on.

'What'd you do?'

'Nothing.' Her explanation fell on deaf ears. Rebecca watched the way he couldn't wait to get out. She followed him down the wide, red-carpeted corridor. 'Lighten up, Kelly. It was coincidental.'

'Will you please call me Commander when there are people nearby?'

'Sorry, I keep forgetting.'

'Stop forgetting. Please.' He put her suitcase down in the corridor near the mess door, and waited while she strolled to meet him. She peered into the dining room but saw little except the large servery because the main hall was separated from the corridor by a partition. The smells from the kitchen were so mixed that she had trouble decoding them and unbelievable hunger surged upwards. 'Would you like a drink first?' he asked. 'You can have anything you want.' She looked into Kelly's dark eyes and smiled. 'You can have anything you want, within reason.' He let her walk into the bar first. She heard a frantic whisper.

'Ducks on the pond.'

Fifteen faces immediately turned and whatever conversation, polite or otherwise, that was in progress came to a sudden halt. The only sound was Paul McCartney and 'Yesterday' from the Wurlitzer in the corner.

'What would you like to drink, Miss Miller?'

'A big, strong, gin squash, Commander Nolan.'

Barry Mannett heard the order and delivered, along with the commander's usual bourbon.

'All facilities here are communal. There's no segregation of rank or gender.'

'*Everything's* communal?' she asked, eyes widening.

'But we've allocated a bathroom for you. I'll show you later. May I smoke?' he asked.

'Of course you can. If you want to die slowly.'

He lit up and ignored the sarcasm.

'Can I have one? I've never tried one of those.'

'You've got a bad heart.'

'I just thought we could die together.'

'You're going to nag me, aren't you,' he said quietly and sighed as if he were used to women nagging him.

'You didn't have to cancel the interview.'

'Ah, but I did.'

'Why? I'm feeling better now.'

A shrug was all he offered.

She got up and walked to the Wurlitzer, inspected it carefully. It was American and took American coins, but the slot was covered by masking tape.

'Choose one,' someone said and Rebecca turned to see four faces perusing her silently.

'All you have to do is press the appropriate number,' one of the men said.

'I know how to work a jukebox.'

She turned her attentions back to the Wurlitzer, and heard the whisper, 'Nice ass,' but she didn't turn to four innocent faces, as they'd expected. She noticed three Australian songs and deliberately chose the most Australian of the three. Rebecca returned to the bar, accompanied by a few moans and John Farnham. Again.

Kelly had taken her seat and was having another drink. Conversation slowly resumed as two voices became raised from the corner, where she noticed there was a piano that looked as old as the building itself. And the voices were becoming very strained.

She watched, stunned, as Kelly turned, judged the distance and threw his full glass towards the would-be fighters. The glass shattered millimetres from each man's nose.

Southern Comfort peace-keeping duty.

Kelly didn't say a word, and nor did the two would-be brawlers. The man behind the bar simply got him another drink.

Rebecca decided she wouldn't complain that he had taken her seat. 'Good shot, Commander,' she said instead and sipped her gin squash.

Kelly looked at her and smiled. 'You should have seen me when I was twenty-one,' was all he said, and waited patiently until she had finished her drink before he asked, 'Can we eat now?' very quietly.

'Please don't throw your plate.'

'Never in the mess. I usually throw knives.'

For a moment she almost believed him, then humour slid across his dark eyes. Again, he allowed her to walk in first. She felt like a sacrificial offering. 'I suppose you open car doors, too?'

'Whenever possible, yes. After you.'

Again, the entire room hushed. She didn't notice the dark red curtains, the polished wood walls or the ornate, high ceiling. She did see the people, all male, some in uniform, the majority not. Most were aged between twenty-five and forty. A league of nations was condensed into one room. Almost thirty pairs of eyes stared at her and the atmosphere was a mixture of curiosity and caution. Curiosity because she was female and caution because each man fully realised what and who she was. What was worse, she wondered, the sudden, intense silence interrupted only by the occasional clatter of a fork, or every eye watching each move she made?

Kelly picked up a tray. So did she. Then came plate. Cutlery. She tried to serve herself but her hand shook. 'Here, keep it still. You're vegetarian, aren't you.'

'Yes, Commander.'

He gouged a hole in a vegetable pasta and plopped it onto her plate. Then he let her take what salad she wanted. Cheese, Broccoli. Rebecca looked back at the servery, her attention drawn to the baked potatoes, her favourite food, and standing on the other side was a very large man who was covered in tattoos. Frank, she guessed. 'It looks good,' she said.

'What?' he snapped, leaning closer.

'It looks good,' she said, louder and watched a smile appear on his weathered face. No one's ever said that before, she thought and wondered why, as she returned his smile.

Kelly finished serving himself and sat down at what appeared to be his normal place. There was no room at his table. She scanned the room. There was no room anywhere that she could see.

Then she heard the sounds. Thump, thump, thump. Crash. She turned and there was one man sitting on the floor, a dazed expression on his face. His friend, with a huge smile, said, 'There's plenty of room for you here now, Miss.'

And Rebecca ate her first meal in the communal mess at Nighthawks anti-terrorist base. She felt at home, and for the first time in her life, accepted without question or reason. 'Would you like a coffee?' came the soft query. She looked around to the man crouching close by, a black American. His skin was so dark that it shone and made the gold chain about his neck glisten more intensely. She remembered his face.

'You're the chopper pilot. You're Harlem.'

'The name's Luke Jeffries, Miss. They call me Harlem. I'm goin' for a coffee. Would you like one?' he tried again.

'I would love one,' she said with a smile.

CHAPTER 6

*S*HE STOOD *by the shore, staring out over the endless stretch of freezing, grey water, wondering if it was as cold as she was inside. Times nothing kept out the cold, nothing warmed her. Not even Mairie's fire. Hannah went back, sat down and pulled her father's coat about her ears. She was freezing as she looked at their best tablecloth, at the rocks she'd spent all afternoon collecting, at the rope she would use to tie it all to her body. Somehow. And then she'd walk out into the water until it took her away.*

And no one would realise she had gone, because even her father didn't recognise her any more and hadn't she said to Mairie she didn't know when she'd be calling again?

Hannah wrapped as many rocks as she could fit into the cloth and was knotting it tightly when she heard and felt the hoofbeats through the marshy ground. Hannah hid her heavy sins in Mairie's basket, got to her feet and turned her back to the loch. She waited to see the rider, coming at a canter over the bare green hill. She would wave if the rider waved and then she would do what had to be done. But as the horse drew close, she knew who it was long before he saw her, the solitary figure by the water's edge. Her heart sank. He always ruined her plans.

Hannah pulled her father's coat tighter about her neck. The wind was roaring into her face, bringing Redmond's voice with it. He was calling her name. He was happy, too, which made her feel worse.

'Is so good t'see you,' he said, and he jumped down off his horse to give her a crushing hug then drew her back, studying her face. Her cheeks were red from the cold. He touched her nose and she didn't react. 'What be you doin' all the way out here then? Collecting for Mairie?'

'Aye. Collecting. It's here I come to think these past months.'

'Hannah, you shouldn'a think. Is not good when you think. Makes y'unhappy.'

She couldn't look at him.

'Are you not pleased to see me?'

'I'm pleased t'see you.'

'Are you not well then?'

'Aye,' she whispered. 'I'd not be well.'

'It'd be that you missed me?' he tried.

'Aye, I missed you.'

'Hannah, will you not tell me what's wrong?'

'You didn't go t'Aberdeen.'

Redmond let go and stepped back.

'Was a lie you told me t'get your way. Is lies you always tell me t'get your way and I love you so much, I believe you every time.'

'I'd not lie t'you.'

'But you canna look me in the face and say, Hannah, was Aberdeen I did go to.'

He looked into her eyes and said nothing.

'How long you been home then?' she asked.

'Oh, a fine welcome. I'd ride for miles to find you, and when I do, you be like this to me? What is it I've done now?'

'I'd see Catherine today at the market and I was wondering why she was smiling so. So I said, cousin, what's made you so happy? Is not peace he gives me, she said. Is no peace at all. And I know what she means by that.'

'So you'd believe her?'

'She said she be sure she's carrying a wee child.'

'Catherine canna have babies. Is a dream she lives in most'a the time. And I'd a'come sooner but—'

'Is not that you didn't come visit, but you lied to me. Two times, you lie t'me that I know about. You say Catherine will not let you touch her like I will and I hear you never let her be. You went to Glasgow, Redmond Innes. She told me. Y'said you'd take me with you if you ever went to Glasgow. It wasn't Aberdeen at all. You went to Glasgow and you lied t'me!'

'The orders be changed but I've come to tell you what Glasgow be like—'

'You come to have your ways again, Redmond Innes. No other thing ever be on your mind but that!'

'Oh, Hannah, you're wrong.' He touched her face so gently that she closed her eyes. 'You know I love you.'

'And did y'bring me anything?' she asked, hope alive in her dark eyes. He looked away from her face. He'd brought her nothing from Glasgow, the place of her dreams.

'I'd not the time.'

'Aye. Aye. Will you not let me be, Redmond Innes? Will you not go back to y'wife?'

Redmond saw the basket close by and he went to it, leading his horse as he walked. Hannah studied her feet as he picked up the weight she'd spent all afternoon making. 'And what be this, then? A new way of goin' fishing or was it you'd planned on being the bait?'

'Just leave me be!' she cried, hot tears scorching her frozen cheeks as he tore the cloth into pieces with his knife and threw the rocks out into the water where they belonged. She'd never seen him as angry. As upset.

'I'd not want you to come back to this place, Hannah. Are you hearing me?'

'Is where I come to think.'

'And what be this you think of? How t'die?'

She said nothing. She started shaking. Crying.

'Oh, Hannah, what's a man to do? Your mother be dead, your father be dying, yes, but you've life yet to live.'

'I'd not have you. Ever.'

'What is it you want me to do? I canna murder m'wife.'

'If you canna choose, will you not let me be?'

'Hannah, is you I love. You must believe me. I'd be wedded a week when I first saw you. Now can you not think how it is for me?' He wiped the tears from her frozen face and he held her tight for a long time. 'I'll take you home. I'll take you home.'

'Home,' Kelly said with a smile that was almost apologetic. Rebecca, suddenly awake, looked up into his face.

'Pardon?'

'Here. For now, it's home.'

She wondered where she was. She stood in a corridor, on pale grey carpet and barely recalled walking up three flights of stairs.

But somewhere she had seen . . . 'Kelly, did I see a statue of Venus somewhere?'

'Yes, you apologised for bumping into it. Do you always walk around with a vacancy sign on your forehead?'

She ignored that one and peered into room nine. Home? 'It's better than the isolation room.' She walked in.

Kelly followed and put her suitcase on the bed. He watched as she studied the room. 'I know it's not a penthouse on the Gold Coast but it's the best we can do for now. If there's anything you need, within reason, let me know.'

'A few plants would be good. Something to read.'

'There's a library downstairs.'

She walked to the window and peered out. There, still in the hazy distance, Salisbury Cathedral. She was three flights closer to heaven now, and had almost a 180-degree view of Broadmeadows woods, Wiltshire farmland for as far as the weather allowed her to see. It looked awfully cold out there. 'Which way am I facing?'

'East. Lights out in one hour. If you need anything my number's two-eight-zero or I'm across the hall. My door's not locked. I'll see you tomorrow.'

'Good night, Commander.'

'I hope so,' he mumbled.

Rebecca unpacked, hung her few dresses in the closet, folded the rest of her clothes away. She put her personals in the bathroom and looked into the mirror. Her face was drawn, lined and shadowed. She seemed to have aged ten years in a few days and she touched the side of her neck. All that remained was a fine pink scar.

She showered and lay on the narrow, hard bed. Kelly had called this room home. His was across the hall, yet she wondered where he lived. *Was* he married? Why was it that she knew so little about him when it was easy to know others with little more than a glance?

There was noise downstairs—mens' voices, coagulating into a blurred growl, now and then interrupted by a laugh or a curse. She must have been given a room in the officers' quarters.

Try as she might, her thoughts always returned, like a boomerang, to Kelly. He was patient, quiet, nearly always gently amused. His dark eyes and subtly tinted skin made her wonder if he had a hint of Indian blood in his background.

Rebecca toyed with her small gold cross while she stared at the ceiling. There was sticky tape. Her predecessor had taped a poster of a naked female to the ceiling. Momentarily, she also knew what he had done on the bed she now lay on. Block it, she thought, as she had taught herself to do. Block it, it's irrelevant.

Below, male voices. Everywhere, men. Soldiers. Possibly mercenaries. 'God, help me make sense of why I am here,' she whispered, drawing the blankets higher and wishing for someone to turn up the central heating. She'd left a Queensland autumn for an English spring and nothing could combat the creeping cold, not even a tracksuit.

He sees.

I know he sees but he won't admit it. He pretends to think I'm crazy.

Soon he asks for assistance.

Sure. Who kills the President? That's what they want to know. Do *you* know who pulls the trigger? I sure as hell don't.

But as she drifted into sleep, a small movie played in her mind. It starred Leon Carter, the CIA man, and she was in the car with him when the brakes failed and his car skidded sideways into the back of a tourist bus. Night. Fog.

She opened her eyes. She was sitting up in bed, sweating. The digital clock on the phone gave her the time. Two-fifteen. Apart from a quickly beating heart, all was quiet.

'Kelly? Wake up.'

He opened his eyes and saw the face in the dim light. Rebecca? Her hand was on his shoulder, shaking him awake. She withdrew and clasped a blanket around her, tightly.

'What's—what—'

'Leon Carter's dead. I just saw it happen.'

Kelly, who had been flying a Sea King over Antarctica at a hundred feet couldn't adjust immediately to what she was saying.

'Kelly, wake up! Leon Carter is dead. I think he was murdered.'

Kelly sat up in bed and scratched his chest vaguely. Rebecca sat too, and continued. 'I saw it happen. I was there. He slid under a Trans Continental double-decker tourist bus. He was driving a black Laser in heavy fog and the brakes had been tampered with and the road was slippery and—'

'Slow down. One step at a time.'

She was silenced. Her eyes were huge and very blue. He didn't know if she was shaking from what she had supposedly seen or from cold.

'How do you know it wasn't some crazy dream?' he asked, trying to see the time.

'I was there, Kelly. I was with him.'

Kelly turned on his light and she squinted at the sudden glare. He expected her to notice the ladies on his wall, especially the one near the bed, but her attention was centred on one thing only—Leon. 'You were with him—'

'And I was there when the President was shot, too. I was standing in the crowd, watching when he was shot. Leon Carter is dead. Kelly. I know it was murder.'

'How do you know?' Kelly asked.

'Because when I met him, when I touched his hand I saw he would live to be a very old man. He had a long, good life. He wasn't meant to die that way, Kelly.'

Kelly thought back to the airport. Now he fully understood the cause of her smile then. So she could touch people and know the length of their lifespan. He didn't doubt anything after watching her with Macpherson. She was capable of more than they knew. Had ever guessed.

'Do you know where this supposedly happened?' he asked, trying to remain neutral.

'A six-lane highway. I didn't see any signs, any landmarks. It was very foggy. I don't like how this feels, Kelly,' she said quietly. 'Something's badly wrong. I can't shake it.'

Kelly knew that feeling as intimately as an old lover's kiss. He reached out and touched her wild hair, then her face. She was cold, sitting there wrapped in a blanket while he was half naked. She wasn't used to the climate yet.

'You thought something like this might happen yesterday, didn't you?' she asked. 'That's why you cancelled.'

Kelly was non-committal. 'We don't know that he's dead.'

'You'll hear about it in the morning.'

'I can only hope you're wrong about Leon.'

'Who's likely to take over his job?' she asked, knowing she wasn't wrong. 'He told me he was the Head of Operations over here.'

Kelly knew she wasn't grasping at thin air. He put his arm around her so that her head rested on his naked shoulder and her hair tickled his nose. And something about holding her felt too familiar. 'I'd like you to trust my judgement here. Can you do that?'

So much was unsaid. So much she knew she'd never hear. 'I'd better let you get back to sleep. Sorry for waking you.'

Rebecca turned back at the door and something about the way she stood, with the hair falling wild and the despair in her eyes, reminded him of his old dreams of Hannah. 'You're the only person I can talk to here, apart from Jamie.'

'Let's hope you're wrong about Leon.'

Then she was gone.

He lay back, turned the light off and sighed. The last time he had met Leon socially, he'd been driving a black Laser but today, as Kelly was returning to the infirmary from assault five, he, too, had seen that black Laser slide into the back of a bus. And Rebecca had been in the car, too.

For the rest of the morning, sleep was as elusive as rational thought.

CHAPTER 7

SHE OPENED her eyes to the sound of the knock at her door and the words, 'Chow's on.'

Rebecca got out of bed and stumbled to the bathroom to wash her face. Her hair was standing on end and there were large dark circles under her eyes but the sun was rising into a perfect day and below, the male voices were blurred again.

She had a vague recollection of shaking Kelly awake, of telling him what she had seen and looking for disbelief to cross his eyes. She'd seen none that she remembered.

But that was hours ago.

She washed her face with freezing water, brushed her hair, changed into jeans and pullover and went down for breakfast. Again, the room hushed when she came in and she sighed, wondering when they'd get used to her presence and vice versa. She took a tray and smiled at the cook. 'Morning,' she said. He grunted at her. Rebecca studied the array of foods and settled on a bowl of fruit salad. She headed for the coffee machine, aware of how quickly the solider before her departed as she closed in.

For a moment she wondered if she had leprosy, and then she heard her name. She turned to the door. Colonel Hamill stood there, and Kelly was with him. 'Can we see you for a moment, Rebecca?'

She scanned the faces. Everyone was watching. Rebecca left her tray on a table. Nothing was offered as she walked between the two, and nothing said until the three were out of the lift at level six. Today there were no thoughts about the elevator stopping, it performed its duty unhampered.

There was no carpet at level six, simply a small sea of black and white polished tile floor. Nor were there bars on the windows. She was led into the CO's office—glass and chrome decor, black leather chairs, large umbrella and happy plants in chrome planters.

It looked like a psychiatrist's office, one who was determined to send his patients crazier than they already thought they were. It was not warm, nor was it welcoming. Then again, Hamill was the commanding officer of an anti-terrorist squad. This suited his image more than flower-power wallpaper. She winced at the artwork on the far wall, grey and black abstract, and at the antique gun collection in a cabinet behind the huge desk.

And on the desk was a chrome eagle taking flight. It was the same eagle that she had seen perched over Kelly's head. The same eagle that adorned the Nighthawks' berets and uniform insignias.

'Take a seat, Rebecca.'

She sat in a chair that swallowed her. Kelly remained by the window and he stood with his hands behind his back.

'Commander Nolan informs me that he had a visit from you at two-thirty this morning?'

'Yes.'

'The visit was about this?' Pete asked and put a readied newspaper into her lap. Page two, a news photo of what remained of a black Laser tangled with a Trans Continental double-decker tourist bus. Rebecca's stomach turned again.

The silence stretched.

'What do you expect me to say?' she asked, shakily. I don't even know what to think.

'Why do you suspect murder?' the colonel asked.

Rebecca looked at Kelly but he wasn't watching. 'Something feels . . . twisted, but this is as much concrete evidence as anyone will get.' She looked down at the photograph. 'This is the end product of what I saw taking place last night. It felt like I was with him in the car. That I was meant to be with him. The road was slippery, he went into a skid, it was foggy and it was impossible to avoid that bus. The car had no brakes. I even heard his last words.' She gave the paper back to the colonel.

'Which were?'

She looked at Pete's ice-blue eyes. ' "God, help me." '

Pete took a deep breath and glanced at Kelly who was still studying his feet. 'I'm informed you can also know a person's life expectancy?'

'Sometimes, yes.'

'Basically, you're telling us that you know when a person is supposed to die?'

'Sometimes I can pick up the number of destined years in that person's lifeplan.'

'And what is a . . . lifeplan?'

'It's a map, if you like, that each one of us is born with and follows while we live.' She didn't want to say any more, of how she believed each person was also guided along his or her individual path. 'Leon had the potential to live until he was in his seventies. I saw him as an old man the moment I touched his hand. All I know, Colonel, is that something went very wrong'.

'Can you *try* to be more specific?'

'No. But suppose Leon Carter genuinely needed my assistance, not my demise? Someone doctored his car—perhaps someone who wanted Leon's job, I don't know, but it makes sense. End of Leon. Even if he had survived, he would probably have been in hospital for long enough to be safely out of the way. What do you think?'

'Anything is possible,' Pete said, watching her closely.

'Leon was supposed to have talked to me yesterday, right? What if he'd been driving me to or back from London? If he had been allowed to interview me, perhaps I would have been with him.' She looked at Kelly and wondered just how much he saw, and knew, and felt.

'As far as I know, and God knows what else you don't tell me, there've been two attempts on my life so far and I haven't been here a week. You promised me it wouldn't happen again. Pete, you promised I'd be protected.'

'And it seems you are a very precious commodity right now.'

'It seems? You've expected this. You didn't warn me of any danger. The most you ever said was, it's not going to be easy.'

'You proved your abilities to us at two-thirty this morning. Rebecca, we need you.'

'No, no. I know very little about Robert Glover's death. Is that plain enough for you? I do not know who wants to kill him, whether it's one or a hundred. I barely know why. All I know is how the man might die. And as I told you, it sometimes changes slightly. I want to go. I want to go back to London, do what I came here to do and go home. I am a healer. How many times do I have to tell you? I want to go home and forget this ever happened.'

'Rebecca, you'd be dead before you made it to Salisbury. If

you walked out now, you would be on your own, without any protection whatsoever.'

Kelly closed his eyes and winced. It wasn't something he would say to someone in her position.

'I also believe you know more than you are willing to relate, which is why you are frightened.'

'No! I'm scared because I don't know a thing!'

'You want to run? Be my guest,' Pete said and he even opened the door. 'I'll let the gate security know you're on your way.'

He meant it. Kelly shook his head imperceptibly.

'There has been one attempt on your life. One. Now whether you would or would not have been with Carter is supposition and has no bearing on what is at this moment. The fact is, you were not in that car and again, in case your theory is correct, you have Commander Nolan to thank. But he will not be accompanying you back to London because if you walk out of this compound now, you are negating our agreement. Whoever is breaching security will be found sooner or later, Rebecca. I'd rather not discover who is responsible by losing you in the process. But I will say, before you walk out, that it won't be a quick death, because whoever these people might be, they will want to extract as much information from you as is possible before you are, as we say, eliminated. I would not wish that on anyone, Rebecca, least of all a twenty-four-year-old and, if I may say so, very attractive woman. But it's up to you. I cannot keep you here against your will.'

Nausea flooded then ebbed as Rebecca tried to read this man. She tried very hard but he seemed to have a barrier six inches thick and lined with lead. To him personally it didn't matter if she lived or died and he was making that very clear.

'Your welfare is our responsibility and from now on, your welfare will be our first priority at all times. We will endeavour to take as many precautionary measures as are deemed necessary and we will hold to these measures for as long as it takes. Do you understand me?'

'Yes,' she whispered.

'I want you to trust me, Rebecca. In trusting me, you have to trust this entire unit.'

Security breaches included? she thought.

'You'll report immediately anything further you might *see*, *feel* or otherwise *know* to either myself or Commander Nolan. No one else, is that understood?'

'Yes.'

'It doesn't matter how trivial you believe it might be.'

'Okay,' she said, voice shaking.

'Now, if you've changed your mind and you're going to stay, you can return to the mess and have your breakfast.'

Rebecca left and Kelly attempted to follow. 'No,' Pete said. 'She knows the way. Let her stew a while.'

Kelly reached for a smoke. He offered one to Pete. Accepted.

'She's better than we thought,' Hamill said.

'No, she's better than we were told. Samperi is not going to take no for an answer. Cite anything you like, Pete. Deny access as much as you want. If he wants her, he'll take her. I know him too well.'

'And that leaves us with what?'

'Nothing,' Kelly said. 'Which is exactly what we had before she came along. When Samperi fills Leon's vacancy there'll be nothing but trouble.'

'What do you mean when? He's already Acting Head.'

'You've made my day,' Kelly moaned.

'Faraday was with her constantly, wasn't he?'

'Yo.'

'Did she talk to him at all?'

'Any information he obtained is on tape, transcribed and filed.'

'Not sent to Washington?'

'No. There was nothing startling.'

'But Gene doesn't know that. Tell Faraday I want to see him.'

'He's on seventy-two-hour furlough. He left the base last night.'

'Is he in contact?'

'I've already tried to get him at home. Knowing Jamie, he's up to his ears already.' Kelly was putting it politely—the way that kid scored women was amazing.

'Go and see if she's okay. We need her cooperation. Just do what you have to. It's obvious she trusts you.'

Do what I have to, Kelly thought, as opposed to what I want to. 'Aye, aye, Captain,' Kelly said and departed.

Rebecca was picking at her fruit salad when Kelly came in, poured a black coffee and stood opposite her. 'Is it safe to sit?'

'Try it and find out.'

Kelly sat.

'You knew something was going to happen yesterday when you cancelled the meeting. What did you see, Kelly?'

'Not a lot. I saw you under a Trans Continental tourist bus and it wasn't a pretty sight because basically you look better with your head on your shoulders, okay?'

'Why didn't you tell me?'

'If the positions had been reversed, would you have told me?' Kelly asked.

'No. I would have talked you out of travelling in a black Laser.'

'Exactly. So I avoided the inevitable and your state of health at the time gave me an excuse to do just that.' He sipped his coffee and studied her eyes. 'But I couldn't tell you that, could I?'

'Do the men here know you have the gift?'

Kelly laughed to himself. The question needed no answer except, 'Well, if they suspect, no one's silly enough to say anything to me.'

'You're Indian, aren't you?'

'A quarter Cherokee but I'm not sure in which quarter it is.'

'So you're no Medicine Man?'

'No, I'll leave the magic to you.'

After a little while, she asked, 'What Pete said before, was it true?'

'I wouldn't have used exactly his words but, basically, yes.'

'Even though I'm here, I'm still in danger, aren't I?'

'We all are to some extent. Every day's a gamble. In a place like this the odds are . . . well, you'll realise that soon enough.'

'I want to go home, Kelly. I want to go home.'

'Rebecca, you can't hide from these people.'

These people who knew that she'd had chicken-pox when she was eleven years old.

'But I don't know anything.'

'Unfortunately, a lot of people believe you do.'

Tears brimmed in her eyes. She dropped the fork she'd been toying with and Kelly took her hand, tightly. 'Why did I let myself do this?'

'You really didn't have much of a choice.'

'What would have happened if I'd said no at the airport?'

'I can't answer that and you know I can't.'

'Would you take me home? Take me to the airport? No one need know. I know you could do it. I know you could get me out of here without anyone knowing.'

'Rebecca, you don't understand the position I'm in. I can't.'

'You can't or you won't?'

'Both,' he replied, quietly. 'Give it time.'

'God almighty, the way things are going, I don't have any time.'

'Will you trust me?' Kelly asked.

She looked into his eyes. His face was blurred.

'Will you please trust me?' he asked again.

'Kelly, you're about the only person here I do trust.'

And he squeezed her hand.

'I hate myself when I'm crying,' was all she said.

'Give us time,' he said again. 'Don't you remember what day it is?'

'No. I don't even *know* what day it is.'

'Well, today is Tuesday and we have the clash for the Nighthawks' Ashes this afternoon.' Kelly gave her a handkerchief and she wiped her eyes, blew her nose and focussed on his face, questioning.

'You get a few Americans in England when cricket season starts and what do you think happens?' he asked.

A hint of a smile crossed her face. 'They burn a baseball bat?' she asked.

CHAPTER 8

REBECCA SPENT the morning in a soundproof room with a technician in a lab coat. Kelly had taken her there and introduced her to, Steve Mason, 'our top interrogator.' He'd left her with a smile of encouragement and she'd felt suddenly bereft.

On the desk in front of Steve was the file containing the details of her original prediction of Glover's assassination. She was given earplugs and placed in front of a microphone, while he asked her, again and again, to describe the scene in detail. He made copious notes as she talked.

'And you are standing where?' he asked for the fifth or sixth time.

'I don't know. It feels as if I'm . . . waiting to welcome him. In the crowd. It's an airbase. He's close enough to touch.' She had told him this so many times she was boring even herself.

'And the bullet comes from where?' He was relentless.

'From the crowd. At least I think it did that first time. Other times it seems to come from above, from a rooftop, or from . . .' she felt her concentration sliding away. 'Sometimes from behind him, or to the side.' She had told him this, too, until it felt like a litany repeated out of habit, without any meaning. 'I'm sorry—the more I try to consciously focus on it, the more it slips away.'

He took her painstakingly through all the other times she had had the vision—usually once or twice a year, more often recently—noting every variation from the first version of six years ago. They went through three long-playing tapes, and still he wasn't satisfied.

'And you don't recognise anyone else? No one in the crowd, in the President's entourage? No one you've met since you've been in England?'

'No.' She was nearing the end of her endurance. 'No! No! No! God—don't you think I'd tell you?' But there were things she couldn't tell him, couldn't put into words. Momentary glimpses of something, someone, half-familiar, and then the fog settling once more, so that everyone apart from the President and his wife, descending from the aeroplane, was faceless, anonymous.

'Okay,' Steve said reluctantly. 'We'll call it a day. I'll go through the tapes, and I might ask you to look through some photo files. Tomorrow,' he added hastily as she raised an incredulous face.

When she got back to her room she saw that someone had left her a tray of salad sandwiches and a jug of lemon juice. She sighed with relief when she found the half-bottles of liquor in the bar cupboard under the window, and poured herself a stiff gin squash.

The bar was closed at two in the afternoon, chairs on tables, chairs on the bar. The juke box was turned off but the piano had lain in wait, it seemed for years, for someone to give it life. Rebecca touched it, slid her hand along the peeling lacquer, touched the dusty bust of Beethoven resting on top.

She hadn't played for years, not since her father had died and she had given the piano away.

Play for me, Becky.

Play for me.

Rebecca took a chair from a nearby table and sat, opened the lid and inspected the yellowing, cracked keys. She winced at the sound of the scales but it wasn't as bad as she'd first thought. Before long, she and the piano were giving each other mutual life and when she played, time was non-existent, and her exhaustion gradually fell away.

Kelly followed the melody he thought he knew from somewhere and discovered Frank Connelly standing by the bar door, back to the wall, eyes closed, lost in dreamland. 'Seen Miller?' Kelly asked, bringing the tattooed cook back to earth with a heavy thud. Frank pointed him to where the music originated and headed back to the kitchen.

The 'Skye Boat Song' was almost over. Kelly stood at the doorway, tossing the baseball from one hand to the other, watching her, listening to her soft, wonderful voice. When she'd finished he said, 'It needs tuning.'

She turned quickly. 'Give me a heart attack next time.'

'You're missing the big game.'

'Is it three o'clock already?' she asked, closing the piano, putting her chair back in place.

'Five after,' he replied. 'We're waiting for you.'

She walked towards him. 'You even look like a baseball player.'

Kelly pulled a spare cap from his pants and put it on her head. 'If you feel up to it, we need an extra man. Person.' He didn't ask her how her session with Steve had gone.

'You want me to play?' She wasn't going to volunteer any information either.

'The losing side needs all the help it can get.'

Words to make her fire. She didn't know if he was teasing or serious. 'I suppose you're on the winning side?'

'Of course I am.'

She walked beside him, down the corridor, taking a left, a right and out into the sudden late afternoon chill. 'I love an optimist, Kelly. The world needs more optimists, just like you. Twenty bucks my team wins this game.'

'Do you always throw your money away?'

'No. But you do. Is it a bet?'

'Aha. There's your team.' He pointed vaguely to a gaggle of men sitting in wait and leaning against the gym wall. Kelly walked off towards the diamond which was also the helipad. He was highly amused.

Rebecca studied the players, then the diamond and momentary doubt hit. What's my big mouth done this time? she wondered as she took her place on the grass beside the other batters. She sat next to Billy Macpherson. He had golden brown hair in the sunlight, and because he was off duty he wore a sparkling diamond ear stud in his right earlobe. His smile was slightly lopsided and his small hazel eyes full of something she did not want to recognise. 'Glad you could make it, Miss,' he said. 'We're going to need all the help we can get.'

'Call me Rebecca. I don't answer to Miss.'

Billy hid his grin. 'Be careful of Nolan's curved.' He offered more advice which she did not comprehend. Rebecca played softball, not baseball and had convinced herself there wasn't too much of a difference. But she hadn't played with males before, either, especially American males.

Ammo Griinke, the umpire, was sipping on a beer can and calling strikes with every ball pitched. Rigged, she thought. Resting near the whiteboard-scoreboard, on a large, empty juice tin on the grass, was a gleaming urn, full of the ashes of burnt baseball bats. She sighed. Kelly was right. 'Who's left a vacancy?' she asked.

'Jamie. He played third base,' Billy said. By the time Macpherson batted, the bases were loaded and two were out. He hit to the left outfield and made it to first base with half a heartbeat to spare.

Oh, hell, Rebecca thought as she picked up the bat and faced the pitcher, whose mound was nothing more than a few bags on the helipad centre.

Kelly pushed his red cap back on his head and smiled at her but there was no humour in it. Twenty bucks, his eyes said. Rebecca knew then that she would rather die from his curved ball than hand over the American equivalent of twenty dollars Australian in traveller's cheques.

And worse, he attempted to waylay her concentration by studying the loaded bases but when he turned back to his next victim, she had her cap on, reversed. She was ready.

The barman was on third, wanting to steal, not able to.

Jamie Faraday flashed into her mind's eye and Rebecca recoiled from the sudden, unsolicited image. Someone yelled, 'Time out' until she was ready again.

Apparently, time out was not an expression the commander enjoyed hearing. 'Give us a homer, Pip,' someone behind her said and three men on the other team laughed.

She faced Kelly, wiggled her behind and was finally ready. Bat touched ground and swung back, ready to wallop.

She's played before, Kelly thought.

The first ball hit the catcher's mitt before she saw it leave the pitcher's hand. It fizzed by her at eye height and the drunk umpire shouted, 'Strike!'

'No way!' she cried angrily amid calls of strong language from five other team-mates who agreed with her totally. Kelly received the ball back from the catcher blindly, with one hand behind his back as he walked around and kicked the bags on his mound. What a bloody show-off, she thought.

Again, she faced him. Again, he smiled and wound up. She had the horrible thought that perhaps he had played this professionally and she had called him an optimist. There was no time for shame.

Help me, Emmanuel.

Someone must have, she thought, because as she swung, bat contacted ball, a minor miracle, and every face, including her own, saw the ball disappear into the distance between first and second. 'Holy shit!' came a stunned cry. Rebecca woke to see Barry-the-barman-Mannett sliding into home, followed closely by the other two.

She decided to run and Harlem, the catcher, ducked before the bat took out his ear. She reached third, looked back and saw the fielder hurtle the missile towards home. Rebecca slid in, feet first, panting and looked up into Harlem's dark eyes. He took the catch and looked down at her, spreadeagled at his feet. 'Do you play basketball, too?' he asked.

'No, but you should see me play cricket,' Rebecca joked. She got up, dusted off and dared glance at Kelly. His face was more than sarcastically amused now. 'Thanks for that, Commander!' she called and sat down on the grass to recover. She should not have run.

'On ya,' Billy said, an attempt at an Australian accent. 'You hit, someone else can run for you, okay?'

Rebecca had never enjoyed a game as much in her life. Three runs to win and two batters out. The battle for the baseball bats' ashes nearing the end. Kelly, who had hit home runs on his first balls so far, took his final stand.

Mannett considered the matter carefully. He'd expect two fasts, one slow. Barry wound for a fast but Kelly was three steps ahead. Rebecca saw the perfect catch hit from a slow and it was coming directly for her. She only had to move ten feet to her left to take it. Take it she did with a joyful scream, while the runner from second tried to beat her to her own base.

'Out!' Ammo cried and Rebecca threw the ball high into the air, yelping with joy while Pugno, the discarded runner, lay on his back between her legs, smiling, until someone gave him a kick in the ribs and the mess bell sounded.

The captain of Rebecca's team made a hasty grab for the urn, someone threw Rebecca over his shoulder and promptly put her down again. Everyone dispersed to the bar, and all was done.

Almost. She watched Kelly collecting the gloves, ball, bats and mats and throwing them all into a large box. She helped because he seemed to be a good loser. The fact surprised her. 'You play well,' he said.

'I certainly hope so. I made it to the state softball team.'

'Now you tell me?'

'I thought you would have known. You people seem to know everything else about me.' Kelly ignored that and picked up the box. He walked to the gymnasium with it and Rebecca followed him inside. 'Aren't you forgetting something?' she asked.

'What?'

'My team won, Commander, and you owe me twenty dollars.' She held her hand out.

Kelly met her supercilious grin. 'You'll have to wait until payday.'

'When's that?'

'Three weeks.'

'You were paid last week and you're broke already?' she asked.

Kelly didn't answer. His wife, Marianne, took three quarters of his pay, possibly to help the boyfriend out of the debt she'd got him into. Marianne didn't like taking money from her father, or so she said. It was only money. The poor worried about having none, the rich about having too much. Kelly didn't give a damn either way. All he'd ever needed was his bike and his art. And someone he could talk to. The last was the hardest to come by. 'Who was helping you?' he asked.

'When?'

'When you batted the first time.'

'No one was helping me.'

Kelly laughed. 'That's why I saw you wearing a Dodger's uniform?'

'I tell you what, Kelly. Next time, let me try whatever it is you've been smoking.' She walked off but stopped when she heard: 'And the gold mist that follows you wherever you go? Is that an illusion, too?'

She turned to him. 'Come again?'

'You heard me. When you healed Macpherson, it was permeating the entire room. I saw it. I felt it.'

'You wouldn't understand if I tried to explain.'

'Why don't you try me, little lady?' He walked towards the exit, his sneakers squeaking on the wooden floor.

'Don't call me little lady. I'm not little, nor am I a—'

Jamie's face flashed into her mind again. The quick, sudden image appeared from nowhere, without warning. Kelly saw her walk into an invisible brick wall. 'What is it?' he asked.

'Jamie.'

'What about Jamie?'

'I don't . . . No! No!'

The scream decalcified his spinal column, reverberated around the gymnasium and, it seemed, into the entire complex.

'Rebecca?'

'Don't touch me! Keep away!'

But Kelly didn't heed the warning. 'Rebecca?' he asked, genuinely concerned, grabbing her shoulder and wishing he hadn't because one image penetrated his brain and remained there in full technicolour glory—Faraday, with half his head shot away. The eyes open, staring and vacant. Kelly let go and stepped back. 'Rebecca?'

'Not Jamie. Not Jamie!' She was gone, at a sprint, kicking open the gym doors, disappearing before Kelly had found traction. For a while, he was a cat on a slippery floor.

'Hey, what's—' Rebecca pushed the soldier aside and ran, trying to remember the way to the front doors.

'Someone stop her!' the Commander called.

Rebecca did not stop when she was ordered. The foyer was a breath away. The front doors. Locked. Out. Out to fresh air, to the evening, to freedom. She touched the main doors. A shrill blast of security alarm split the air. Cameras on. People coming. 'Rebecca! Step back, now! Away from the doors! Now!' Uneven footsteps approaching. The scent of the man hit in a violent, overwhelming cloud of dust, death, pain. She saw crumbling stone walls. Prison walls. Hannah's walls. The alarm kept screaming, so did her mind. She screamed silently for the doors to open.

They exploded, outwards. Cold air hit her face but she didn't feel it. She took the twenty steps, running as she'd never run before, not down the driveway or into the carpark, but into the thick woods to the north.

She screamed as hands grabbed her pullover. She turned and kicked wildly. The hand let go. She heard a curse, foul, grotesque, and a call in a voice she knew—*Keep away from the fence!*

Running again, still pursued until arms flung around her waist and a great pushing weight hit her body. Grass met her face and all air was crushed from her lungs. The world spun in a blanket of colour. She couldn't breathe. She was barely aware that Kelly was there, pulling her to her feet now, breathing hard himself. But she couldn't stand. Her knees crumbled. He held her upright. Shook her. So angry, so angry and upset.

'What the fuck are you trying to do!' he yelled, giving her a good shake.

Still she couldn't breathe. She couldn't talk. Blood poured from her nose. It was salty, hot in her mouth. Breath eventually returned, a hard struggle.

'What is it with you? I'm trying to help you, girl. I'm trying to help you! Why are you trying to kill yourself?' He picked up a stick and threw it at the fence. The stick exploded into flames on impact. 'What the hell am I going to do with you?'

Rebecca looked up into Redmond Innes' eyes. And passed out into Kelly's arms. He caught her. A dead weight.

'What the hell's—' Barry Mannett asked.

'Take her,' Kelly said, thrusting his burden at Mannett. 'Who else saw—' His words failed. Half the squad stood at a safe, stunned distance. Quinn reluctantly stepped forward.

'Commander? We've got no power. Security's out, everything is out. She's blown the whole system.'

Kelly glanced back to the asylum. Total darkness, save a gas lamp illuminating the mess. And torches inspecting what was left of the front doors.

'How'd she do that?' Barney's voice was a squeak of disbelief. It was one question Kelly didn't want the answer to.

'Get Pete back here. Now.'

'We don't know where he is.'

'Fucking find him!'

'Here. Drink this.'

Eyes like a wary animal's, watching each movement, hearing each breath, feeling each silent question in the dim, dark, quiet. There was the red-head who shared the commander's table in the mess. Someone called him Creedy. The pilot, Harlem. Ammo who was suddenly sober. Two others she hadn't seen before.

'Come on. Drink this.'

Joel. Her flight companion. In his hand was a glass of clear fluid for her to take. Rebecca took the wad of tissues away from her bleeding nose and drank the bitter liquid silently. Joel put his hand on her head and turned to the others.

Rebecca wiped at her eyes and held her nose again. The only small comfort was Harlem, beside her. She could feel his apprehension, too. The commander kept watching her. She felt it everywhere—the stunned confusion. But no one was more stunned than Rebecca.

The air coming in from the demolished doors was freezing but no one would let her move. No one noticed she was cold. Shaking. She looked at the doors, at the burnt wood, the scorched brick. At the firefighting equipment and the foam on the carpet. 'How did that happen?' she asked.

Harlem turned to her, surprised. 'You don't know?'

'No. I was running? I was running and . . .' Memory returned instantly. 'Jesus. It's Jamie. Jamie's dead.'

Every face turned to her.

'Jamie is dead. I saw it happen. He'll come back here with a sign around his neck. It says "Return to sender".' Rebecca rested her head against the wall. She was past crying, beyond exhaustion, her head spinning, the soft questioning voices around her another blur. She wondered what was in that drink. Whatever it was had numbed her completely.

Then the car lights appeared and the very air grew colder with her trepidation. She knew who was coming. Kelly turned to her. 'Get your ass upstairs, now.' Rebecca didn't question. 'Macpherson. Make sure she goes nowhere.'

Billy obeyed, pleased at the escape. 'He thinks I'm going to run away again.'

'Are you?' Billy asked as he walked her up the stairs.

'There's nowhere to go. I'm sorry but I saw . . . I panicked.'

'Mightn't seem like it but he's doing you a favour.' Billy didn't say anything else, he didn't have to. He opened the door to her room. Emergency power was on.

He closed the door and sat outside with his back against the wall, staring down the length of the corridor, still not believing what he'd seen half an hour before. By the others' faces, they didn't believe it either.

Nor did she.

The colonel wouldn't. Billy waited and waited for the inevitable and soon enough he heard it:

'What has happened here!'

Four muffled, disbelieving words.

Rebecca clutched the spare pillow tightly and stared at the bars on the window. She could hear them downstairs. Hear the voices, if not the words. Kelly was taking full responsibility for what had occurred. But it wasn't his fault. Somehow, she was spiralling out of control. Out of the control so bitterly won after so many years. And, in its suppression, her strength had grown, apparently, monstrous. Oh, Jamie, she thought. Why you? Why did it have to be you?

Footsteps along the corridor. She wiped at her eyes, quickly. 'That'll be all, Mac.' Billy's footsteps receded. There was one almighty knock on her door and it opened. The room was suddenly lit. 'You're wanted,' Kelly said quietly.

Rebecca got off her bed and tried to speak. Apologise. Anything.

'Save it for the colonel.'

'I'm sorry, Kelly.'

'I said, save it.'

Kelly stood behind the girl he'd fallen in love with years ago. A girl who saw people as they died and made him see the same things. A girl who'd seen Robert Glover die years before he came into office. Years before anyone knew who he was. There were truths in what she'd foreseen. Too many truths to ignore. She was shaking, from fear or cold, again he wasn't sure. He wanted to hold her, calm her down if he could, but he kept his hands behind his back the entire time. He watched Pete Hamill carefully. How he would react to this was anyone's guess. Now that the shock of the damage she had caused had worn off, Pete was taking it fairly calmly. Kelly, though, felt an explosion was nigh. And when it came, it would fall on him.

'Why?' was all Pete could finally ask. 'You agreed to cooperate.'

'I am cooperating.'

'And running away? Is this how you cooperate?'

'I had reasons.'

'Reasons,' he mumbled, closing his eyes. 'This helps, Rebecca. You destroyed two and a half million dollars worth of electronic security systems. You annihilated our entire communications network, and you say you had reasons?'

Rebecca studied her feet. 'I'm sorry,' was all she could say, so softly that he didn't hear.

'Furthermore, eleven personnel have each told me all you did was touch the—' Pete paused, beheading the expletive before it emerged. 'Touch the door.'

'I'm sorry, Colonel—' Rebecca said, fighting a losing battle with her anguish. 'I wanted the door to open and it did. I don't know how I did it. I just . . . thought it open.'

'You *thought* it open?' Pete glanced at Kelly. Kelly shrugged. The colonel took a huge breath. 'What do you suggest I do with you, Rebecca?' he asked, although it wasn't a question. He already knew what he'd do with her—at least, what he was tempted to do.

'Let me go home before I damage anything else?'

Kelly sighed. Pete couldn't look into her eyes for long. If she was trying to joke, her timing was lousy. 'Get her out of my sight, Commander, quickly.'

'There's been another death because of me. How the hell am I supposed to react!'

Pete looked up quickly. 'Another death?'

'Jamie Faraday,' she said, voice breaking, eyes filling with tears. 'A woman killed Jamie.'

The colonel's face paled. 'You knew of this, Commander?'

'Vaguely,' Kelly said.

'It's not his fault! Don't you bloody dare—'

'That'll be all, Commander.'

Kelly didn't want to leave, but he had no choice. The door closed quietly.

'Talk to me, Rebecca. Tell me what has happened.' Pete was trying for a sympathetic tone.

Kelly stood in the corridor for well over half an hour. Not a sound emerged from Pete's office until the door finally opened and Rebecca emerged with a soft, 'You don't believe me.'

'It's not a matter of belief. It's a matter of proof.' To Kelly, he said, 'In my office when you've finished escorting Miss Miller back to her room.'

The walk back to the officers' quarters on level three was slow and for a time, silent.

'Now you're in trouble.'

Kelly tried hard to smile.

'You saw it, didn't you? You saw it when you touched me,' Rebecca said softly, stopping for a rest on the stairs.

Kelly couldn't reply. He sat beside her and nodded.

'I liked Jamie. I liked him a lot.'

'Yes, I know. I just hope to God you're wrong this time. Come on.' At level three, finally, Rebecca reached to open her door. Kelly put his hand on her wrist. 'I didn't mean to hurt you,' he said, trying not to look at her swollen nose. It seemed to her that she'd heard that before, somewhere, that she had seen that look in his eyes before. 'I used to play gridiron, too.' He was trying hard to apologise and went to touch her face but she pulled back.

'I know you used to play football. You also had a motorbike, wore a leather jacket and thought you were tough. Now all you want is a fishing boat and some peace because you've had enough of fighting other people's demons.'

'What else do you think you know about me?'

She looked into his eyes. She didn't mention the wife she saw now, somewhere in the States. 'I know nothing. It's the safest way to be.'

'If there's anyone you'd like to talk to—'

'And what would talking do? Will it bring Jamie back? Will it bring Leon Carter back? Will talking get me out of here?'

'No.'

There was a moment's silence.

'Do you really think I want you here, caught in this mess?'

'You might feel safer with the colonel. He wants to see you.'

'He'll wait.'

Rebecca looked down at her arm, felt his warm, reassuring touch. It was all so familiar. Achingly familiar. For a stranger, he knew her so well. 'I can't stay here, Kelly. This place is driving me crazy.'

'You'll get used to it.'

'I don't want to get used to it. I never realised it was possible to . . . Something's happening to me here. Something frightening.'

'The damage will be repaired.'

'And everyone will sidestep me now. They'll think I'm some kind of freak.' Just what she'd trained herself for years to avoid.

The turning away. The muttering. The sudden silences.

'No. The boys'll get used to you. They're curious more than wary.'

'Jesus, Kelly, *I'm* frightened at what I did.'

'Well, that's you, but with us it's a simple matter of adaptation to a new situation. Okay, granted, this paranormal stuff has never happened to us before, but our eyes are open.'

'Kelly, why do you keep lying to me?'

'I am not lying to you.'

Rebecca thought she was drowning when he touched her hair, swept it away from her eyes. 'Oh, come here.' Conceding defeat, she had won the battle of the pleading looks. Kelly held her and rested his chin on top of her head. 'You'll get through this. We all will, and that includes Robert Glover.'

'I wish I had your faith,' she said softly into his chest.

'Try and get some sleep,' he said and drew her back before she got too comfortable and he started reacting to her presence. 'Then again, if you can't sleep, I'm still across the hall.'

Rebecca refused to acknowledge the open invitation in his eyes. 'Good night, Commander.'

The door closed in his face.

'Hannah! Confess, confess . . . tell them anything, lass, anything.'

His mind was screaming but nothing was heard. The words halted, frozen in his throat as the inquisitors coated her crushed feet with grease and suspended her over flames. She was screaming again. 'What is it you want me to say?'

Kelly sat up quickly. He was covered in sweat, his heart thudding in his ears. He hadn't realised he'd been asleep until the nightmare. Hannah again.

Hannah.

He looked at the clock. Time to get up anyway. Another day. God, another day.

Rebecca ate a solitary breakfast in the darkest corner of the mess and nobody ventured near. Now and then she would glance at the commander who sat alone, too. She knew he hadn't slept either.

I hope to God you're wrong this time.

But he had seen, too. He sees more than I do, she thought. He knows more than I do yet he won't admit it, not even to himself.

The mess was unusually quiet except for the BBC's early morning news emanating from the small speaker above her head. The very English voice.

Rebecca felt weighted by a thousand rocks. Frank's fruit salad had no taste, the coffee was bitter.

She was waiting for what she knew would come.

And she heard the voice as it echoed from the back door of the kitchen. The cook was calling the cats like he did every morning. But today, Frank Connelly couldn't find the cats.

He found Jamie Faraday instead.

CHAPTER 9

KELLY STARED down at the lifeless, naked body that had once housed Jamie Faraday. It was propped by the industrial waste bin near the kitchen doors. The face was almost recognisable to those who'd known the kid. And Kelly had seen this, some of it. Just like Rebecca had.

Around him he heard a few whispers, but mostly the silence was very loud until a quiet, shaky voice said, 'Just like she said, man. Just like she said.'

It was Harlem, hand over face, turning away. Kelly quickly scanned other faces, too. Most were deathly quiet.

'I want to see Miller. Now,' Pete said and rose to his feet. He walked by Kelly and slapped something at him. Kelly looked down. A piece of thin cardboard, string. Etched in blood, three words. *Return to sender.*

Rebecca was still in the mess, head in hands. She looked up when she heard Kelly's uneven footfalls. Despair had intensified the colour of her eyes. She was shaking. He didn't blame her. 'CO wants you.'

'For what? I told you. I told him. No one believed me—'

'Now, Rebecca.' His voice was different. Quiet. Hand reaching down with the same gentleness he had shown the night before.

'What did they do to him?'

'You already know,' Kelly said.

Rebecca wore jeans and yesterday's pullover as she stood silently in the CO's office, waiting until he had finished his phone conversation. He indicated that she sit. 'Commander, get us all a coffee.' Kelly left the room.

Pete's blue eyes searched hers for a short time, but the thoughts there were not for her, or of her. His thoughts were on Jamie Faraday and returned to her momentarily when the gaze changed its expression to one of pity. Then curiosity. Confusion. And for a fleeting moment, fear, but he hid that expertly. For a second, Rebecca had the strong feeling that this man knew Robert Glover. As a friend. As something. Something.

'You will tell me everything you saw. Every last insignificant detail. Anything you can think of.'

'I've already told you all I know. All I saw.'

'You'll tell me again.'

'Is that an order?'

'It's a request,' Pete said because he thought he knew where she would tell him to place his order. 'Please?' he tried with half-hearted sarcasm in his voice and his eyes. He seemed dual-edged. A face for every occasion. And again she couldn't read him.

Kelly returned with three coffees and took his to his usual place, by the window.

'I want a cigarette,' she said softly.

'You don't smoke,' the colonel said.

'I do now.'

Kelly offered her a cigarette, lit it for her and stepped back. She hadn't wanted a smoke for two years and certainly never at this hour of the morning. She remained quiet for a little while, trying to form her words. 'Colonel, I don't want to see it again.' She inhaled on the cigarette, her lungs rejected it. 'I don't want to relive it.'

'Faraday was twenty-two years old. The Nighthawks were all the family he had. That's what we are, Rebecca. One family. By now you should be aware of that. I want to know who was responsible and where this took place, so steps can be taken to rectify the situation accordingly.'

All so very formal. 'You're not police. I know how you intend rectifying the situation. The eye for an eye kind of justice doesn't work. A thousand years ago, perhaps, but not now.'

'Who and where? You've done this many times before.'

'I was helping police! There's no comparison!'

'You will not speak to me in that tone of voice.'

'I'll speak to you any bloody way I want to. I told you what I had seen but no, no, you needed proof. Well, you've got your proof. Jamie's lying in a body bag because the poor bastard got to know me. If these people can't have me, they'll take the next best thing, like the medic who spent so much time with me. Right?

Am I getting close yet?'

Kelly sighed to himself and sipped his coffee.

'The terms of your agreement state—'

'You can't bring him back!'

'Who and where? It seems you already know why.'

He would keep her here for hours, calmly, coldly asking the same thing. Who and where? Kelly's deep, heavy silence was contagious. Powerful. She looked at Kelly and he was watching her intently.

'What I'll say won't help.'

'I'll judge. Tell me.'

'I'll need something he was wearing constantly. His dog tags would do.'

Kelly left to get them. The office was remarkably quiet but there was a great deal of underlying tension.

'And what exactly do you know, Rebecca?' Pete asked, trying to remain neutral.

'Pertaining to what, exactly?'

'Robert Glover.'

'You already know. I've told you a thousand times. Haven't you listened to the tapes?'

'I'd like to hear it again.'

She told him, again, but this time the colonel asked his own questions. 'Do you know from which direction the bullet originates?'

'From his right, usually, but I'm not a ballistics expert. By now you guys have probably got guns that can fire around corners. You've got everything else.'

'I am trying to be patient with you.'

'Don't worry. It's mutual.'

Blue gazes locked and neither wavered.

'How does this psychometry work? Do you know?'

'When I hold an object and tune to it, I get images in here.' She touched her forehead. 'Pictures. Scenes. I feel what's happened. I feel the emotions, and in situations like this, the fear associated with the deceased, the way that person died. It's the residual memory I tune into.' With help, she thought. Now was not the time to mention Emmanuel, even if she could see his hologram-like figure standing directly behind the colonel. Pete turned to see what she was looking at, but there was nothing there. The colonel rubbed his neck. He was a very worried man. She could have taken his discomfort away with a simple touch but she did not offer. Touching him would be a mistake. She clasped her hands in her lap and remained silent.

It seemed to take an eternity for Kelly's reappearance with Jamie's dog tags. He put them on the desk and stepped away. She took up the tags. Nothing happened for a little while and then it flooded in. Sudden, strong. She rose, and paced the room. 'He was wearing them when he died. Bear with me, I'm trying to sort through the images.' There was a pause. 'He's waiting for someone. We're at some kind of pub. Tavern. It's evening and it's late, too. But she's here now. Coming closer. Is she Indonesian? Filipino?'

Kelly and Pete exchanged a glance as if she was confirming something they already suspected.

'I'm getting odd sensations. Sexual anticipation. He can hardly wait to get her into bed but that's all he thinks about anyway.' Rebecca's eyes were open but blinded by a blank stare the other two associated with combat fatigue. Kelly's spine tingled. The room was suddenly oppressive with static. From the corner of his eye he saw a gold flash. Gold, purple. Then it was gone, and it reformed as a sphere of gold mist which hovered constantly close to her head. Emmanuel? Kelly wondered, not knowing where the name came from, and as if in reply, the sphere brightened momentarily in confirmation. Shit, he thought. She does have a spook friend.

Pete saw nothing. Felt nothing.

'She wants to go. Her English is terrible. I can barely understand a word she says. I suppose language isn't a barrier for what Jamie has in mind . . . And her name. It sounds like a bird.'

'Thuy?' Kelly asked, pronouncing it Twee.

'Yes. Thuy. Don't interrupt me. She's promising . . . Good God, no wonder he wants to go.'

There was a moment's silence as Rebecca tried to make sense of what was forming behind her eyes. She decided not to tell them what Jamie was doing while the woman tried to drive. 'She's driving. It's her car. Jamie left his outside a tavern. I don't know where exactly, but it's a pub close to a river. No, it's London. It has to be. We're in a narrow street now. It's not a residential area but it's near water. I can smell it. It's foul. Looks like a warehouse of some kind. I can see cranes. Some kind of dock.

Shipping containers. Does that make sense to you?'

'Don't stop now,' Kelly said quietly, thinking of Tri Star Lines on the Thames. A CIA front.

'I think I'm . . .' The pause again, it seemed endless.

'What have you got now?' Pete asked.

'Jamie thinks she's kinky and he's asking why here? Something feels wrong. Really wrong but she . . . oh, God.'

'What's happening, Rebecca?' Kelly asked.

'Putting it subtly, she's changing his mind, Commander. And she does it so well.'

'Oh. Right. Carry on.'

There was another long pause. 'Yes, it's definitely a warehouse on docks, on a river and it's low tide, that's why the smell is so bad. There're rusty shipping containers. Tri . . . Tri . . . Star . . . Something. The symbol is three inverted triangles. Red, white and blue. Does that make sense?' she asked.

'Carry on. You're doing fine.'

But there was silence and Kelly looked out of the window. He could almost see what was happening, too. Maybe he *was* seeing it. Feeling it right along with Faraday and Miller. He shifted uncomfortably. He could see them both making love, standing up, in a dark corner inside the warehouse. Jamie was making her laugh.

Until three shadows appeared and took Rebecca by surprise. 'Oh, shit,' she whispered, bringing the two men in the room to complete attention.

'What?' came two voices at once.

'Jamie's being dragged away and she's laughing.'

'Calm down and tell us what you see.'

'There's a gun at his head and she's laughing. There're three of them, dragging him up metal stairs. Spiral stairs. He's pushed into the wall and there's a light. The light. It's very strong—' She winced again, moved her head. 'There's a gun at his head. Can't see it, know it's there.' Her breathing grew quick and heavy.

'Rebecca, are you feeling this?' Kelly asked.

'Yes.'

'You are not Jamie. You are a witness. An observer.'

'It doesn't help, Kelly—'

'How many are there?' Pete asked.

'Two. Maybe three . . . yes, three.'

'Can you describe anyone for us?' Pete asked.

'I can't see. The light . . .'

'What's the woman doing now?'

'I don't . . . I don't . . . she's watching. Just watching.' Rebecca's voice took on Jamie's accent. *'Why's she doing this? I can't identify the voices. They're just outlines of faces in the dark. The light's so bright. I can't see the faces! What the fuck is going on here?'* Rebecca's strained breathing slowed, regulated. She was trying to catch what was happening in her mind, trying to separate what she witnessed from what Jamie felt. But it was far too quick. Too quick.

And when she spoke again, it was her voice, her accent. 'There's someone there he seems to know. I can feel it. It's so strong. He's questioning. Asking, why? Jamie is trying to get away. There's so much fear, so much hatred. Terrible fear now. They hold him. Hold him tight so he can't kick. He's already hurt someone. God, he can fight!'

'Can *you* see any faces!' Pete yelled.

'No! All I can see is her! Thuy! She is all he will look at!'

'Are you getting any names?'

'No. Just voices. Questions. So many questions. About her. About me. Yes, questions about me. Someone's saying—"what do you mean, she read it in a newspaper"? Please, Pete, I can't do this—'

'You can and will.'

A long silence followed. A deathly quiet. Rebecca stared into nothing.

'Rebecca?'

'There's nothing.'

'What do you mean there's nothing? Is he dead?'

'No. He's alive. But he's suddenly calm. So very calm. He's not answering anything now. He just repeats his name and his number. Over and over and—'

Rebecca crumpled to her knees as if she'd been punched in the belly. She started coughing. Gagging. Kelly tore the tags from her hand and caught the image, too, just before a booted foot caught Faraday in the groin for the second time and the reflected pain of it almost sent him to his knees on the carpet beside the psychic. But the pain was gone as quickly as it came. And Rebecca was still on the floor, crying now. Kelly helped her to her feet.

She was shaking.

'No more, Pete. For God's sake, no more. We have enough.'

'Sit her down.'

Rebecca sagged like a rag doll into the leather chair, and drew her feet under her. Her face was grey and she peered around the room, disorientated, trying to readjust to this sudden, new environment.

Kelly offered her another cigarette and she took it, gladly, looking up into his eyes and seeing more than concern there. The hand was on her shoulder again, reassuring, kind. 'You should have told us you also feel it.'

She had, but Pete Hamill either hadn't cared or hadn't realised what would happen.

'Now, when you saw Faraday die—'

Rebecca looked at the colonel, who was masking any feelings, if he had any, with a six-foot layer of ice. 'I heard an American male say, "Kill the useless son of a bitch", and I saw the woman put a gun at the side of his head and she shot him.'

'Would you recognise her if you saw her?'

'Oh, spare me, please.'

'Would you recognise her!' the colonel barked.

She looked at Kelly, who was back by the window. Having a smoke, too. He seemed to sense the gaze and he nodded. 'She has short reddish-brown hair. It's cut in a bob. She has large dark eyes and a little mouth. A heart-shaped face.'

And the colonel nodded to the commander and although nothing was said in this silent exchange of information, no words were needed. But Rebecca understood.

'You low-life bastard. You knew who she was all along. You didn't need me at all.'

'You may escort Miss Miller back to her room, Commander.'

'So the Indonesian woman's going to have an accident too? Is it going to be the same kind of accident poor bloody Leon had? Untraceable?'

'You may escort—'

But Rebecca was gone, leaving in her wake one exploded fluorescent light.

Kelly had to move quickly to catch her and when he did, he was repaid by a mis-aimed kick to the groin. He stopped her immediately with a simple twist of her wrist and she squealed.

'Let me go!'

'Listen to me, Rebecca. We are endeavouring to keep Robert Glover alive, do you hear me? Faraday has been the second to die and this doesn't include the attempted hit on you. It seems obvious that anyone who has had any contact whatsoever with you is in danger. Do you understand that?'

'Do I understand?' She pulled out of his grip. 'All I understand at this point in time is that there are numerous people who want to know what they believe I know about each of them. I don't think it's some huge conspiracy to kill the President. I think we have a situation here of a few people who want him dead for reasons we can only guess at. Head of CIA Operations died by accident. Someone you didn't want me to speak to is taking over that position, right?' Kelly didn't reply. 'Right?'

'Keep your voice down.'

'I will not keep my voice down! Who runs Tri Star shipping company, Kelly? The CIA? Who runs this outfit, Kelly? You told me it was the Defence Department. How many more lies do I have to hear? You people don't need me to avert any assassination. You're using me to draw out the fucking enemy. A few scattered people who don't want Robert Glover as President because he's too much of a threat to them as individuals. Leon died conveniently. I ask myself why and I realise he must have been a good guy. Honest. Fair. He was a friend of yours too and I haven't seen any remorse!'

'Can you please slow down?' he asked quietly, motioning for silence.

'When Jamie was questioned, there was someone there he knew. But he told them nothing because he knew nothing. Just like me. I know nothing! Who was it there that he knew, Kelly? Was it someone from Nighthawks?'

'Rebecca, please. Slow down.'

'Why? Am I being monitored? Am I being bugged now?'

Kelly didn't say a thing. He didn't have to.

CHAPTER 10

*R*EDMOND LIFTED *her face. The beauty of the child in her heart glowed within the dark eyes. 'You'll not offer me some of your father's ale before I go then?'*

'There's none left, nor is there much food. Da's ill; each day his mind grows poorer. He asked me who I was today. Seems I'm a stranger to him now. I don't want to be alone and now you tell me you're going away again. What am I to think?'

He put his arm about her shoulders and walked her into the house. 'No more of this nonsense. I'm not goin' to Glasgow and you'll promise me you'll not go back to the loch?'

'Aye. I canna dare think it now.'

He kicked the door closed and the ginger cat caressed his ankles. He pushed it away. 'Oh, Hannah, you're a beauty,' he said, resting his arms on her shoulders, staring down at her. There was little passion until he saw her, touched her. It was always the way. She was not on his mind when out of sight. But in sight, he was powerless. 'So your da be sleepin', then?'

'Aye.'

'I'll tell Catherine to bring you both some food.' He kissed her neck, his hands pulling at her blouse until he found soft, hot breasts.

'No, not today. I'm unwell.' He took no notice. 'Redmond, no. Please, no. Please, you're hurtin' me!' She pulled away, closed her blouse and held it together tightly.

She looked sad. Worried. Her bloody father again. Redmond wished the old bastard would die, give him some peace. 'You canna deny me. How am I to know how long I'll be gone? What if I don't come back?'

'Perhaps it's for the best if you don't come back.'

'You'd look me in the face and say it?' She tried to but what love she had was too strong. 'So let me take what may be a man's last joy. You canna deny me now.' His mouth at her neck,

his beard scratching her skin. She tried to push him away but his hands only held tighter.

Hannah closed her eyes. 'I am with child,' she said. It was almost a whisper. He looked into her eyes. They were filling with tears. 'I be the one carrying a baby, not y'wife.'

'This be the reason you wanted t'die?'

'No. I'd not know then.'

Redmond stepped away. He was upset. He didn't want this news. 'You carry no child. This is pitiful, Hannah. Next you'll say it'd be mine.'

'But it is. It is yours. There has been no one else. I canna make up something like this. I know, Redmond. Inside me, I know. I am ill because of the baby. I canna eat a thing and even water—'

'No one else, you say? Every man for miles has had you!'

Hannah slapped his face.

Kelly cringed from the ghost of a sting. For a moment, his cheek burned. 'Kelly?' The sound of a familiar voice broke the haze. Familiar air now. The mess. He looked down. No tartans or wool coats, no swords or dirks. No small stone cottage a mile from the village. No pregnant, underage mistress. Just a late, greasy breakfast congealing on a plate and fingers wrapped around a coffee cup. The coffee was cold. 'Kelly? Anyone home?'

'Huh?' Kelly mumbled and looked up into Barry Mannett's face. From the corner, Rebecca was watching him. He felt the stare.

'Can I ask you something?'

Kelly remained silent, waiting.

'Did she really see Faraday die?'

'Why?'

'Curious. If she does see this stuff, it's no wonder she keeps to herself. What's she really know about each of us? Have you ever wondered?'

'Don't be too curious. It doesn't pay.'

'Stafford told us what they'd done to Faraday. He seems to think we might all be targets, but Faraday and you were about the only two who have really talked to her. Know her. You know what I mean?'

'Thanks for the warning, Baz. I'm already aware of the situation.'

'The shit sure doesn't take long to hit the fan, does it?'

Kelly simply nodded and Mannett took a table. Kelly picked up his cold coffee and turned his head to the corner where Rebecca sat now. Alone. She wasn't eating, either. It had been a rough morning for everyone. And she'd had another session with Steve, fruitlessly poring over photo-files of possible conspirators and known terrorists.

Rebecca caught the gaze and Kelly felt an odd sensation tingling in his gut. Almost every time he looked at her lately, he could feel that Hannah girl lingering in her eyes. He took his cold coffee, tipped it into a nearby pot plant and refilled his cup. Before he knew it, he was standing next to her. 'I need to talk to you, Rebecca. Take a walk with me?'

Outside, the air was brisk, the sun fighting its normal battle for supremacy. By midday, she thought, it'll be raining again. Rebecca thrust her hands into her pockets and followed Kelly. His suggestions were as deniable to her as his orders were to a subordinate. 'What's on your mind?' she asked as he came to a thoughtful standstill near a garden bed of neglected roses.

'What I suggest you do for the rest of the day, is go to your quarters, stay there and keep the door locked.'

'Expecting a missile attack from me now?' she asked.

'If it was war I think you'd be our main weapon.' He smiled at her.

'When my anger is out of control—'

'Yes, I've noticed. Remind me never to stand you up for a date.'

Good one, she thought.

'Rebecca, I'd like you to stay in your room when I'm not around.'

'Ah. Going to visit someone, are we? She wouldn't happen to be an Indonesian lady, would she?'

'I'm doing what must be done.'

'You're going to make things worse.'

'I didn't ask you to come out here to argue.'

'I'm waiting.'

Kelly searched her face and said nothing. At times like this she was impossible to talk to. After a moment's silence, he said, 'I've had Quinn put closed-circuit in your room. The bathroom's fine, so don't get paranoid. The camera's there for your own good.

And there's new locks on the doors, thanks to someone, anonymous of course, who blew the hell out of our electronics systems when she got . . . upset.'

'Now that you know what I'm like when I *am* upset we can all avoid expensive situations, can't we, Commander?'

Kelly sighed. Why was she so defensive? Why did she make him try so hard? 'Here's your access number. Don't lose it or forget it.' He gave her a scrap of paper with a series of eight numbers on it.

'I'll keep it close to my heart forever.' Rebecca slipped the scrap into her bra. 'I'm not even safe here, am I? I tell you what, if you're as good as everyone seems to think you are, I suggest you remain on full red alert. Keep that third eye open at all times, Kelly, or someone might give you a fourth, just like Jamie's.'

'I didn't know you cared.'

She met his gaze and a tiny smile appeared on her face. 'You lie, too. What's on your mind?'

'It's a personal query.'

'You mean there's something about me you don't know?'

Kelly ignored the sarcasm. 'Does the name Hannah mean anything to you?'

Rebecca studied his face. 'Should it?'

'If I knew, would I ask?'

'Take my advice, Kelly. Don't ask.'

'Okay, I won't ask. I'll tell you. Hannah is a teenage girl, who's pregnant and—'

'She burned in the name of God during the Scottish witch-trials about 1662 and whatever you think you know, congratulations but I don't want to hear it.'

'But she's been haunting me for years.'

'Is that why you dragged me out here?'

'I was hoping you could help me make some sense of it.'

'Okay. Tell her to leave you alone. Send her to the light. Find yourself a ghost hunter. Anything. Just leave me out of it.' Rebecca began to walk away but a large hand gripped her shoulder.

'She's not a ghost. You are her. You *were* her. Hannah. Don't ask me how I know. I just . . . do. It's like it's the same . . . the same girl but it's a different place, a different time. Somehow, I'm there, too. It's as if I'm tied and gagged and I want to help her so badly, but I can't. Rebecca, you have to talk to me. You understand this. You have to help me. This is driving me crazy.'

'Join the queue.'

'I was seeing you eight years before I knew you existed. The woman I married looks so much like you—'

'Thanks. I needed that.'

'You don't understand. I was searching—'

'I don't want to know.'

'No. No, I can't believe that. There is one thing you cannot do to me, Rebecca, and that is lie. I can see lies before they emerge.'

'Why? Because you live in a lie?'

'Oh, give me a break!'

'Why should I? I know what you are, Kelly. I know what you always have been. I know about your wife.' She did, suddenly. 'I know she has another man. That she's in America and you're here and while someone else is making her happy, the heat's off you. I know you'd rather face Attila the Hun than have to come to terms with who you are. What are you going to do when you find there's nowhere else to run? Nowhere else to hide? Let go of me, I bruise easily.'

Kelly let go and she walked away.

'You're not going to help me?' he called after her.

Rebecca turned back and the wind blew her hair across her face. 'So you can watch me tied to another stake on another bonfire? Why the hell should I? Nothing has changed.'

Harlem was waiting when she came in. 'Morning,' he said and followed her down the corridor. He was behind her when she came to a stop at the stairs.

'Everything all right, Harlem?' she asked.

'Fine.'

Rebecca stopped on the fifth stair. Harlem was still following her. 'Are you sure everything's all right?'

'Yo, ma'am. Fine.'

'Why are you following me?'

'Orders.'

'Whose orders?'

'Commander Nolan's.'

Rebecca groaned and kept walking. He was right behind her

all the way. She stopped at her door, reached into her bra for the scrap of paper and studied the newfangled lock. She'd never remember eight numbers.

'I'll be right out here if you need me.' He smiled at her. She touched the door without hitting her access code. It opened. She walked in and it closed in his face.

Harlem touched the door himself where she'd put her hand. It was hot. Very hot. Nothing happened when he pushed.

Rebecca looked up at the camera positioned high in the opposite corner of her room. There was a mat near the door. It hadn't been there this morning. She looked under it. A sensor pad. She looked at the camera's red light. She gave it a sultry smile, a Marilyn Monroe pout.

And Barney Quinn sent her a kiss in return and watched, enjoying the show as she took off her shoes and lay on her bed. Rebecca folded her hands on her chest and closed her eyes.

You would turn your back on one needing help, compassion and understanding?

Don't nag me, Emmanuel. I'm not in the mood.

Were he Billy you would turn your back?

No, but—

Buts negate. Deceive. It is time for amends to be made.

CHAPTER 11

KELLY AND Joel used infra-red enhancers to confirm the presence in the fourth floor flat. The Indonesian woman was alone, walking from one room to another. She's packing, Kelly thought.

'Well?' Joel asked.

'Tails.'

They tossed. Heads. Kelly's face remained as expressionless as always. Joel gave him the boxed yellow roses from the back seat. Kelly studied them in the dim light. 'Might get Rebecca some of these,' Kelly said. 'Think she'd like roses?'

'She'd probably jam them up your ass.'

'True,' Kelly said. 'Could be painful.'

Kelly put his red baseball cap on, pushed his sweatshirt sleeves to his elbows, and took the roses to the fourth-floor flat. He knocked on the door. He knocked again, louder.

'Who is it?' came the sweet voice.

'Delivery. Flowers, ma'am,' he drawled in a deep-south accent, borrowed from his wife's wonderful family.

'Who they are from?' she asked.

Kelly referred to the make believe-card. 'From . . . let's see here. Gene? This is flat sixteen, isn't it? Or have I got the wrong place again?'

A box of yellow roses obliterated the man's face. Thuy opened the door and barely had time to think. She was caught by one hand around the neck. Kelly Nolan kicked the door shut and held her fast against the wall. Recognition was instant in her eyes.

'Not leaving us, are you?' he asked, throwing the roses to the carpet and not expecting a reply. One suitcase sat by the entry door and what looked like airline tickets lay near a travel bag on a kitchen bench. She had just showered and was wearing, he was surprised to note during his quick body search, absolutely nothing under a silk bathrobe. No wonder Faraday was brimming with anticipation.

'How you been, Thuy? Heaving Gene aside for the occasional Nighthawk?' he asked, pulling her one-handed into the flat's kitchen and inspecting the airline tickets and passport. 'No? Going to New York? That's a good idea. I tell you what, we can have a calm little talk first. How's that sound?'

She nodded. But she would agree to anything. For a price. Kelly studied her face, its angelic beauty and loosened his grip long enough to allow her to breathe. 'Remember Jamie Faraday?' he asked.

The dark eyes widened with horror. 'I see you do. Good. Now I could kill you slowly and believe me, I'll enjoy every long hour of it. Or I could do it quickly. All you have to do is give me some names. Mainly the three who were in the Tri Star Lines warehouse office the night Jamie Faraday was shot. That's not so hard, is it.'

She attempted a pitiful kick to the groin. Kelly held on a little tighter. She started to gag.

'Names,' he repeated, quietly.

The pressure around her throat relaxed enough for a little more air to be dragged into searing lungs.

'Ten seconds before I start making it hurt. I can make a woman hurt in ways even you didn't know about. Nine. Eight. Seven.' He paused to take a knife from his boot. It had an ornate, carved handle. Kelly hit the release and a four-inch blade appeared close to her eyes. 'Six. Five—'

'Leth . . . Leth . . .'

'Tommy Lethbridge?'

She nodded and winced when the blade touched her nose lightly.

'Well, I'll be. All this time I thought Tommy was working hard for national security. This *is* Tommy from the Pentagon?'

'Yes. Yes.'

'That's one down. Two to go.'

'I see nobody else.'

'No buddy, huh? You've got a very pretty face, Thuy. I could make it ugly. I could make it so ugly only a blind man would want you.'

'I not know others!'

His knee thudded up and parted her legs. 'Gene,' she squeaked.

'Not the Gene we all know and love? We'd better be specific, here. Gene who?'

'You know!'

'No, Thuy. You're going to tell me.'

Terror in her eyes. 'Samperi. No hurt me. Please, no hurt me.'

'That's up to you. One more name.'

'But I not know! You know!'

The knee between the thighs had no effect this time. 'No, no. I not know.'

'You know. Describe him. What's he look like?' Kelly touched the face lightly with the blade—nose, cheeks, lips.

'It was dark, no see. Please, I tell you what you want. I have no choice.'

'What did he look like?' Kelly asked calmly, the point of the knife tickling under her ear. And it bit.

'Old!' she squeaked. 'Fat. No hair. Glasses. Rich, very rich. He say nothing, he do nothing. He watch. Listen. But you know him. Yes, yes, you know him well!' She was crying now. Amazing what a drop of blood would do, especially when she felt it trickling down her neck. The description fitted Marianne's father. Kelly pushed the thought aside.

'Okay, this man with no name listened to what, Thuy? What'd Faraday say about Rebecca Miller?'

'No-thing. He say no-thing. He say she tell no-thing. She know no-thing. Please, no do this, please—'

'What were you paid for killing Faraday?'

'No money. Ticket, identity. New York apartment. I tell you all I know. She will die. Great danger.'

'She's a danger to who, Thuy?'

'Everyone.'

'Everyone who wants the President dead, right?'

'Yes, yes. I have said all.'

Kelly heard a strange noise from the next room. It sounded like a baby waking.

'Please, you will go?'

Kelly walked her into the bedroom. A tiny girl was trying to crawl out of a cot and the kid looked like Gene. Thuy begged him in her native tongue not to hurt the child. And worse, it looked up at Kelly and grinned.

Kelly let the woman go and she swept the baby into her arms, still unsure of what he would do. He was unsure himself until Rebecca's voice replayed, over and over in his mind, *I know what you are. I know what you always have been.*

'I'll be back in an hour. God help you if you're still here.'

Rebecca was enjoying the music in the bar until Ammo decided to play an extremely loud video game and Fleetwood Mac was drowned by attacking Martians. Kelly came in and was immediately handed a Southern Comfort. He scanned the occupants of the room, leaned against the bar and sipped his drink in solitude. He was not in uniform. He wore faded, tight jeans and a pale blue Idaho University sweatshirt with the sleeves pushed to his elbows. He finished one drink before he turned and with his back against the bar, and in an obviously casual pose, he nodded towards Rebecca. The barman caught the silent message and the refill was put onto the bar, not into the waiting hand.

Rebecca bit back a smile and studied the ice melting in her glass. She felt her face heat, as if he'd known she'd been staring at him. Wondering. Then he was beside her. 'Ah,' he said. 'They're playing our song.'

Rebecca looked up into his face and knew, deep inside, how this evening would end. The knowing produced a slight shake of her hand as she sipped her gin squash. I am not ready for this, she thought. I'll never be ready. She wished he wouldn't stand so close.

'Can I talk with you somewhere quiet? You can bring that. You might need it,' Kelly said, indicating her drink and turning away, as if knowing she would follow. She did. He walked in silence towards the stairs which led to the officers' quarters and her hesitation grew until he stopped at the library, opened the door and turned on the lights. 'After you. Take a seat.'

She went in. Now that the room was not full of monitoring equipment, she could see it clearly. Rows of unread books hugged the four walls. There were five dusty, long tables, a scatter of wooden chairs and half a dozen heavy leather recliners. Floor ashtrays, a gleaming brass spittoon. There was a dart board on the back of the library door, which had obviously been removed for her last visit. It had a photocopied picture of Pete Hamill taped to it. Kelly looked at it and smiled as he closed the door.

'That'll be me up there come March.'

Rebecca tried to smile and sipped at her drink.

'You were right. He does want a posting to Washington.'

'And what about you? If I could grant you one wish, what would it be?'

Kelly smiled and thought it over. 'A fishing boat and some peace. Sit.'

She sat on the edge of a reading table. He seemed another person out of uniform. Happy. Casual. Then the officer surfaced again and her illusion shattered. 'Rebecca, I need to ask you certain things without you getting upset or misconstruing what you're about to hear. Do you agree to be rational about this?'

'If you answer one question before we begin.'

'What do you want to know?'

'Did you kill her?'

After a moment's hesitation: 'Who?'

'The Indonesian you questioned today. The one you took a box of yellow roses to.'

'Who have you been speaking to?' he asked, warily.

'No one. Did you kill her?'

'No.'

Rebecca sipped her drink again and noticed that Kelly was warming his thoughtfully. 'But you were going to.'

His glance was icy.

'What's so important that no one else can overhear? What's so personal you know I'll get upset before you even ask?'

'I've been requested to teach you basic principles associated with self defence and surviving interrogations. And how to use a weapon.' He added very quickly, 'it's for your own good.'

'Whose idea is this? Pete's?'

Kelly nodded. 'I agree with him. Partly.'

'I won't be a party to violence of any kind.'

'It's self defence.'

'I can take care of myself.'

Kelly watched the way she sat on the table, idly swinging her legs. So outwardly calm. So very pretty. So alive and radiating a cloud of camouflaged confidence. If she had been in his grip and not Thuy, it would have been over in ten seconds, not ten minutes. How easy this girl would be. The thought was disturbing.

'Rebecca, you can't take care of yourself in situations which are alien to you.'

She regarded him coolly. 'You sound like a text book.'

'You have no idea at all.'

'About what? You? I know you're capable of killing with your bare hands. You don't need a weapon to take life. It's not something I'd brag about, but I'm not you, am I?' You needed no hands then, Kelly, she thought. Redmond. All it took were a few accusations and someone else gladly tossed the torch into the bonfire. Her black skirt rose as she slid off the table and walked towards the first row of books.

'One thing lacking here is trust. Why won't you let me in? Don't you know me yet?' he asked, the officer receding quickly.

'Sometimes I don't want to know you. Did you cut her face? Is that how you force a female to talk? You go straight for the face?'

'You don't understand.'

'I don't want to.'

'What I am endeavouring to do here is—'

'Toughen me in case I'm suddenly landed in her situation. To prove how wonderful you are at protecting me. If that's the case then Robert Glover doesn't stand a chance.'

Kelly slowly, silently, counted to ten.

'What have you seen now that you don't want to tell me?' she asked.

'It's a feeling.'

'It's possible for you to feel? You who can kill with his bare hands?'

'Stop it!'

Rebecca shied at the sudden yell.

'I am sick of this bullshit! I am trying to help you. I am trying, whether you realise it or not, to keep you alive. I am trying to find some trace of the woman I hoped you'd be in the eight years it took me to find you but all I get, day in, day out is crap which would sound more mature coming from a five-year-old kid! What have I done to you, Rebecca? What makes you run hot and cold? Is it some cerebral disorder? What have I *done* to you?'

Rebecca stared at him, her eyes wide, her heart thumping, inwardly cringing as he came closer. Kelly shook his head and reached out to touch her hair. 'Sometimes I just don't know what to do next where you're concerned.' He slid the lock of hair between his fingers. Yes, it was as soft as it looked. 'Do you equate me with Redmond Innes? Is that it? Do you really think we can be the same person?'

Rebecca tried to escape. He was too quick on his feet. He knew Redmond's name? What else did he know?

'You can't tell me anything about that Scottish soldier that I don't already know. Forget him. But you can't forget because you don't want to forget.'

'How can I when I'm reminded of him every time I look at you? I look into your eyes and I see him!'

'No! You see what you want to, not what was. You can't recall the good, Rebecca. You can't recall the feeling, the magnetic bond they—we—shared. God knows I feel it every time you're near me. I felt it before I knew you existed. I saw this girl in my head and for eight of the longest years of my life, I prayed she was real and I wasn't crazy. Now she's here and I don't know what to do with her.'

'Don't do this to me, Kelly.'

' "Don't do this to me, Kelly," ' he mimicked. 'Have you ever considered how I feel? Where I might fit?' He seemed tormented. Torn. And no, she hadn't properly considered Kelly's role in this. It was so easy to blame him for her confusion and frustration. One moment she was tempted to reach, hold and never let him go—it had to be the bond he'd mentioned and felt himself. But the thought of Hannah; of what she knew of the long distant past forced her to run away. Hide. Tell herself it must not happen again. But it seemed that no matter what lengths she took to avoid this, Kelly would try harder to understand it; treat the cause, not the symptoms, in his own way. And his way was to face it in the only manner he knew.

He put his hand on her shoulder and it was not the touch of a friend. It was an ageless sensation. How many times have we done this? she wondered. How long have we been doing this, over and over, each time hoping we would finally get it right? She grabbed his hand and held tight. The gesture brought him closer and she turned, burying her face into his shoulder.

'Once upon a time you had to kill me. Now you have to keep me alive. That's what this is all about.'

'Maybe that's true, but you're not the same person and nor am I. He was a soldier who played around on his wife and got some little girl pregnant. He stood back while she burned. There is no way in hell I would allow that to happen. I'm not the one running away. Not this time around. I know who I am. What about you? Who are you, Rebecca? Who do you want to be? Someone who's been dead nearly four hundred years or the lady who's with me now? It's your choice, but I'll tell you who I'd rather have. And it has to be you.'

She said nothing.

'Forget the past. Leave it where it belongs. I know enough to realise we should live for now. Circumstances change. People change.'

His touch hadn't. It was so familiar. Warm. Strong. He was rubbing her back as if he knew somehow that was what she needed, and it was much more than a fragment of a past memory. For a little while she smelled heather. Saw bare rolling hills. An expanse of water. Someone loping towards her. Redmond. But the soul shining through the eyes as she was exalted, lifted on high, was Kelly's. *Circumstances change. People change. You don't recall the good, the bond. Who do you want to be?*

Kelly gently pushed her away and took her hands.

'What do you want from me, Kelly?'

'I'd like to know what you're so frightened of.'

'This,' she replied quietly. 'I don't want to do it again. I don't want to be some poor, stupid female who loves the wrong man and ends up dying because of it. Can't you understand that?'

'Yes. I can but—'

'Kelly, it's futile.'

'No. I don't believe that. I have very strong feelings for you. Can we at least try? This is meant to be.'

'Pain and misery are never meant to be, but they happen when you and I are together. There's never anything else.' She pushed him away and walked for the door.

'Because you don't want anything else! You like being miserable! The past can't hurt either of us now unless you want it to. It's over, it's done. Let it rest.'

'It's not resolved! It haunts me!' She tried the door. It was locked.

'Looking for this?' Kelly was dangling the key.

'You bastard. You had this planned.'

His smile was disarming.

'You're more psychic than I am!'

'Okay. I admit it. I see, I hear, I know. It has its uses. And drawbacks. Mostly I try to ignore it. What we have to do is live for today. Not tomorrow, not yesterday.'

'But you're married again and there's still a bonfire! It's not an accusation of devil's work this time, but I'm still stuck in the middle of someone else's mess and, just like Hannah, I can't find a way out. I have no control. I'm at someone else's mercy. History is repeating. We are back on the same roundabout. Can't you see that?'

'Yes. But I also know it can and will work out this time.'

'If it doesn't?'

'I'll know I tried. Do you realise how hard it's been for me knowing you're so damned close and I can't do anything about it? Every guy on this base idolises you. They all wish. Well, I wish too, but I can't touch you, I can't even talk to you because when I try you push me away. Why? Because of what you think I must have been so long ago? What's the purpose of life, Rebecca? Isn't it growing? Learning? Loving?'

'Yes, but—'

'But nothing. I can't even kiss you, dammit. I never know how you're going to react.'

'You've never tried to kiss me. All you ever do is talk!'

She had a point. Kelly was taken aback.

'Don't you think I haven't wondered? Don't you think I feel what you do? Don't you think I'd like to . . .' She turned away quickly and wiped stinging tears from her eyes.

'So why fight it?' He bent to the kiss and discovered to his amazement that there was no resistance. Her fingers laced in his hair. He smothered the faint protests with another kiss. Words she would never believe yet a touch, he realised, evoked her fire. Her nearness, her very presence was enough to evoke his.

Every time I see ye, touch ye, it seems as a new day.

Kelly lifted her pullover over her head and threw it behind him. Rebecca closed her eyes at the touch of his hands unbuttoning her blouse. 'Kelly, I don't—'

'Shh. Later. Much later.' He opened the shirt. 'It's okay, no one will know.'

He was reading her mind. What if someone found out? Overheard? Came in? She closed her eyes to the touch of his ingenious, warm hands and another soft bourbon kiss.

Hannah, you're such a beauty. A man canna keep his hands t'himself.

But someone might come along and . . .

She sighed when his fingers cupped her breasts. Kelly's touch was a luxury—the hands and the mouth alternating along a soft trail, the length of her shivering, exposed body. Silencing her doubts. 'Kelly, I haven't . . . any . . oh, God.' He was on his knees, now, and she closed her eyes to the expert caresses, barely noticing the cold, hard door at her back, only half aware of what he was doing to her, arousing her body to a riot of quick, powerful responses until she was quickly past any elusive point of no return. Nothing else mattered and she doubted anything ever had, except this.

'Hold on to me,' he whispered and lifted her, holding her weight effortlessly.

Rebecca wrapped her arms around his neck and her legs around his hips. Her thoughts echoed with his rhythm—let this have no end. She was lost inside his heat for long minutes that seemed infinite until gradually, it lessened. The only sounds now were of two people falling back into their respective realities. Ebbing back to normality.

Kelly sighed, a little shaky, and rubbed his face against her breasts. Her fingers were locked around his neck, her legs still around his hips. 'You can let go now,' he whispered, face still muffled.

Go now. Before Catherine comes back. Go. Go!

Rebecca let go. Kelly eased her down to the floor gently, only to feel the weight of her body against his again, the arms around his waist, tight. Clinging. He held her close for a little while, realising too late that she deserved and needed more than some quick, heated, stand-up copulation. She needed wide soft beds. Soft pillows. Soft lights. And hours, not stolen moments before lights out.

'Next time I promise it'll be different.' He kissed the top of her head and tended to his clothes. Rebecca stepped away, not able to look into his face for fear of what she would see. A simple touch was all it took for this man to win, and shame rose quickly—shame that she didn't seem to have changed at all.

She pulled her skirt down and held her blouse together, tight. The words she'd needed to hear then and now were not forthcoming. She thought she might wait forever to hear three words, spoken with sincerity, with truth.

She turned her back to him and buttoned her blouse, rapidly, cringing away from the hand on her shoulder and his efforts to hold her close again. 'No.' She found her underpants in the corner where he had thrown them. She slipped them on and rearranged her skirt once more.

'What's wrong?' he asked.

'Let me out of here,' she said quietly.

'Rebecca, talk to me. I can't read minds. Not the way you can. Tell me what you want.'

'I want to get out of here. Now. Don't make me angry.'

He took his time unlocking the door. 'Maybe I have trouble saying what you need to hear right now, but I can prove it if you give me half a chance.'

'That's what I'm frightened of,' and after a fleeting glance into his dark, confused eyes, she fled down the corridor.

'Rebecca, what the hell do you want from me! A declaration signed in blood?'

But she was gone and Kelly kicked the wall, savagely.

He tossed fitfully until one-thirty in the morning. He was too confused to sleep properly; his body, his brain was on overload. She was across the hall, not across the planet any more but she'd been closer when she lived half the world away.

She is Australian, I am told . . . yes, Australian. The blonde hair, the blue eyes, very, very pretty and younger by ten years but you will know. Here, the old gypsy had said and reached aross the round table and touched his chest. His heart. Kelly looked from the arthritic fingers back to the jowled face. *Here your spirit lives and will know as it always has known. The day you see her you will know, for the spirit takes flight.* Old, fat fingers fluttered towards the ceiling. Kelly gave the old lady a dumb look. It was all so very disturbing.

He was nineteen back then and on leave from aviation officer candidate training. At a Norfolk fairgrounds, he'd been dared by

Richardson to go into the Tarot reader's tent. He was drunk enough to try anything once.

You have the sight yourself. Why you here, sailor?

A dare, ma'am. But I don't believe in this garbage.

Lies, lies. All believe who have the flame. Your flame is this big. Growing. Growing.

Kelly saw the hands spread to eighteen inches apart and he didn't know what she meant. All he wanted was out. Quickly.

How much do I owe you, ma'am?

For you, with so much ahead, so much to do for the world, you owe me nothing.

The old gypsy winked at him, his hair stood on end and Kelly departed. The roller coaster was safer territory.

She came out after him, yelling, *You are special, sailor! Special and chosen! You will remember this day!*

'What was that about?' Richardson had asked after Kelly had run off like a frightened dog, dragging his mate with him.

'Nothing'. Kelly had barked.

He woke again in a cold sweat. The asylum was quiet. Deathly still. He could not rid himself of the 'knowing' that something was wrong. Terribly wrong. His knowings were rarely amiss. What would be the real harm in appearing beside her bed at this hour of the morning? She'd done it to him once. No, he thought. No. I can't push it. The more I reach, the further away she pushes me.

Kelly wrestled with the impossibility of the situation for another sleepless hour before pure compulsion overruled his logic. Security was on. One attempt to disengage the lock on her door would have scramble sirens splitting the air. Only Barney, Pete and himself knew her code. But as he keyed it in, his heart was already in his ears. The door opened with the normal release signal—a long, high-pitched electronic buzz. As he stepped on the sensor mat the camera in the corner activated into infra-red mode. Kelly hit the light. The bed was still made.

Rebecca was not there.

CHAPTER 12

REBECCA OPENED her eyes and tried to focus. Wherever she was, it was dark. Cold. It wasn't her room at the base. Where the hell am I? she asked silently. Her brain was foggy.

Billy Macpherson. She remembered Billy telling her everything would be fine once she decided what she'd do. Billy didn't want her to walk back to her quarters alone in the dark. Billy was the last person she remembered seeing. She tried to move. Weighted. For a dazed moment, she thought she'd been shot again.

She smelt cigarette smoke. 'Kelly?' she croaked into the darkness and, turning, she saw the silhouette by a window. The only light was from a glowing cigarette. The silhouette was not Kelly's profile. The hair was longer, curly at the ends, the stature was smaller.

'He's not here now,' a soft American voice replied. Then there were footsteps approaching.

Rebecca remembered nothing more until she woke again, to sunlight streaming across her face. She peered up at the low ceiling and lifted her head slowly. Heavy colonial furniture. As heavy as her head. Pottery vases and jugs and plates and shiny trophies on a mantlepiece. The entire wall shimmered.

Somebody's house? Outside, she heard a cow bellowing. Someone's farm.

Farm?

She was lying on a couch, there was a pillow under her head, a blanket covering her. She wore the same clothes as yesterday—the thin floral blouse tucked into a short black skirt. Her shoes were missing, her feet were cold.

She saw a coffee table covered in pale gingham cloth, empty cans of Pepsi and an overflowing ashtray. And a man watching her. Rebecca squinted. Behind him, she could see heavy drapes of maroon velvet, drawn aside, letting the morning sun in through a bay window. Her first thought was the bathroom. Her head spun long after she put her feet to the floor.

'Stay where you are.'

Rebecca tried to focus on the man. Light brown hair to the collar, wavy at the ends. The eyes were blue and the gaze was indifferent.

'What do you want?' she asked, speech slurring. 'What am I doing here and where *is* here? More to the point, who the hell are you?'

But he only stared at her some more, then finally he said, 'Your name is Rebecca Louise Miller, correct?'

'What's going on?'

'Is that your name?'

'Yes—'

'You're the psychic who has assisted the Queensland and Australian Federal Police on more than one occasion?'

'Oh, God, not again.' Rebecca put her head on her knees. She hadn't consumed enough alcohol to deserve this hangover.

'I asked you a question.'

'Yes—' Rebecca moaned and rubbed at her face. She felt as if she'd been dragged by a galloping camel across miles of desert sand and again the room spun.

'Why?' he asked.

'Why what?'

'Why did you assist the Queensland and Australian Federal Police?'

'I wonder that myself,' she mumbled.

'I asked you why.'

'I don't know,' she snapped, impatience rising. 'I volunteered. I knew I could help and I did. Who are you?'

'You *knew* you could help?'

'Yes! Are you deaf?'

'And now you are helping the World Council, the National Security Council, the Central Intelligence Agency and certain other departments of the United States Government divert a much prophesied assassination of Robert Glover. Is this correct?'

'Why did you say much prophesied?' she asked, head suddenly clear.

'You're not the only one who has, shall we say, foreseen this. However, you are the one with the best track record of success and voluntary cooperation.'

No, she thought. I'm possibly the most dispensible. She studied him, unsure of what to do or say. Hadn't Kelly mentioned something about self defence and interrogation? Was this what he had foreseen? Samperi trying to get access to her. Samperi taking over Leon Carter's job. Rebecca knew who this man was now—he no longer needed introduction.

'Why are you assisting these organisations?'

Rebecca thought of many things almost at once. Pacing the balcony so long ago, not taking her father's advice. Why? Could it be one reason only—she had never really overcome the hopeless desolation she felt as she 'watched' that black man die?

'Why are you assisting these organisations?' he asked again.

'You breathe to stay alive, I agreed to assist for the same reason. Gene. Or do I have to call you Mr Samperi?'

Blue gazes met. 'You know who I am.'

'Maybe I'm psychic. How did I get here? I was under the impression the Defence Department had denied your access to me.' Not your organisation, Gene, you, personally.

'What bullshit story have they fed you now? I'm an alleged suspect in a Pentagon witch-hunt? Is that it?' He laughed. 'It's crap, honey. It's all crap.'

She found it difficult to read this man. 'If you had official access to me, why was I kidnapped?'

'Who said you were kidnapped? Don't you remember how you got here?'

She tried to think, backtrack her movements. Kelly, making his presence and intentions known. He'd loved her, however frantic the union and for the next hour she'd tried to fight the realisation that she had enjoyed it. But Billy Macpherson was the last person she had seen. In the middle of the basketball court, she'd cried on his shoulder. *I don't know what to do, Billy* . . . The rest was a blur.

'What do I gain by harming you, Rebecca? "Trust me", are the only words you've heard lately. It must be the Nighthawks' latest motto. What have you gained by trusting them? I'll tell you. Nothing. Their degree of competence when it comes to keeping you safe and healthy is negligible. The most they have given you is a false sense of security. Believe me, Rebecca, that attempted hit at Heathrow did go wrong. They didn't plan on actually shooting you, simply frightening you. They were hoping for a typical civilian reaction—'

'Oh, for God's sake—'

'Who would you run to, Rebecca, if someone started shooting at you? The good guys in the Allies' uniform? I'm told you were hit because of the crosswind, not because of a marksman's bad aim.'

'They have no reason to harm me. We're working towards a common goal.'

He smiled at that. 'Psychological warfare, whose side you'll take, depending on the initial story you were fed. Most people who had just stepped off a long flight are tired, disoriented. Not thinking properly. They knew the type of person you were months before you got on that plane. They might call you a sucker, but I'd call you compassionate. You have a remarkable depth of affinity with life. All kinds of life. They know that now, they knew it then. So tell me, Rebecca, would you have agreed to this if you'd been approached two days after your arrival in England?'

There was no hesitation. 'It's possible.'

'Ah, so it's true. You are here to serve humanity in whatever way you can and to hell with yourself as number one priority, right?'

Rebecca did not know what to make of this man or of this situation.

'Maybe it's time you did put yourself first, 'cos you sure as hell can't serve humanity if you're dead.' Gene rose to his feet, lit a cigarette and reached for a black leather case hidden behind the recliner he sat on. He opened it. Rebecca saw it was full of micro tapes. He chose one at random and threw it to her. It was dated, timed. 'Everything you have said since you arrived at Broadmeadows has been recorded. Pertinent pieces of information are relayed directly to Washington and/or Zurich, where they are analysed and recorded.'

Rebecca didn't have to hear the tape to know what it contained. This recording had been made the day Jamie had been killed. She was back at Broadmeadows, near the CO's office, level six. Sprouting about her theory of individuals wanting the President dead. She focussed on Gene's face. He nodded at her silent question. Yes, everyone knew about Kelly, too. Everyone knew what she did and said twenty-four hours of each day. A large, heavy rock settled in her belly and hot stinging tears fought at her eyes.

'I know how you feel. Cry if you want to. If I were you.

I sure as hell would. There's something else about false security, honey. They will attempt to give you what you need the most to keep you as happy as possible.'

She could still smell Kelly. Taste his kisses. Feel the small callus on his right hand as it tickled her skin, fired her senses. She opened her eyes quickly but hot tears had blurred reality. Gene was there, offering her a hanky. She took it and he stepped away.

'If you can assist them when Glover makes his stopover—if he lives long enough to stop over—good. But if something goes wrong—and that's bound to happen—or if you and the other one hundred and twenty-nine psychics who have seen the same thing are wrong, you, I'm afraid, are dispensable. You know too much, Rebecca. Solitary foreigners who decide to change their intinerary and suddenly trek across the continent sometimes get lost. That's their plan. You know too much about organisations and people who are not supposed to exist.'

'I'm not listening to you.' Rebecca rose unsteadily to her feet and threw the tape back at him. 'You make no sense. None of this makes any sense.'

Gene watched as she searched for an exit. 'You're not assisting anyone. You're being used to flush out suspects. No more, no less. You're just a decoy.'

Rebecca calmly opened the nearest door. It led to a linen closet. The next room was a large, sprawling kitchen but that door to the outside world was locked. Any trace of calmness disintegrated when she heard her own voice on tape:

'I don't think it's some huge conspiracy to kill the President. I think we have a situation here of a few people who want him dead for reasons we can only guess at. Head of CIA operations died by accident. Someone you don't want me to speak to is taking over that position, right?'

She walked back into the living room to find Gene was still sitting there, legs casually crossed, his foot tapping. On his lap was a small cassette player and on his face, a smile. 'I'm the one they didn't want you to speak to. Gene Samperi. Pleased to make your acquaintance.' He fast-forwarded the tape for a few seconds.

'Leon died conveniently. I ask myself why and I realise he was a good guy. Honest. Fair. He was a friend of yours.'

'Can you please slow down?'

She closed her eyes at the sound of Kelly's voice. No wonder there had been unconcealed panic in his eyes.

'But when Jamie was questioned there was someone there he knew. He told them nothing because he knew nothing. Just like me. I know nothing! Who was it there that he knew, Kelly? Was it someone from Nighthawks? Am I being monitored? Am I being bugged now?'

Gene smiled slightly and he hit Stop. He didn't have to speak. He let her think for a little while.

'This isn't happening.'

'Do you want to know a secret?' Gene asked. 'They're listening to us right now, too.'

'How?' she asked, voice shaking.

'The ear studs. That cross around your neck. I'll prove it if you like and after that, we can have a coffee, something to eat and a nice little chat. How does that sound? I'll even show you where the bathroom is. I'm sure you'd want that more than anything else right now. Am I right?'

Rebecca looked away from his eyes. 'You're lying. I know what you're trying to do and it won't work. It will not work. I know there's a breach in their security. Whoever it is has been feeding you this information. Giving you those tapes. Kelly wouldn't let this happen. I know him too well.'

Gene stopped laughing long enough to say, 'Do you really know him? Do you really know what he is? He is an assassin. A killer. He is the best the Nighthawks have. Do you have any idea at all what he is trained to do?'

'I don't want to know!'

'I have seen the end product of his work, Rebecca. Look, give me the jewellery, then maybe you might believe what you see instead of what you hear. Come on, what have you got to lose except a few illusions? Honey, I know. You're the one in the dark, here. I'm doing this for you. Only you.'

Rebecca reluctantly removed the chain and took the earstuds out and gave them to him. He put them on the coffee table, took a pocket-knife and extracted the tiny ruby from the centre of the crucifix. Set under the stone was a minute electronic device. He extracted it with tweezers, put it on the coffee table and crushed it with a hammer. 'I know this was your mother's. I know what this means to you and I'm sorry I had to do that but believe me, you're safer without it. I'll replace it for you if you want.'

Just then her beloved cross meant nothing. He crushed one opal stud and Rebecca stared down at another squashed but recognisable minature electronic device. It emitted a little squeal before it died completely. 'Seeing is believing, right? Every second of every day. No matter what you do, or where you are. Edited tapes are sent immediately to Washington and also Zurich. Now I can prove that, too, if you want.'

'Sent to who?' she asked, devastated.

'Would you like to talk to the World Council parapsychology department? How about a call to the Secretary of Defence office? Would you like to file a complaint of privacy invasion? Do you honestly believe your own government would agree to what has been happening to you? More to the point, do you think these friends of yours would be bothered with your government?'

'I thought they knew. I thought the World Council—'

He laughed again. 'The World Council of Nations, Rebecca, is a little like Nighthawks anti-terrorist squad. It doesn't really exist. But my organisation does.'

'My government doesn't know what I'm doing here?'

Gene shook his head sadly.

'But I signed an agreement at the airport. The guy who gave it to me was from the—'

'Australian High Commission? I doubt that very much. What you signed, Rebecca, was a waiver. You didn't read it, did you? Would you like to answer my questions and then if you are willing, listen to my offer?'

'Offer?'

'Alternative arrangements, Rebecca. Help me, I'll help you. Whoever these alleged assassins are, they're running scared. Very scared.'

'Of me?'

'Personally, no, but scared of what you can do, and what you may know, yes. Very.'

'Who the hell are you!'

'I told you. Gene Samperi. Central Intelligence Agency. Acting Head of Operations for Northern Europe.' He flipped open some kind of identification but she didn't look at it. 'And I didn't want Leon's job. I was hoping to get back to the States.' The blue eyes clouded for a little while. 'He was a very good friend of mine, Rebecca. I know now that you were supposed to be in that car with him. But I think you know that, too, already. Now, I have my suspicions as to who might be one of these frightened individuals you refer to constantly on tape, but we can talk of that later.' Gene watched her face pale further as she digested his words.

'We'll talk about it now.'

'Kelly,' he said simply.

'No. No way.'

'In situations like this, it's normally the least obvious with the best motive who has the most success. Who are you supposed to inform of everything, Rebecca? Who is the one you're most likely to confide in? It's obvious to me. I've listened. I've heard. I know the guy. You only think you do. You are his means to an end. Who is he married to?'

'I know he's married.'

'I asked you who he's married to.'

'Someone called Marianne.'

'That someone called Marianne is a senator's daughter. A senator from the south who does not want a black President. Has Kelly told you of his next posting?'

She said nothing.

'Kelly Nolan is heading for the Pentagon. Why do you think he married into wealth and power in the first place?'

'Pete Hamill is being transferred, not Kelly. Kelly wants a fishing boat.'

'Who told you that crap? Kelly? Jesus, you *are* gullible. Believe me, everything he has done and said has been very well planned, organised and—'

'No! I don't want to hear any more!'

'Well, that's up to you.'

I know what you are, Kelly. I know what you always have been! He betrayed me once, she thought. He'd assured her that history would not repeat. What was this if not another bonfire? *He's the lethal bodyguard. Married to a senator's daughter?*

Nausea rose at the memory of him making heated, passionate love to her only a few hours before. She could still smell him on her body.

'Now, I have to say this, but we will discover who is heading this assassination conspiracy with you or without you. Best for everyone if you remain alive and cooperative. I'm sorry, Rebecca. I am very sorry, but I think you're right. What was it again? Something about being tied to a stake and burning?' Gene watched her face drain of all colour. 'I could go a coffee. How about you?'

She nodded. 'Where's the bathroom?' she asked shakily.

Gene showed the way and waited for the door to close before he threw the final earring to the floor and his boot heel crushed it to powder.

'We've lost her,' Barney said quietly. 'He's destroyed the remaining device.' In communications, Barney gave up trying to retrieve a signal. He took the headset off and sat back with a shaky sigh and dared not look at Kelly.

'Who was the last to see her?' Kelly asked, outwardly calm.

'She was with me until twenty minutes after lights out.' It was Billy Macpherson, and Kelly turned to him. 'I was going back to my quarters and I heard her crying. She was in the gym so I stayed with her a while. She didn't know what she was going to do about you. About this whole deal.'

'What the hell did you say to her?'

'Nothing. You know what I'm like with women. She just needed someone, I guess. She was crying a lot. She said she knew what she would do and she thanked me. And I wondered what the hell she was thanking me for. I offered to walk her up to her room but she said no so I didn't pursue it. Jesus Christ, I should have gone with her.'

'What time was that?'

'I don't know. I'm guessing about midnight.'

'You were with her for an hour and a half while she cried?'

Billy nodded and studied his fingernails. 'She needed someone.'

'Hamill's ETA?' Kelly asked.

'Thirty minutes.'

'Range of the transmitter?'

'Forty miles.'

'It's still operational?'

'Still have a signal.'

'Thank you for suggesting another device in her watch, Quinn.'

'Call it good timing,' Barney said, trying hard to joke.

Kelly felt sick. Forty miles. Forty miles included Salisbury, included hundreds of farms and numerous villages. 'Can we *please* get a satellite fix on that fucking transmitter before the turn of the century?'

'We should have a fix by the time the CO gets in. It's malfunctioning. She plays havoc with electronics, Kelly,' Barney said, agitated himself.

Kelly chewed his thumbnail and tried to control his blazing emotions. Malfunctioning. Yes, she tended to interfere with electronics but why now, of all times? 'Quinn, did you get all that crap on tape?' he asked. Confirmed with a nod. 'Good. Relay it immediately. I'm going to kill that bastard. I'm going to take him apart one piece at a fucking time.'

'We'll get her back, Kelly.'

Kelly looked into Billy's eyes. Billy, in his own way, quietly loved her. Maybe everyone did. Everyone she had touched, at least. He turned to Quinn. 'Call me when you get a location.'

'Yes, sir.'

Kelly headed for the door. 'Kelly?' He turned back and examined the four faces staring back at him. Quinn. Barrett. Macpherson and Stafford. '*We* know he's full of shit, man,' Stafford said.

'Yeah. Thanks. But you're not her, are you?' Kelly left communications quickly, praying that he would be within killing distance of Samperi when he stepped off the edge completely.

Kelly kicked the main doors open. He stood on the baseball diamond, quietly seething in the morning sun, needing something to punch as he waited for Harlem to bring the commanding officer back from London. The CO who was, no doubt, bringing confirmation from the White House absolutely denying Samperi access. A little too late. Conveniently too late.

But Thuy had described Corey Leibermann. What had she said? You know him. You know him very well? Jesus, Kelly thought. My father-in-law is involved? The more he thought of it, the more it made sense. Corey had hated him on sight. Kelly had vaguely suspected it was his Indian blood. He'd even joked to Marianne once about her old man sneaking out at midnight to don the white hood, which she emphatically denied he ever did. And Kelly knew by then that whenever she emphatically denied something he was close to the truth.

He turned his head when a small party of troops jogged by

and Ammo asked, 'Any news, Commander?'

'No. None yet. You'll be informed.'

They moved on. A three-a.m. assembly of fifty-two stunned soliders. No one was missing except the commanding officer.

Kelly looked at his time. An hour had gone by in a flash, or so it felt. He had planned, however vaguely, to begin the challenge of teaching the girl basic defensive techniques whether she agreed or not. How to fire a weapon without killing herself in the process. He was under orders from Pete. *She's to be issued with a weapon.*

She won't like it.

I don't care if she likes it or not, Kelly. She will be issued with a weapon for her own protection.

Something you're not telling me?

I'm taking precautionary measures. No more, no less.

You expect me to tell her she's to carry a gun?

Yes, Commander. This is an order.

'Sure,' Kelly said to himself, and closed his eyes from sheer frustration. 'Will do.' Then a farmhouse flashed into his mind's eye—a clear image, that remained long enough to be committed to memory. He took a notebook from his jeans pocket and used the miniature pen attached to sketch, hastily, the two-storey cottage with its thatched roof. Stables to the side, oaks along the drive. Rolling hills encroaching. Sunrise or sunset. Either way, it faced east or west.

Kelly looked at the sketch until the real image appeared again, in glorious colour, in his mind. And into this scene ambled a Jersey house-cow, grazing lazily, and he watched it walk away, towards a fence. On the other side of the fence, lying immobile in the long grass, was a body. Bleeding. A bare foot tangled in a barbed wire snare. It was Rebecca and she looked very dead. The clothes were torn—the same clothes she was wearing the night before, when he . . .

'Oh, Christ. No,' he whispered.

'A coffee, right?' Gene asked as she reappeared from the bathroom.

'No. I'm not very well.'

'Look, I know how you must be feeling.'

'Spare me this, Gene. I'm not in the mood.'

'Toast?' he offered.

'No.'

'Bacon, eggs?'

'No!' Rebecca attempted to go into the next room and stopped when she heard, 'No. You'll stay with me at all times.'

'I can't stand the smell of meat cooking,' she lied. 'I'm sorry but if I stay in here I'm likely to throw up. I am not going anywhere. How can I, if I don't know where I am?'

'Sit in there where I can see you.'

Rebecca walked into the living room, sat on the seat at the bay window and looked out at the surrounding countryside. It was flat, and very green. She faced east but she couldn't see any sign of Broadmeadows, nor could she see Salisbury Cathedral.

Deep inside was a knowing. It was strong, ineffable. Samperi was simply at work on her emotional vulnerability, her innocence in matters of political machinations, and Kelly was his obvious victim. Kelly was not a Presidential assassin. He was a *warrior*, not a political intriguer. Time to think. Reason. That was why Gene had to be in the kitchen, within sight but giving her space. Space and time to think.

Okay, fine. Kelly was a Nighthawk. But everyone in the Nighthawks squad was a trained killer. He hadn't been searching for a senator's daughter to marry. Just someone who looked like . . . Why did Samperi choose him for this attack that sounded like truth but felt like lies? The answer came quickly. Kelly loved her. Deeply. And Samperi knew it, knew how vulnerable she would be to that.

She watched Gene cooking what appeared to be his breakfast. He was playing on her emotional fragility, no more, no less. But what was his motive? Nothing came to answer that question.

She had the dark, aching feeling that she would never see Kelly's face again. She knew where she belonged and what felt like home to her now. All she wanted was to see the asylum again. No one would know she'd gone because they would allow her to sleep late, knowing she had a free morning. Frank would probably have kept her a special brunch.

The thought of food turned her stomach again. She was still shaky and weak. Worse was the sight of her shirt buttons, still askew. She had hoped a quick wash would cure her ills but the cold water alleviated nothing. She looked a mess. She felt worse.

Rebecca put her head back against the window pane and wiped

prickling sweat from her upper lip. She felt the weakness seeping in, the tightness deep in her chest. It was hard to breathe. She needed her medication for the first time in days. And she had none.

'I have to go back. Please. I need medication and it's at the base.'

'Nice try.' Gene finished his breakfast, opened the fridge and drank juice straight from the carton. 'Heal yourself,' he said, wiping his mouth and putting the carton back. 'I hear you're magic.'

'The magic only works with some things,' she said tiredly. 'I have arrhythmia. I've never found a way to heal that myself. I'm no use to anyone if I'm dead. You said that yourself.'

Gene came in and sat beside her. She didn't look all that great. He reached to touch her face. She was clammy. Sweating. Cold. He could see a pulse visibly pounding in the hollow of her throat. Gene touched. He shouldn't have. She knew immediately who had been at the airport when she arrived, assembling a sniper rifle with a laser sight. She saw herself running in the rain, being pulled along by Kelly. An orange glow hitting her side, her breast, her shoulder. Kelly throwing her bag, turning, and pushing. Hard. She saw herself stumbling, bouncing on the tarmac.

Rebecca weakly pushed his hand away. 'Please take me back.'

'No. No. First, you'll tell me what you saw when you were eighteen.'

'I saw a black man shot. He was on the top steps of a plane. A Learjet. And he lifted his hand to wave—You've heard the tapes.'

. . . and the first bullet hits him between the eyes, the second on the right side of the head. The woman beside him and two bodyguards also fall and amid the chaos of screaming people, a bunch of roses is trampled and a red shoe rolls from a hasty kick.

The President's wife lies in a huddled mess at the bottom of the stairs beside her husband. She's trying to say something. Reaching for his hand . . . 'No, Robbie, no—'

'And?'

'What?' Rebecca asked, sweating profusely now, needing air badly.

'After he waves, what?'

'He falls. He's dead.'

'And you read who he was in a newspaper?'

And she knew then who had kicked Jamie Faraday in the stomach. Who had put the gun into Thuy's willing hand and ordered her to 'Shoot the useless son of a bitch!' And she knew why he wanted to return to the States. The woman, Thuy, was already there. Waiting for him. Waiting for her lover's reappearance.

Rebecca choked on a scream when the hand clenched her face and turned it, hard. She saw death in those pale blue eyes—the eyes of a frightened man whose barriers were down, who was exposing himself unknowingly to what she discovered from a simple touch.

'I asked you a fucking question!'

'Please, I don't feel well. And I've been over this and over it. So many times . . .'

'You read who the black man was in a newspaper? Yes or no!'

'The *New York Times*. Wednesday. December 10, 1997. "President Robert Glover is dead." '

'Is that all?' he asked, disgusted.

'Yes. Yes. I swear. I glimpsed a news-stand. That's all.'

'Who'd you tell?'

It was becoming harder to breathe. She forced her head back against the window pane and struggled for air.

'Who did you tell?'

'My father—didn't want me to . . . Leave it be. Leave it be—'

Gene, on his feet, towering over her, asked, 'Who will kill the President?'

'I don't know.'

'That's bullshit! You do know! You must!' He grabbed her shirt and pulled her up but her legs refused to hold her upright. Cloth tore. 'Who did you see in the Tri Star Lines office?'

'No one.'

'Who did you see!' he yelled, shaking her. Rebecca had no strength left to resist.

'Her. Your woman. Her. She told them. She told them who was there.'

The grip loosened and she fell.

'Who did she tell?'

Rebecca, on the floor, closed her eyes and saw Kelly, half naked and hanging by his wrists. Then Kelly turned into Hannah, surrounded by hooded men, touching her, stabbing at her with . . . 'No!' She tried to crawl away.

She yelped when his foot kicked her flat and then crushed her hand. She looked up into his face.

'Who did she tell?'

A soft blanket of calm descended upon her. 'She told Kelly.'

A hint of panic flickered across Gene's face. He mouthed Kelly's name and more fear touched his eyes.

'She told him everything. They know now. They know about you and if they could hear us before you destroyed the transmitters then they'll find us. And God help you.'

His face drained of colour.

Rebecca lay there, weak and unable to move.

'Who else do they know of?'

Rebecca shook her head and tried to focus on the hazy image of the gun pointed at her face.

'Who else!'

'I don't know!'

He cocked the Browning. 'One last chance, lady!' Rebecca closed her eyes to the image of a steel band wrapping around the man's forehead and tightening. Tightening. There was a crack and a shattering noise as the bullet hit the lightshade, ricocheted.

A thump. Nearby.

She opened her eyes. He was on his knees, trying to scream, not able to make a sound. Blood poured from his nose. His ears. The gun in his shaking hand was pointing vaguely at her, then it dropped from his splayed fingers and, with his head clenched in his hands, Gene fell on his face beside her. He kicked, and was still.

Rebecca stumbled to her feet, dazedly working her way towards the locked door. Without knowing what she did, she touched the handle and the door swung open. Once outside, she collapsed.

Sun on her face. Tiny daisies beside her. She rolled to her side and dragged herself weakly to her feet again.

A cow lowed and she yelped. But it was beyond the fence, staring at her. Her senses were numb till she heard the unmistakeable sounds of rotor blades slicing the still, morning air.

She squinted into the early sun. From out of the glare came the sound of Harlem's Kiowa and she knew who was in it. Her bare feet found instant wings. She ran over grass, over gravel, half afraid Samperi would crawl from the farmhouse and finish it, as he had intended.

Rebecca didn't see the fence until she'd hit it and careered over it. Her clothes ripped again, her flesh tore. Her bare foot was caught, looped tight in barbed wire. With her skirt up around her hips, she lay on her side in the long, green, wet grass, feeling nothing but agony and the warmth of fresh blood running down the length of her leg.

The grass buffeted. Three men in black assaults leapt out of the helicopter—one coming to her, running like the wind, his head down. The other two sprinted towards the house. She heard a familiar voice calling her name.

'Kelly?' she whispered, and then there was nothing.

Kelly skidded to a halt on the wet grass, almost tangling in the fence himself. He looked down on the scene he had witnessed in his mind barely fifteen minutes before. She looked dead. He touched her throat and felt a weak, thready pulse. He tried to extract her injured foot from the barbed wire without causing any more damage, and turned her over gently. He looked behind as Macpherson closed in. 'She's alive. Get Stafford back here, now!' Billy retreated, hollering for Mitch.

Kelly picked Rebecca up effortlessly and carried her towards the Kiowa. 'Where's Samperi! I want him!' he barked at Stafford and Billy as they returned from a needless clearance of the farmhouse and Kelly set Rebecca into the chopper.

'Samperi's dead,' Mitch said. 'Looks like a massive cerebral haemorrhage.' He pushed Kelly out of the way.

Billy's face paled as he watched, guilt rising because he felt it had been his fault. If only he'd walked her to her room, this would have been avoided.

Rebecca opened her eyes to the scissors cutting what remained of her blouse away. Three faces hovered above. Faces she knew. Faces she loved. 'I killed him. I willed him dead—'

'Shh. Not now. Not now,' Kelly said, soothing her while the medic did the best he could with what little was available. Kelly looked at each of his friends' faces in turn. Harlem, Billy and Mitch. They had all heard. 'Take us home, Harlem.'

CHAPTER 13

'BUT I *canna take no more of the questions.'*

'Tell us what it is we'd know.'

'I canna do that. I'd not know what you'd know, James Daley.' She looked up into the judge's eyes. He was so much like her da was before he grew old and ill, before he lost his mind and couldn't recognise her. A good friend of her da's, James Daley. Came regular to visit, especially when his wife was so ill. Came for the herbs. Now he'd come to visit at the end of the day but he couldn't go into the cell. He stood on the other side, whispering, as if hoping no one would hear. The only one likely to listen was the madwoman, Isobel, next door.

'Confess, Hannah, lass. I'll do all I can t'help but my hands be tied unless you confess.'

'But I'd not do this that they say. Where is my Mairie gone? I've not seen her days now. Where's my Mairie? Can ye not tell me where she'd be?'

'Hannah, Hannah, will ye not forget Mairie and agree to what they ask ye? Agree. Please.'

But there were footsteps outside and James Daley had to cover his face and go quickly away before the door opened.

Isobel, the madwoman from Nairn, squashed her wild face against the bars. 'Ah, so it's not just Redmond Innes taking favours but the judge himself too?'

Hannah looked up. 'He'd be a friend of my da's. Known me since I was a wee thing.'

'Ah, and your da had many friends callin' at his door then at all hours of the day and night?'

'The widow McTaggart's been teaching me the way of herbs and medicines and the workin' of things and the sick come see me if I canna go to them. Times my da's too ill and I'd not want to leave him. Is only the ill come visit.'

'Aye, aye. Terrible sickness in your village, Hannah Dougall.'

'How is it you know my name?'

'I know all about everyone.'

'Go away with ye. You'd be mad.'

'Aye, aye. Watch for that child inside ye, Hannah my pretty one, for it takes the fat of an unbaptised bairn to make ye fly.'

'You'll leave us be!'

'Your Mairie, the old blind hag? I know where she be.'

'Where then?'

'She burned days ago now.'

'No! She'd do no harm to nobody!'

'She burned!' Isobel sang. 'She burned alive and is only the bairn stops you from the fires! Confess and you burn. If you don't you'll still burn. Confess, confess, con—'

Redmond came in, picked up a rod of iron and whacked the madwoman's bars. She sank down, suddenly quiet. 'Touching,' she mumbled. 'The lover's returned.'

'You'd not listen to that, Hannah. Is not true what she says.'

The persistent beep was familiar, annoying. It crept in as she pushed up through the grey, swollen, sticky mass, growing louder as she fought for the surface.

Rebecca broke through with a gasp. The beeping was loud, piercing, fast. A hundred razors sliced her body and she couldn't breathe until the mask came down. Cold oxygen was drawn in and she was greedy for it. 'Aye, lass. Easy, easy.'

When her savage need for air was satisfied, the oxygen was taken away.

'All's well.' A Scottish voice. A gentle voice. *James*? Rebecca tried to focus on the face above. 'No, lass. I'd not be Jamie.' Mike McLaren put his large, soft hand on her head. 'You're back with us. You'll be safe, now.' Her right foot was on fire. Both thighs. Arms. Hands. Breasts. Even her chin stung.

Rebecca tried to sit up. 'Nay.' The reassuring touch became restrictive. She tried to push it away and discovered why he didn't want her to move, what the persistent beeping was. An ECG. No more damp, stinking, cold castle cells. The present had returned and this was not a farmhouse. Rebecca touched the sensors firmly glued to her skin. Her wrists were bandaged, blood seeping through. Her foot was strapped yet screaming.

'Aye, it's a mess you're in, lass,' the MO said as he injected her IV with pethidine. 'Pain'll go soon.'

It lifted almost immediately. For a while she thought she was flying. 'Kelly?'

'Aye, he's hanging about outside. Nearly everyone is.'

'Let me see him?'

'Soon, lass. Soon.'

'Now? Please?'

'I'd not want you upset.'

'Let me see him!'

Mike sighed at the angry tears forming in her eyes. At least, he felt they were angry tears. 'Aye,' he said softly. 'Aye. But not for long.'

Kelly was leaning against the MO's desk when the Scot appeared and the small crowd that hung about for news parted like the Red Sea. 'The lassie's a wee bit stronger than she looks, lads. Get your lazy butts back to work now.' Sixteen men reluctantly moved off, conversation growing into a hum, punctuated by boots on tile until the gaggle had ascended the stairs. 'She's wanting you. Kelly. Five minutes.' Mike picked up the phone to inform the CO that the woman had regained consciousness and Kelly cut the call before it had begun. Mike looked into Kelly's eyes. 'Aye, aye. Ten then.'

Kelly headed for isolation and Mike noticed Billy Macpherson still lingering. 'She's not dying, Billy. Off ye go.' But Billy remained with his arms folded, contemplating the intricate web of boot laces at his feet.

'She *can* do it, Captain.'

'What?' Mike barked impatiently.

'She healed my arm. Eight guys were watching. Ask the commander.'

'No. No more of this rot. You'll not expect a man to believe the lass heals by touch. Is a fallacy. Illusion. 'Tis wishful thinking, Macpherson. Your wounds must have looked worse than they were. You've been watching too many fantasy movies, is all.'

'Give her a chance.'

'Go back to work now before I have you cuttin' the lawns with scissors.'

'What'd he *do* to her?' Billy demanded and Mike lost what little patience he had left.

There was no reply when Kelly tapped on the door so he opened it slightly and peered in. She was propped on a mountain of pillows, her eyes were closed. Kelly saw the bloodied and bandaged foot peeking out from the cover of the sheet. Bloodied at her thighs, her breasts and arms. She must have hit the top wire at chest height and flipped, he thought. Rebecca lay as his grandmother had for the last night of her life—the old half-Cherokee woman he'd called Mom all of his life. Until now, the only woman he'd ever truly loved without pretence.

'Rebecca?'

She turned to the voice and Kelly stepped into the room, closing the door behind him. On the red beret in his hand and his black assault uniform were sewn many different emblems, including gold eagle wings with an anchor and Neptune's trident. A God of the Sea. Pilot's wings, too. Rebecca looked into his dark eyes. He had never told her that he was a pilot. He had hardly told her anything at all about himself, nor had he asked very much about her. How could she love someone who seemed so calmly disinterested? Was Gene right when he had said that everything had been planned? That they'd had four months to study her, like a virus under a microscope? That he didn't want a fishing boat? That he was married to a senator's daughter? If he had wealth, he didn't brag about it. Kelly bragged of nothing.

He simply stood there, nervously fumbling, not courageous enough to speak. The chasm between them felt bottomless—he on one side, she the other. He couldn't interpret what lay behind her blue eyes. He wanted to run yet his legs refused to move in any direction except forward.

'I killed him,' she said quietly. 'I killed him by thinking about it. What kind of monster am I? What am I capable of doing?'

'You're no monster.'

'He knew that I knew about him. He was the one who tried to kill me at the airport. He tried to convince me that it had been some kind of—'

'Yes, I know.'

'But I almost believed him.'

'That's understandable given the circumstances.'

'An alien situation. You were right. I didn't know what to do and it was an alien situation.'

Kelly looked away from her eyes.

'He was there when Jamie was murdered. Gene gave her the gun and he said, "Shoot the useless son of a bitch". It was him. He was one of the assassins all along. You were right, Kelly. But you didn't want me to know.'

Was that supposed to make him feel better? Kelly studied the Nighthawks insignia pinned on his beret and wondered when she'd raise the topic of the wife and father-in-law.

'Why won't you come closer? Am I so much of a mess you can't look at me now?'

Kelly came closer, near enough for her to reach out a bandaged arm and touch his hand.

'Was loving me some kind of farewell present because you knew what was going to happen and you didn't expect me to come back?'

'No!' He stepped back, quickly.

'What did you expect him to do to me, Kelly?'

'Rebecca, please—'

'Why did you lie to me?'

'I haven't lied to you, Rebecca. I swear I have never lied to you.'

'But you never told the truth either. Why couldn't you have told me that half the population of Washington was aware of every move I made? What about my privacy?'

'Rebecca—'

'What about you loving me, Kelly? Haven't you any shame? How could you have touched me knowing so many people were listening in? What sort of man *are* you?'

Kelly took a deep breath and closed his eyes. How could he explain that he'd simply *forgotten* she was being constantly monitored on tape? That for once all his professional vigilance had deserted him? It was only later that he'd remembered with a jolt and rushed, red-faced, to try and wrest the tapes away from a sympathetic and equally embarrassed Barney.

'Would you like to hear the rest of those microtapes we took from Samperi's briefcase?' he asked. 'They're interesting, Rebecca, if you like static silence. All we have been sending to Washington is conversation relevant to this situation. No one there hears you taking a shower or . . . or . . . whatever else is worrying you. We edit them here. I'll prove it. When you're better, I'll take you to communications. You can hear the tapes. Is that what you want? Or do you want me on my knees begging forgiveness for something I had no control over?'

'You could have told me.'

'I was under direct orders not to, but I tried to warn you.'

Was that the reason for his hand signals for silence, for his grimaces? His sudden frowns and winces? Most of all his non-committal silences?

'Rebecca,' he said with a small smile. The dark eyes were on fire, moist and tormented. She felt the hand sweeping the hair from her face, caressing. Warm and kind and expert. 'I was so worried about you.' His quick scan of the medical monitoring equipment confirmed the truth in his eyes. 'We all were. Amend that. We still are. It was like Grand Central Station out there a while ago. None of us fully realised the effect of having you here until suddenly you weren't here. Can you remember what happened after we . . . after lights out last night?' Kelly was looking at the bruised hypodermic entry near her right collarbone.

'I think I'd made it to the top of the stairs when someone grabbed me from behind.'

'Macpherson was the last person to speak to you, is that right?'

'It wasn't Billy.

'Yes, I know. He's left-handed. Whoever did that to you was right-handed,' he said and pointed at the hypodermic bruise.

Rebecca touched it. 'How do you know that?'

'I teach them how. It would have been a left hand across your face, pulling your head back, and right hand stabbing with the hypo. There.' Kelly touched the mark.

'Hypodermic—' Rebecca realised now why she felt so hungover. 'Am I still bugged?' she asked.

'No. But there is a transmitter in your watch. We got a satellite fix on your location.' Eventually, he thought.

'Gene didn't know about that, did he?'

'No one did except me and Barney Quinn and it was Barney's idea. Each of us has a tracking device on him at all times. We do consider you a part of the family. Here.' Kelly fumbled to pull out his dog tags. 'See? But I assure you that you won't be bugged again, from this moment on,' Kelly said with a half-hearted smile. He hadn't liked the idea from the start and if that were not believed, then remaining quiet was his best ally.

'Would you hold me?' she asked, taking him completely by

surprise. As did the sudden sound of a throat clearing. McLaren was standing there, watching from the doorway. How much he had heard was anyone's guess.

'Your ten minutes was up five minutes ago, Commander. Best you be on your way. She has another visitor.'

The colonel had brought roses again. Big red roses. Hamill was wearing civilian clothing and he looked very tired. Almost worried. 'This must be serious,' she said. 'More roses?'

'I was in London when I was informed of the situation. What can I say except I am sorry? I can understand how you must feel. Betrayal is often the worst . . . okay. I'm sorry.'

'What do you want now?' she asked, knowing he hadn't come simply to say he was sorry.

'I want to know from your own lips if you killed Gene Samperi by thought alone.'

Her eyes clouded and she turned her head away.

'Did you, Rebecca?' he asked again.

'He was going to kill me.'

'That's not an answer.'

'What *is* the answer? If someone points a gun at your face you don't stop to ask questions. You told me that yourself.'

'I need to know exactly what happened. From you.'

'No. *You* don't need to know. The White House does. The Pentagon does. The non-existent World Council over in Zurich needs to know. And if you tell them that yes, I did kill by thought alone, this base is going to be swamped with more non-existent World Council parapsychologists all wanting a piece of me for scientific study and if that's the case, Colonel, you can—'

'Commander Nolan has told you.'

'Told me what?'

'Oh, Rebecca,' Pete said with a sigh and sat on the edge of her bed. He came a lot closer than Kelly had dared to but not close enough to touch. 'You did kill him, didn't you? Just yes or no. I don't want to hear any hows or whys at this stage.'

She nodded and Pete reached for her hand. 'Well, between you and me and these walls, I'll just say we've been after that bastard for five years. Thank you.' He patted her hand and rose slowly.

'Where have you been? Why are you never here when something goes wrong? Why's Kelly always left holding the lid of the garbage can?'

'Meaning?'

'You're supposed to be the commanding officer but you're always somewhere else. I don't know much about chains of command, Colonel, but I know who's left with most of your work.'

'Rebecca, keep on your side of the fence,' he said and looked away from her.

'Do you really think I can be placated with a few hybrid flowers? Will roses make all this worthwhile? Do you know what I have been through?'

'You're not the only one here who is upset. I'm disgusted and ashamed at what has been happening. But if you really do want to hear some truths, I suggest you be quiet and listen, if it's possible.' A spark of anger lit her eyes. He carried on, unperturbed. 'What I was doing, *again*, was endeavouring to plough through miles and miles of red tape so we can keep you here without interference from any other organisation. I had the orders, finally granted after careful consideration of a new set of circumstances—mainly the deaths of Carter and Faraday—which would have denied Gene Samperi access to you. I was called in London at some ungodly hour of the morning and informed that you had been abducted during my absence. Now this might surprise you, Rebecca, but I don't want you here, almost as much as you don't want to be here. Unfortunately we have to make the most of a lousy situation. I can compromise, providing you do your job and let me do mine.' His blue eyes were an immobile glacier. 'And that will include both of us continuing to cooperate with the paranormal researchers from King's College and Zurich.'

'When?'

'That will be up to you,' he said with a smile. 'When you're ready. I suppose it's futile to ask how you feel?'

'Is it futile for me to ask if you'll be promoted before you're posted to the Pentagon or after you're there?'

'What's this about?' he asked, surprised.

'Aren't you wanting to go back to the States?'

'You must know something I don't.'

'I thought—' It was a rare flash of insight into the colonel's motivations. His tiredness had let his guard drop slightly, she thought.

'What?' His voice was hostile, defences all back in place.

'It's not important.' Rebecca gave him a tired smile which faded completely when the door closed. I just want to know how many people are lying to me, she thought. But nor did she know who was being truthful.

CHAPTER 14

I'D NOT lie to you, Hannah. I'd not. Tis you I love. You and no other.

Rebecca pushed the past back where it belonged. Her mind was a mass of dark confusion. She could barely think clearly as she lay immobile on the narrow hard bed in isolation for the second day. There had been a staccato influx of visitors. Billy was one of the first and the most memorable. She had imagined them all taking numbers and waiting their turn.

Billy was a man of very few words. Shy. Worried. He had many things to ask and no courage to ask them. He appeared with bandaids on his left hand and a small maiden-hair fern in his right. Perhaps he had seen her wandering about in the gardens, or admiring the occasional plant scattered throughout the asylum complex.

She knew he was on a time limit, the cranky MO possibly had a stopwatch out as well. How many times had she heard: *You'll not be annoying the lassie now!* when she needed company the most?

'What have you done to yourself this time?' she asked to relieve the uncomfortable silence between them.

'Oh, just a few blisters.' He didn't say what from—six hours of cutting grass with nail scissors.

'Let me see.' Rebecca beckoned him closer and Billy ripped the bandaids off quickly, wincing. He expected her to hold his hand and cure him with another miracle and his eyes closed from the magic touch.

'Ask Frank to steam some cabbage in milk for you and when it's cool use it as a poultice for about ten minutes.'

He was disappointed until he realised she'd kept hold of his hand.

'And what about you?' he asked. 'Can't you take away your own pain?'

'Sometimes. My wounds tend to heal quickly, anyway.'

'Why don't you heal yourself totally like you healed me?'

'Billy, don't nag me.' It was easy enough to help others—it came naturally. But herself? No. No. Gene had been right. She did not believe she was here to serve herself.

'You like being a martyr. I'll bet you could heal your own pain if you tried. If you wanted to.' He looked at his hand, now numb and tingling. 'You can touch me and it's instant relief. You can take away the pain for me, or anyone else who's hurt or sick but when it's yourself, you won't. Sometimes you have to put yourself first.' He retreated shyly. 'I wish to God you would, Rebecca.' Then he was gone.

And if she had put her own welfare first, she would not have been gullible enough to believe she would be doing good by helping a security force keep a black man alive. If she had any real degree of selfishness, she would not have had the incredible need to help people who could not help themselves. How often had she been told it was her compassion which heralded these 'miracles'? Just like Hannah's never-ceasing trail of people coming to the stone cottage half a mile from the village. People she cured with her herbs and spells. People who had turned on her so swiftly out of fear. For what they could not understand they would destroy. Hannah, an innocent who burned.

Rebecca, cast again into a like situation. For what they cannot understand they will destroy.

. . . running scared.

Of me?

Not you personally but what you can do, what you know. Yes.

She had always had the power to heal, to give and maintain life. Now she had to come to terms with the fact that she could just as easily take it away. She remembered Gene Samperi's surprised eyes as his nose bled. As the pain grew intolerable. As every blood vessel in his brain exploded under pressure.

Put yourself first.

Even the man she'd killed had advised that.

Rebecca stared at the ceiling and wondered if Gene Samperi, Leon Carter and Jamie Faraday would still be dead if Robert Glover's skin had been white. Would he be the first black man to take his reserved seat on the World Council of Nations or would the World Council of Nations really prefer him dead?

If he was so dangerous, so able and willing to cause many tremors, then whose job was it to avert the inevitable earthquake?

Robert Glover's first mission, as stated by himself, was to regain order within his own nation initially, and build new foundations for a new way of life. To cater first to the needs of the individual, hoping the individual would assist his neighbour.

Glover with the overview. Glover who knew exactly where to begin. And thousands, if not millions of people, instinctively sensed the changes about to unfold and were crying impatiently for action. For change. But such changes would not cater to the needs of a few individuals who also were in positions of power . . .

Tears formed in her eyes. Tears of physical pain. Painkillers at four-hourly intervals. Another half hour to wait, if she could. She thought of Kelly, because not focussing often helped. He had not visited since the night before. The captain said he was probably busy, not to bother him so much. He had enough on his mind. But he hadn't even given her five hurried minutes at lunch time. The walls were closing in.

She had no one else but Emmanuel. And she cried quietly for his help. If she could sleep there would be no pain. No pain. And the mists gently rolled in, as surely as the fog obliterated the Wiltshire sunrise. In sleep, there were fields of endless, eternal flowers, with colours indescribably beautiful. She walked through them with Emmanuel who held her hand and spoke without words in a way that touched her core deeply.

Emmanuel's world, entered in dreams, was scented with music, and colours that were feeling. It was a world where she felt complete. Total. But it always ended. Always. He would turn to her, as he did now, his blue eyes touched with sadness.

Go now. Much remains undone. Here you do not belong, here you are only a visitor.

And again she tried to protest as his world receded and his image clouded.

No, don't make me go back—

Emmanuel lifted his hand in farewell and turned away.

She awoke quickly when something clattered to the floor in the next room. She lay in a tight curl for a little while until she realised it was not painful to move her legs.

She touched her chin and looked at her finger. The gash there was no longer weeping. She sat up quickly. There was no pain. She could move freely. She untied the paper gown and let it fall, picked the skin tape off.

The six lacerations from the barbed wire were nothing but bright pink, itching scars now. Rebecca touched her breasts and thighs to make sure it was no illusion. The eight stitches on her left wrist had dissolved.

All you need do is ask.

And then receive.

She was discarding the mountain of bandages on her right ankle when Mike came in, fully armed for the daily ritual of wound dressing. 'What the hell are you doing?' he asked.

She froze momentarily and huge blue eyes peered up at him. 'I'm getting out of here is what I'm doing.'

His grunt needed no translation. She knew he didn't believe. He never would, no matter what he saw, or felt, or subconsciously knew. He spoke of God, sure enough, but in matters of stethoscopes and scalpels, he was the ruling deity.

'I'm discharging myself, Captain. Thanks for your help but I'm fine now.'

'You'll be staying put.'

'Mike, I'm healed.'

He mumbled something incoherent.

'See?' She held up her wrist for the inevitable inspection and the huge soft hand took her arm. He grunted with disbelief and attempted to reason away what he could not accept. He pushed her flat and after a quick search, he scratched his head and glared at her.

'What the hell have you been doing behind my back, then?'

If you knew you still wouldn't believe, she thought. 'Nothing. It's a miracle. Can I go now?'

Mike studied the bright begging eyes, the silent female plea he was so accustomed to. After a final encompassing examination: 'Aye,' he admitted. 'But you'll keep off the foot now.'

'The foot's fine. It's not fractured.'

Mike checked her right ankle. The swelling had receded, the tissues healed. He manipulated it. She sat there, watching him, and only once did she flinch. It still felt slightly tender.

She can do it. Captain. She healed my arm. Macpherson's words echoed in his brain. And when Mike touched her shoulder to help her from the bed and steady her swaying body, he noticed that the constant simmering of his own peptic ulcer diminished. He retied the gown and put his hands behind his back quickly. The pain returned but not as intensely. He touched her again, the pretence to keep her balanced, and as before, the ever-present acidic gnawing dispersed into a warm, tickling tingle.

Rebecca put her hand on her stomach and looked up into his eyes. She was about to ask about his ulcer when he said, 'Get out with ye.' She grabbed her dressing gown, Billy's fern and fled, limping, but glad to be free again.

Kelly heard the knock and took no notice until the door remained shut. 'What!' he barked, impatiently. Nothing except footsteps receding. Soft, uneven footsteps. Rebecca? he thought. No, impossible.

But impossible was a nonexistent word where she was concerned. He left the paperwork and opened the door, peered out into the corridor. Rebecca was walking away towards the elevator, limping very slightly. 'Rebecca?' he called.

She turned, saw nothing but his face and two hands as he held the partly opened door aside. Nothing would defeat the sudden glow that she knew lit her eyes, too. 'If you're busy it can wait.'

He was busy, but . . . 'Come on in. I could use a break anyway.'

He returned her smile and watched her walk towards him. She had her hair in a ponytail and wore a blue floral dress. And one shoe. She limped towards him, carrying the other in her hand. 'Something tells me I shouldn't ask why you're out of the infirmary so soon. Does McLaren know you're out?'

'He signed the release but I'm still on probation.'

Kelly grinned at her and opened the door wide. 'I was coming down to see you after dinner. I've been busy . . .' Small talk.

Rebecca walked into his office for the first time. It was as large as Pete's, more cluttered, less touched by interior decor. But she knew that someone surely worked here and that he enjoyed his work.

On top of a filing cabinet was a rigger in a bottle and without asking she knew it had taken him almost ten years to complete. She also saw a woman, halfway through a heated argument, pick the model up and threaten to destroy it. She shook the impression away.

On the wall which separated his office from the colonel's was a beautifully framed oil painting of a wild restless sea. It seemed to show her what he tried to hide from the rest of the world. The calm he exuded was all surface and pretence. He had painted this, just as he had created the rigger in glass.

'The painting's very beautiful.'

He accepted the compliment silently and fought the urge to close the door, lock it and hold her tight. It was very good indeed to see her, almost back to normal. He closed the door and reached for her. He studied her hand. Her arm. He touched her chin. 'Should I ask?' he asked. Rebecca smiled at him. 'You're incredible.' His finger tickled her face and he lowered his head and kissed her and as he kissed her he quickly untied the shoestring strap at her shoulder.

She pulled away. 'You're supposed to be working.'

'Would you like a coffee?' he asked, not wanting to agree too soon.

He smiled at the way she fought to retie the strap and excused himself while he went to find some milk and sugar—he took his black.

Rebecca was left alone in Kelly's office and she sat on the only available chair after she moved aside a box of papers.

Letters.

As soon as she touched the box she knew who they were from. Love letters bound by a thick rubber band.

And everything Gene had said flooded back and again nothing made sense. Just when she thought she knew what she would do . . . But touching the letters would be invading his privacy. These paper secrets were his own, she had no right to know, or torture herself with her need to know.

She stared at the box again. One touch was all it would take to reveal . . . possibly too much. But curiosity was overwhelming and like a child wanting reassurance, Rebecca touched the rubber band.

An impression came—swift, vague. A striking woman with fashionably wild, pale hair, a woman of class, of wealth. She was immaculate. She was the same woman who had threatened to shatter his model ship.

The senator's daughter.

Rebecca folded her hands in her lap but the box called. Called.

A magnet to her curiosity. She rose quickly, put the box back on the seat and resumed her place by the filing cabinet. Suddenly, she wanted to run away. Then Kelly's phone rang and startled her.

She stared at it, unsure. It buzzed persistently until she picked it up and answered with a soft, 'Commander Nolan's office.'

She heard an echoing silence until a woman with a very drawling accent repeated the number she had called and Rebecca checked off each digit as it was relayed. 'Yes, you have the right number.'

Silence again. Rebecca's heart beat in her ears because she knew it was Kelly's wife. That she called him regularly. And vice versa. She picked up a red biro and wrote down a series of eight numbers. 'Yes, I'll tell him.' Then she heard the dial tone.

When Kelly came back with two coffees in hand and a packet of biscuits under his arm he could see immediately that something was amiss. He said nothing, but gave her a coffee. She tried to smile. Another bad sign. He opened the biscuits and she shook her head at his offer. Kelly resumed his previous position behind his desk, remaining quiet, waiting for the reason for her visit.

'You make a good coffee.'

'Something wrong?'

'It's all changed now, hasn't it?'

'Sorry?'

'The phone rang while you were out. I took a message. Hope I didn't breach National Security in the process.' Kelly waited expectantly. 'She didn't leave her name; she said you'd know who she was. Actually, she said, you *should* know who she was and she left the number. There.' Rebecca vaguely pointed to his desk. 'And what I came to tell you in the first place, is, the figures you need to complete the requisition for the armoury are on a piece of green paper under last week's security roster.' Rebecca put her half-finished coffee on his desk. 'You make a good coffee, Commander Nolan. You make coffee like you make love. It's good, but if you really tried, it could be much better.'

Kelly watched her walk out. He heard the door close quietly. What the hell was that about? he wondered, and looked down at the phone number, written in red on a Nighthawks memo pad.

Marianne's parents' unlisted home number. An invisible heavy weight settled on his shoulders and he sighed. He took today's letter from his breast pocket, the letter he'd meant to store with the others after mail call before he'd been sidetracked.

He opened it again. Two pages of a flowery hand, countless euphemisms to describe her incredible loneliness. Again. The same emotional plea to come home, come home. I need you. Written when she was drunk, alone, remembering, half meaning it. Sober, she felt differently. On the first reading he'd made it to the second paragraph where his absence was likened to desert survival without water, when his phone had rung. Griinke had received 300 pairs of wool blend socks instead of the requisitioned Armalite ammo. And so Kelly's plans to visit Rebecca in the infirmary were waylaid again and Marianne's letter was stuffed into its envelope and into his pocket, forgotten until now.

The timing couldn't have been better. Rebecca, who had probably never answered a phone since her arrival, chose today and his office to be present when his wife called. He felt as if he was being set up.

Instead of returning Marianne's call, he looked for last week's security detail roster and sure enough, the figures he had been searching twenty minutes for lay in Griinke's hurried scrawl on a small scrap of green paper.

Asking how she did it was useless. Asking how she was back on deck in so short a time was also futile. McLaren had been more than concerned about possible infection of her wounds and the onset of pneumonia and he'd judged her time in the infirmary would take at least seven days.

Kelly sat back and picked up his coffee and a biscuit. He'd begged them from Frank. They were Rebecca's favourites, or so the cook said. Chocolate-coated mint slices. Kelly ate four before he contemplated returning the call. It was evening in Georgia and by now, Marianne would have consumed half a bottle of scotch. So, she was back with her parents.

Kelly hit the series of numbers on the memo pad. He spoke animatedly with the black housekeeper for a short time—the one jewel in the Leibermann family crown of thorns was Ella. Her favourite expression—*I knew you was coming. Come see what I baked.* Kelly scored a huge Black Forest cake each visit.

He waited while Ella located Marianne. Kelly knew where she'd be. She'd have taken an evening skinny dip in her daddy's heated pool, her hair would be blanketed in a monogrammed towel, one long tanned leg drawn up, she'd be inspecting her knee as she talked in her slow drawling voice.

He closed his eyes.

He could feel her reluctance. 'Come and show me.'

'But it's so cold in here and what if Catherine should come back?' Hannah looked to the door, terrified that her cousin would return.

'She's not here. Do I ask so much? Is this wee thing so hard to do?'

'You've been at the inn. You been drinking again. I'd not like you when y'been drinking. Y'make me do things that aren't right.'

'But I just want t'see.'

'And then you'll touch and you hurt me when y'been drinking.'

'Show me or I'd be thinking it's lies.'

Hannah pulled her dress over her head. Then she pulled the thin shift off. 'Is not lies, Redmond. I be carrying your baby.'

He smiled at the defiance in her eyes. 'Step into the light, I canna see ye there.'

'Had you not been drinking you'd see better.' She walked from the shadows into the thin patch of sunlight struggling to brighten the untidy room. He noticed her belly was getting bigger each time he saw her of late. Dark circles under her eyes. He sighed. She was losing her beauty to this baby she swore was his. 'Redmond, if Catherine should come back—'

'She won't. Come closer. I want to touch. It moves yet?'

Hannah looked down at her feet. 'Aye. He moves.' She reached for her clothes but he was too quick and he threw them into the doorway and barred the door by leaning across it. He was smiling.

'You'll let me go now before my cousin comes back. She finds me here she'll hang us both. And I've a feeling my da needs me. I've got to go now, Redmond. Is true.'

'Your father can go t'hell. Catherine can too. God, give me a knife now, I'll cut out her nagging tongue and throw the ugly cow into the bog.'

'You don't mean that. Don't say it.'

'I want you, Hannah. Is me who needs you, not your da. Is me who'll have you.'

He took her arm and pulled her down to the bed. 'Let me be!' His touches were cruel and impatient and she couldn't get away from the smell of whisky. It seemed it would never end. And then Hannah heard her cousin's scream:

'What's this you be doing?'

Redmond froze as something hit him across the shoulders. Once, twice, three times. His wife was screaming.

'No! No, Cathy, no! Is she!' He was on his feet, as naked as Hannah. 'Is she bewitchin' me! She'll not leave a man be!'

Hannah tried to shield her face and body from the impact of the broom as it hit, again and again, until she cried, 'No, Cathy. You'll kill my baby!'

Catherine, holding the broom high, let it fall and Redmond snatched it away as Catherine screamed at her cousin to get out, get away.

Hannah was thrown out into the cold without her clothes. It was market day in the village and all heard the commotion. Laughter followed her as she tried to hide and all heard the fighting from the Innes house, too.

'What have you done?'

'Cathy, you canna understand what she does to me—'

'She's with child! She's with child! You're off sowing y'seeds all about except in me!'

Redmond flinched as his wife flailed at him with the broom.

'Kelly, I've been waiting forever. Why haven't you called me? Why haven't you written me? Who the hell answered the phone?'

'Marianne, slow down.'

'Since when have the Nighthawks had women in the ranks?'

'Is something wrong? If not, I am very busy right now.'

Silence. 'Is she still there?'

'No, she's not here.'

'She's English.'

'No, she's not English and I can't tell you why she's here either. Now, has something happened?' Have you trashed the Mustang yet? he wondered.

There was silence.

'Marianne, will you tell me what you called for?'

Silence again. She sipped on a glass of malt. He heard the

ice tinkle. 'Know what I'm doing right now?' she asked in a husky voice. She took a suggestive deep breath, preparing to tell him.

Kelly lit a cigarette. His hand was shaking. 'Marianne, don't. The calls are being monitored.' She didn't care.

'For Christ's sake, Marianne, stop it. Tell me what you want or I'll put the phone down.' This was one of her favourite sick games when she was bored. It no longer got to him.

'Daddy's going back to London, Wednesday week,' she said quickly. 'Will you see me if I come visit? Please, Kelly? I need to see you. Talk to you.'

Wednesday week. Kelly closed his eyes and said, 'Sure. Call me when you get in. We'll meet somewhere.'

'Promise?'

'I promise. I'll see you Wednesday. Call me first.'

Marianne hung up, took some ice from her glass and put it into her mouth. Tommy Lethbridge took it with his tongue.

'She's going to die because of you! Can you never, never keep your mouth shut?'

'But she stole you and you be all I have!'

'A body canna be stolen! Is you I be married to! You! You've killed her. Your own cousin!'

'She'd not be dead yet.'

'Aye, but she'd wish to God she was soon enough. Do ye know what it is they do to them up there in the tower? Do ye know what they did to the Widow McTaggart? Is a madness about, Cathy. A madness and you and Nell be keeping it alive!'

'They'd not hurt Hannah while she be full of child.'

'Aye, aye, but it canna stay inside her forever. Is you I blame for this. Is you I blame! To hell with ye Cathy. Tis a hell you've turned this into!'

He looked down at his wife, on her knees, crying. Oh, and so she should, too.

'Why'd you tell Nell of Craigmore? Why? What else is it you tell Nell?'

'She'd be the only friend I have. Hannah killed Nell's wee son.'

'Her wee son was good as dead the day she birthed him. I heard you say it. Is a shame, y'said. Such a shame.'

'I'd not know it'd come to this! I'd not know! What is it you want me to do? She canna keep the wee one when it's birthed. But we can. You be its da. Is all I've wanted, a wee bairn. You know that. Is our chance, Redmond. Is our only chance. We'd take the wee one. Be ours, he would. Be ours . . .'

Redmond looked down at Cathy, clinging to his leg. He pushed her away.

'Was you who said she bewitched you! Was you said she had the mark!'

Rebecca stared out of her window and into infinity. Despair had an edge keener than a razored blade. This has to be a nightmare, she thought. Dear God, let it be a fantasy.

'You okay?' The question came from the doorway.

Rebecca flinched at the sound of Kelly's quiet voice. Tears filled her eyes.

'I need to talk to you.' Someone, anyone, he thought.

'Why?' she asked, staring out at Salisbury Cathedral which was almost lost in the hazy distance.

'Rebecca, there's things we have to do. Most of all, I need to get out of here for a while.' He came closer. 'I think you do, too.' He tried to see her face but she turned away. He knew she'd been crying. 'Come on.' He sensed that he again was the cause of this latest bout of distress and he put his arms around her. 'It'll work out. Somehow,' he said quietly. 'Come on. Let's get out of here.'

He took her outside to the car park behind the infirmary where half a dozen army jeeps sat in wait. Kelly took a set of keys from his belt and helped her into one of the vehicles. He put the key into the ignition and glanced at her. 'My wife'll be here in England next week. I'll be taking a day off to see her. Talk to her.'

Rebecca had no comment.

'But for now, I have to take you out to the firing range.'

'Do I get a blindfold?' she asked.

'No,' he said with a smile and he drove off towards the training grounds. After five minutes of a rough ride through thick bush, the narrow dirt road suddenly opened into a huge clearing. Kelly stopped the jeep with a sigh. 'You're going to hate me for what

I'm about to do, so we'll get it over with as quickly as possible.'

In the distance was a row of targets reaching to infinity, perhaps beyond. To her right, on the edge of the clearing, was a building that looked like a cottage, without windows, without a roof. 'What's that supposed to be?' she asked. Kelly walked her into it—just a shell of a house until he hit a switch. Stiff cardboard cut-outs of evil-faced males and females sporting cardboard machine guns leapt out from all directions. A few obviously innocent civilians appeared as well.

'It's a kill house,' he said simply.

Rebecca backed out, quickly. 'Do you realise what you're really doing when you practise this?'

'We don't practise, we simulate.' Kelly's voice was tolerant but she knew she was encroaching on very dangerous ground now—his job. 'Come on.'

She followed to the indoor firing range. Targets attached to hooks, the distance variable. She sighed. 'You have to be kidding me. Is this Pete's order for the day?'

'Yes.' Kelly thrust earmuffs at her. 'Now this,' Kelly said, taking his own gun from his belt, 'Is called a—'

'Beretta. A model 92 if I'm not mistaken.'

Kelly rolled his eyes and carried on. 'I realise how you feel about guns and death and destruction, however I have my orders.' He took a clip from his belt.

Rebecca sighed and folded her arms. Her foot was aching again, badly.

'Now, this is a clip. It holds bullets, right? You know what they are?' he asked and smiled at her unamused face. 'Said clip loads as such.' He slipped it in. It locked. He slipped it out, slipped it in.

The earmuffs didn't help a lot. Every time his gun fired, she felt the impact as the paper target was hit. Fifteen times. The paper man was heading towards her now. There wasn't much left of his head and his chest was riddled with small holes. Not many were out of the first tiny circle. She looked at Kelly. He was teaching her nothing. He was simply showing off. 'There was no need for that. One was enough.'

Kelly handed the gun to her. Rebecca put her hands behind her back and stared up defiantly. 'Now what? I know you can shoot.'

'That might be true, but I won't touch that gun.'

'Rebecca, he's a paper man. He does not bleed. I'm only asking that you do this once and then I can judge what type of handgun to issue you for your own protection.'

'Good God. Now I have to protect myself. I pity Robert Glover. I really do.'

'Give me a break here. I'm only doing what I have been told.'

'This is never going to end, is it?'

'Everything ends eventually. Please. For me.'

Rebecca took the Beretta, the clip, loaded it, locked it, cocked it, took proper stance, proper aim and emptied the gun into a paper target more distant than his. The weapon had more kickback than she expected but its accuracy was good. She passed the empty gun back. 'My dad used to call me Annie Oakley.'

'No kidding,' Kelly said quietly. 'What else can you do that I should know about?'

'When I was eighteen I almost made it to America for the world Skirmish titles.'

'Skirmish? You?'

'I also have three trophies for competition shooting. Philosophies change as we grow older and wiser, you see. I see the irrelevancy of this and do not partake any more. But, it's a little like riding a bike. I thought I'd forgotten. Nice to know I haven't lost my touch.'

'What stopped you reaching the titles?'

'My father took eight months to die. You could say he was my first priority.'

'Oh. Right,' Kelly said as he inspected the target and then her face. 'Only three trophies?'

'Only three competitions.' She went on, 'I often wonder what I'd be doing now if I'd gone to the States, but nothing would be achieved by thinking that way. So I decided I'd enhance the real gift I had. After my father died, I studied alternative medicine. In my heart I know it was the right choice.'

'Absolutely.'

'I wish Captain McLaren held your view.'

Kelly reached to touch her hair. Rebecca felt another kiss looming and she knew what his kisses led to. She tried to walk away but the large hand on her shoulder halted all movement and all intention of escape.

'I want you,' he said quietly. 'Not her.'

'Do you always get what you want?'

'Usually, yes.'

'You don't know me, Kelly. You only think you do and that's true deception.'

'I know what I feel. I know what you feel. One moment it's yes, the next it's no. No, because you fear what might have happened once, in a different life. No, because you don't want it to happen again. Yes, because you know you love me and that it's reciprocated. The last thing I want to do is hurt you, Rebecca, so how about a confirmation? Tell me if I am what you want and I'll tell you what you need. It's the same thing.'

She said nothing. He tilted her face up to his and the looming kiss became real. Soft, sure and very warm. Fingers tangled in her hair. Fingers fumbled with her clothing. Hands warmed her breasts. He was kissing her neck, as hungry as ever and if she didn't pull away now, she never would be able to. The man was electric. He knew exactly where and when to touch.

'No. No, don't.' Rebecca pulled away, plucking at her clothes.

'No one's here and no one's likely to come.'

'Kelly! No! Do you know what the word means?'

Pure frustration hit his eyes. 'But I can't get you alone any other way.'

'No!'

He acted as if no one had ever denied him before. Ever. But he wasn't angry, just confused.

'I think we'd better get back to the basics here. Now, can you decide what type of handgun you want to issue me now that you know I can shoot or do I have to partake in a kill house simulation as well?'

'No—'

'Well? What am I being issued with, Chief Instructor for Everything?'

'You have a preference?'

'A GP 35 will do fine. It'll grow cobwebs from lack of use but we'd better keep the colonel happy and completely unaware of what is going on within his own company, right? Can we go back now?'

'Rebecca, I do care about you.'

'Is that all? You care?'

'I am *trying* to make amends here.'

She shook her head sadly. 'Keep trying. Just remember I'm not like your wife.'

'Would you be here with me if you were?'

Rebecca turned away.

'Go on, run. Enough's enough. I am not taking any more from you. Wait outside, Miss Miller. I need to expend some energy and I'd rather you didn't witness it.'

Rebecca pushed the door open with a heave and stepped into the mild, struggling sunshine. From inside came the quick succession of cracks from the Beretta, but Rebecca heard nothing.

She found herself in a bright, colourful crowd. She looked about, momentarily disoriented until she realised what was happening. She was slipping into another reality again, a reality yet to occur. Noise. Cameras, media. Barricades. A Learjet, not a Presidential 767. At the top of the stairs were two bodyguards. One turned, assisting the First Lady, who emerged squinting and putting sunglasses on immediately. She wore red and blue and turned back to her husband. She reached for the hand which was not waving to the crowd and the moment fingers locked, the first bullet hit Glover between the eyes. Before the President crumpled, a second bullet hit. More shooting. Two bodyguards fell, and a screaming Elizabeth Glover was the last to die. Then the image dissolved slowly and Rebecca became once more aware of the training ground in Wiltshire. Of the cracks as Kelly continued his target shooting.

She walked back into the building and waited for Kelly to expend his excess energy. He had emptied four clips and was reaching for his fifth when he sensed the presence and turned. 'It's changed again,' she said, shakily. 'Last time, it was different. Different.'

'What are you talking about?'

'Glover's wife is shot, too.'

'Tell me what you saw. Don't omit a thing.' Kelly took her out into the sun and sat her down in the long grass. She slowly related what she had seen, cooperating willingly.

'He has a bandaid across his nose. It's broken. For some reason, his nose will be broken. Kelly, if he comes to England wearing a bandaid on his nose he's going to die and so will his wife.'

She rested her head on his shoulder, all anger forgotten in her reason for being there in the first place.

They sat in the grass for a long time, thinking. Kelly had his arm around her, lazily. When she moved, the pressure increased slightly, as if he were silently telling her that yes, he realised she was still there and was still important to him.

'We'll keep this to ourselves for a while,' Kelly said his voice rousing her from a meaningless reverie. 'At least until there's news of the President's busted nose. Okay?'

At dinner that night, the TV news silenced the mess.

Robert Glover, while playing with his four sons on the lawns of the White House, had been accidentally hit in the face by a baseball. His nose was broken.

CHAPTER 15

'MITCH?'

Stafford looked up from his *Playboy*, saw who was coming around the corner and slipped the magazine into a drawer. Then he realised such a move was ludicrous where Rebecca was concerned. One look and she knew what he'd been fantasising about. 'What can I do you for?' he asked.

'Is Captain McLaren about?'

'I can't help you?'

'Ah. Not really.'

'Try the gym. He's probably working out.'

He was, with six others who watched her limp into the gym amid calls of *incoming wounded!* Mike broke rhythm, saw who was coming towards him and began his weights again.

There was a basketball game in progress on the court and Harlem begged her to aid his team. While he was begging, the other side scored a basket. Rebecca dodged one wild ball and its chaser and Mike, lifting thirty kilos on a bench press, turned to her. 'Aye lassie?'

'I need to talk to you, Captain.'

'You've a captive audience now then.'

'No. It's a private matter. I can wait till you've finished here.'

Ten minutes later, Harlem's team lost by a wide margin. Rebecca knew they would play better if they had no female form to ogle, but being neutral, she barracked for both teams, clapping and whistling when each scored.

Mike emerged from the shower dressed only in black shorts and a T-shirt. Not only was he heavily built, but also heavily muscled. He wasn't exactly the sympathetic father figure even if he had six daughters. 'Come on, then.'

She hobbled along beside him and down the stairs to his office in the infirmary.

'Is the ankle troubling you?'

'A bit. It's not important.'

He opened his door and she walked in under his arm. 'Would you like a cup of tea then?'

'If you're having one.'

Mike put the jug on and found his tea bags. 'What is it, lass? Seems like the worries of the world've landed on you.'

Rebecca sat down. 'Can I trust you to keep this to yourself?'

'I would hope so.'

Rebecca studied her fingernails. 'I have a suspicion I might be pregnant. Nothing certain, just a suspicion.'

The captain's smile died a quick death. 'You'd be pulling an old man's leg then?'

Rebecca shook her head.

'You'd not be on any kind of contraception at all?'

'No,' she said softly, eyes brimming with tears. 'The Pill's out because of my heart condition. And I wasn't otherwise . . . prepared.'

'Aye, aye,' he mumbled, aware of her medical history. 'I shouldn't be asking, but it's Kelly, is it?'

She nodded and kept studying her nails.

'Aye, I thought so. Lass, it'd be none of my business but are you sure you know what it is you're doing?'

'I'm here asking you to help me, not judge me. I feel bad enough as it is.'

'Lassie, I'm not judging. Just a wee bit concerned, is all.'

'I have to know for sure. Can you do a pregnancy test or is it too early? If I am pregant I don't know the effect the arrhythmia medication would have on the baby.'

Mike sighed. 'A confinement's not something I deal with regularly,' he said with a smile, but she was not in a joking mood. 'How often, then?' he asked and turned the jug off, made the tea and gave her a mug. 'Is it a regular thing you two have going?'

'No. It's only happened the once,' she said quietly. 'Only a few days ago. But it was at the worst possible time. Mid-cycle. I've been feeling different ever since. I'm nauseous in the afternoons now, food doesn't stay down very long. Sometimes I can't face a glass of water. I thought my breasts were swollen and sore because I fell through that fence, but now that the wounds have healed . . . it's getting worse, Mike. Every day I'm feeling lousier.

I'm already retaining fluid, too. Look at my feet. I feel fat, and ugly and I'm cranky.'

Mike saw the tears in her eyes. He was the one who felt like crying. 'Surely it's way too soon to be feeling it?'

'All the signs are there and inside, I know. I just *know*.'

'I see the alternative medicine canna help you now?'

She didn't answer.

'Have you told Kelly?'

'How? He's married. He doesn't need this right now.' If ever, she thought. 'I came for a conference, I end up here. I fall in love with a married man and the first time he touches me—bingo.'

Mike put his hand on her shoulder—any excuse to touch, he realised, because his ulcer was giving him hell again. 'Best we do nothing for six weeks. 'Tis too soon to know. You'll not worry until we've something to worry about.'

'And my medication?'

'Lass, you have to take it. I'll check for side effects and if you don't hear from me, you'll know it's fine.'

'Don't tell anyone. Will you promise me Kelly will never know?'

'And can I ask why you'd not want him to know?'

'I have my reasons.'

'Rebecca lass, are you sure you know him?'

'Of course I do!'

'No, no. If you knew him, you'd not hide this.'

Rebecca stood under the shower with her perfumed soap in hand, the hot water helping the aches—physical and emotional.

If you knew him you'd not hide this.

She finished washing, dressed and peeked out of her door. The light was on in Kelly's room. She hesitated. Did she need an excuse? Why couldn't she just visit? But he would know something was wrong because she had been taking great pains to avoid him completely. Hiding when he walked by.

Anyone seen Rebecca? No, Commander. Try the garden.

Try the garden while she hid in a storeroom two feet away from him, sighing with relief when she heard him walk off. Why am I hiding? she'd wonder.

If he could see auras the way she always had, then he would know she was pregnant. Perhaps he would even be happy about the news? God knows, she thought, I can't go much longer without seeing him again. She had avoided him for days now, since she had spoken to McLaren.

She chewed her thumbnail. It was, until now, easy to pretend she needed no one. Pretence could only stretch so far before it became absurd. He knew her far too well. It was almost impossible to hide from him for any length of time. Nor did she want to. She only felt somewhat whole when he was nearby.

She knocked on Kelly's door and waited forever for him to open it. He had a towel wrapped around his waist and shaving cream all over his face. But he gave her a smile of welcome—as if he had known she would eventually come. He scanned the blue jersey dress she wore so well. 'You look good.'

'I just want to talk to you.' She said. 'Unless you're otherwise engaged.' She wondered why he was shaving at this hour of the evening.

'No, no. Give me five,' he said and beckoned her in. He disappeared into his bathroom and she followed and propped herself against the wall.

'We didn't tell the colonel what I saw at the kill house,' Rebecca said, studying the muscles on his dark back. 'I thought I had to tell him immediately.'

'Not a lot has changed.'

'But four people die now.'

'Yes, you told me.' He kept shaving. What was death to him?

'Nothing affects you greatly, does it? You act as if you're used to this sort of thing. As if you couldn't care less about all this . . . dying.'

'Is that what you think?' he asked, watching her in the mirror as she leant against the wall and studied his discarded boots with detached interest.

'I suppose you *are* used to it. Unaffected by it.'

'No, girl. You learn to live with it.' He tapped his razor in the water and continued, unprompted. 'A lot of folks have asked me how many people I've killed. I suppose they think I have notches on my gun. I usually walk away from those questions. Which is probably why I don't relate to civilians very well. And vice versa.'

'Am I still a civilian?' She couldn't read the silent reply in his eyes. 'Kelly, I haven't been totally honest with you.'

He kept shaving.

I'm pregant, damn you. I let you have your way once and what happens? her mind silently screamed. Kelly kept shaving, waiting for her to elaborate on her 'dishonesty'. 'I've seen this assassination in five different forms since I've been here and I don't know which one to believe. In one, the man is alone. In another, his wife is with him but she isn't shot. In another she is . . .'

'But in each, the President does die from either one or two bullets to the head. Right?' He'd heard her daily taping sessions with Steve.

'Yes. But his wife—'

'Is a variable. The constants haven't changed. Don't panic. Is there some other problem?'

'Kelly, listen to me. My main worry is that if I fail to help you people, it'll be my fault that Robert Glover dies. I couldn't handle another death.'

Kelly washed his face and she handed him a towel automatically. 'Do you really think that the President's life or death lies in your hands alone?' He reached for his jeans and put them on.

'Right now, yes.'

'All we ask is that you help as much as you can and we'll take care of the rest. Okay?' He turned towards her. 'You worry too much about the wrong things.' He ruffled her hair and reached for two glasses and a bottle of Southern Comfort he kept in his bathroom cupboard. 'Ladies first,' he said with a smile.

They sat in his bedroom and for the first time she saw the painting of herself on his wall. At first she didn't recognise it, only felt that the haunting face was deeply familiar in some way. She got up and went closer to examine it. 'Who is she?' she murmured, half expecting him to reply that it was his wife.

'You should know,' he said, watching her intently.

'She looks a bit like my mother.'

He sighed and turned away, staring out of his window into the darkness. 'It's you, Rebecca. You in 1989, when I first saw you.'

She started to protest, then looked again at the portrait. Yes—it could be her. Not the way she saw herself, but perhaps the way someone else might see her.

'Remember I didn't know you then. I'd paint you differently now.'

'Would you?' It was more a request than a question. He turned back towards her eagerly.

'What do you want me to do?'

'Sit down here on the rug.'

She did as requested and he posed her, propped comfortably on her elbow, against a mountain of persian cushions, her hair free-falling over one shoulder. He slipped the dress down her arms and asked her to draw her left leg a little higher so that the dress gathered at the thigh. Yes, her body was covered but it may well not have been.

'How long's this going to take?'

'Two minutes.'

'That's a bit quick, don't you think?'

Kelly took a polaroid photograph and waited for it to develop. 'No, don't move yet.' He peeled the negative off and crouched behind her. They both studied the effect and reached agreement.

'Is that all I have to do?'

'Yep,' he said and attached the photo to his easel, found his pencils and paper, began the basic outline, describing the process as he worked—how he would do an initial sketch, colour it, and if she approved, he'd begin the major painting when he had time.

Time. That elusive, precious commodity.

Rebecca sat up and leaned back on the cushions with her legs tucked under her. She listened to him as he spoke, sometimes with a pencil in his mouth, sometimes not.

'Redmond Innes was an artist, too,' she said.

Kelly looked at her quickly.

'It's true. He'd take her out to the loch to watch the moon rising and she'd touch his hair and say it was the colour of the moon. And he always promised he'd paint her one day but I don't know if he did or not.'

'Maybe some promises can't be broken and last forever.'

'What's your wife like?' Rebecca asked, finally.

'Well, sometimes we make mistakes that we spend years paying for, if not lifetimes. Marianne's a lot like you to look at, I guess. But she isn't you. You're not demanding, materialistic, egocentric. You give, she takes.'

'Does she love you, Kelly?'

'In her own way, maybe she does. Or she did, once. But it's like you said that day on the range. Philosophies change as we get older and wiser. She's never been a friend, Rebecca, and when all else is gone, friendship remains. Marriage is supposed to be companionship for life. If you're lucky enough to find a true friend who's a lover as well, you end up with the potential for a real marriage.' Kelly sighed. 'Or so the experts say. I'm impossible to live with. I need too much space—personal and otherwise. I can't stand having anyone clinging to me—anyone who should know better at least. It feels like a noose after a while. Maybe that's why she's in the States and I'm here.'

'Do you ever go home?' she asked.

'Once a year. I'm there for two hours and I want out. I can't get away from there fast enough. That's my marriage.' And why has it taken you all this time to ask me? he wondered.

'How long was your initial posting for?'

'Five years.'

'How long have you been here?'

'Two.'

She waited for him to tell her that he really wanted a posting to the Pentagon, but nothing came. 'Why did you marry her?'

'Honestly? She looked like you.'

Something bit hard and deeply and Rebecca tried to ignore it.

As he worked, he enjoyed the comfortable silence that lingered until she asked:

'Is it true that her family connections could get you into the Pentagon?'

'What is this? "Let's interrogate Nolan" day?'

'Just asking. You never talk about yourself.'

That's right, he thought. I wait to be asked, just like you do. 'Put it this way. The thought of a Pentagon position once crossed the Leibermann family collective mind. When something crosses that mind, girl, you can bet the thought becomes manifest.'

'Is your father-in-law really a senator?'

'Oh yes. Corey owns half of Georgia. He couldn't own me, though.'

'Why?'

'Why? I'm quarter Cherokee. Maybe he only hated blacks until his daughter fell in love with a little Indian blood.'

'Was she disinherited for marrying you?'

'His little darlin'?' Kelly imitated a deep south accent. Just like his wife's. 'Marianne's the only Leibermann offspring, legitimate at least, and what she wanted, she got. Then I came into her life and a bored, spoilt little girl knew she could throw petrol onto hot coals. We came back from Vegas married. Dorothy, that's Marianne's mother, took the news okay, actually I think she liked me, but Corey . . .' Kelly fell silent for a while, remembering. 'The only time I ever asked my father-in-law for financial assistance was when my mom was dying. I needed fifteen hundred bucks a day to pay for her three months in intensive care and the hospice after that. Well, Corey obliged. He handed me an open cheque with conditions attached. The main one was never to taint the Leibermann line with any Cherokee blood.'

Kelly paused for a while and Rebecca recognised a long-hidden need in his eyes. A need for a real family. Here was this man who believed he had married the nearest he would ever find to the woman who haunted him for eight years, only to find his beliefs a lie.

'You spoke of choices out there on the range. I made mine and I have to live with them. So that's partly why I haven't divorced his one and only little ray of sunshine. And as for the senator, he couldn't buy me as easily as everyone else around him. He never got accustomed to that and I've never forgiven myself for letting that old woman die so slowly because I never took his money. If I had, it would have made the end easier for her. But he would have owned part of me forever. Do you hate me yet?' he added, needing to know.

'No.'

'I must be doing something wrong.' He came back and poured himself another bourbon.

Kelly resumed his seat by the easel and studied what he had accomplished so far. Rebecca rose slowly and walked to him. She saw an enlarged outline almost identical to the photograph. Kelly would give this piece of art more life, more feeling. More of himself again.

'I like it already,' she whispered, resting her hand on his bare shoulder and feeling the tension which had virtually locked his muscles in an inescapable cage. 'When was the last time you relaxed?' she asked.

'I'm relaxed now. Why?'

'It doesn't feel like it.' As the soft massage began, his breathing grew slower, deeper. He put his head back. Her hands worked slowly across his chest and the sparse scattering of body hair.

Rebecca closed her eyes and into her head appeared an Indian warrior astride a grey horse, lance held high in his right hand. She wondered who it was and an image hit her mind immediately. A huge black wing. 'Kelly, who is Black Wing?'

'Sorry?' he asked, brought back from the trance her massage had induced.

'Who is Black Wing?'

'My great-grandfather on my mother's side. See that on the wall there?' he asked, turning to indicate the Indian lance. 'It was his. I never knew him. He was dead twenty years before I was born. But he's always fascinated me. Always.

'It's all or nothing with you, isn't it?' Kelly said, suddenly, sliding his hand up and down her arm. 'That's why you denied me last time.'

'That's how I am.'

Kelly stilled the hands that fired his senses, rather than eased them and before she knew it, she was on his lap. 'No, Kelly. It's not that I don't want to, that's not true. But you need this massage. I promise you'll be a new man by the time I'm done. Please?'

Kelly kissed her, slowly, and set her free.

Rebecca began slow, steady and confident work on his forehead, his scalp, his face, his neck, until his head felt so heavy . . . so heavy. She took his hand and gently coaxed him to his feet. He needed no persuasion to discard his jeans and lie face down on his rug with a pillow under his chest.

Kelly didn't question. Her touch was pure magic—fingertips, palms from the small of the back to the shoulders and across, strokes flowing upwards, over and over, unending, until he couldn't take any more and he rolled over and listened to her sigh. 'I've barely started. Why are you so impatient?'

He beckoned her closer and as she leaned towards him, he unzipped her dress. 'We shouldn't be doing this,' she whispered.

'Absolutely not.'

Rebecca, on her knees, peeled the dress over her head. Kelly pushed the long blonde hair back over her right shoulder and let the back of his hand rub the reddened nipple.

'Stay with me tonight.'

'Kelly—' she whispered.

'Please?' he asked. 'If you don't want to make love, fine. But stay with me. Please. I've never had the chance to hold you all night long. Please.'

'I—'

And they both looked up as the lights went out. The odd curse filtered up from the floor below. And a moment later a warm, soft female body was close to his. He was pleased to find again that she was scared of sudden darkness. Arms enfolded her and he felt her hot breath on his chest, her breasts squashing into his side.

'You're still afraid of the dark.'

'I'm not afraid of anything.'

'Prove it,' he whispered. Her hands were already exploring his eager nakedness.

Rebecca couldn't help herself—she grasped and held, fully, hearing his sudden intake of breath and the way he expelled it slowly. Small hands alternated with her mouth until he touched her shoulder to halt her. And he wondered just who was the impatient one, now. 'Yes?' he asked.

She kissed him again as she sat astride, lowering slowly, keeping him a tight prisoner, straightening her back with a shudder of a sigh. She could barely see his face in the darkness but felt his hands on her thighs. Fingertips between her legs and touching as she leaned forward again and began to move slowly, in time with her own private song, in harmony with Kelly's for a little while at least. She relinquished her fleeting dominance when, still together, they rolled off the red Persian rug and on to the carpet. His easel toppled with a crash but neither heard a thing.

Kelly did not stop and nor did she want him to. Eyes accustomed to the dimness now, she watched his face while he loved her, taking all his own weight on his hands. She ran her hands along his muscled, tight arms. He barely felt her touch. His eyes and his thoughts were closed to any reality except this. On and on and on and on. His final surge was a powerful one, so powerful that she cried out. Then he relaxed, and breathing heavily, became fully aware of her.

Kelly put his hand on her chest—her heart was thudding. 'You okay?' he asked quietly.

'Fine,' she said softly, half expecting he would say she could leave now if she still wanted to go. She sat up slowly but his warm hand pulled her down again. Bodies pressed tightly together.

'You're cold. You should have said something.' Kelly reached up and drew back the covers on his bed. 'Will you stay with me?' he asked, again.

'I'd like that,' Rebecca replied.

She looked up, vaguely aware of the people watching, recognising the faces but not really seeing them. Had they no shame? No mercy? Hannah screamed at the next engulfing convulsion—the pain alone she thought would surely kill her. But before it did she had to push this thing from her body. Push as hard as she could with all the strength she had left. Days now. Days and days. And Catherine there, telling her she was sorry . . .

'Is coming! Is coming! I see the head!'

Redmond came in time to see his son expelled onto the fouled straw. Catherine pushed him away with the cry, 'Is a boy!' And Hannah, thin, weak, ill, sat up and reached for the inert baby. Catherine's hands almost touched it. Hannah screamed at her, with eyes that were wild now the pain was done. Forgotten. And her boy, her son, bloodied, slippery. Blue. He didn't cry. The cord was wrapped around his tiny neck. He didn't breathe. Hannah pulled the thick umbilical away and wiped the baby's face, just as Mairie had shown her, but he slipped from her shaking hands and plopped again to the straw. Once more she tried to pick him up and hold him.

'Is dead! Is dead!' Isobel cried happily from the adjoining cell.

'No! He canna be dead!' Catherine screamed.

A pitifully weak squeal silenced them all. The son. The baby. It had a shock of red hair, like every boy sired by an Innes and it came into life as angry as any Innes, too. Redmond looked into Hannah's eyes and his heart died again as Catherine pulled the infant from her arms.

'You canna take him. You canna take him—'

But take him they did. Wrapped him in the sheet that Catherine had brought. And Catherine ran away with him but Redmond stayed.

'Is not allowed. James Daley fears what you'll do to the bairn. So I said I'd take it, if it lived, for the bairn be mine. I promise

we'll take . . . we'll take . . .' His words failed.

'What more can ye take from me?'

Redmond retreated, too.

Kelly woke because she moved suddenly. 'Beck?'

She was sitting on the edge of the bed now. 'Go back to sleep.'

Kelly watched the way she fumbled in the dark for her clothes and dashed for the bathroom.

He got out of bed, pulled his jeans on hurriedly and stood by the closed door. 'You all right?'

'Fine. I'm . . . oh, God.'

He was undecided whether to go in or not. 'Rebecca, are you sick?'

At the basin, Rebecca washed her face with cold water and tried not to look at her reflection in the dawn's dim light. I have to tell him, she thought. I have to.

Later.

Later.

'You're vomiting,' came the voice beyond the door.

'It must be something I ate last night,' she said. 'Go back to bed.'

He seemed satisfied with that. She put her dress on and appeared in the early morning light. He was sitting on the bed, crosslegged and waiting for her to tell him.

'I'd better go back to my own room. I'll see you later.'

Kelly nodded.

Rebecca looked up from her breakfast when Kelly came in, acknowledged her with an unsure smile and sat at her table. 'How are you?' he asked. 'Do you have anything planned for today?'

'No. Just Steve with his endless questions and photos.'

She wondered how long they would persist with the sessions. Surely they were as sick as she was of hearing the same information repeated over and over again. At least the sessions were getting shorter now—she thought Steve was finally running out of steam.

'Would you like to watch an exercise after that?' Kelly asked.

'Will you be in it?'

'Absolutely. We'll be gone most of the day, so I'll tell Frank he has another mouth to feed. Tell Steve you're in a hurry.'

Rebecca felt the stare coming from a distant corner of the mess. Mike McLaren was watching intently. Rebecca went back to her breakfast. She hoped that today it would stay where it belonged.

CHAPTER 16

MARIANNE PUT the phone down, took a cigarette from her father's gold case and Tommy lit it for her. 'He's not there, Daddy. He's on exercise. He doesn't want to see me. I know he doesn't.' She looked at Tommy—Tommy who would do anything for her. Anything. 'And I know why. It's that Australian. Why's she still alive? If she wasn't alive, I know he'd want to see me. It's going to make this hard, Daddy. You don't know him like I do.'

'You go pack, Mary. You know I need you to help me here.' Corey's voice was soft, persuasive, fatherly and she dared not resist. Damn it all, she thought and glanced at Tommy again as she went out of the study. He deserved his promotion, she needed a man and Daddy needed Robert Glover dead because that one was surely going to put a stop to her daddy's selling arms from the Middle East to South America. And so far Kelly and this Australian she'd overheard so much about were spoking everyone's wheels.

Killing Kelly on duty would save a lot of annoying problems for everyone, too. First of all, hers. But she wasn't supposed to know too much—it was safer not to. It had always been safer to feign deafness and sometimes blindness.

And every time the phone rang, she expected it to be Pete Hamill, telling her the terrible news. She'd rehearsed her lines so often she wasn't sure if she could act distressed on cue.

When his daughter had left the drawing room, Corey Leibermann said quietly, 'Find out what is happening over there. Now.'

'There hasn't been any contact yet, sir.'

'I said find out what's happening! If that fucking Australian fortune teller's . . .'

'Yes, sir. I understand the problem she poses.'

Problem? She was supposed to die with Leon Carter so Gene could take over. God knew, Corey needed him in charge. A good man to have, Gene. 'She's screwed me three times.'

'Yes, sir, I know.'

'She was supposed to die before she left *Heathrow* for Christ's sakes.'

'Yes, sir. I know.'

'How difficult is it to kill one woman?'

Tommy had no simple answer—when the old man was in a mood like this, agreement and silence in turn were often the right tactics to employ. 'Sir, she . . . I didn't want to tell you this, but she can kill by thinking about it. I heard what she did to Gene, sir. I heard it was like decompression without the implosion. Not many want to get involved now. And Kelly's making it impossible. We can't get near her.'

Silence permeated the skylit study and Tommy stroked the old man's telescope.

'What do you mean it was like decompression?'

'Basically, she caused a massive cerebral haemorrhage.'

'How the fuck can she blow up someone's brain?' Corey asked.

'I don't want to know,' Tommy said. 'She blew the shit out of their electronics by thinking about it. She's scaring a lot of people, sir.'

'Does this mean you're deserting me, too?'

'No, sir. Definitely not. I'm simply outlining the situation we have here.'

Corey opened his file and extracted a surveillance photograph—courtesy of the Defense Office—of the Australian psychic. A pretty, ethereal looking girl, a little like his own daughter.

'No one's sure exactly what it is she can do and that's the main problem. She's been studied by Swiss and English parapsychologists, and they're pretty excited by her. That's all the information I can get. Sorry, sir. I wish I could tell you what you want to know.' I wish I fucking knew myself, Tommy thought.

'I'll tell you what I want, Tommy. I want both of them dead. I want her dead because our time's running out and I want . . . you know what I want.'

'We're already working on that right now, sir.'

'Looks like you're standing in my house bullshitting me, Tommy. I want that Indian *dead* before Glover starts tripping off to Europe. The only chance we have is in England. If the President's going to cut security, he's cutting his own throat.'

It was the first time in three months that Tommy had seen the senator genuinely smile.

'I want my son-in-law dead.'

'As I said, sir. We are working on that right now.'

Rebecca sipped at a mug of coffee as soon as they arrived. After all her complaining that she went nowhere, she had agreed without thinking to Kelly's invitation to watch a few simulations—there was little to do at the base to combat welling boredom—but now that she was able to venture out into the cold, Wiltshire air, all she wanted was the warmth of her bed and rest. Rest. But she'd felt some compulsion to come, from the first.

Rebecca, dressed in jeans, sneakers, pullover and Kelly's parka, stayed by the personnel carrier, out of the biting wind. She looked at the twenty soldiers—a mixture of army, navy, air and otherwise special forces from around the world (at least, those nations in accord with aims of the World Council of Nations).

A doomsday feeling lingered heavily like a mercury-filled cloud. She had not been able to shake it for two days now, nor could she locate a cause, except for the knowing that today someone would be hurt.

She watched Kelly organising his contingent into four groups, barking at them about the primary objective of each manoeuvre. A Huey was coming in from the north, and one group was harnessing for an assault on an abandoned, five-storey building which had been used as a prison for the criminally insane. Before it had been burned to a skeleton.

Another group was 'taking' the train which lay in wait for its next hostage situation as it had done for the past fifteen years on a regular basis.

A third group was waiting to do the same with an ancient 747 passenger jet.

The fourth was to begin on the Mother—a series of three obstacle courses. All in rotation. Like a child's party game.

What does my father do?

She imagined a little boy coming home from infant's school, asking the magic question.

Why doesn't he live with us? Didn't you love him enough?

Kelly turned to her as if, from afar, he had felt her thoughts.

He was putting on a harness, about to join one of the small assault squads at the waiting chopper.

Rebecca's grip tightened on the enamel mug. A slide show began in her mind. Quick, instant pictures of what would soon be. Of men, freefalling on ropes from the Huey, landing on the prison roof, attaching grappling hooks and abseiling, feet first, into the old building. The final soldier, suspended twenty metres in the air above the prison roof, suddenly fell. The rope attached to the chopper simply let go.

By the time she had found her feet, the Iroquois was filling. Rebecca ran, as quickly as she could, not aware of her screaming ankle, not aware of her own voice screaming, either.

Kelly saw her stricken, panicked face, and against all reason as opposed to instinct, signalled to the crewie to abort.

Rebecca watched the chopper come down and shielded her face from billowing dust. From the grey cloud, a black-clothed soldier emerged. 'What!' he roared.

'Sabotage!' was the only word she could think of to force his attention.

'What?'

'Sabotage! Who jumps last?'

'Me!' Kelly roared in return.

'Don't jump today! Please! I've seen you fall!'

He'd seen that look in her eyes before. He'd seen it when she had seen Faraday die, when she spoke of Glover dying. Kelly nodded to her and turned to the chopper, gave it the thumbs up and watched it lift off.

But the feeling of impending disaster did not retreat.

Rebecca watched the cover of the smoke grenades and the chopper birthed its blackened young.

Fly and be free.

First down his rope in a freefall spin, just as she had seen, was Billy. He ended on the A-shaped roof without tangling this time, without being repeatedly bashed against the brick wall. This time he was successful, attaching rope and grappling hook to the roof, abseiling down and into the top floor where he was lost from sight. The next two to go also completed the simulation within the time allocated.

But her premonition of tragedy grew incredibly stronger. Why? Kelly was beside her, watching too. 'Who's next?' she asked.

'Henschell.'

Kelly had no sooner spoken the name when Henschell's rope let go. The young soldier hit the prison roof at an angle, bounced and tangled in Billy's abseil rope. He attempted to grab at the rope and cling and he did for a while. Then the hook released its hold. The young soldier bounced on to the mossy flagstone below.

Rebecca stared down at where the young man lay on his back, blood pooling at the back of his head, blood trickling from his mouth. The eyes open, staring.

Kelly looked up at Rebecca, saw her paling face and shook his head. Brett Henschell, a Nighthawk of eight weeks' service, was dead.

'Get him back to the compound,' Kelly said to the circle of stunned onlookers. 'Debriefing in thirty minutes.'

And Rebecca, with her arms folded tight, turned and threw up. A hand on her back. Billy, whispering reassurances as best he could until the commander appeared and ousted him. Nothing was spoken or needed to be said until Kelly took off his harness and saw the name engraved on an inside buckle.

Henschell.

Henschell had been using Kelly's equipment.

'She what?'

'Saw it. Henschell took my equipment by mistake.' His mistake, Kelly thought, my life.

'What the hell was the woman doing out there in the first place?'

'My idea,' Kelly said. 'An attempt to give her another perspective on what we do and the reasoning behind our actions.'

'Well, this would have helped, Kelly. She saw Henschell die.'

Kelly said nothing.

'She's a civilian, for Christ's sake!'

'All right! You want the truth? I don't know what the fuck made me ask her to come out there, okay? All I know is she tried to save my butt! Happy now?' Kelly thrust Ammo's initial findings at the commanding officer and turned away. He didn't make it to the door.

'It was personal with you at the start, wasn't it?' Pete said, eyes icy. 'I tried to warn you.'

'Spare me the lecture, Pete.' All Kelly wanted was a drink.

'Do you honestly think I don't know who she is? Jesus, you were fantasising about her when we were on the *New Jersey*. She's all over your walls, man. I've half a mind to pull you out, right now. Letting a fucking civilian . . . what's wrong with you?'

Kelly turned away. Too much of the past welled too quickly.

Didn't know you could draw, sir. Who is she?

I don't know.

Can you sketch from photos, too, sir?

Maybe.

Would you do one of my girl for me? Here. She's nice, huh?

Yeah, Kelly said, looking at the Hawaiian sailor's mangled photograph of a smiling girlfriend. Yeah, she's nice.

The news spread throughout the ship at the speed of sound.

Show me, Pete said.

Show you what?

These drawings you do. Why didn't you tell me you were an artist?

You never asked.

'You think I don't realise how much this female resembles your wife? I knew you were making a mistake by marrying her. She's been on the phone constantly for the past two days, Kelly. Now either you face this situation with Marianne and you get your personal life back into some semblance of order or you are out. Are you hearing me? I can understand how you feel about Brett, but Henschell is dead, not you. I am giving you an hour, Kelly. One hour. Send the female in. That'll be all.'

Kelly departed quietly and Pete picked up Ammo's report on his initial findings. The release pin had been sawn through, Henschell's body weight added the final touch. Pete rubbed his hand through his short blond hair and heard the soft knock on the door. He knew who it was, no man ever knocked that gently. 'It's open,' he said and watched her come in, turn and close the door. She was wearing the commander's windproof. Pete closed his eyes and slowly counted to ten.

'You wanted me?' she asked softly, resigned again. The only

time she ever spoke with the commanding officer was after another disaster. She barely knew the man as a man—a being behind the uniform.

Pete indicated the seat opposite his desk.

'He's in trouble, isn't he?' she said, referring to Kelly. He had been awfully quiet, almost shellshocked since the accident. And since being called to the CO, his eyes held a depthless amount of sadness. Despair . . .

'Rebecca, you are here to advise.'

'Not turn everyone's lives inside out. I know.'

Pete rubbed his face again, rose and paced the room. 'I can't say your presence has caused any major disturbance because the changes in the personnel are too intangible to describe, let alone understand.' He studied her for a little while. 'You're a peace lover, right? You abhor the notion that the military is a fact of life because you believe the world would be a happier place without it.'

Rebecca wondered what he was trying to say as she agreed silently with his words.

'And yet you agree to observe that which goes against your very nature. Your deep beliefs. Why?'

She still did not know what to say because even she had no answer to that question.

'Are you in . . . love with Commander Nolan? Is that why you went out there today? To be close to him, if that's the phrase to use here?'

Love. What would he know of love and closeness? 'I'm here to advise, not give you details of my personal life or my feelings. My feelings are my own and I won't share them with you. I went out there today because I knew something disastrous was in the offing and I had mistakenly thought I could avert it. I failed. A man I didn't know died even though I had seen it happen five minutes before it did happen. Whether you want to believe it or not, Colonel, that is the reason I watched those exercises today.'

'You convinced Kelly not to jump, is that correct?'

'The man I saw die was the last to come out of that chopper. Kelly was to go last. I even had a diagram of what had caused that fall.'

'Diagram?'

'A mental image. A flash. I saw the rope, the attachment on the end. It had been cut through and the soldier's body weight caused it to snap while he was suspended in the air.'

'And?' Pete asked.

'No. I know what you want me to say. I won't be responsible for another's death.'

'In other words, you are now telling me that you know who is responsible for the commander's safety equipment being tampered with.'

She said nothing.

'You know who is responsible for abducting you, too, don't you? You know who the security breach is, and you refuse to tell me. Who *will* you tell, Rebecca?'

She didn't answer him.

'Don't you trust me?'

'I don't trust anyone any more.'

'Because of Gene Samperi?' he asked.

Again, she said nothing. Why agree with the truth?

'You killed the man who destroyed our credibility. Doesn't that in itself count for anything?'

'No. He was going to kill me. It was self-defence and you know it.'

'Who is the security breach, Rebecca?'

Nausea rose while the colonel continued:

'Whoever is breaching security—'

'Was the cause of the attempted hit at Heathrow. I've heard it all before. It makes no difference.'

'And how, tell me, girl, how am I supposed to keep you alive if you refuse to cooperate? I am supposed to send progress reports to the White House. How the hell do I explain this sudden refusal to assist?'

'I tell you what you need to know. No more, no less, and the reasons for that are my own and possibly beyond your comprehension. What are you so upset about, anyway?' she asked, voice shaking. 'It's not you on the firing line. It's Kelly. It's me. You're doing all right. If Robert Glover dies and the CIA he wants to dissolve is magically reformed, your position at the Pentagon will magically reappear, too. Correct?'

'Rebecca please—'

'Why should you care about me when you'd like to see Robert

Glover's brains spray painting a Learjet four seconds after he arrives in England?'

'If I were you, I'd be extremely careful of making accusations which have no basis in fact. You asked why I'd care? I care as much as any man here about your welfare. Perhaps it might interest you to know that yes, yes, I do intend going back to the States, but that was something which you had foreseen. I hadn't. It might also interest you to know that the Nighthawks will possibly be disbanded under the new President's proposed changes to the military system. Glover intends not only dissolving the CIA, but also withdrawing all American troops who are not involved with United Nations and NATO organizations. So no matter what eventuates, I will still get back to the States. As of this moment, our situation remains unchanged. You are here to help us avert a possible assassination attempt while Glover is on English soil. Now, I am asking you for the second and final time, who is the security breach? Time is running out and it's in your own best interests to tell me now.'

'So the matter can be rectified accordingly?'

'What are you afraid of?'

'I told you before. Another death.'

'If I told you it would be a court-martial situation? Rebecca, you are protecting the wrong person. It's Stafford, isn't it?'

She looked up quickly and blue gazes locked, but she said nothing.

'Oh, come on. In eighteen police cases you correctly pinpointed the motives of twelve offenders!'

'You've already decided Mitch will take this fall, innocent or guilty.'

'Rebecca, I am fast losing patience. Help me, and I will help you. I know that Stafford was responsible for the safety equipment, that he was the last to handle it. Now I know that Australians have one unfortunate, seemingly hereditary trait which for the life of me I cannot fathom. Your aversion to what you call dobbing. I call it a responsibility to this squad.'

Rebecca studied her hands. 'When I was abducted, all I remember is a certain scent. Two people use that aftershave.'

'Who?'

'Mitch Stafford and you.'

Her eyes bored into him for a moment but he kept his gaze steady.

'If you search, you'll find a Swedish hacksaw blade in his locker. If you can have forensic tests done, you'll find it's responsible for weakening that steel pin. But I don't know who was paying him and I still don't know who is going to kill the President.'

'Paying him?' Pete asked, an expression of disbelief crossing his eyes.

Of this he apparently knew nothing. But he had led her to believe he knew everything. 'Look, if you knew I had chicken pox when I was eleven years old, surely to God you can find out that Mitch Stafford is being paid to breach your security. Now, if you don't mind, I am going to go to my room. I'd rather this day never happened.'

CHAPTER 17

KELLY WAS not in the bar before dinner and nor was he in the mess during dinner. No one had seen him all afternoon, although someone had seen him coming down from the CO's office around five. He had also missed the basketball game and had not been forgiven because his team had lost.

Rebecca ate as much as her stomach allowed, asked for a raincheck on Billy's offer of an after-dinner drink and took the stairs to her room. The light was on in room eight across the hall.

When a man endured that amount of despair, she knew better than to barrage him with questions. Perhaps he was feeling his own mortality after watching Brett Henschell die in his place. Perhaps he was simply painting. Needing precious time alone.

She should have known better, yet she knocked on his door.

Kelly was packing.

'Can I ask what's going on?'

He studied her for a little while before he stepped aside and let her in. 'I was going to tell you last week, but you have this barrier I can't seem to break down.'

'What barrier?'

Kelly folded an assortment of clothing—civilian clothing—and put it neatly into a kit bag. 'Your barrier,' he said, simply. 'I'm tired, no more, no less. I'm getting away for a while.'

Getting away or running away? she wondered. 'May I ask where you're going?'

'I'm meeting my wife in London tomorrow morning and I'll probably take her to the Jersey Islands for a week.'

Rebecca stepped back without realising she had moved. She wasn't wounded, she had never felt anything quite like it before. An implosion perhaps, where something died inside. A slow, lingering death. She couldn't look at his eyes.

He was talking barriers? Didn't he know how much she loved him? Hadn't he almost admitted he felt the same way to her on more than one occasion?

Almost.

That was the key word.

Echoes of Gene's voice:

I know him. You only think you do. You are his means to an end.

Echoes of a long distant past:

I love you, Hannah. 'Tis you I love and no other.

Rebecca could almost feel flames licking at her feet again.

And as she stared—stunned, hurt, aching—she realised that he had even talked about his wife before he had made love to her, a week ago. Two weeks ago, the phone call in his office. He had known about this holiday for two weeks and he had said nothing? And what about all her love letters?

No profanity she could think of suited the occasion.

Rebecca opened his door and slammed it shut when she left—the most violent thing Kelly had ever seen her do, voluntarily at least.

One slamming door echoed her true feelings.

Kelly sat with a thump on his bed. He didn't know what the hell to do any more. It was take this forced leave of absence or be declared psychologically unfit for further duty. And how to explain that to Rebecca?

Rebecca limped to her window and looked down on the car park. Kelly's bike sat there in the drizzling rain. He was always promising to take her for a ride one day. He probably rode that bike like he made love, fast, furious. But his gentle side when it showed . . . No, she thought. I can't let these thoughts surface. I can't afford to.

His wife.

Meeting her in London. Taking her to the Jersey Islands for a week. The other woman who had loved Kelly, who'd married him despite the opposition of a very powerful parent, would soon be in England. Why else would she have called him but to tell him she was coming? Why hadn't he told her then that it was all over?

What did he think she would do?

Cry?

Beg him not to go?

Make him choose?'

Make him choose when she had never been able to have what she wanted the most: him. Always, always, someone else had taken him first. Always.

Hopelessness welled and tears rolled as gently as the landscape misting on the horizon. She was nothing. Had she ever been anything where Kelly was concerned? What changed? Whatever *really* changed? she asked herself. She was no better than the creature she'd been three centuries before—a poor, simple little girl who would never had lost her innocence even if she had lived to be eighty. But innocence was a quality Rebecca doubted she had ever known. Her innocence was lost the night her mother died. And she had told her father five minutes before the hospital rang.

That night, her adopted brother ran away. His threat made good. *When she dies, I'm outa here!*

And Hugh Miller was left with constant memories of a wife's lingering, wasting death. With the worries of an uncontrollable, runaway youth and a seven-year-old girl with haunting eyes. Haunting eyes like her mother's. A girl who should never have been born and was reminded of it all her life.

Why couldn't it have been you! he'd yelled to the child who'd looked at him, questioningly and tried to hold his hand because he was so upset.

We were told we couldn't have a child. You shouldn't have even been born!

Rebecca stared out at Salisbury Cathedral until hot tears stained her vision completely.

What more must I do to repay whatever debt it is from whatever sin it is that I've committed? she asked, silently. What more?

'Where's my baby?' she asked when James Daley came in again, his face tormented, ashamed.

'It had to be done, lass.'

'Where's my baby?' she asked again, her dark eyes pleading. So innocent.

'The doctor's said you're strong enough now.'

'I need my son. I want to touch my son.'

'Hannah, confess now and you'll be spared the pains of the tower.'

'The tower? Is that where my baby be?'

'Catherine Innes has your baby and he does well! Now, will you confess!'

'I'd not do the devil's work. I do the work of the Lord. A kind Lord is mine.'

'Take her away.'

The nausea was back. It hit with a venegeance and Rebecca barely made it to the bathroom in time. She hugged the bowl. Its chill was almost kind, almost curing the heat of desolation. At that moment, she wanted to die. She would have invited it, welcomed it like a long lost lover.

But all she heard were the footsteps on the tiles. Uneven footsteps. Redmond Innes had walked unevenly. 'Leave me alone,' she whispered after another onslaught had attempted to relieve her body of her entire stomach.

'Why don't you ask Mike for something?' came Kelly's dull question. There was barely a hint of life left in his voice.

'Go away—'

His knees protested as he crouched beside her and put his hand on her head. 'I don't want to go, Rebecca. I don't want to leave you here but I have no choice. I'd talk to you if I thought you'd be receptive but all you ever do is push me away. I don't understand you but I wish I did. I wish you'd let me in because it would make my decision easier.'

'Seems you've already decided,' she said limply, flushed the toilet and struggled to her feet. She ran cold water and wanted to drown in it.

'I know what she wants to see me for.'

And since when has discussion of an imminent divorce taken a week in the Jersey Islands? All she needed now was more lies. 'It's not my problem. I didn't marry her. You did.'

'This isn't easy for me, Rebecca.'

'Well, it should be. You've done it before. It should get easier with practice!' She hit him and he barely flinched. Anger alone prompted the second assault, and despair, the third.

Kelly just stood there, staring vacantly over the top of her head, allowing her to do whatever it was she needed to do. 'What am I to you! Nothing? An occasional lay while your wife's unavailable?'

'Is that what you think?'

'It's what I know!'

Kelly had to look away from the tears, each one searing like acid deep inside him. 'And if I said I would willingly die for you? That I have never loved anyone the way I love you? Would you believe me?'

'I don't know what to believe any more. I don't know what to do!'

Still, he waited to hear the words which he knew would never come until he had forced them from her. 'I guess I'll see you in a week's time, then.' He walked slowly to the door, hoping she'd say something. Anything.

'Please, don't go.' But it was too late.

'I have to,' he said without turning around.

CHAPTER 18

THE NEXT morning she woke half hoping Kelly would call and say he'd changed his mind, that he was coming home. But she knew it was impossible. He would be away for a week, and she just had to wear it. After breakfast a smiling Pete Hamill took her to the library for her second appointment with the team of parapsychologists. She sighed when she saw their paraphernalia already set up and waiting. They hooked her up and left her there, and began by asking most of the same questions over again. As if they thought the answers might have changed, she thought bitterly. Then they set out the spoons. After a few tries, she managed to make one curve slightly, but that was all. Their disappointment was tangible. She didn't care. She only cared that she couldn't be with Kelly.

Professor Gottsbaum sighed heavily into his microphone. 'You are not tuned in this morning, is that it?'

'You could put it that way,' she said, picturing Kelly at the airport, or some hotel, waiting to meet his wife. His wife. She looked at the clock and wondered how much longer it would take until they got sick of it and went away. But the professor was clearing his throat again.

'Your healing powers. You will demonstrate this please?'

'On who?' For a wild moment she wondered if they'd deliberately injured someone so that she could perform for them.

Then Nicky Pugno came into the room and his eyes were frantic. Her hands started to burn immediately. She could see his pain, a mass of it, lingering like a huge, black cloud and almost obliterating his entire face. Toothache.

'Do you want me to help?' she asked, always getting permission first.

'Want my gun?' he replied, the humour apparent but receding with each banging throb from the abscess under a tooth.

Rebecca stood slowly, trying not to disengage any wires or sensors and momentarily forgot she was being seen and heard. 'How long have you been like this?'

'Since Monday,' he moaned.

'Why haven't you done anything about it?'

He moaned. 'They asked me to wait for you,' he said. Anyway, he would rather die than sit in a dentist's chair.

'Sit down, keep your feet firmly on the floor and trust me. All right?'

He sat, planted his feet and sighed the instant her hands touched his face. Nicky soon floated away into his little private heaven and Rebecca's only physiological changes showed in heart acceleration, and increase in body temperature. Her eyes were closed, the Nighthawk moaning softly as his pain faded away and the abscess disintegrated. He was aware of nothing at all, just her calm, her sweet perfume, her touch and insurmountable relief. And Nicky Pugno realised why everyone was in love with this girl. He wondered what making love to someone like her could do—possibly blow more than just one's mind. It took ten minutes to complete the 'healing' and another two for her eyes to reopen. Brain patterns reestablished normality, heart-rate decelerated, temperature decreased significantly.

Rebecca took a deep breath, patted Pugno's shoulder and asked, 'How's that feel now?'

'It's not there.' He stuck his finger in his mouth, daring himself to feel that abscess. It wasn't there. He wanted to hug her but everyone was watching. His smile was enough.

After Nicky had left they allowed her to rest for a little while. Then they began their questions again. What did she believe caused the bombproof doors to explode?

'Fear,' she replied.

'Fear for yourself?'

'Just fear.'

How did she do it?

'I thought about it. I was upset, frightened and hardly aware of it happening.' She imagined the colonel holding his head in his hands. 'It's the same with the elevator. If I go near it, it short circuits.'

'Do you know why this is?'

'Not really.'

'You are what is known as electrically sensitive.'

More questions came like miniature battering rams. Only one she couldn't answer quickly and it was the one she knew was the sole reason for this episode.

Would she intentionally take human life?

'I would never do that.'

'She's lying, definitely,' Michael said.

The question was reworded. Again she replied in a negative, although her body's reactions betrayed her. Her mouth was awfully dry. Emmanuel's voice echoed in her head:

Remain calm.

'Suppose you were in a position where there was intense—'

'The answer is still no!'

'But the instinct to survive is overwhelming. Would you concentrate your efforts on killing a human being who posed a threat to your survival?' It was Michael, and his voice was excited.

Rebecca became very hesitant, frightened to reply. Jesus, Jesus, they know I killed Gene Samperi by visualising it, that my power increased through fear alone.

'Would you intentionally take a few lives to save that of many millions, Rebecca?' the professor asked.

'Look, you know and I know that psychic power alone can be extremely destructive. Directed properly—'

'You will answer the question, please?'

'Colonel Hamill, I don't want to continue.'

'Tell us what is on your mind, Rebecca,' the professor persisted. 'Please to answer the question.'

Her heart said no. No. 'No.'

'We are here to help you.'

'Bullshit!' she yelled. She looked at the cameras, felt her own horror at what she'd wanted to do and had done, to Gene. And these guys were here to help?

'Please, we feel this is important.'

Psychic weapon, she thought. That's what they want me for. A weapon. Someone to cause embolisms. Someone with the psychic power to defuse or activate bombs from a distance. To travel unseen. To spy. To exert pressure on another's will. And all this and more she was apparently capable of doing, voluntarily. At will. 'No!' she screamed.

'Rebecca, you will answer the question.'

'I will not be what you want me to be!' she screamed and

started ripping off the sensors, the wires. 'Leave me alone! Why can't you just leave me alone!' Michael came running in to save the equipment but after one glance at the subject he retreated after she screamed, 'Don't you come near me!'

'Okay, that's it. This is as far as she goes.'

'Colonel, we have barely begun. This young woman is phenomenal.'

'This young woman has had enough. She has been under too much stress already.'

'She is not working to full capacity?' the professor asked, astounded.

'She's had enough.'

Rebecca had never been as pleased to see Pete Hamill when he came in. She looked at the professor. They were standing in the library, talking about her now as if she wasn't there.

'We have not finished, Colonel Hamill.'

'As far as I'm concerned you have.'

'We need to study her in more detail. Much more detail. We would like to use her in Zurich—'

'*Use* me?' Rebecca asked as she put her pullover on.

'She is not the subject of clinical experiments, she is an integral part of my unit. She is not going to Zurich, she is needed here. Turn those cameras off.' No one moved. 'Now!'

They moved. 'It is not yet over,' the professor said. And finally, he left with, 'You will hear more of this.'

'I seriously doubt that,' Pete replied. 'We've complied with the terms of your agreement, and you've found out nothing more about the death of the President. It's a waste of time.'

Quiet settled on the library after they had departed, taking their equipment with them. Rebecca watched the colonel come back in and she fidgeted, nervously. 'I blew it,' she whispered. 'I'm sorry. I blew it.'

'You lasted longer than I would have,' Pete said.

Rebecca looked up into the colonel's eyes. He wasn't angry at all, just pleased they had gone. She wished he could be Kelly, because all she needed now was someone's arms around her, tight. 'Why does everyone think I'm so damned important? Special? I'm not. Anyone can do what I do if they'd only believe.'

A thousand things he could have said about her importance, specialities and beliefs remained unspoken. 'Let's eat.' He walked with her in silence for a little way. 'The idea of violence and killing hurts you a lot, doesn't it?' It was a question that needed no answer. She studied her fingernails with deliberate intent. 'Would you kill again if you had to?'

'If I had to. If there was no alternative. If my reaction was unthinking.'

'It must be difficult for you here. With us.'

Difficult?

Pete caught the facial expression and laughed, too, despite himself, it seemed.

The smells of roast beef, steak and kidney pie, sausages and onions wafted down the corridor from the kitchen and hit her full force. She was starving even though she still felt allergic to food. The allergy grew immense when she walked into the mess and looked down at Frank's culinary delights. Every day of late he would make something especially vegetarian—it was almost as if Jamie's words had been a dare. *Now he has a vegetarian to experiment on.* A pregnant one. If Frank knew that, he would be force feeding her three immaculately balanced meals each day when she could barely eat one. There were enough worries for these people without adding a pregnant psychic to their list.

'Sit with me,' Pete said as he heaped his plate and she chose a salad. The CO indicated the seat beside him. Rebecca took the seat opposite. 'Rebecca,' he said eventually. 'You've never lied to me, right?'

'Have we ever stopped clashing long enough to converse like normal people, let alone lie to each other?'

Pete ignored that one, even if she was right. 'What is it between you and Kelly?'

'Seems we've been over this before. What it is, Colonel, is none of your business.'

He put his cutlery down and sighed. 'You think I don't know? Do you think I'm blind as well as stupid?'

'No. I don't think you're stupid.'

He tried to ignore that, too. 'I would like us to be friends.'

'Can we just try to tolerate each other and see what happens after that?' she asked.

'I'm willing.' He sighed, as if his willingness was duty, too. Or there was something heavier preying on his mind. Rebecca waited patiently. 'Kelly is a very good friend. I don't want him hurt.'

She wondered what he was trying to say. 'I wouldn't like to see him hurt, either. Sending him away because you believed him incapable and psychologically unfit is not solving a thing. It's making it worse. If he's in hell, I did not make it for him. He's quite capable of doing that himself. Aren't we all?'

'I'm concerned, that's all.'

'Concerned I'm screwing up his life?'

'No. Just concerned.'

'That's very noble of you. Has he ever offered his concern about all your illicit affairs? The effect that betrayal had on your wife? Your kids?'

Quietly, Pete said, 'I can see the point you're trying to make but—'

'But, Colonel, the world would be a much calmer place if everyone became the master of his own universe before dabbling in someone else's. One, you can't tell me what to do with my personal life. Two, I am not a Nighthawk you can order around. You have no power over me. I am a civilian who's finally found someone who means a great deal to me. Sometimes he means more to me than life itself.'

'It won't work.'

'That's right. You don't want it to work!'

Heads turned in her direction. 'Would you please keep your voice down?'

'What are you trying to achieve here, Pete? Are you hoping I'll either be dead or back in Australia when Kelly reports for duty again? If you keep us separated will that cure your main problem? Is it personal ambivalence here towards me? You don't want to lose your second in command to some Australian? What is it exactly?'

'For God's sake, Rebecca. Kelly needed time.'

'Who else needs time? Whoever was paying Stafford? Is he paying you too?'

'I have warned you about accusations—'

'You must be the only person on this planet who can look me in the eye and lie at the same time!'

Voices hushed because of the force of her yell.

'Kelly sees, feels and knows as much, if not more than me! You know it, I know it. Didn't he save your life once because he'd seen your plane ditch into the ocean?'

'He told you about that?'

'He didn't have to. How many people in this room right now are still here because of Kelly? Come on,' she said, loudly. 'Hands up. Let me see them!'

Rebecca counted eleven hands poking hesitantly into the air. Thirty per cent of the people in the room.

She looked back at Pete. 'I need him with me when the President comes and I tell you, Peter Hamill, it feels as if you're doing all you can to make sure the President *does* die. It makes me wonder just who the real security breach is and who better than the commanding officer? Who'd suspect him? Is he getting paid too or is he doing this for a promotion? What do you think he'll be, Pete? Will he be a Brigadier General or a Rear Admiral once he hits the fucking Pentagon?'

The back of the colonel's hand swung, contacted her face and knocked her out of her chair. But the colonel, too aware of his sudden mistake, heard every chair scrape back and every man stood, waiting, almost defying him to move suddenly.

Pete looked down at Rebecca, at the bruise already forming on her cheek. At the bloodied mouth she was wiping on her sleeve. He had never hit a woman before in his life.

'The commander will be back in one week's time. And you will never, never speak to me in that manner again.'

He walked by, narrowly avoiding her hand. She looked at the faces of the men as they sat again and continued with their lunches.

'Rebecca, there's a call for you.' It was Billy. He put his hand down and she took it. He heaved her to her feet.

She walked out with Billy, internally shaking but outwardly calm until he suddenly pulled her into the empty boozer. She'd never seen him angry before. 'What the hell did you say all that for!'

She looked at the phone near the bar. 'Which line?' she asked, touching her mouth again.

'There is no call.'

'But you said—'

'There is no call!'

Rebecca had seen fear before and glimpses of it showed in Billy's hazel eyes. 'What the hell are you trying to do?' he asked. His question had no answer.

'Something you had better know, Rebecca. Pete Hamill and

Robert Glover went to the academy together. Are you listening to me? For Christ's sake, they flew sorties over Iraq together! The CO was his wing man!'

'Oh, shit,' she whispered. But she wasn't wholly convinced. Men change, she thought. Friendship gives way to personal needs, ambitions.

'What the hell am I going to do with you?' Billy said. 'Are you crazy, girl? Who are you, Rebecca?'

CHAPTER 19

SHE KNOCKED softly on the CO's door and heard the voice granting admission. Rebecca opened the door one-handed and came in, limping softly.

Pete's groan was barely perceptible as he looked at the intruder and pushed away from his computer terminal. He wondered what she had behind her back, one hand was hidden. On anyone else, he preferred seeing both hands at any given time.

Even men he knew.

But there was shame lighting her blue eyes, shame that almost matched his own.

'No one asked me to come. I'm doing this voluntarily.'

Doing what? he wondered.

The hidden hand produced a rose—one of the white ones from the garden near the gym. He'd seen her weeding it on occasion. Then he realised he hadn't noticed any roses blooming there for two years.

'I couldn't get a white flag,' she said quietly.

'Didn't you try Ammo Griinke?' Pete asked, not wanting to look at her bruised face very long, if at all.

'Yes, I did try the sarge but I didn't have a serial number for the two forms he said I'd have to fill out.' She smiled in spite of her split lip. 'My father was in the army for a while. He used to tell everyone about how he once requisitioned a black dog for an old man he knew whose dog had died. Three months later, a black dog actually arrived. I couldn't wait three months for a white flag to arrive on this base where surrender is not an operable word.' She handed him the white rose, partially in bloom. 'It's not a Peace rose, but it's the best I could do. Sir.' She smiled again.

Sir. She was calling him Sir. Pete rubbed his aching head. 'Thank you, Rebecca. It's not every day a pretty girl gives me a rose.'

'Sometimes I don't know what to think, what to do, or what

to say. If you want me to apologise to you in front of your men, I will.'

'There's no need. The men have seen and heard worse than that.'

But did the offenders live? she wondered. 'I am sorry. Can you understand the position I am in?'

'No, Rebecca. I am not you and you are not me. I think we're both slightly thankful for that small mercy. Okay?'

'Okay.'

Silence fell and he wondered what she wanted.

'You're writing to Brett Henschell's parents, aren't you?'

Pete reached for a cigarette and offered her one. She declined.

'What do you say in situations like that?' she asked.

He laughed, albeit with resignation. 'It's the usual form letter. Sacrifice for the country.'

'The normal propogandist bullshit. Good old America.'

'Brett was English.'

More silence. She wanted to talk but didn't know how. She felt it was important to try to get to know this apparently impenetrable man. 'What's the . . . mortality rate like in a squad like this?' she asked.

'What's on your mind, girl?'

'Kelly,' she said, eventually.

'I take it you can't decide what to do?'

It seemed an understatement.

'You need to go home but you need him, too. Which is the greater need? Is it a mistake, is it right . . . ordinarily, I wouldn't have understood your position until my wife hit me with her dilemma last night. She can't take any more of being the officer's wife. I'm away too much. I barely know my own kids and she can't take any more of England. She wants to go home, too. But she still needs me.' Pete sat back, put his feet up on his desk and ground out his cigarette. 'I am what I am, what I've always been. She knew what I was when she married me and she made the mistake of believing she had the power to force me to change. But it helped her to know that we'll be back stateside soon.'

'And if the squad's not disbanded, Kelly will be the CO.'

'What I'd like you to do is answer me honestly. Will you do that?' Pete asked.

She nodded.

'What was Kelly when you first met him?'

My memory is not that long, she thought. We were probably amoebas sharing the same drop of water in the first ocean.

'Kelly was a married navy officer, second in command of an anti-terrorist squad.'

'And he still is providing he gets his act together. I can't afford to lose him.'

Nor can I, she thought. The ball is literally in his court now.

'Rebecca, sometimes we don't always get what we think we need.'

Fate, though, had its own devices to segregate needs from wants. Somehow, she knew that the choice she would soon be faced with would be the most important one of her life. And Kelly's. It was a choice either to resolve or ignore.

And if it were ignored, the circumstances would only repeat. And repeat, each time becoming more difficult to endure. Until eternity if need be.

'Kelly saved my life in 1986, Rebecca', Pete said quietly. 'I was flying Hornets off the *Enterprise* in the South Pacific at the time. I'd never met him before. So I didn't know who the hell he was the morning he knocked on my cabin door. "Don't fly today, Major", he said. I asked him why not. He told me if I took my plane out, she'd ditch on take-off. He looked me in the eye and said again, "Don't fly today, Major." And he just walked away. We ditched on take-off and he was the first diver in.'

She looked at Pete Hamill, his jungle greens accenting the blue of his eyes. Perhaps he understood little of what she knew, and understood much of what she didn't. He had remained on his side of the illusory fence and how many times had she crossed the line into his territory? For the first time she was able to feel something of the real man behind the slightly amused eyes. 'Can I ask you something?'

'Shoot.'

'Was Robert Glover the pilot when your plane ditched?'

Pete pointed to the door. 'That will be all, Miss Miller.' And as she opened his door he said, 'Your apology has been filed for future reference.' His defences were in place again, and they were unbreachable. He must have spent a lifetime building them. Perhaps several lifetimes.

Kelly checked the time. Quarter after one. Again, he winked at the kid sitting opposite and received a devious grin in return.

A two-hour delay was now stretched to two and a half; the five-year-old boy helped alleviate boredom. He had been warned countless times to, 'Leave the man alone. Dad will be here soon.'

Five seconds to a five-year-old was too long for any form of soon, shortly, or, 'Don't nag me, Johnny!'

There was a brave new world out there waiting to be explored. Kelly knew that impatience so well. He remembered the games too. Playing his own games with his partner—a packing crate. That box had taken him all over the world. It had been a pirate ship, it had been a B52 bomber. It had been whatever he had needed it to be.

His partner now was a five-year-old Johnny Unknown, shooting an imaginary gun at him. Kelly shot back with an imaginary pump action shotgun while the mother wasn't looking and he winced as the child, rolling around on the carpet, taking too long to die, was heaved by his collar back to the seat and told to stop misbehaving.

Kelly roamed a little, watched a few jets land. Johnny Unknown was beside him, mimicking. He was followed to the men's room and back to the waiting lounge where he was in trouble again for wandering off with strangers.

When the heat dissipated, Kelly stopped the boy's whining for a while. He took three coins from his pocket and, aware of the boy's eyes not missing a beat, performed one of a few party tricks he kept literally up his sleeve. Three coins between four fingers disappeared with the flick of a wrist and appeared by magic on a protruding tongue.

The little boy's eyes widened, his mouth opened in awe and the magic of the moment disintegrated when the arrivals poured forth.

Kelly watched the boy's reunion and waited to face his own. Marianne was searching for him amid the crowd and he didn't recognise her as instantly as he'd thought he would. In a strange, alien way it was almost good to see her again.

The platinum blonde hair had been savagely cut to within half an inch of its life. That in itself seemed a silent message because he had preferred her hair long. Feminine. Her face was heavily made up and not a lot had changed because she still waited for the right moment to be someone's centre of attention. Even if it was her own. He wasn't sure what she would do to welcome him. He never really knew what she would do from one moment to the next.

She wasn't sure herself. When she touched his hand her nails were like claws—more deliberate pain intended than warmth of welcome. 'Oh, Kelly. You're looking good enough to eat. It's too bad I'm on a diet.' Her voice rang with insincerity. Southern charm wearing thin.

'Hello, Marianne,' was all he could think of to say.

She kissed him, perhaps she believed she had to.

'Where are you staying?' he asked.

'The Hyatt. I'm going back tomorrow, Kelly.'

Incredible joy flooded him and he hid it expertly. Six days in Jersey, alone. If he survived tonight, he would survive anything.

'Try Leibermann. My daddy's secretary made the booking two weeks ago.'

'Ah, yes,' the receptionist said. 'That would be for Miss Marianne Leibermann?'

Marianne looked back at Kelly and shrugged. 'You know what Millie's like. She's always getting things wrong.'

'No problem,' Kelly said. 'I can come back later if—'

'No, no. We have to talk some time. Better sooner than later.' Marianne took the key and Kelly followed to her room.

Hannah woke to the footsteps, one heavier than the other. The cell door squealed when he came in. She stared at his boot and drew the stinking blanket tighter around her broken body. James Daley's words echoed still:

How say you, prisoner? Guilty or not guilty?

I've done no wrong in the eyes of my God.

Then you will taken at four o'clock on the morrow to the village square and there you will be burnt alive and your ashes scattered to the wind.

Kelly turned away from the hotel window and the grimy view

of London. Marianne was ordering a lunch for two from room service and he hoped, how he hoped, she would not order champagne as well.

No champagne. Malt scotch instead. After two glasses, they'd be arguing. For the second time in his life he was sick to the stomach and afraid. Afraid of a loss he could not avoid. Perhaps Rebecca was right. He would rather face Attila the Hun than have to face who and what he was. And perhaps they should eat first before he asked her how Tommy was these days. It was the question foremost in his mind, on the tip of his tongue. But it was all a matter of timing.

'I guess you know why I came,' she said.

'No, I never could read your mind that well.'

'Kelly, I'm caught in the middle of someone else's grudge. Daddy won't give an inch and you're just as stubborn and stupid as he is.'

Corey's face came to mind.

Rich, rich. Fat. No hair. Glasses . . . You know well. Very well. No do this, please, no do this!

He still felt Thuy's fear. That woman had been bought, too. How many others are out there? he wondered and took his attentions back to his wife.

'I never thought he'd hate you 'cos you were Indian. I knew it wouldn't be easy but I really thought he'd get used to the idea once he got to know you.'

Kelly wondered where her palm cards were hidden.

'Now, I know he ranted about me having mixed-blood babies and I know that's what upset you the most. But we never talked about it, Kelly. Hell, I don't want babies.'

Kelly shook his head and turned away.

'I know you've got another woman.'

'It's news to me, Marianne.'

'Oh, come on. Don't be coy. What do you think I'll do? Cry? I know you been unfaithful. I know coming home's just a chore for you. But I want to know, is this Australian nice? She don't talk funny, does she?'

'What Australian are you talking about?'

'I know who she is, Kelly!'

Great, he thought. She's getting angry. 'And who told you all this garbage? Your daddy?'

She almost said yes, then remembered she wasn't supposed to say a thing. Kelly's thought processes split. Part of his attention remained on his wife and what she would soon ask of him—freedom—and the other part of his mind leapt steadily away, back to a Georgia mansion and forward to the White House. 'Does Corey know I'm meeting you here?'

'Kelly, he wants this over with as much as I do. I want a divorce. I want a divorce now before I start hating you. But you have to promise me you won't ruin my daddy. You can't.' Her voice shook, her hand shook as she poured herself another drink and cursed because she couldn't get the ice from the tray in the refrigerator.

'I know you're screwing her and I know you must love her if you bed her, so where's that leave me?' She fought on with the ice tray and in a fit of anger threw it to the floor. Ice cubes sprayed across the tiles and she swore again. 'God damn it, Kelly! I know she looks like me! I want out! I want out now before I go mad. I'm going crazy!'

'I tell you what. I'll let you and your daddy off the hook if you tell me two things.'

The glass at her lips ceased further movement and she turned her head towards him.

'I want to know if your father was in England on the tenth of March.' The day Faraday died.

'Maybe.'

'What do you mean, maybe?'

'It was March, sure, but how do you expect me to know which day? He was gone a month or more.'

'Who's screwing you, Marianne?' Kelly asked calmly. 'Is it Tommy Lethbridge? Is he going to marry you as soon as you're divorced? What's your old man promised him?'

And he knew by the way she so vehemently denied it, that Tommy Lethbridge was definitely the man of the moment. The man of the past twelve months.

Kelly shook his head sadly and picked up the ice tray from the carpet. He twisted it and cubes popped. 'You'll get a letter from my lawyers next week.' He kissed her forehead and walked out.

Kelly used the public phone in the foyer but Pete's lines were engaged. He left a message with Creedy that he'd try later and when he hung up, he sensed the presences closing in. He also sensed the crowded hotel foyer.

'Don't think about it, sunshine,' came the whispered threat in a voice he had not heard for two years. 'We'll do this quietly.'

Kelly turned slowly.

Tommy, and beside him, smiling brightly, was Thuy.

He woke slowly. He was on his side on a stinking, damp wooden floor. His body was aching and alternately numb; his hands restrained behind his back. He looked behind and followed the rope to a crossbeam on the ceiling and a pulley.

His eyes adjusted quickly to the darkness. It wasn't a natural darkness. It was still daytime. Tri Star Lines. The trademark was everywhere.

He remembered little, except for the Indonesian's hand taking his, being poured into the back of a limo, and seeing a face which was sickly familiar. Then there was nothing. Until now.

He heard feet—a heavy set of male feet, shoe soles labouring up . . . he counted . . . twenty-two metal stairs. Spiral stairs. And he heard the familiar wheezing, the strained breathing followed by one voice: 'What the hell did they put him up here for?'

Kelly closed his eyes voluntarily, wincing a little in anticipation of what would come.

An Italian leather shoe with 230 pounds behind it kicked him square in the kidneys.

'Hi, Daddy,' Kelly whispered.

Rebecca was watching the pre-dinner basketball game when she felt a strong pain in her lower back. It had felt like an invisible kick. 'Rebecca? You okay?'

Billy beside her was concerned. And so was she. Concerned for the baby.

'What the hell is it?' he asked.

But she didn't reply. The kick came again, strong enough to thrust her forwards. Billy caught her arm before she landed on the floor.

She saw Kelly with the same sign around his neck. 'Return to sender'. 'Kelly,' she whispered. 'He's there, Billy. Tri Star. No, no, it's Tri Star *Lines*. It's the warehouse where Jamie died. It's near docks somewhere. They've got Kelly now.'

Kelly looked into Corey Leibermann's eyes. Corey James Leibermann, his wife's father, was not only a long way from home but, it seemed, he was also on very familiar ground.

Kelly was hanging with his hands behind his back, twisted. The weight of his body was dislocating his shoulders each time he moved. Breathed. 'What're you waiting for, Corey? The rest of your triple-K senate team to arrive?'

Corey moved his tired, obese, tweed-suited body across the attic. Pale, late sunshine tried in vain to penetrate a tiny, taped window behind Kelly's head. It was enough to make the fat man squint when he turned his attentions upwards. 'Kills with her mind, does she, this new woman of yours?'

Perhaps she could, but Kelly could kill with his feet. One kick to the chest and he could rupture the heart. But Kelly's shoulders would dislocate and he knew Corey wasn't alone. He couldn't see, but Kelly sensed the presence of others. How many was anyone's guess. 'Samperi died of cerebral haemorrhage,' he managed to say. The fat man grabbed at the bound feet and twisted. The only screams were internal until he heard what Corey said next.

'And how would you like Rebecca to die, son? It's easy enough to get her here, but you know that. I could hang her right there beside you, couldn't I? I could let Thuy or maybe Tommy have some fun with her first. Would you like that, son?'

As if answering a silent call, Kelly heard the sounds of high heels clacking on the steel stairs. Thuy appeared and gave him a huge smile. 'I have been waiting for you,' she said softly and lowered him to within a few inches of the floor. 'I can kill you quick or I can kill you slow. So you will talk to us now. Now it is your turn to talk to me about the woman, and who and what it is she knows.'

Kelly closed his eyes. 'She knows nothing.'

'I have all the time in the world, son,' Corey said. 'And so has Thuy. We have at least a week, haven't we, boy?' Kelly watched as his father-in-law nodded to the Indonesian and he went down the spiral stairs.

Some things he did not want to see.

Rebecca was half aware of discussion, argument, conjecture and Billy Macpherson's arm about her shoulder, constantly. He was giving her strength. Telling her that, yes, they would find him now. He had his tracking device in his dog tags. They'd find him. But there were too many talking at once, too many questions which had no answers. 'How many are there?' the colonel asked.

'Three,' Rebecca said softly. 'The Indonesian, Marianne's boyfriend and her father.'

'Senator Leibermann?'

'Is he fat? About sixty? Does he wear a tweed three-piece suit? Does he chainsmoke? Does he keep his cigarettes in a gold case?'

Pete Hamill's face was paling quickly.

'It's the same place where Jamie died. I *know* it is. I saw the Tri Star Lines name and symbol again. Kelly told me it's a CIA front. How many times do I have to tell you where he is? Do something before he dies!'

'Your name!'

'Hannah.'

'Higher!'

And the two pulled on the ropes. Hannah, naked, hands bound behind her back was strung by rope to a hook in the ceiling of the tower. Her shoulders were dislocating. Another weight was put on the rope at her feet. She was tearing in two and there was too much pain to scream.

'Your name!'

'Tell me what it is you want me to say!'

'Your name!'

'Hannah!'

'No! No! I want the name you were given by the abomination!'

'Hannah is my name—'

The impact of ice-cold water jarred him awake. Kelly focussed on the face. Thuy again. Where the hell was Tommy? Waiting until he was at his weakest?

'You ready to talk yet, sailor?'

'Nolan, KF, Commander, United States—' the repeated recital was interrupted by a shriek of agony as she heaved him higher.

'You starting to piss me off, sailor.'

'Great,' Kelly tried to say. 'I can't help you, Thuy. Sorry, but I can't because I know shit.'

'I think you know more than shit.'

Kelly felt cold female hands coating his bare feet in something greasy. Cooking oil. A small electric radiator was put on the floor and turned upwards. The plug was jammed into an extension lead. Kelly watched the bars glow a deep orange. Then he felt the warmth. A warmth which would become heat. And then it'd burn. One quiet minute later, he was asked, again, 'What does she know about the President's shooting?'

'Shit. She knows shit.'

'What does she know? I hear she has seen it happen and she has seen who too does the shooting.' Thuy lit a cigarette. She studied it with great interest. Kelly could feel his soles blistering.

'She has not seen the assassins. If she has she hasn't told me.'

'But she tells you everything.'

'No!'

'I can bring her here tonight. You would like that?'

'No—'

'I can bring her here, make her ugly. All over ugly with this.' She held up the cigarette, took a slow drag and blew the smoke up into his face. And like a dancer, she took something from her boot. Just as he had done to her, she released the blade close to his face. 'Or all over ugly with this. Like you.' The blade seared down his cheek.

'I'm going to fucking kill you this time!'

Thuy laughed and stepped away. 'What does she know?'

'Nolan, K.F. Commnder, United States Navy—' Kelly prayed she would come closer while he rattled off his serial number. Just a little bit closer, come on honey, just a little closer . . .

'Which airbase?'

'Nolan, K.F. Commander—'

'Does it happen during the President's stopover in Britain?'

'Nolan, K.F. Commander, United States Navy—' Kelly was losing consciousness again until he felt the blade tickling at his ribs.

'Why did she kill my Gene?' Thuy asked and she seemed a little disappointed when suddenly, his chin hit his chest.

For a moment, Thuy thought he was dead. 'You wake up!'

Nothing.

Thuy released the pulley and Kelly hit the floor, crumbling. He felt cold hands on his chest, trying to feel a heartbeat while he freed his hands from the tangle of knots at his wrists.

'You wake now!'

It took Kelly half a second to snatch the knife and drive it into the Indonesian woman's heart, push her away. And as he heard Corey's voice, 'What's goin' on up there?' and the slow step of the fat man echoed on the spiral stairs, Kelly cut through the rope at his feet and moving faster than he believed was possible, he crouched by the stairs, waiting for Corey to make it to the top.

'Thuy?'

Kelly heard the heavy breathing and waited for the legs to appear. He drove Thuy's switchblade into the back of the senator's left knee. He didn't hear the squeal of pain. He didn't feel the thud as the huge body literally shook the floorboards on impact. He searched for a weapon he knew must exist amid the clothing, found it, pulled the knife from the leg, and heaved the fat old man to his back. He vaguely heard the pleas. His instinct, against reason, was to kill. Jam the gun into the pleading mouth and shoot. He had no witnesses. He could make it look like suicide. Reason overrode the need. Kelly could cause more damage by leaving the senator alive to face inquiries. Inquiries which would destroy the lifestyle which meant more than his life. Kelly lifted the gun away, rose unsteadily, and reached for the rope which had been used on him. 'You fucking breathe too loud, I'll kill you,' he rasped. 'Sit up.' The senator tried to get up, hurrying when he felt his own gun crunch against his teeth again.

Kelly, one-handed, tied the old man's hands behind his back and pushed him onto his face. He trussed him, stuffed a monogrammed handkerchief into the mouth and left him to stare at Thuy's open, permanently surprised and dead eyes.

Kelly tried to stop his face bleeding profusely as he limped on his blistered, bare feet silently down the metal stairs, trying to find a way out of the darkened warehouse, through the packing crates and storage containers. He heard the door opening, was blinded by the sudden light. He swallowed rising nausea as Marianne came in, closed the door, stopped to light a cigarette and walked on.

'Daddy? Is he dead yet?'

There was no answer except a muffled voice from upstairs.

'Daddy?'

Kelly watched her take the stairs and he heard her inevitable scream. 'Come on, Daddy, you've gotta walk! We have to get out of here! We gotta go!'

Kelly imagined her trying to untie her father—hopeless, she couldn't untie a shoelace—and he imagined her old man telling her to get out, get help. Instead, he heard:

'Get Tommy, girl, go get Tommy.'

Marianne came down alone and Kelly was waiting at the bottom of the stairs. She squealed again as an arm folded across her shoulders and she was pulled across the floor. 'If you scream I will kill you,' he whispered in her ear. 'Where's Tommy?'

'Who?' she squeaked, unable to move because when she tried, his grip tightened.

'Where is Tommy?'

'Outside in the car but I didn't . . . It wasn't my idea . . .'

'Why does he,' and Kelly motioned to the floor above her head, 'Want Robert Glover dead?'

'It's nothing to do with me. I don't know. What you gonna do?'

'Why do you want me dead, Marianne?'

She tried to laugh. She tried very hard. And when she tried to move, his arm started to choke her. 'Jesus, Kelly—'

'Tommy fucking Lethbridge.' His voice was full of disgust.

'What about her, huh?' she whimpered. 'What about that fortune teller?'

'You will tell me how you know about Rebecca Miller. You will tell me now or I will fucking kill you just as easily as I killed that Indonesian upstairs.'

'Daddy told me. Said the NSC and Defence Department brought her over to help find the people who want the President dead. That's what he said. He also said you were screwing her and the only way I'd ever get Tommy is if you were dead. He said you knew too much to be safe alive and divorced.'

'Do you want Tommy so bad?'

'Kelly, don't hurt me.'

'Is your father one of the people who want Glover dead?'

She wouldn't answer. Kelly, holding her tight, dangerously tight against him as he stood with his back to the wall, was overwhelmed by her perfume.

'Is it because of his arms deals? Because Glover's dissolving the CIA?' Kelly whispered into her ear. 'Or does he want him dead because he's black?'

'Kelly, what you gonna do to me? Will you let me go? I'll call Pete, I'll tell him where you are. I'll do that. Just let me go. Please, let me go?'

The warehouse was illuminated again. Sudden blinding light from the doorway. Tommy Lethbridge walked out of that light, his hands were on the back of his head and he was followed.

By Pete.

Pete and four others.

'Clear,' Kelly called. 'The place is clear.' He pushed Marianne away and into Ammo's waiting arms. 'Get her out of my sight.'

'Where's Leibermann?' Pete asked.

Kelly used the Browning in his hand to point to the attic. 'He's waiting for Thanksgiving. The Indonesian's dead.'

Without a word, Pete sent two men upstairs.

'You okay?' he asked. Kelly nodded and took two steps towards his friend. His legs ceased to hold him upright and he hit the floor, face first.

CHAPTER 20

'COME WITH me, Hannah,' Redmond said quietly.

'I canna walk.'

Redmond looked down at her legs, her feet. They were twisted. Crushed by iron claws; burnt from the fires.

'Ah, look at this. The lover's here again. 'Tis so sweet to see. Is Catherine too busy to accommodate you now, what with the bairn and all?'

Redmond ignored Isobel—the one who had incriminated others so freely with words as lethal as the plague itself. Just like Nell. Just like Cathy.

Nothing mattered now.

He lifted Hannah into his arms. She was very thin, weighed nothing. He wrapped the blanket around her and carried her away deeper into the castle where all was still and quiet at this small hour. The hour of reckoning.

Redmond barricaded the door. Let them never be found.

He sat with his burden in a dark corner and held her against him. She whimpered in his lap. She couldn't breathe without pain. God knew what they had done to her this time because there was nothing left in her eyes. Nothing at all.

'Hannah?'

She looked up at him. His fingers enveloped her entire hand. Pain shot through her body—all her fingers, too, were broken. There were tears in his eyes, the big man was crying. Then the tears were gone, wiped away on a sleeve. 'The boy's growing,' he said. 'Is true what they say. He looks like me but it's you I see in his eyes.' He touched her face, the huge fingers so delicate. 'Smiles a lot, he does. He's a happy wee thing an' he loves me an' I canna take it. I canna bear to go home. I canna bear the way he looks at me. Tis as if he knows. I canna bear lookin' at Cathy. Canna bear what it is I've done. Is a pain I canna take.'

Hannah's eyes closed, her head lolled in the crook of his arm and his heart was very loud, especially when he held her tighter. The flagstone was cold and damp against her bare legs. My son, she thought. My son's happy.

'Hannah?' The eyes flickered open and tried to hold on his face. 'This should never'a happen. None of it. But you had the marks and you wouldn't confess . . . Is no stopping the Puritans now. Is a madness about. Nell of Craigmore, she's not stopped since her baby died.'

The eyes closed again. She hated seeing him cry.

'I love you, Hannah, you must believe me. Tis you I'll love forever. And only you.'

His words meant nothing because she heard little. She kept losing his face.

'This evenin' they'll be comin' to take you and burn you. You won't confess so you'll be burnt alive. Was William McTaggart to tell me. I come as fast as I could, try and stop it. But I canna. Have pleaded with James Daley. He says his hands be tied though he let me come to you now. But I canna let 'em do it. Should never'a got this far. Should never'a happen. You with child then. Should have saved ye.'

The baby, she thought. My son.

'I'd make it right if I could but have my time with you again. You believe that, Hannah. Please?' Her eyes closed. 'You must believe me. Will you not look at me?'

There was silence. It was still, deathly except for the sounds of two people breathing. She lay broken, fragile in his arms. Every breath for her was agony.

'God help me, it shouldn't be this way. Can you hear me, Hannah? Will you not look at me?'

'I hear you, I see you—'

'God, help me make it right,' he whispered.

'Just let me die. Let me go—' And there, beside him, she could see her father. He looked so well, so bright, as if he were but waiting. But he was so ill. Dying. 'Da?'

'You da, no, he died weeks ago. I'd not told you—'

'Da?' she asked, happy. So happy, suddenly.

'He be dead, Hannah.'

'No, he be here. He be here. Can you not see?'

Redmond tried to follow her gaze. He could see no one. He

looked down at her. Her eyes were bright for the first time in six long, agonising months.

'May God forgive me for this I do,' Redmond whispered, casting the filthy blanket aside, reaching into his boot. He took his knife and held it to her heart. He tried to look into her eyes and for a brief moment, she seemed to know, and by God, there was no fear. 'I'll love you forever, Hannah.'

'Aye—' she whispered. 'Aye.'

He drove the knife in, hard. Her eyes widened. Blood poured from her mouth. Odd noises escaped her throat. But she didn't die. He thrust it in again, and suddenly she was dead.

Redmond held the lifeless body close but there was no relief from his agonies and nor would there ever be. His love hung across his lap like a rag as he sat there a long, long time with his head back against the stone wall. 'I'd make it right if I could,' were the only words he could say. A litany fused with tears. 'God help me make it right, even if it's wrong I do.' His fingers blindly touched her face, her throat, the knife buried to the hilt in her breast. He pulled it out and plunged it deep once more into his own.

Kelly woke from the sudden pain in his ribs. And as breathing returned, so did reality. This reality.

A heart-shaped face framed by long, wild hair was looming above, barely recognisable through the dense fog. He felt as if he were drowning, slowly. Kelly fought to remain awake. Forced himself out of the depths to pain in his face, his ribs, his back. His feet felt raw. And when he tried to move, agony shot through the shoulders he'd dislocated.

Memory returned in a heated flood.

'Marianne?'

It was the only name he could think of. Her terrified face was his last conscious memory.

Rebecca stepped away from the bed. Her excuse—to let the doctor through. And I believed he loved me, she thought with a breaking heart.

All my beliefs have been lost. Somewhere the person I used to be has become hopelessly lost. All my beliefs, my ideals.

Always be kind.

(To people who saw kindness as a weakness, not a strength.)

Love as much as you can.

(People who reciprocated the intensity of feeling by throwing a torch to the bonfire. Standing back. Relieved it was over. For then life could go on.)

Help those who cannot help themselves.

Help those who will in turn help others.

All my beliefs, she thought. Where are they now?

He wakes and the first name he utters is his wife's.

'Marianne?'

Where there is life, there is hope. Always. Always. Why did she feel so dead inside?

'Aye, laddie. Be still now,' Mike said, his tone unusually gentle. 'Marianne's off havin' a wee chat to the FBI and a few secret service boys who came over, specially to visit.'

'She wanted me dead—'

'Aye, aye. We know.'

And as Rebecca listened quietly, she felt her heart beginning to come to life once again.

'Corey—'

'Aye, we know that, too. It's out of our hands now but I'll be betting you a hundred quid, lad, that before the year's out, the Corey Leibermann story will be a tele-movie. Aye?' Mike said with a smile.

Which Kelly tried hard to return. 'How'd you know? How'd you find me?'

'It's the lassie you'd best be thanking for saving your miserable butt this time.'

'Rebecca's here?' he asked, dazed. He didn't know where here was, until the room suddenly cleared, and behind McLaren, with her thumb in her mouth, Rebecca. She looked as though she'd been forced to walk barefoot through a minefield.

'I'll leave you for a wee time. You'll not move, Kelly. And you'll not upset him,' Mike said to Rebecca on his way out.

She didn't know what to say, what to do. His ribs were strapped because X-rays had shown three were fractured. His shoulders had been dislocated. His feet were covered with infected, broken blisters. There were rope burns on his wrists and ankles, he had bruised kidneys and the facial laceration had required twelve stitches.

'I told you not to bloody well go,' she said with angry tears in her eyes.

Kelly beckoned her closer and reached out, despite the pain, to touch her face. It seemed that he already knew what had happened but no questions surfaced. There would be time enough for questions later. 'It's so good to see you.'

When she touched his hand, he felt this pain slowly dissipate into a dull, almost numbing sensation. 'Don't leave me,' he mumbled, and his eyes closed. He could fight no more.

Rebecca kept hold of his hand and silently pleaded for help.

Mike came in fifteen minutes later to find her sitting on the narrow bed. 'Please, Captain. Not yet. Not yet.'

And the big Scot retreated because Pete Hamill had shown him a certain videotape which should have explained how the girl healed with a touch.

But watching that tape left the Presbyterian doctor thinking again about miracles.

'How long is it you'd be needing, lass?'

Forever, she thought. 'I'll let you know.' She turned back to Kelly and heard another's voice from the doorway:

'I thought you'd be here.'

Pete was still dressed in his black assault uniform; he looked younger in black and more handsome if it were possible. They had talked of an extraction, not a rescue. Apparently the location she had given them was indeed a CIA import/export company, also located via satellite fix from the tracking device within Kelly's dog tags.

'I've come to thank you, Rebecca. Without your foresight we would never have known until it was too late. Thank you, again.'

Pete stepped closer and looked down on Kelly's peaceful, sleeping face. Sometimes he wondered what it would be like to see exactly what this girl saw. Know what she knew.

'I just received word from the White House. The President will be making his stopover in England in twelve days' time.'

'Twelve days?'

'Twelve days. Will you believe me if I said it's been different having you here with us?'

Rebecca smiled at the colonel. 'I haven't left yet, Pete.'

Kelly woke to a strip of bright sunlight blinding him. He felt a female's hands on his body. Some kind of soapy cloth, too. 'What the—'

'Morning,' Rebecca said as she continued the sponge bath. 'I haven't done this for years.'

Kelly tried to sit up, to protest. Futile. 'What day is it?' he barked.

'Friday.'

'What happened to Thursday?'

'You slept for twenty-eight hours. How do you feel now?'

'Good enough to be out of here and bathing myself. Do you mind?'

Who's being modest now? she wondered. 'Captain's orders.'

'Let me out of here. I've got to go.'

'Where?' She enjoyed this reversal of situations.

'You know where.'

'Oh, *that* where. Here you are, Commander.' She gave him a spouted receptacle. Kelly took it and threw it across the room. He heaved himself from the bed and limped his way to the bathroom.

Angry.

'Is it something I've said?' Rebecca called, loudly.

There was no answer until Kelly reappeared and began hunting for his clothes.

'Your clothes are in the laundry. I asked if this foul mood was caused by something I said.'

Still he hunted for something to wear, apart from the paper hospital gown.

'Kelly, I am talking to you!'

He turned to her with a gruff, 'What?' hitting her with what the boys normally called the death stare.

'What have I done now?' she asked with a sigh. 'Is this change of attitude because of me? Something I said, something I did?'

'Absolutely. You've got ten days left here. Ten days, then you're gone. What were you going to do, Rebecca? Write me? Send me a few annual photos?' His anger was gone, replaced with something she had never seen before. He was in pain, but not physical pain.

'Kelly, what are you talking about?'

'You think I don't know you're pregnant?'

She felt as if she'd been punched. 'Who told you that?'

'Oh, for Christ's sake. Look at you.'

She looked down at herself. She didn't think she was gaining any weight yet.

'Look at your face. Your feet. Your . . . How far gone are you?'

'Who told you!' she yelled and again he mimicked her.

'No one told me. No one *has* to tell me. But I have been waiting for you to have the guts to tell me what it seems you can't. I may as well wait for fucking ever.'

'I was going to tell you.'

'When? Thirty seconds before you got on your plane? See you next life, Kelly? By the way, I'm having your baby? Goodbye? Is that what you were going to do?'

She couldn't face the devastation in his eyes.

'I was going to tell you, but there was never a right moment. If you weren't on duty, you were in the wrong mood. Kelly, you have enough to worry about without me adding to it.'

He didn't believe her. 'No. No, you were afraid of how I'd react. Have you ever considered I might enjoy worrying about you? That I only worry about people I care about?'

Her silences were always confirmations.

'What are you planning to do?' he asked.

'Go home, I suppose.'

'And raise the kid yourself. Alone.'

'Thousands of women manage being sole parents.'

'So I'm not the kind of father you'd want? Why? Because I don't wear flowers in my hair and stand on street corners waving placards that say stop the wars? I kill people instead?'

'You know that's not true.'

'You've never considered me, have you? What I might want. What I might need. What'd you think I'd do, Rebecca? Deny it and light another fire?'

'It should never have happened.'

'Oh, right. It should never have happened. What's this mean? The love and light lady's going to abort now?'

Rebecca fought the urge to slap his face.

Gazes met and held. Anger in hers, confusion in his. 'Don't you love me?' he asked. 'You think I don't know that if it wasn't for you I wouldn't be here right now? I wouldn't be alive? Jesus, Rebecca, all I have ever wanted was you. You and a family.'

'What about your wife, Kelly!'

'What about her?'

'You have to choose. You have to choose!'

'I already have. I told her I was divorcing her.'

'Because you knew I was pregnant?'

'Even if you weren't, I'd still want you to stay.'

Kelly heard the soft voice ask, 'Why can't you say you love me?'

'Isn't showing it enough?'

'No.'

'When I said I would willingly die for you, I damned near did.'

But she needed to hear more. He could see that in her eyes.

Kelly told her that he loved her and that this time he'd make it right. And he held her while she cried.

CHAPTER 21

REBECCA WOKE when he stirred and the warmth of his long, naked body was no longer curled into hers. 'Kelly?' She sat up in his narrow bed and squinted into the darkness as he pulled a uniform from his closet. He didn't say a thing. 'What are you doing?'

Nothing.

Rebecca pulled the bedcovers tighter and watched him dress. It was almost midnight. What on earth was he doing this for?

'I will come back. I'd like you to have faith in that.'

'Kelly, what—'

Scramble alarms split the stillness.

Rebecca grabbed her dressing gown and was still pulling it on when Kelly bolted from his room but he didn't hear her call—the alarms were too piercing. When she made it to the door, red flashing lights strobed in the corridor but Kelly was already gone, down the stairs. She followed, dazed.

On the second stairwell, someone bolted past her, hit her shoulder and she rebounded into the wall. She heard the apology but the man had disappeared down the stairs before she knew who he'd been, and thundering through the noise, she felt more than heard the choppers coming in.

Halfway to the mess she hugged the wall as six black-clothed bodies shot by. By the time she reached the gym, she did not know who was who amid all the black-clad soldiers.

The clock gave her the time. It was five past midnight.

'What's happening?'

She was ignored.

'What's happening! Someone tell me what's happening!'

It wasn't a simulation. It felt real. Very real. One of the thirty-strong team looked back at her and nodded.

Kelly. *I will come back.*

And they were gone.

I will come back.

I'm not the kind of father you want cos I don't wear flowers in my hair. I kill people instead.

No, Kelly, she thought. This is my fear. My worst fear. That one day you will not come back to me.

All was quiet until she heard the squeak of boots on the polished wooden floor and the Scot's gentle voice, 'Come on then, lass.'

She looked up into Mike's eyes. 'What's happening?'

'There's a siege at the Israeli Embassy in Kensington. We're working with Alpha.'

'Alpha?'

'Another outfit a mite like ours, lass.'

Kelly had known. Again, he had known. Stay with me tonight? he had asked again. Please stay with me tonight. And while she had slept so soundly, amid gentle dreams, he was awake. Awake and watching the clock. And waiting. How could she pretend that he was anything but what he was? He was everything she had ever despised about humanity yet he was the man she loved. Deeply.

And the Scot must have read her thoughts.

'Perhaps you'll be handy in the infirmary but I hope you won't be needed.'

Rebecca sat on the bench where she had sat to watch them play basketball. The terrible emptiness crept in again. Somewhere she must have mislaid the person she used to be.

Mike sat down beside her and put his arm around her. Rebecca accepted the offered shoulder. He didn't say a word for a long time. 'Come lass, we could be watching it on TV while we wait.'

The TV on the wall in the bar interrupted its telecast every half hour for a live cross to South Kensington. She sat, still in her dressing gown and barefooted, with Frank and Mike. The handful of men left behind were quiet. Very quiet.

The stalemate had begun at midday. This terrorist group, calling itself The New Freedom Order, was led by a Shiite moslem, Omil Niazi.

'N.F.O? Not fucking original, either,' someone mumbled.

Omil Niazi's face appeared on the screen with a brief, if not illustrious history. He looked so young. So terribly young. But there was something *more* about this Arab's face, too. Rebecca felt the pang of fleeting familiarity, as if she'd seen him before. *Somewhere. Somewhere.*

He was barricaded with an as yet unknown number of terrorists and hostages in the generator room on the roof of the Israeli Embassy in South Kensington. No demands had been or were likely to be met. It wasn't really news. It was almost an everyday occurrence somewhere in the world. Now, Rebecca was close enough to touch and feel the reality of it.

She wasn't watching this on the six o'clock news at home, thousands of miles away, virtually untouched by a drama that others enacted. At home she could turn the TV off in case her esoteric philosophies of reasoning, objectivity, cause, effect, and Love Conquering All Darkness suddenly took flight.

The TV's off switch would not bring back people she cared about. People she loved. Nor could an off switch deny reality. Kelly was right. Her perfect world was an idealistic fantasy.

I know it's not the kind of world a person like you is used to but there's precious little I can do about that.

She looked about at the faces of those who, for some reason, this time hadn't rolled. Most of them wanted to be there. It was their job. Their life.

The reasons for the regular live crosses to South Kensington lay on the concrete at the bottom of the Embassy stairs. Two now. Two bodies tipped from the roof. The first was an old man's, the second even older. And there they lay. Anyone attempting to retrieve the bodies was shot at from the bunker. That's what they called it now. It wasn't a generator room any more. It was a bunker. And it was war and innocents were dying. One hostage for each hour of delay. They had begun with the old, next would be the young.

One of the grounded Nighthawks cursed. The TV showed to the eager populace footage of the first body dropping to the ground. Rebecca closed her eyes. She couldn't look. Pain choked her—the pain of injustice. The pain of pity for the innocents. It was never the innocents who wanted the violence, the hate, the death. What was wrong with humanity? What was wrong with these men here? They were all discussing what they would do if they were the OC.

'There's no hope of getting those people out. Not from there,' Mike said quietly. Rebecca looked into his eyes. The captain was planning his own strategy. Was he missing this? Was he too old to do this now? Was his only job to tend the wounded when they returned? He may have been the Nighthawks MO, and a father of six daughters, but he was also a soldier and for the first time, Rebecca saw that soldier gleaming in his eyes. All trace of the healer was gone and her heart was breaking. Then Mike grabbed her hand. 'You see that, lass? They've got a bunker on the roof and all the hostages in with them. Drove 'em to the roof they did.'

'But they're only mentioning the Alpha Assault Group.'

'We don't exist,' someone else said.

'But how do you know who's who in a situation like that? You all look the same.'

Kelly recognised Ammo by the bloodshot eyes. He was allergic to his own sweat under the respirator eyepieces. There were eighteen civilians locked on the roof of the adjoining building and an ancient elder tree impairing views from one rooftop to the other. The terrorist count in that small steel bunker was a guess. No one knew the exact number.

While clearing the embassy, Alpha had taken out three terrorists on the third floor and four hostages had been fed through the library window. One was picked off during the retreat and he still lay down there alongside his rescuer—one of the Alpha boys who'd lost the back of his head.

These boys had anti-tank weaponry. There was no way to the roof apart from the series of flying foxes already linking the buildings. Infiltration from the air was impossible. Choppers couldn't get close enough.

What they needed was to blow the crap out of that steel structure. And everyone inside would die. Macpherson, Alpha's expert and the regular army bomb team did not think such a move a good idea, not with eighteen hostages in a twelve-by-twelve area. No, Kelly thought. We need to strip it bare. Peel it like a banana. Pick them off. We need Rebecca here to drop that door, just like she dropped the doors at the asylum. That's what we need, he thought.

'Kel?'

He looked back at Ammo, mask off now, wiping his eyes.

'We need the pipsqueak here to do her stuff and knock that fucking door down. She's done it once, she can do it again.'

Kelly didn't reply.

'Have you seen the tapes of the PSI testing?'

No, Kelly had not seen the tapes. He didn't have to.

'It's for you,' Mike said and held the phone out to her. Rebecca's face drained of colour. She shook her head. Mike was quietly adamant. Rebecca, shaky, took the phone.

'Kelly?'

'You get bullet and flameproofed and get here! We need you!'

'What?'

Kelly cringed behind the rented truck and screamed down the field phone words she'd understand and hung up. One of Shiites had been using him for target practice from the ventilator shaft of the bunker as he'd weaved his way back to the temporary command post. Pete was crouching with him. 'Can she do it?' came the question.

'What do you think?' Kelly said. 'If she's upset enough, anything is possible.'

'Is there an alternative?'

'Depends how much of a body count you want.'

'There are four small children up there, Kelly. One is the son of the ambassador.'

Kelly took three deep breaths before replacing his respirator and he ran back out into the line of fire, weaved his way across the narrow street and into the diplomat's residence.

'Lass?'

Rebecca put the phone down. 'He wants me there. I have to get bullet and flameproofed and I have to go. They need me. Harlem's coming back to get me right now.'

Mike ran her down to the armoury and found the smallest flameproof they had. It seemed eight sizes too big. The bulletproof the captain helped her into first wasn't as heavy as she'd thought it would be. It hung to the top of her thighs. He helped her into the black coveralls, rolled the sleeves back to her wrists. He put a balaclava over her hair and pulled the hood over her head.

After the thick socks came a pair of black lace-up boots, far too big. Then came yet another coat of body armour. This one reached her knees.

'And don't you look a sight,' Mike joked.

'What do they want me to do?' she asked, huge blue eyes alleviating the ferocious image that the assault gear always conjured up. Rebecca could barely lift her feet.

'I thought you were the psychic?'

'Come on, Mike, I'm frightened.'

'Good. I hear that helps you work these miracles.' He bundled her out of the armoury and out to the helipad at the back of the gym. They waited in the cold darkness for Harlem to arrive. As always, the wait took forever. 'Are you cold?' the captain asked. The girl was shaking, her eyes were still huge. She didn't reply. Mike put his arm around her and gave her a warm fatherly hug, after which she clung to his arm.

'If they assault to clear, God knows how many civilians will die. That would be a last resort and Omil knows it. He's quite secure where he is. He has the advantage.'

'But what can I do?'

'Think of yourself as a liberator. You've nothing against Jews?'

'Oh, Mike—' She was close to tears now.

He held her again, a little tighter this time. 'Just do what you did to our front doors and the lads'll do the rest.'

'You make it sound so easy.'

'For you, lass, it is.'

As the chopper lights approached and descended, she looked at the captain's face. 'God be with you.' He tapped her behind and off she stumbled towards the chopper. No sooner had the door closed than the chopper was lifting, banking. And Mike whispered to himself, 'But God's always with His own, isn't He, lassie?'

Far too late she realised that this had nothing whatsoever to do with the safety of the President of the United States. 'What am I doing here!'

Harlem's dark eyes widened as he dared a glance at her. He had a fair idea what they wanted her for, but word had it she was pregnant to the commander and Harlem could not believe

Kelly would get her into a situation like this. He remained quiet. The best thing to do with any of the commander's wild ideas. Wild ideas that always worked, somehow.

She was studying her hands as if she had never seen them before and a look of abject terror was in her eyes. She grabbed Harlem's hand and held it tightly. His eyes widened further.

Rebecca did not pick up a thing. No images, no impressions. She looked at Harlem and he tried not to squirm. He had no aura.

She pleaded for Emmanuel's help but all she received was an echo mixed with resounding static.

The bulletproof was interfering. It had to be the body armour.

Harlem saw her unbuckle the seatbelt. He almost spoke, then his eyes widened. She was unfastening the armour, lifting it off. She looked at her hand again. She grabbed his hand. 'What's going on?' he said. 'What the hell you doing!'

Rebecca slipped out of the coveralls and took the armour off. He saw a splash of white breast before she crawled her arms back into the overalls, zipped it up and replaced the hood. 'What the . . . what are you doing?' His voice was so piercingly high he squeaked.

'Trust me,' she said and grabbed his hand once more. The relief was overwhelming—she had a clear image of Harlem when he was young, racing about a basketball court and stealing a bicycle. She let go and closed her eyes in thanks.

'Rebecca, you gotta put that armour back on!'

'No!'

Harlem was on the radio to the CO. He thrust the headset at her, Pete's voice was crackling through. 'What the hell are you doing! Put the armour back on!'

'It's interfering with the electromagnetics and the electrostatics! Trust me! I know what I am doing!'

The colonel started cursing so she handed the radio back to Harlem. And now he was in trouble until the radio suddenly had a few transmission breaks—something Harlem was expert at causing.

London stretched for miles and miles, as far as she could see, or dared look. The closer they came to Kensington the more calm descended upon Rebecca. She followed Harlem's pointing finger and she peered down.

All was a hive of activity a safe distance from the embassy.

Police. Army. Media. Rebecca saw the short bursts of orange fire from the rooftop of the embassy. Someone was shooting at those below from the bunker on the roof. She could not collate what she had been watching on TV with what she was witnessing here now, until a spatter of bright orange fireballs shot up towards their hovering Kiowa. Harlem mumbled one obscenity ten times in three seconds, then thrust the radio at her again. 'For you. Make it quick, for Christ's sake.'

'What now?' she spat into the radio.

'Can you do it?'

'Not from here. What the hell do you think I am? I have to be close. Very close. You know that.' After a pause, she said to Harlem, 'Put us down.'

Harlem landed in a vacant car park a block away from the embassy and kept nagging her about the armour.

She was met by Pete and with him were four others in one uniform or another—police, two from special police squads, another anti-terrorist group officer. All eyed her with some apprehension. They know, she thought. They know about me. Some secret I'm supposed to be.

She won the argument with Pete Hamill concerning the body armour by stating what she knew to be fact: 'Nothing will happen if I wear it. You have to trust me. We don't have much time.'

'How close do you have to be?' Pete asked.

'As close as possible.'

She listened calmly to what these men had to say—much the same as Mike had said, half an hour before. Rebecca chewed on her thumb. 'That roof,' she said, pointing to the adjoining building, the diplomats' residence, where fifteen Nighthawks were already in wait, unseen from below, shielded by the elder tree and one-a.m. darkness. 'Is there anyone on the top floor of the embassy? Men who can get up there as soon as the structure goes down if not before?'

'Yes.'

She looked into Pete's pale eyes and swallowed a rising lump that she suspected was her heart. He seemed to be trying to smile back. 'Well, we'd better do it then before someone else dies.'

Pete had her by the arm, shielding her as best he could from the intermittent machine-gun fire as they dashed, weaving, across the deserted street, the footpath, and up the stairs into the building next to the embassy. Billy Macpherson was waiting to pull them inside.

Once inside, Rebecca leaned against the wall. Her heart was on fire. Her face was white, her eyes cavernous. She'd thought the uniform would have left some trace of courage in the cloth. But she felt none of it now.

'You all right?' Pete asked. 'No extra holes?'

How could he stand there joking? 'Are you ready?' he asked.

'As I'm ever likely to be.'

Billy led the way up the stairs to the roof, and Kelly swung towards the sudden movement. He didn't know if he was pleased to see Rebecca or not. There wasn't a lot visible under the hood apart from terrified eyes.

'They're going to wax another hostage in three minutes,' Pete said. 'Alpha's ready.'

'Where the hell is your armour!' Kelly asked as he crouched beside her, behind the cover of a chimney stack.

'I can't wear it. It interferes.'

For the first time in his life, Kelly was indecisive.

'I can do it. I know what has to be done.'

Something shone in his eyes. Something she didn't comprehend.

'Ammo's on the smokescreen. You'll let us know, give us some warning. You use this signal,' and he extended his thumb into the air, 'Before you know the structure is going to fall. Right?'

'Right.'

'And you will stay as low as you possibly can.'

'Right.'

From where she crouched, Rebecca could see the small, inch-thick steel structure clearly. It seemed as large as her flat's living room. God, she thought. Let me be home watching the Pacific on the horizon. Let me be anywhere but here.

She could feel women crying. She closed her eyes and repeated to Kelly what she saw inside. 'Fourteen women, four kids, one baby and one man but I think he's already dead. Yes. He's dead. He's been pushed into a corner.'

'What else? Kelly asked.

'Five, no, there's six men I can see. Three have Uzis. I don't know what the others have. There's one at the ventilator shaft and he's going to shoot again.' She broke concentration as the shooting began. A quick spatter. 'It's so crowded in there, Kelly.

The people are being moved around, constantly. There's one lady about as old as me. She has a little boy, about three.' She could see and feel that one woman screaming. Rebecca closed her eyes again and grabbed Kelly's knee. 'Omil has her son. They're going to kill her son.' She saw Omil. So young, so cold. Taking a boy, no more than three years old, tearing him away from his mother. Dragging him to the door, putting a pistol to his head. There was no time.

Rebecca ran out low, slid onto her belly, put her arms over her head and watched in her mind's eye as the bunker roof tore open like a sardine tin. Two walls and the door fell outwards.

Then she gave the signal and almost drowned in acrid fog. Fifteen Nighthawks used the smoke cover to fox it across as the roof peeled off the bunker.

Rebecca covered her ears at the sound of tearing metal; the sound of machine-gun fire. From the sound of the screaming. From the sound of death. She knew that anyone with a weapon was a target. There was no escape.

And twenty seconds later, there was no more shooting. The smoke had cleared, letting through the cries of a baby, of the shocked. Just cries from out of the stark, loud silence. Voices. American and English. Male voices of reassurance.

Rebecca lifted her head slowly, weakly. A police chopper hovered overhead, floodlighting what remained of the generator room atop the Israeli Embassy.

Where that little boy was wandering, dazed, amid the clearing smoke. He was crying. Kelly put his hand on the boy's head, the child looked up and clung to his leg. And with the machine gun slung across his back, he picked the boy up and took him down to join the others, to find his mother.

Rebecca put her face down on the asphalt. She couldn't move any other part of her body. She could only feel the booted feet coming closer, quickly. It was Billy. 'We've got to go. Now. Quickly.'

'I can't move,' she said.

'Are you hit?'

'No, I don't think so.'

Billy carried her from the roof. Shock, he thought. It's only shock. He set her down in the foyer of the diplomats' residence and balanced her until she found her feet again. 'You look like shit,' he said quietly.

'Did anyone . . . did anyone—'

'It was successful. Now come on, we have to go. Keep your head down and don't speak to anyone. Don't look at anyone. Understand?'

He walked out into the cold early morning air. Rebecca followed. The echoing street which she had weaved her way across was now crammed with people. Above, more choppers in the air. Rebecca walked beside Billy with her head down, through the crowd of police and army. To her right, she glimpsed the barricade and the multitude behind it, the gaggle of TV cameras, the flashes of photographs.

Billy climbed into the back of a rental truck, turned and offered his hand. She took it and was heaved inside. The doors closed and the vehicle moved off.

Nobody spoke. She was surrounded by twenty-five elite killers and no one was brave enough to look into her eyes. Kelly was not among them, nor was the colonel.

There were a few coughs, drowned by the noise of the engine. Mostly there was silence. It was uncomfortable, alien. They were never this quiet as a rule. Never.

Rebecca was suddenly aware of the cold, her teeth chattering. Billy put a thick blanket around her and she collapsed against him, crying quietly at what she had done. And he tightened the blanket around her and held her until she stopped shaking.

'I want to go home,' she cried softly. 'I want to go home. I can't take this, Billy. I can't take it.'

'It'll work out. You'll be . . .'

She heard no more of Billy's reassuring, kind, almost loving voice. For the rest of the journey he kept the blanket tight around her as she slept, her head on his lap.

Billy wished the journey could have no end, but everything had to end. Even hopeless love. Better a friend than nothing at all.

Kelly looked down at her, still dressed in the assaults. Boots, too. He almost laughed at the sight as she slept on top of her bed with nothing but a blanket and a uniform she despised to keep her warm.

What had one of the Alpha boys said? *Would you rent her to us?*

He touched her face—no reaction—and, tiredly, he went to

the door and turned the light out. It was four in the morning but Kelly did not sleep. He watched the PSI videotape instead.

And as he watched, he knew she would never forgive herself for what she had done.

Would you intentionally take a few lives to save that of many millions, Rebecca?

I will not be what you want me to be!

The news, honey, Kelly thought, is all bad.

CHAPTER 22

BEWARE THE *man bearing flowers.*

Yes, Emmanuel. That makes sense, thank you very much.

The man bearing flowers indeed. She sat alone on a drum near the fire station at the Enfield base, watching air force personnel stroll by. Some even stopped, to do more than smile. One airman asked if she was lost. No, she'd said. Just waiting. He walked on, out of luck.

She swung her feet and glanced up to the rooftops, trying to accommodate this location to the one she'd seen in her mind. It didn't fit. Unless it was a mirror image or reversed. Or a cosmic joke. Lately she couldn't differentiate reality from fantasy.

She closed her eyes for the hundredth time, trying to capture the scene. Which one? All her impressions had been bullied into disrepair.

The red carpet, the people without faces standing at the bottom of the steps. The open door of the small jet, the minder stepping out first. Then Robert Glover, bandaid and all. His wife. A tall, striking woman. Four shots and both are dead.

The ex-model loses a red shoe.

It wouldn't help to tell Kelly she would probably know the details of the hit in its entirety thirty seconds before it happened.

Soon, this place would be overflowing with people and media. Uniforms everywhere. No Presidential 767. No cargo planes touching down a day before. No elaborate security. Too much change, she thought. That's what frightens people the most. And if the President dies . . .

Pete was walking towards her. Kelly was with him, as well as the CO from Enfield, a couple of others, Captain McLaren strolling behind everyone. Rebecca slid from the drum she was sitting on and Pete beckoned her.

The only person in the group she could read clearly, even at a distance, was Colonel Carl Lindberg. He was upset because his stepson had smashed up his new Volvo. He certainly didn't want any assassination of the President to happen on his base, either. He was not having a good day and he didn't care who knew it.

And at the bottom of all this fuss was Robert Glover's one unfortunate personality trait—he cared. He actually liked people. He would often stroll off into a crowd and talk for too long to people who didn't really matter. Or so his minders thought. His obvious humility and touching sincerity drove his security staff to despair. He'd talk about harmony and unity, the progression of the human race towards a common goal of total peace—disarmament was not a tactful word, not when others made too much money from war in general. And he loved children. He had enough of his own. He was playing with four of them when his nose was broken. His security team thought he was crazy. Perhaps some people thought he was insane. And being black certainly didn't help matters.

Everyone's blood was red.

An FA 18 taxied by and killed her reverie. The colonel had been talking to her and she hadn't heard a word he'd said. She was watching the plane. There was something odd about it. Something wrong.

'Just take your time,' Pete said over the roar of engines and walked back to his official huddle. Kelly remained with her on the tarmac.

'What did he say?'

'Rebecca, do you ever listen when anyone is talking to you?'

She regarded him blankly. 'Does that plane look all right to you?'

Kelly turned around. 'Yeah, fine. Don't worry about the Hornet. Just concentrate, that's all you have to do.' But he looked back to the Hornet. A dark mist seemed to surround it. Not a good omen.

'Concentrate . . .'

She was in the centre of a colourful crowd behind a barricade. To her right, armed people on the rooftop of Aircraft Maintenance One. Directly in front of her, the jet. The red carpet. Standing by the stairs in his navy dress uniform, Kelly. Pete. Three others, one of whom was Carl Lindberg. A Rolls waiting close by. Television news cameras to her left. One was from the CNN

Network. Beyond that the control tower.

The control tower caught her attention. 'There,' she said to Kelly, pointing. 'From there.'

'Which shot's this?' Kelly asked.

'Side on. Mrs Glover's shot from there, too.' Rebecca touched her neck and turned in her imaginary crowd, stood on tiptoe to peer over imaginary heads. She was facing the fire station and a fire truck. In her head she heard sirens. She followed the sounds of a disabled fighter coming in from the south. 'A plane's going to crash-land,' she said.

'What?'

'A plane is going to crash-land.'

Kelly looked back at the Hornet taxiing for takeoff. Yes, it was definitely surrounded by a dark mist. 'Can you see it? Hear it?' she asked.

'No. No, but I believe you.' Kelly was quiet for quite some time.

'Something's funny,' Rebecca said softly.

Kelly felt far from laughing.

'There's a fire truck with a one-man crew and the plane is going to crash-land but the fire truck is not moving, Kelly. It should be and it isn't.'

Kelly thought suddenly, for no reason, of Tommy Lethbridge, who was supposedly back in the States and locked into the Leibermann inquiry. There was a sour taste in Kelly's mouth and the longer that Rebecca stayed in the open like this, the more bitter it became.

'There are two assassins, Kelly. The man in the fire truck and one in the tower. They're both using weapons with laser sights.'

'Rebecca, don't mention the Hornet to anyone else.'

'But—'

'Trust me. Do not mention the crash landing.'

'What are they doing over there?' The Enfield CO asked the Nighthawks commanding officer.

Pete glaced at Kelly and Rebecca. 'Conferring, by the look of it.'

'Conferring. Right.' Carl Lindberg took a hanky and blew his nose. 'Now Nolan, sure. I can accept that he's a little twilight zone, but you're seriously trying to tell me that *that* little girl there is a mind-bender.'

Pete looked back at Rebecca, standing there with the wind tossing her hair. She looked as lethal as the Easter Bunny, which was a mistake too many people had made. 'Uh-huh,' was all Pete said to the question and walked back to where Kelly and the girl stood.

'Do you want the good news or the bad?' Rebecca asked and Kelly gave her a nudge. 'It's changed again. Each time I learn something new, the whole scenario changes.'

'What?'

'What I'm saying, again, is this can't be avoided. The only way to avoid it is to stop the President coming. Or divert the plane to another base at the last minute. If he touches down here, he's dead. Can't you call him? Let me talk to him?'

'What do you mean it's changed again?'

'I just told you. Each time I'm shown something, the scene changes. It's as if nothing is fixed. The only thing that's fixed is now. Whatever is done now affects what will be. We can't stop this happening. I'm sorry, but if he lands here—'

'You will stop this destiny bullshit and you will tell me what you saw. Now.'

'She's telling the truth. When I touch her, I see what she sees. She's a catalyst, Pete,' Kelly lied. 'There is nothing we cannot handle providing full measures are taken.'

Pete stepped back, annoyed. 'I'll see you both in my office back at base at thirteen hundred.' He walked off with Carl Lindberg mumbling about wastes of time.

Kelly glanced down at Rebecca. She was pale, shaky. She looked up and asked, 'Kelly, why did you lie?'

He didn't reply.

'What are we going to do?'

'I think you already know.' Kelly walked her back to where Harlem was waiting in the Kiowa to take them back to base.

Kelly put his arm around her once the elevator's doors closed. 'It'll be okay,' he said quietly. 'If you let me do the talking.'

'I feel so useless.'

'Maybe it's got to be that way. Maybe it's up to us now,

not you. Have you ever considered that possibility? Rebecca, haven't you done enough?'

'But what if we're wrong?'

'Rebecca, only worry about things you can change.'

'I don't want Robert Glover to die. He's special, Kelly.'

'The constants haven't changed. He's still waving at the top of the stairs, right?'

She nodded.

'Right. For now, you let me do the talking.'

'We're supposed to tell Pete what we know.'

'I think that's why it keeps changing.'

Rebecca stared up at him, open-mouthed.

'I heard, Rebecca. I heard about your argument in the mess. What you said to him. Please, trust me on this one because where there's doubt, silence is best. So you keep quiet.'

A few moments later, she was seated in the CO's office with the unbearable need to hug a pillow. Pete was shouting. 'How could it be from the tower? The tower could be crawling with people, it isn't possible . . .' on and on and on, while Kelly's voice too, grew louder as he tried to convince him.

'He's already in the tower!' Rebecca yelled. 'Stop this fighting! I can't stand the fighting!'

Two faces turned to her. Two voices at once:

'What?'

'There's a walkway thing around the top of the tower. Somewhere below that walkway there's a crawl space. An air conditioning vent, something like that. The assassin is already there, waiting.'

'Why didn't you tell us four hours ago!' Pete roared.

'I didn't know then!' she screamed in return and the overhead light applauded with a considerable explosion. Rebecca covered her face and tried to calm down. Her stomach was churning.

'How long are you staying?' Pete barked. 'If it's for very much longer for Christ's sake let me know so I can have a skylight put in!'

Rebecca's jaw ached from tension. 'Don't humour me.'

'Humour you? I am serious!' Pete was immediately on the phone to Enfield. And because he was on that phone, Rebecca knew it had all changed again. Another dice had been rolled. She hadn't let Kelly do the talking and she knew if he bit his lip any harder he would soon taste blood.

She listened in complete, shamed silence to the conversation with the Enfield commanding officer. When the colonel hung up, Rebecca refused to wilt in anticipation of the next onslaught. She took a deep breath and met the icy gaze.

'How can it keep changing?' he asked, trying to be calm. Trying very hard.

'We alter our own destinies all the time. But whatever is in the true plan will happen no matter how many diversions there are. I have tried to explain this before but you don't understand. I don't know what this man's destiny is because you won't let me speak to him. If I spoke to him I would know if he's to die now or not. And please don't ask for a rational explanation.'

Pete sat down. He had to.

'I know it sounds absurd, but I know it is not impossible. If the man was indeed sent progress reports on me, then surely to God I can speak to him on the phone. Please. It'll be too late for should-haves tomorrow night, Colonel.'

Kelly watched Pete very closely. He was being expertly cornered and he knew it.

'You,' Pete said, on his feet and pacing. 'You want to talk to the President! Do you know how difficult that is to arrange? You just think you can sit there and demand to speak to the President?'

Rebecca's anger was growing. She tried to keep her priorities in perspective without letting the trivia of personality clashes override necessity. 'He knows about me anyway. I'll remain calm. I won't overstep your boundaries of etiquette.'

Pete stopped pacing, looked at the time and studied Rebecca for a little while.

'Please let me talk to him? I know that you flew sorties over Iraq together. I know that you went to school together too. I know he is a friend of yours. Please.'

Pete rubbed his hand through his short hair, apparently thinking fast. 'Get your butt back in here at sixteen hundred. That'll be all.'

Rebecca went back to her room and lay on her bed. She knew what Kelly would say when he came in. He would say, 'You were right.'

She stared at the ceiling. Why do I despise that man? she demanded silently. I am not supposed to despise anyone. He is

Kelly's old comrade and I cannot bear the sight of him. It's clouding what little judgement I have left. She closed her eyes and tried to calm down but tension rumbled inside like a miniature volcano.

When Kelly eventually came in, he sat on her bed and stared at the floor. 'You were right. Base security at Enfield found some guy with a sniper rifle. He also had a cyanide capsule and no identification. He's dead.'

'Another one.'

'Another what?'

'If I hadn't said anything this wouldn't have happened.'

'And Robert Glover's brains would be spray painting a Learjet. Look at priorities, girl.'

'All life is my priority.'

'Even Gene Samperi?' Kelly asked. She looked away. She had to. 'It's fine thinking every man's an equal,' Kelly said softly. 'But it doesn't work like that, not in the real world.'

'I don't like your real world, Kelly.'

'Yes, I know.' Kelly took her hand. 'There's nothing wrong with what you want, Rebecca, but sometimes you've got to open your eyes and see what's really here instead of what you think should be here. Look, I've seen glimpses of your little heavens too but unfortunately, I have to live down here amid the crap. Not everyone's good on the inside and not everyone wants what you call good—peace and love, stuff like that.'

'Don't you want peace?'

'I'd be the first to lay down my arms if it was possible. I'd be right in there with you. The idealism's great, honey. But not everyone can hear your words, least of all understand them. And even fewer listen when they *could* understand and maybe that's worse.'

'Why won't they listen?'

'They feel safe in their comfortable niches and they don't want anything upsetting that security. Now, to you, it might be wrong but to them, it's right because it's comfortable.'

He stopped talking for a little while. Rebecca said nothing at all until, 'You don't understand either?' All this time she had thought he knew what she knew.

'I understand what you're saying, I understand where you're at. I've just got a different perspective. My idealism nearly died the night John Lennon was shot. Then, seventeen years ago, I went to the memorial service in Central Park. The guy standing right in front of me was shot dead. Two people died there that day. Did you know that?'

'No—'

'And that was the end of Nolan's wonderful world. Maybe I agree with you that someone like Glover comes along far too rarely. Yes, maybe he is special. I don't know. I do know that you are special, too. You're doing what you think is right. But that kid who was holed up in the tower at Enfield thought he was doing something right. Nothing here is black or white but there's infinite shades of grey and that's where I fit. Your God might very well exist, honey, but till we can all call it by the same name at the same time this is going to go on and on and on. So I just do my job and that's taking the life you think is sacred and I try not to think about it too much.'

'But that's—'

'No. You've got a job to do and you've got a threat coming at you and that's what he is. He's not human. He's a threat, a target. You can't afford to let him be human. You know something else?' he asked and touched her hair. 'Maybe if the world was full of people like you, I wouldn't even have a job. I could go fishing. I'd like that.'

She was still aching. Confused. Her world seemed a lot better than his, safer. Nicer. Prettier. 'And yet I've caused people to die. I can't forgive myself for what I did the other morning. All that damage. All those people . . .'

'Would be dead if not for you. Why not see it as eighteen lives?'

'I can't, Kelly. I can't.'

'You're taking the shortcut to the funny farm if you persist in taking on everyone's sins, everyone's pain, and everyone's guilt. You're not God. You are not an angel of mercy. Maybe you come closer than anyone else I know of but you are still only human. You have no expectations of others and you accept others as they are so why the hell are you so hard on yourself?'

'Habit.'

'And that's taking a slow crawl up a very steep and rocky Mount Perfection. You be careful you don't slip off because you're getting close to the top. I don't have to see any parapsychology videotape to realise that.'

'Why do you twist everything so it makes sense?'

'It's not twisting. It's another perspective. Maybe you need grounding. I'm not saying it's wrong to be a dreamer but you have to keep your feet on the ground at the same time. We live in *this* world, Rebecca. You feel it under your feet every day. This is where you belong. Here, with me, not dancing with angels, even if they're real.'

'Hold me?'

'Will it cure the world?'

'No.'

'Good,' Kelly said and lay down beside her. Nothing was said for a long time. His heartbeat was very loud, very strong. He kissed her. 'You're probably the best thing that's ever happened to me. No, hell no. You *are* the best thing that's ever happened to me. Would you marry me when I'm divorced?'

'I leave the top off the toothpaste.'

'That's a hanging offence. Keep trying. I'm waiting for a reasonable excuse I can argue with.'

'Kelly, I have trouble living with myself. I need space.'

'The commanding officer's residence has seven bedrooms and fifteen hectares of land. Is that enough space?'

'You're not the CO yet.'

'I'm not divorced yet, either, but by March, all, as they say, will be well. Don't leave me.'

'I've never been able to.' Again, there was silence.

'What are you going to say to Robert Glover?' he asked.

'I don't know. What do you say to the President of the United States? Hiya, Bob, don't come to England wearing a bandaid on your nose?'

'Sometimes I wonder about you.'

'Join the queue.'

At ten past four, Pete handed her the phone. She took it. Struth, she thought. He's eating. It's probably a hamburger on the run. Robert Glover said, 'Make it quick, doll,' with a very full mouth. She looked at Pete. He shrugged and turned away. You wanted him, you've got him.

And now that she had him, Rebecca didn't know what to say to this man.

'You're the psycho, huh?' he asked after swallowing.

Psycho? 'Yes, sir,' she replied, secretly wondering how elastic his sense of humour was.

'How good are you?'

'Ask me something.'

'What am I wearing?'

Rebecca closed her eyes and repeated what she saw this tall dark man wearing as he sat on a very large bed in the White House, nibbling lettuce off an open hamburger. His wife walked by with her arms full of clothing and indicated that he take his boots off the lace bedspread. He didn't. 'I see you're wearing a pale blue shirt with white pinstripes, dark brown pants, black socks, black elastic-sided boots, a thermal vest and flourescent orange and blue underpants your eight-year-old son gave you for your birthday last week. And they're a size too small, sir, sorry—Mr President. You shouldn't eat those onions, either,' she added quickly. 'And the mustard will give you heartburn.'

There was a cough from the other end of the phone followed by a thoughtful silence. 'And what do you want to tell me?' he asked.

'Well, sir, that depends on what you want to hear. If you want the truth it's not going to be nice but I suppose I could lie, like everyone else close to you seems to be doing at this time. So I'll leave it up to you to decide.'

She heard a silence again and the inevitable clicks on the line. His private phone was being monitored. 'Talk to me,' he said.

'Come to England alone. Don't bring your wife.'

'Why?'

'She'll die with you. Was she going to wear a navy blue suit with a red blouse?'

On the lace bedspread was Elizabeth's final bag. She walked into the room and again tapped at his boot. This time he took his feet off the spread. 'What were you going to wear?' he asked her. Elizabeth came back with a navy blue suit and a red blouse. He waved her away and to the softly-spoken young woman on the other end of the line, he said, 'Well, yes, she was.'

'Don't let her come and please don't wear that bandaid on your nose either.'

He touched the bandaid that he wore in private only. 'Are you telling me to cancel?'

'No, sir. I am only advising you not to bring your wife and not to wear a bandaid. If you could do that, then perhaps you will live to be a very old man. That's all I can say to you.'

'I'll keep it in mind. Put Peter back on.'

Rebecca handed the phone over and she walked from the room, still unsure, still doubting. Something still felt very, very wrong.

CHAPTER 23

IT WAS two a.m. and deathly still. In three hours' time she would be on her way to Enfield. Sleep had not come and nor was it likely to. Across the hall, Kelly was having bad dreams. She didn't have to be close to feel his torment but the narrow corridor seemed as wide as the Himalayas were tall.

She didn't want to go home.

But she could not stay here, either.

Each time she looked into his eyes she felt his silent pleas. *Don't go. Don't go. We'll make it this time. History won't repeat. I'll never let any harm come to you. This time we'll do it right.*

If only he could be an ordinary man, with an ordinary job. If only their worlds could touch and blend and not collide.

Ten past two. She could bear it no longer.

Kelly's door was unlocked. He wasn't in bed. He was sitting by the window, as if he'd known she would come. Eventually. When, like him, she could take no more.

But he looked at her as she came in, and then away again, quickly.

'You're still intending to leave, aren't you,' he said quietly, not even a question.

She didn't know what to say.

'Do you know what we are?' he asked. 'We're different leaves on the same branch of one tree, that's what we are. I don't want you to go. But I have the feeling you will. It's not who I am so much, it's what I am that bothers you. Rebecca, this job is all I know. Before you came, it was my life.'

'You told me you wanted a fishing boat.'

'I still want that, but I also have another three years of duty to serve. If the squad's disbanded, I'll go back to the States. Would you come with me? No matter where I am, or what I'm doing?'

'Don't ask me to decide now.'

'Will you ever decide? Three years girl, and I'm out. I'm away from what you hate so much. Is three years that long?'

'No.'

'We could get a house in Salisbury until—'

'Kelly, no. Right now, I don't want to have to decide anything.' She put her hand on his shoulder.

'You can't see past tomorrow either, can you?' he asked.

'I don't think we're supposed to. Whatever is meant to happen will happen no matter what we do or what we know.'

Kelly reached for her hand and pulled her close.

Two and a half hours was all they had until the dawn.

Enfield Air Base. Most of the Nighthawks contingent were in plain clothes, a minority in greens. The commanding officer in dress blues. Second in command in dress whites. The commanding officer of Enfield and Mrs Lindberg were also part of the queue and beside her, the Chief of Defence Staff, Lord Howell, ready to personally escort President Robert Glover to Whitehall, where the Prime Minister waited.

It was ill advised, security-wise to have both national leaders at this one location, considering the circumstances. Protocol was forcibly disarrayed already for the arrival. The bulletproof Rolls was waiting.

According to tradition—one he could not avoid—the President would stroll down the stairs of the plane, greet the welcome party in order of their importance and wander off towards the crowd.

A few schools were represented by a gaggle of kids, ages ranging from six to seventeen. They had the opportunity of a lifetime.

See a man die. Eyewitnesses to history in the making.

Maybe, Kelly thought.

The tower was covered. The fire station covered. Every rooftop covered. Everyone coming in had been body-searched and identified. Even the kids.

Recognisable faces mingled in the crowd. Rebecca wore jeans and a white jumper with a koala on the front. Her long hair was wild in the wind. Every time Kelly looked at her, she was talking to a swarm of kids.

She looked up to the sky before anyone else's head tilted and thirty seconds later, the white Lear came into sight.

As it touched down into the crosswind and taxied back, the

fire truck pulled out, and engine idling, it obliterated the view of the station.

Bingo. Kelly watched Ammo, Jay and Barry wander off towards the fire truck. The three were casual, unnoticed by the TV reporters who had cameras already focussed on the approaching Lear. Kelly lost the three from sight. Mrs Lindberg's hat was caught by the wind and Kelly saved it for her. As he bent to pick it up he heard the voice:

Beware the man bearing flowers.

He barely blinked. He hadn't heard that voice for years.

What? he asked, silently.

Beware the man bearing flowers.

The only people with flowers were the kids behind the barricade. Flowers for Elizabeth Glover. Something wasn't right.

Rebecca looked at the fire truck. There was no one in it now. Jay appeared, alone, and nodded, smiling, to Kelly. Situation controlled. She'd never felt relief quite as intense and she tried not to imagine what Barry and Ammo were doing to the fire-truck 'suspect'.

Kelly had asked her to talk to the entire squad before they left and she'd told them all what she expected to happen in two hours' time. They had all listened, there was not one disbelieving face. Pete was the only person not present—he was already at Enfield.

And she looked to the sky again just as the Learjet parked and the engines cut.

Seconds later, sirens split the air. There was movement. Lots of movement. And above, the disabled FA 18 was coming in—trailing black smoke across the mid-summer sky. Any moment now, she would see the parachutes.

Two of the news crews diverted, half the crowd tried to divert as well. Base security kept them back as ambulances and fire trucks raced towards the disabled fighter. There was no movement from the Presidential plane. Rebecca knew the cause of the delay.

Robert Glover was watching from the window, mumbling to himself about kid pilots. 'Eject, dammit, eject!' And as if the order had been heard, two parachutes appeared moments before the fighter came down in a fireball.

'Are you ready now, sir?' the newest of his three aides asked. 'We're already behind schedule.'

Robert Glover finished his drink. 'Two pilots could be injured, if not dead and you tell me I'm behind schedule?' The secret serviceman looked away from the stony gaze and mumbled an apology while the President took a mint from his pocket, straightened his clothes and stepped out, a smile appearing on his face even though the magic of the moment had been stolen by some kids crashlanding a multi-million dollar airplane.

His new bodyguard was beside him on the way down the few stairs and four more brought up the rear. 'Can you smell whisky?' came the question under the smile, the wave of the hand.

'No, sir. You're fine.'

'Crowd me this time and you'll be on a queue for another job. Understood? That goes for every one of you.'

'Yes, sir.'

'I'm getting sick of the sight of you all. Man can't even take a piss alone these days.'

The President waved to the kids behind the barriers first and he saw the Australian woman in the crowd. As he took the final step, still intact and thankful for that mercy, the kids cheered and screamed as if he were a hero.

More flowers, he thought. Great. Everyone in his security team could certainly be alert with their arms full of flowers. He waved to the kids and turned to the welcome party.

The British Chief of Staff, Lord Howell. He shook the hand and didn't hear the apology for the Hornet's mishap. 'I've downed the odd airplane in my time. They'll learn to fly or die trying.'

He moved on to Carl Lindberg. Another clasp of hands. 'I want to see those boys before I leave here, Carl. I don't care if it's in the back of a goddamned ambulance, I will see them.'

'Yes, Mr President.'

Mrs Lindberg received a polite handshake and a compliment about the colour she was wearing.

He moved down the line to Pete. 'I'll talk to you later in London,' he said very quietly. 'Some fool's been advising me to disband your unit.'

Kelly was next in line. Nighthawks second in command.

Commander, U.S. Navy. Eyes met, gazes held. 'Don't I know you from somewhere?' Robert Glover asked.

'The *Enterprise* in '86, Mr President.' Glover had been meant to be in the same plane as Pete, on the day of Kelly's warning.

Something passed between them during the touch of hands. The President's eyes fired with a trace of humour. 'Guess I still owe you one, Commander.'

Robert Glover walked by with his little troop on all sides and he backtracked to Kelly. 'I heard about Kensington. Leibermann. I'd like to meet this girl of yours.'

Before Kelly could comment, the President turned back to Carl Lindberg. 'If those boys are under fifteen hundred hours between them, someone's ass is going to get kicked.'

'Yes, Mr President,' Carl said.

'Train these kids on biplanes for Chrissakes, then they'd know what it is to fly.'

'Yes, sir.'

'Would you give a seventeen-year-old a Ferrari, Carl?'

'No, sir.' Just a Volvo, he thought.

Kelly followed Glover's party as it strolled towards the crowd and the President took some flowers from a couple of girls, patted a few heads, shook a few young hands, ingested the compliments, the idolatry.

Beware the man bearing flowers?

The only one with flowers was Glover and he wasn't going to shoot himself. He did not look suicidal. Not yet, anyway.

'Where's your wife, Mr President?' one of the kids asked.

'She couldn't make it. Maybe next time.' Glover walked on, passing most of the flowers to the closest secret serviceman so his hands were free to touch more hands.

Kelly was hit by a volatile flood of adrenalin.

The bodyguard.

The ambulance carrying the two unfortunate pilots came to a stop. Kelly followed the President's party away from the crowd and this time, he kept close to the blond bodyguard.

'How old are you, boy?' the President asked one of the pilots.

'Twenty-one, sir.'

'Do you drive a car like you fly a plane, son?'

'No, sir.'

'That's something to be thankful for. You ejected too damned late, I was watching. You ejected too late.'

'I thought I could bring it in, sir.'

'Know what happened to thought, son? How many hours have you got?'

The young pilot saw the CO behind the President, mouthing something. 'One thousand, six hundred and one, sir. Well, almost.'

'How old are you again?'

'Twenty-one, sir.'

The President turned to Carl Lindberg. 'Sleeps up there, too, does he?' Before Carl could open his mouth to say a word, Glover was walking off. Again.

'Mr President, we're already twenty minutes behind schedule.'

'Schedules, schedules. Think I give a damn about schedules? Whitehall's been there long enough, I'm sure it won't crumble if I'm an hour late.'

Oh, shit, Kelly thought. Another forty minutes of this?

The door of the Rolls was open and the Chief of Staff was waiting impatiently. Glover looked back to the crowd and saw the Australian standing nervously in the middle of the swarm. He ventured forth, his barrage of human shields trying to keep pace as he stepped over the barricade. People immediately surrounded him.

'Excuse me, Mr President? The car's waiting.'

'Good, it can wait a little longer,' he said to Carl who was also nervous about this unexpected diversion.

The reporters converged in the usual swarm. He buffeted questions about the Zurich meeting on disarmament. Mostly he had no comment except on the weather. But there was one question which startled him. 'There was a rumour, Mr President, about an attempt on your life here today. Do you have a comment?'

Yes, he had a comment. He laughed and shaking his head, walked towards the blonde girl with the big blue eyes and the koala bear on her sweater. The crowd parted.

Rebecca tried to smile. He approached, so tall, so huge, overwhelming in presence, and a large dark-skinned hand reached out and clasped hers very tightly. She saw little except his smile, his radiance.

He wasn't wearing a bandaid, his wife was nowhere to be seen, he had walked down those stairs without being shot, and his touch, his presence was overpowering. His smile captured every cell of her being and kept it prisoner. Prisoner for life: 'No wonder people voted for you.'

He thought that was funny. For a very short moment of time, everything she had endured was worth every last trace of pain, every last tear, every ounce of humiliation and anger.

'Honey,' he whispered, hugging her to his massive chest as surrounding cameras flashed excitedly, 'Thanks.' He planted a kiss on her forehead, and he turned to his bodyguard. 'Give this young woman my flowers.'

As the secret serviceman stepped from the background of milling people, she saw the gun, the bullet and the President falling towards her with surprised, dead eyes. 'He's got a gun!' she screamed, pulling her own, kicking the President aside as the man bearing flowers caught a 9mm bullet between his eyes. The bullet destined for Glover's head misdirected into the crowd and a bystander crumpled. Rebecca tried to push towards the injured man but someone tore the gun out of her hand and someone else took her in an armlock. The air was filled with screams, confusion, panic. She pleaded for release, she could help that man, but no one heard her. No one listened.

People were trying to help Glover to his feet and he fought off all attempts. He roared one word—Nighthawk!—and the man trying to break her arms suddenly released her. There were apologies, her gun was returned.

Robert Glover's eyes met hers and a moment later, he was bundled off into the bulletproof Rolls.

Rebecca was disorientated. She felt the gun in her hand, saw the people crouching around the body on the tarmac. The flowers were crushed, strewn, being kicked by feet, blown by the wind. But there was no red shoe.

Then she fainted.

And the Australian psychic, pictured above with the President moments before the assassination attempt, remains unidentified.

Rebecca put the paper down and covered her face with her hand. 'They put my bloody picture in the paper,' she groaned.

She found it amazing that no one had wallpapered room nine with the front page of the late edition *Times* newspaper, making her walk into another nightmare the moment she arrived home.

Home. She was calling Broadmeadows, the asylum, home.

'It's a good photo,' Kelly said as if that would make her feel better. She looked at it again. Front page headlines.

Psychic saves President.

And there it was, a large glaring photograph of Robert Glover crushing her to his massive chest. It was all Rebecca wanted to remember. She'd been awed to silence by the sight of him.

'I didn't kick him, surely. Tell me I didn't?'

Kelly nodded.

'It wasn't me. Tell me I didn't shoot that assassin.'

Kelly turned to her window and looked out at the view. She had the sunrise, he had the sunset. Perhaps they could share midday? 'Rebecca, leave it. Leave it. It's over.'

'Over? Kelly, did you read this article?'

'Yes, I read it.' He didn't say that every TV news report world wide would be replaying her acrobatics, the assassin's death, the wounding of an innocent bystander and the President kissing the tarmac. She had made the news.

'You *knew* that Glover was going to dissolve the CIA? That he wanted to withdraw all American troops from overseas except the ones in the United Nations Peacekeeping Forces?'

'Yes. I knew.'

'This summit is about global nuclear disarmament!'

'Isn't that what you want?' Kelly asked. 'It is over. Leave it.'

'Where's Pete?'

'In London.'

'You knew Pete was involved? You *knew*?'

'We knew something. That he was at least leaking information to Samperi. That Stafford was his boy. He recruited him personally.'

'But—his own men. Jamie . . .'

'I don't think he sanctioned that.' His face darkened, he really didn't want to talk about it. Then he saw her face, struggling to understand, and realised he owed her some explanation at least.

'We think the whole thing was planned from the States—my esteemed father-in-law being one of the ring-leaders. Pete had his own scenario—I don't think they told him everything that was going on. They knew he'd object to some of it. In fact I think they deliberately misinformed him about Glover disbanding Nighthawks.'

'But why, Kelly? Why did he get involved at all? Greed? Ambition? What?'

'I don't know. But who knows what motivates a man like Pete? Perhaps it was simply what you accused him of—that he couldn't bear to think of a world where people like us might be outmoded. A world that denied everything he'd ever lived for. It's what I was saying before, Rebecca. There are a lot of grey areas. I'm sure he thought he was doing the right thing, for whatever reason. Now, no more questions. Leave it. It's over.'

There was a gentle rap on the door and a delivery arrived via Billy Macpherson. It was the largest spray of flowers she had ever seen. 'Another crisis must be looming. Every time I get flowers something goes horribly wrong.'

Kelly took the card, nodded to Billy to depart, which he did, hesitantly, and he gave the card to her. She opened the small envelope and read the typed words:

You can't go until you've seen the painting.

Rebecca looked at him, standing there, looking shy for the first time since early March. 'Is this painting finished yet?' she asked.

'No.'

'How long's it likely to take?'

'Oh, I'd guess two and a half, maybe three years.'

'I suppose you know of a place in Salisbury that's for rent, too?'

She'd seen that smile before, many times.